A CERTAIN FREEDOM

When Hamilton Forsyth leaves the family ironmongery, Walter, his son and heir, seems set to manage the business and marry Clarissa Pinkerton. His sister Belle will do the accounts and keep house. Their youngest sister Morna needs an occupation and, in 1909, the best occupation for a woman of her class is to marry, but when Walter announces he is to marry their pregnant housemaid Sarah, the sisters find their plans have to change. When Morna finds a job and Belle makes a scandalous marriage they find that women can be just as strong as men in this changing world.

To my husband, Jim, who deserves a gold medal but will have to settle for this book instead.

A CERTAIN FREEDOM

by

Evelyn Hood

Magna Large Print Books
Long Preston, North Yorkshire,
BD23 4ND, England.

British Library Cataloguing in Publication Data.

Hood, Evelyn
    A certain freedom.

    A catalogue record of this book is
    available from the British Library

    ISBN   0-7505-2482-0

First published in Great Britain in 2005 by Time Warner Books

Copyright © Evelyn Hood 2005

Cover illustration © Gordon Crabb by arrangement with
Alison Eldred

The moral right of the author has been asserted

Published in Large Print 2006 by arrangement with
Time Warner Books

Magna Large Print is an imprint of Library Magna Books Ltd.

Printed and bound in Great Britain by
T.J. (International) Ltd., Cornwall, PL28 8RW

Acknowledgements

The fictitious summer camp at Portencross referred to in the book is based on a very successful summer camp held during the 1930s at Lunderston Bay, Gourock.

The suffragette quilt referred to in this book was made in Paisley, not Saltcoats, and is now on display in the Sma' Shot Cottages – the weavers' cottages owned by the Old Paisley Society.

I am indebted to the staff of Ardrossan and Saltcoats Libraries for their help in researching material for this book.

My thanks to Kathleen Degnan, the brains behind the title of this book. Bless you, Kathleen!

1

'Parenthood,' Hamilton Forsyth announced, 'is the necessary evil of a marriage.'

He stood in his favourite pose before the fire-place in his well-appointed drawing room, hands behind his back, sturdy body blocking out most of the heat from the room, and continued as three shocked faces turned towards him, 'And since my marriage has now ended with your dear mother's demise and you are now old enough to look out for yourselves, I consider that any obligation I have had towards you has also ended.'

'Father?' Belle quavered uncertainly, while her brother Walter said at the same time, 'Really, Papa, I hardly think it seemly to speak like that to us only hours after laying Mother in her grave!'

'You never were able to come up with the right comment for the occasion, were you, Walter? This is the perfect time. Another ten minutes and it will be too late.'

'What do you mean, Papa?'

Hamilton's face softened and he smiled at the youngest of his three children. Morna had always been his favourite, while Walter had been his wife's. Belle, the firstborn and plainest of the three, had never been anyone's favourite. 'I mean, Morna, my dear, that in ten minutes ... nine and a half,' he corrected himself, consulting the fob watch he had just taken from its pocket in his black silk waistcoat, 'the cart will be arriving to take my belongings to the station.'

A murmur of consternation swept through the room. Walter, Belle and Morna glanced uneasily at each other, then Belle ventured, 'You are going away on business, Papa? At a time like this?'

'Not on business, my dear. I am leaving.'

'Leaving Saltcoats? Leaving home?'

'Saltcoats, Walter, is your home, not mine. It was never my home. This...' Hamilton swept out a hand to indicate the comfortable parlour, '...is no longer my home. It is the house I came to when I married your mother, and now that she has gone and I am no longer tied to the vows we made to each other, it is time for me to begin a new life.'

'Elsewhere in Ayrshire?' Belle struggled to make sense of what her father was saying.

'Certainly not in Ayrshire. Possibly Glasgow or Edinburgh or London or Paris.' Hamilton rubbed his hands together and smiled at his offspring, clearly relishing the prospect of his new life. 'This fine twentieth century we now live in is a mere nine years old. It's time the four of us seized its new prospects and carved out our own destinies.'

'But ... but what about us?' Walter asked feebly.

His father's dark, well–shaped eyebrows lifted slightly. 'Why ask me? You're all adults now; you no longer need me. As I said earlier, you were the necessary result of our marriage. You gave great pleasure to your mother when you were small, and I will admit,' Hamilton said, his eyes resting for a moment on Morna's flower-like face, 'that there were times when I myself enjoyed your company. But now I must see to my own life and leave you to yours.'

'When will you return?' Belle asked, and her father gave the slightest of exasperated sighs before saying patiently, 'My dear, I do not expect to return, ever. That is what I am trying to explain to you. Frances is dead, you are all grown, and so our relationship is at an end. You have the house, which belonged to your mother and is now yours by right, not mine. You have the business that your grandfather started, which is also rightfully yours. And you have your mother's money. All I have taken for myself is the payment I earned by running the shop.'

'But ... but...' Walter began to stammer, while Belle protested, 'You can't desert us – what will people say?'

'I don't care what people say. I won't be here to listen to them tittle-tattle. God knows I got enough of that in the shop during all the years of my marriage. It will be a relief to be free of it. Walter, you can run the business now, with Belle's help, of course. And if you decide against that, as you have never seemed all that interested in earning your own living,' Hamilton said with a sudden cold edge to his voice, 'it must be a comfort to you to know that since you are already promised to marry Clarissa Pinkerton you will be able to live in comfort on her father's money. It was a great relief to your mother when you and Clarissa became engaged. It was what she had wanted since you were toddlers together. Belle, you can no doubt continue to see to the bookkeeping in the shop, which you have done with great efficiency in the past. And as you also took over the running of this house after my poor dear Frances was forced to take to her bed, you will probably continue to do that as well. Who knows, perhaps one day you will find a man will ... worthy,' Hamilton corrected himself swiftly, 'to offer you his hand and his home. As for you, Morna...' Again, his face softened. With her slender but rounded figure, her thick fair hair and her wide hazel eyes, Morna most resembled her mother. 'You,' Hamilton finished briskly, 'will have no bother in finding a suitable husband, although I would counsel you against Arthur MacAdam, since I have never considered him to be good enough for you. I trust that your brother will advise you when it comes to making your choice.'

'Father...!' Walter bleated, but was ignored as Hamilton consulted his watch again.

'No more time for discussion, Walter, and in any case, I have said all that I have to say and now I must be off.'

'But surely ... a forwarding address...?'

'Anything I leave behind can be disposed of, Belle, for I have no more need of it.' Hamilton pulled on the bell rope to summon the live-in maidservant. 'The cart will be here at any minute to collect my luggage. I shall walk to the station; the exercise will be good for me. I have always found funerals to be claustrophobic. Ah, Sarah,' he went on as the door opened, 'a cart will be calling in five minutes to collect the trunk from the front bedroom. Please ensure that the man handles it carefully. My hat and stick, if you will be so kind. Goodbye,' he said with one final glance at his family, then walked from the room, leaving them gaping at each other in silence.

'There now, that's them all done at last.' Annie McCall put away the last plate and shook out the dishcloth before hanging it in front of the fire to dry. 'What else needs seein' to before I leave?'

'Nothing else.' Sarah Neilson finished stacking the uneaten sandwiches. 'They'll likely not want much tonight. Folk never have an appetite after a funeral. I've got cold meat left, and pickle, and there's always cheese. You get on home.'

'If you're sure. He'll be in from the dockyard and our Maisie's such a dreamer, I can't trust her to have his dinner ready. She'll have the potatoes burned and the fish dried to leather if I know her.'

'Here...' Sarah reached up to the high mantel-shelf, where Miss Belle had left the money to pay the heavy-work woman. 'Thank you for obligin' us today, Mrs McCall.'

'Och, you'd never have managed everythin' on your own, hen, not with it bein' such a big funeral.' The woman counted the money with a swift sweep of her eyes before stowing it carefully into the deep pocket of her apron. She took her shabby coat from the hook on the back door and began to struggle into it. 'Mrs Forsyth was well liked.'

'She was a good employer,' Sarah agreed bleakly. 'It'll not be the same without her.'

'You're no' worried about yer position, are ye? You'll be all right, lassie, they'd not be able tae manage without ye. I can't see that Miss Belle dirtyin' her hands in the kitchen, or the younger lassie either. They werenae raised tae it.' Annie's

13

broad hands, the skin red and cracked from continual immersion in hot water, were clumsy as she buttoned her coat. Some of the buttons were missing, making the coat gape open in places.

'We never know what the future might bring,' Sarah said, and suddenly realised that she had laid one hand over her belly. She turned back to the table hurriedly, before the washerwoman's sharp eyes noticed, and began to wrap a generous handful of sandwiches in newspaper. 'Here, take these home with you.'

'Are ye sure?' Annie asked, her hand already reaching out for the packet. 'Ye'll no' get intae trouble for givin' them to me?'

'Nob'dy'll notice. Anyway, they'll probably not want tae eat leftovers from the funeral.'

'Rich folk can afford tae be fussy, but the likes of *us* can't. Thanks, pet,' Annie nodded and turned to the back door. 'I'll be in on Monday tae help with the washin' same as usual.'

Sarah wasn't alone for long. Five minutes after the washerwoman had gone she heard three quiet taps on the outer door. Her heart leaped with joy as she ran to open it.

Samuel Gilmartin slid into the kitchen and made straight for the fire, spreading his hands out to its warmth. 'I'm frozen ... and starved intae the bargain. Is there anythin' tae eat?' He pulled his cap off. 'There's surely somethin' left over from the buryin'.'

Sarah cast an anxious look at the door leading to the rest of the house. 'Hush, Samuel, you don't want them tae hear ye.'

'Och, they're too busy with their own lives tae

14

bother about what happens in the kitchen.' He pulled her into his arms and kissed her, then released her with a hearty slap on the backside. 'Go on now, girl, and get me some food. And a cup of tea wouldnae go amiss – unless,' he added hopefully, 'there's anythin' stronger left over from the funeral?'

'They'd never store strong drink down here, but I've got some sandwiches.' She had hoped that he would look in this evening, as he often did. Samuel worked as a delivery man for the greengrocer who supplied the Forsyth household, and the very first time she saw him Sarah had been bowled over by his wavy auburn hair, sparkling brown eyes, and ready, charming smile, not to mention his lovely Irish accent. She laid a plate of sandwiches on the table and watched him bite hungrily into the bread and meat. 'You're eatin' that as if you've not had food all day.'

'It's little enough I get. The mistress's carthorse eats better than I do. So,' he said through a mouthful of food, 'how did it go?'

'The funeral? The house was filled all afternoon. The last of the mourners went away not much more than an hour ago. Annie McCall came tae give me a hand. She's not long away.'

'I know that.' Samuel picked up another sandwich. 'I saw the two of ye through the window, chatterin' away like a pair of old biddies. I had to wait out in the cold until she'd gone.' He rose from his chair and rounded the table swiftly, reaching out for her and pulling her roughly into his arms. His lips gleamed greasily and she could taste roast beef when he kissed her.

15

'Mmm,' he said against her throat, 'you feel soft and warm. Like a loaf fresh from the oven. My bonny wee cottage loaf...'

She struggled to release herself. 'Samuel, supposing Miss Belle comes in and finds you?'

'Let her.' He captured her wrist and sat down, drawing her on to his lap, his free hand roaming over the soft outline of her rounded bosom. 'The way I feel tonight I can manage the two o' ye. It'd do her good – I'll wager she's not had a man yet, that one.'

'Samuel!'

'I'm only speakin' the truth. Mrs Smith sent me into Forsyth's the other week tae buy something for her, and Miss Belle was sittin' behind that wee window of hers at the back of the shop, handin' out change to the customers with a mouth on her as if she'd just caught the smell of a bad egg. Plain as a pikestaff, too. No wonder she's never found a man of her...'

Sarah squealed and shot off his knee as one of the bells on the wall jangled. 'That's the parlour – I'll have to go through.' Her frantic fingers buttoned the blouse that Samuel had begun to unfasten. 'And you shouldnae stay here. Someone might come in and find you!'

He settled himself more comfortably into the chair, grinning lazily up at her. 'Sure, who's goin' tae come in here when they can ring the bell every time they want you tae do their biddin'? Off with ye, woman, and see what yer masters desire. I'll just wait here for ye in the warmth.'

'Samuel,' she pleaded, and then, realising that he would not be moved, she fled through to the

16

main part of the house, tweaking her apron bib into place as she went, then patting her hair to make sure it was still neat.

He was half-asleep in the warmth from the range when she returned ten minutes later. 'So what did they want this time?' he yawned, stretching his arms above his head.

'It's the master, Samuel. He's gone.'

'Gone where?'

'To the station, and it looks as if he's goin' tae be away for a good while. The carter came, and him and his lad had tae haul the big trunk that's only used for holidays all the way down the stairs. It was awful heavy – full tae the lid if you ask me.'

'So that's what the noise was.' Samuel scratched at his stomach with both hands. 'He'll be off somewhere on business, mebbe. How about another cup of tea before I get back to the lodging house?'

'D'you not think it's unusual tae be goin' away on business the very day he buries his wife?'

'Who knows the way the gentry think? And who cares?'

'He was still in his mournin' clothes.'

'Well, he would be, since he's just been widowed. Tea,' he reminded her.

'The rest of them looked ever so upset.' The big tin teapot was empty and Sarah's work-reddened fingers automatically went about the business of measuring out tea leaves from the caddy, her mind full of the scene she had witnessed upstairs. 'After I'd fetched his things and helped him on with his coat and brushed it down the way I always do, they all came out into the hall as he

17

left, and then Mr Walter followed him out to the gate. It looked tae me as if they were arguin', and Miss Belle and Miss Morna were standin' at the door, watchin' them. Then Mr Forsyth started walkin' towards the station and Miss Belle told me to get back to the kitchen at once. Very snappy, she was.'

'These folk are as different from us as chalk from cheese. Change the subject, for any favour,' Samuel said, bored.

Sarah bit her lip and then, putting the battered tin teapot on the range to simmer, she sat down at the table and carefully folded her hands in her lap to stop their sudden shaking. Her heart began to beat harder and faster.

'Samuel, I've not been feelin' right these past few weeks.'

'It's probably to do with your mistress fallin' sick and dyin'. Funerals can upset women. You should hear the way the womenfolk weep and wail at funerals back home.'

'It's not that – at least, I don't think so. I think...' Sarah said, and then swallowed hard to control the sudden nausea rising in her throat. Now her heart was banging around beneath her clean apron bib like a small bird caught in a green-house. 'Samuel,' she said, her voice little more than a whisper, 'I think I might be expectin'.'

'Expectin' what?' He had settled down in the chair again, his long legs stretched across the rag rug and his hands linked comfortably over his belly.

'A b-bairn.'

'What?' He jerked upright, staring across at her.

18

'A bairn? You? How did ye manage that, ye daft girl?'

'You should surely know how.'

'Are you sayin' it's mine?'

'It can't be anyone else's.'

'Oh no!' Samuel scrambled to his feet, staring down at her. 'Ye'll not blame this on me, my girl.'

'But you're the only...'

'And how do I know that?'

'Because I'm tellin' you, that's how,' she began, and then, hearing a sound from beyond the inner door, 'Someone's comin'. Hide, quick!'

As he threw himself across the kitchen and into the tiny room where she slept, Sarah sped round the kitchen, lifting his plate and mug from the table and putting them on the draining board.

'Sarah? Oh, there you are,' Walter Forsyth said, from the doorway.

'Yes, Mr Walter. Do you want something?' Please God, Sarah thought, don't let him be wanting *that* – not tonight, not when Samuel was hidden in her cupboard of a room, listening to every word.

But for once, Walter had no thought of personal pleasures. 'Go upstairs immediately and strip the bed in the big front bedroom,' he ordered coldly.

'The master's room?'

'And when you've done that, clear everything of my – of Mr Forsyth's from the wardrobe and the chest of drawers. Everything,' Walter said tightly. 'You can pile it all on the bed for the moment. I'll arrange for boxes to be delivered from the shop tomorrow. You may leave my mother's clothes and possessions where they are for the time being.'

'But what'll the master say when he comes back from...?'

'Just do as you're told, girl!' Walter almost shouted. 'And do it now, do you understand?'

'But it's nearly time to get your supper ready.'

'We'll not be taking supper tonight. For goodness' sake, Sarah, can you not just do as you're told?'

'Yes, Mr Walter. At once, Mr Walter.'

'That's better,' he snapped.

As the door closed behind him, Samuel emerged from the little bedroom.

'He's in a right pet, is he no'?'

'I told you that somethin' had happened. I'd best do as he says, Samuel. He'll only come back if I don't get upstairs right now.'

'And I suppose I'd best be off myself.' He gave a longing look at the teapot, now puffing steam into the air, then made for the back door.

She ran after him, catching at his arm. 'Samuel, about what I just told you...'

He disentangled her fingers from the sleeve of his jacket. 'And I told you, Sarah, it's nothin' tae do with me,' he said, and then, as she began to protest, 'I'm not ready tae settle down, and anyway, how could I house and feed a brat on the pittance Mrs Smith pays me, let alone you as well? I live in a lodgin' house as it is, and there's no room there for you. I'll have tae do better in life before I can even think about marriage and fatherhood.'

'But what am I tae do, Samuel?'

'There's ways and means, and women know about them. That sort of thing's no' a man's busi-

20

ness.' He took her hands in his. 'Get rid of it, sweetheart, an' let's get back tae the way we were.'

'Samuel...' she began to beg, then stopped as the back door closed quietly but decisively behind him.

2

'I'm going to the shop tomorrow,' Walter announced as he and his sisters prepared to retire to their rooms. 'I see no sense in sitting around here.'

'What will folk think of us, going out in public so soon after laying Mother in her grave?'

'My dear Belle, what will folk think of us when they find out that Papa's gone? How can we mourn properly now? We have too much to do.'

'Perhaps he'll come back tomorrow,' Morna ventured, and her brother gave her a withering look.

'You saw the luggage he took with him. There can scarcely be anything of his left.'

'You must go to the bank tomorrow, Walter, to find out how much money we have,' Belle said suddenly.

'You're right ... what if he's taken it all?' The colour ebbed from her brother's face and one hand flew up to stroke his silky moustache, as always happened when he was worried or upset. 'What if he's left us with nothing?'

'Didn't he say that he had taken nothing but

the money due to him for running the shop?' Morna ventured.

'And how much would that be? For all we know he might have decided that he was entitled to every penny we have!' Walter began to pace the comfortable parlour. 'I must call on Mr Pinkerton at once!'

'Tonight? But he won't be in the bank at this hour, he'll be at home, and how would he be able to tell you what's in our account?' Morna wanted to know.

'She's right, Walter. In any case, if you call on Mr Pinkerton you'll have to tell him about Father. Best to leave it for now,' Belle said anxiously. 'As Morna says, he might come back. And if he doesn't, we need to have time to decide what we're going to tell people. We must put on a united front, whatever happens. We're all we have in the world now.'

'Except Aunt Beatrice,' Morna suddenly remembered, and they looked at each other, horrified.

'I had forgotten about Aunt Beatrice,' Belle confessed. 'We have to tell her what's happened before she hears it from someone else.'

'This is our business, not hers. We will deal with it.'

'Walter, you know that anything that happens within this family is Aunt Beatrice's business. We must tell her – tomorrow,' Belle rushed on as her brother tried to object. 'We must! There's no other way. Sarah can take a note round to her house first thing. I'll see to it now.'

'I'll do it. You two go to bed, it's been a

distressing day,' Walter ordered, making for the writing bureau. 'And while I'm at it, I'll tell Sarah to keep quiet about Papa leaving.'

It was just as well that the floor of the short, enclosed passageway between the hall and the kitchen had been left as unadorned wooden planks, because it meant that Sarah could tell when someone was approaching. She dashed the tears from her eyes as she recognised Walter's heavy tread, and was busy polishing silver when he came in.

'Ah, Sarah.'

'Yes, Mr Walter?' She stopped the work she had just started, and scrambled to her feet. 'Would you like some supper now? There's cold meat, and I can heat some soup.'

He tossed the offer away with a wave of his hand. 'We don't want anything to eat. We're all going to bed, and I suggest that you do the same.'

'Yes, Mr Walter.'

'Here.' He held out a sealed envelope. 'I want you to take this round to Mrs McCallum's house tomorrow morning, as soon as you have served breakfast.'

'Yes, Mr Walter.'

'You've cleared my father's room, I hope?'

'Yes, Mr Walter, I stripped the bed and then put everything of Mr Forsyth's on it, as you said. There wasn't much,' she ventured.

'I'll arrange for the shop boy to bring some boxes on the delivery cart tomorrow. You can pack everything into them. And you can serve breakfast at the usual time, since I will be going

23

to the shop.'

Her eyebrows shot up in surprise, but her voice, when she said, 'Yes, Mr Walter,' was expressionless.

He studied her in silence for a moment, and she was readying herself for his usual suggestion when he said instead, 'By the way, Sarah, you know when to hold your tongue, don't you?'

'Oh yes, Mr Walter.' She folded her hands behind her back and stared fixedly at a point just below his chin. If there was one thing she knew, it was how and when to keep her own counsel.

'So you will not mention my father's departure to anyone, will you? Not to a single soul. Do you understand?'

'Yes, Mr Walter.'

'Good,' he said, and then, coming round the edge of the table and putting a hand beneath her chin, tipping her face up towards his own, 'You're a good girl, Sarah.'

'Thank you, Mr Walter.'

'Mmm.' He stared down into her brown eyes, and wondered how it could be that a mere servant could have such perfect skin. Then he leaned forward and brushed her lips lightly with his own before releasing her chin. 'A very good girl,' he said as his hand moved down to shape itself over the delightful swell of her bosom beneath her apron bib. For a moment he hesitated, his fingers tightening and the tip of his tongue slipping out to moisten his lower lip; then he reminded himself that this, after all, was the day of his mother's funeral, and turned away.

At the door, he paused. 'Sarah...'

'Yes, Mr Walter?'

'From now on,' Walter said, 'I am the master of this house. You must address me as "sir".'

'Yes, Mr ... sir.' She bobbed a quick curtsey. He nodded, pleased, and went out.

Sarah heaved a sigh of relief. She was too worried about Samuel's visit, and his rejection of the news she had blurted out, to be bothered with Mr Walter's soft wet kisses and his clumsy fumblings tonight.

She turned the envelope over in her hands and then laid it on the table and picked up the heavy silver tablespoon she had been polishing. Her rounded face and smooth brown hair, parted in the middle and then drawn back behind her ears, were reflected in a strange, bulgy way on the back of the spoon. She stared at it, wondering what she was going to do.

The very thought of doing as Samuel wanted and visiting one of the local women known to help single lassies who had fallen into trouble made her shiver with fear. Sarah was an orphan, raised by an aunt and uncle. Her closest friend had gone to one of those women, and had died a long and agonising death as a result. Sarah had been with her in those final, terrible hours, and the memory of it – the sounds, the smell of blood, the sight of the girl's pretty, laughing face distorted by pain and fear into an inhuman mask – was enough to make her gorge rise.

She dropped the spoon and fled to the sink, where she retched helplessly for several long minutes. Finally, the paroxysm over, she straightened and spat before fetching a cup and filling it from the single cold-water tap.

No, she couldn't bring herself to do as Samuel wanted. But what if he refused to do as she wanted? What if he refused to recognise the child she carried as his own, and to make an honest woman of her? She knew that she couldn't go back to the relatives who had raised her; they would only throw her out into the gutter and tell her that that was where she belonged. And she would lose her job for certain.

She paced the kitchen, her fingers laced together across her belly so tightly that the knuckles were bone white.

What was she going to do?

Belle moved quietly along the passageway from her own room to her parents' bedroom. The varnished door swung open under faint pressure from her hand, and she stepped inside. The room smelled mainly of the pomade her father used on his hair, with a familiar, underlying scent of her mother's lily of the valley toilet water

She closed her eyes, inhaling deeply and willing herself back to the safe days of her early childhood, when this room had been a magic, warm place. She could recall her father, not dressed in mourning black as she had last seen him, but relaxed and smiling in his shirtsleeves and waistcoat, fondly watching her mother as she sat at the dressing table, brushing her long fair hair until it crackled.

Her eyes still closed, she turned towards the large bed with its ornate carved headboard, seeing in her mind's eye, her mother propped against a

26

mound of pillows, her hair tied back with a ribbon, a frilled bed jacket around her shoulders. A shawled bundle was cradled in the crook of one arm while her free hand reached out to Belle.

'Come and see your new brother, my darling,' her mother had said, and eighteen-month-old Belle toddled across the floor. Her father's strong hands swept her up and placed her on the bed, where she snuggled into her mother's shoulder and gazed down at the tiny face floating in a snowy sea of silk and wool.

The second time it happened, she had been four years old and able to clamber on to the bed by herself. This time, the baby had been Morna, pretty as a doll.

'A little sister,' Frances had said, and then putting her free arm around Belle, 'my two beautiful little daughters!'

Belle opened her eyes and returned to the present to find that she was facing the long mirror her mother had loved so much. For a precious moment the glass showed her Frances's slender, graceful figure and delicate, pretty face; then the image broke up and re-formed to reflect Belle herself, with her father's heavier build and a combination of both parents' colouring. As a result, her hair was an indeterminate mousy brown, always worn in a 'cottage loaf' style, knotted at the top of the head. Her heavy-lidded eyes were brown and her mouth small and anxious.

'My two beautiful little daughters,' Frances had said, but if there had been any fairy godmothers at the Forsyth christenings, they had given Morna all the beauty while Belle's gift had been a strong sense of duty.

It had stood her in good stead. After his marriage, Hamilton Forsyth had started to work in his father-in-law's ironmongery, and had proved to be more than worthy of his employer's trust. When Frances inherited the shop and Hamilton took sole charge, the business prospered even further under his shrewd management. He had eventually bought an adjoining shop and persuaded Frances to change the name above the door of the now impressive emporium from 'McCallum' to 'Forsyth'. He had taken his son and his elder daughter into the family business as soon as they left school; Walter to learn how to run the shop and manage the half-dozen employees, while Belle tussled with the bookkeeping.

She enjoyed the work and her natural skill with figures had, for the first time in her life, won her father's warm approval. It had given her secret pleasure to see that Walter, who was of a lazy disposition, was less successful as a pupil, and scarcely a day went by without him getting into trouble with his father.

She had been content with her lot, but now, she felt a sudden stab of resentment. Walter, being a man, was now the natural head of both household and business, when she herself would have been the better choice by far to run the business. Why should men automatically take charge of everything, even when they were less able than women?

'What are you doing?' Walter asked just then from the doorway. Belle spun round as though caught in wrongdoing and then gestured to the bed, stripped to its mattress, which held the few possessions her father had left behind.

'I was just looking. You were right, he took almost all his own things.'

'I've told Sarah to pack everything away tomorrow. I will dispose of them. You'll have to see to the shop for me, Belle, while I do that and go to the bank. I must speak with Mr Pinkerton as soon as possible.'

'What about Mother's things?'

'You and Morna can attend to them. Keep what you want, and find someone who can make good use of what you don't.' He strode to the dressing table and removed the black velvet case that held their mother's jewellery. 'She would have wished you and Morna to have something to remember her by, but first I will select a few pieces for Clarissa. I'm sure Mother would have wanted my future wife to have her jewellery. I've written a letter to Aunt Beatrice and told Sarah to deliver it as soon as she's served breakfast. I said in it that Papa had to go away on business and that we had a matter that we wanted to discuss with her. I asked her to let me know when it would be possible for me to call on her during the day.'

'You think she'll wait for you to call?'

'I made it clear that I would prefer to speak to her in her own home. In the meantime...' Walter returned to the open doorway and stood there, waiting in unspoken invitation until Belle, with a last look around the room, passed him and went into the hallway.

'Will you move into that room?' she asked as he closed the door.

'Of course, but first it will be repapered and

painted according to Clarissa's wishes, since it will be her room, too, once we are married. Goodnight, Belle,' her brother said.

'So – this is a pretty kettle of fish.' Beatrice Mc-Callum swept into the room where the three Forsyths had just started eating breakfast, unclipped the leads on the two King Charles spaniels she had brought with her, and ordered, 'Romeo, Juliet – sit!' As the dogs obeyed she added to Sarah, 'Bring another cup, lassie, and some toast. Hot, golden brown and with the crusts cut off.'

'Yes, ma'am,' Sarah gasped, and retired as Walter stumbled to his feet, almost knocking his chair over in his haste to draw out a seat for their visitor.

'Aunt Beatrice, I said in my letter that I would call on you later today.'

'I know that. I *can* read! And I can smell a scandal when it's right under m'nose. D'you think I'd just sit around and wait for you to call?' The chair gave a faint, protesting squeak as Beatrice settled her ample body on to it. She drew her gloves off and smoothed them before handing them to Walter. 'Put them on the sideboard, neatly. Now then, what's this nonsense about your father going out of town right after buryin' his wife? It must be very important business to take him away at a time like this. Is the shop in trouble – is that it?'

'The shop's fine, as far as we know. Belle's going in this morning while I go to the bank.'

'So it *is* trouble. I knew that Frances was too trusting, but there was no reasonin' with her. What did we know of Hamilton Forsyth?' Beatrice swept on in her booming voice, more used to calling dogs to heel than to drawing-room conversation. 'He wasn't a Saltcoats man – he didn't even come from Ayrshire. Frances and her father were daft, lettin' a complete stranger take over the runnin' of that shop as if it were his own.'

'It's nothing to do with the shop,' Morna piped up. 'It's Papa himself. He's left Saltcoats and he says he's never coming back.'

'Never? What d'you mean, never? What's upset the man? Stop scratching, Romeo!'

'Nothing's upset him, as far as we know.' Belle toyed nervously with the cooling slice of toast on her plate. 'He just said that now Mother's gone he has no reason to stay here. He's starting a new life.'

'At his age? Stuff and nonsense!' Beatrice snapped. 'He has a good business and a comfortable home here. What more could any man want?'

'He said,' Morna's pretty face crumpled, 'that we are the necessary evil of marriage, and now that the marriage is over he's washed his hands of us.'

'Well, now, I can't argue with that,' Beatrice mused. 'It's the one blessin' of my own union with your uncle – that we were never landed with children. Dogs are more intelligent. But even so, most folk stand by their obligations.' Then she asked sharply, 'So what's he taken with him?'

'Very little, as far as we can see,' Walter took the floor, 'apart from his own clothes and possessions. He said that he was taking the money due to him for running the shop, but no more than that. That's why I must see Mr Pinkerton this morning, to find out how things stand with us,

31

and Belle will go to the shop to see if everything's in order there.' He stopped abruptly as Sarah tapped at the door.

'I made fresh tea, Mrs McCallum, as well as the toast.' She set a tray down before Beatrice, who examined it minutely, laying the back of one hand against a slice of toast.

'Nice and hot,' she commented. 'You even remembered to bring a clean cup. More intelligent than the usual serving lassie. You may go,' she snapped, and Sarah fled. 'Morna, a little milk and one spoonful of sugar in that cup, if you please. If what you say is true,' the old lady went on, helping herself to a slice of toast, 'there's going to be a right scandal in the town. Behave yourself, Juliet, you know that you never get fed from the table. Belle, you can pour a cup of tea for me. You know what this town's like – pick a feather up from the pavement, and before you get home it's all round the place that you've stolen a chicken.'

'We can weather a scandal if we have to,' Walter said as his aunt spread butter liberally over her toast, 'as long as the shop and the bank account are safe.'

'Talkin' of the bank, what about your intended? How's Allan Pinkerton going to feel about his daughter marrying into a family abandoned by its father?'

Walter's cheeks reddened and one hand began to move towards his moustache before he caught himself in the act and forced it to join its companion behind his back. 'I must trust that Mr Pinkerton and Clarissa do not believe in visiting the sins of the father on the children,' he said, and

32

his aunt gave a sudden bark of amusement. The two spaniels, sitting obediently on the carpet, lifted their heads swiftly and then lowered them again.

'It's to be hoped that you're right. Your mother had her heart set on that marriage, Walter, and so has Mrs Pinkerton. They'd the two of you promised to each other before you even went to dame school. And the marriage won't do the business any harm, either. But best prepare yourself for a disappointment.'

'I – all three of us – may have to prepare ourselves for more than one disappointment.'

'That's true. D'you want me to go to the bank with you?'

'I'll go on my own, Aunt Beatrice,' Walter said firmly. 'Now that Papa has gone, I'm head of this family.'

'I suppose you are. Well, it's one way of making you grow up,' Beatrice said, and bit fiercely into the slice of toast. 'I'll be keeping an eye on things, of course, for the sake of your poor mother, should you need me.'

3

'Life,' Walter announced after his aunt had left them to finish breakfast, 'is about to change for all of us.' He sliced the top off the boiled egg that Sarah had just delivered and salted it liberally.

'I don't see why.' Morna was toying sulkily with

a piece of toast. 'We've still got this house to live in, haven't we? And the shop.'

'But we don't have Mother to run the house, and Papa no longer runs the shop,' her brother pointed out, digging his spoon into the soft egg yolk. 'We are orphans now, the three of us.'

'But Papa is still...'

'Orphans, Belle,' Walter interrupted firmly. 'As far as I am concerned – as far as this *household* is concerned – Hamilton Forsyth is as good as dead and buried. Our father no longer exists. You heard him wash his hands of us; now we must formally wash our hands of him. We must all be agreed on that.'

'It seems so final, though,' Belle protested. 'What if he were to take ill and come back to Saltcoats in need of our help? After all, we're his flesh and blood, you can't deny that.'

'For my part, he would be shown the door and reminded that he wanted to live his life in his own way,' Walter snapped. 'And there's no need to look shocked,' he added, glaring at his sisters, 'for we're our mother's flesh and blood too, and what d'you think she would make of the way he's treated us? To say nothing of the way he's treated her memory.'

'Walter's right,' Morna chimed in. 'Papa doesn't deserve any kindness from us. I vote that we attend to our own lives and leave him to his, whatever it may be.'

'I'm glad you said that, Morna, because I was about to raise the question of your own situation.'

'What do you mean, my situation?' Morna began to feel slightly uneasy. With both Walter and Belle established in the shop there had been no need for Morna to follow suit. Instead, she had stayed at home to keep her mother company and, as a hobby, attended weekly drawing and china painting classes at Miss Nairn's establishment for young women in Caledonia Road. She had a fairly busy social life, playing tennis, attending soirées and sometimes whirling around the roller skating rink in Glencairn Street in the company of Arthur MacAdam, one of her more regular suitors. Although at times she felt quite bored, she enjoyed her life of leisure and she didn't relish the prospect of change.

'If the money's still in the bank, and the shop is still ours,' she suggested hopefully, 'then nothing needs to alter, surely? We can go on as before, only without Father.'

'I doubt that,' Walter said ominously. 'Whether we like it or not, we're all going to have to make changes. You've been staying at home because Mother needed a companion. But there's no point now in you sitting around the house all day.'

'Sitting around?' Morna's voice began to rise. 'Do you really think that that's all I do?'

'It is, as far as I can tell, and that was all very well when Mother and Papa were here, but I think that Belle will agree with me that you can't expect us to keep you in comfort.'

Tears rose to Morna's thick-lashed hazel eyes. 'If Mother could hear you say such harsh things to me she would be most upset!'

'Mother is not here, and as I said, our lives have changed. It's time for reality to sink in, Morna – time for you to start contributing to the household expenses.'

'Belle, are you going to sit there and let him speak to me like that?'

Belle had carried on with her breakfast, quietly enjoying the discussion between her brother and sister. Since the day of Morna's birth she had lived in her young sister's shadow. While Morna was given piano and art lessons, her father had taught Belle arithmetic and bookkeeping in preparation for her duties in the shop; he had always made it clear that although he had no doubt that with her looks, Morna would have her pick of eligible male suitors, Belle would almost certainly have to learn to support herself.

'Belle!' Morna said sharply.

'I'm afraid that I agree with Walter. We must all earn our way. Remember that once Walter marries Clarissa you and I will have to become more independent.'

Morna put down her uneaten toast and looked from her sister to her brother in disbelief. 'You seriously think that I should go out and work?'

'Belle and I find employment pleasant enough.'

'But you're both needed in the shop. There's nothing for me to do there, is there?'

'Not unless you're willing to become a salesgirl, though I'm sure you could find something more agreeable than that.'

'Helping Aunt Beatrice to care for her beloved smelly dogs? Taking up nursing, or going on the stage?' Morna suggested sarcastically.

'I doubt if you're qualified for the stage, and nursing is a vocation. Teaching, perhaps?'

'I have no desire to teach. In any case, teaching

is a vocation too.'

'I'm sure that many teachers take the work on as a means of feeding, clothing and housing themselves, rather than for the love of it,' Walter said dryly. 'There's a certain pleasure in knowing that you are earning your own way in the world, Morna.' He dabbed his mouth with his napkin, consulted his pocket watch and rose to his feet. 'You may even learn to enjoy the experience.'

The small town of Saltcoats in North Ayrshire, which began as a cluster of sixteenth-century cottages huddled on the shores of the Firth of Clyde, took its name from the local 'salt cottars' who harvested sea salt to cure fish caught by the local fishermen.

As time went on coal mining came to the area, and by the late nineteenth century the growing town, built on a large curving bay and with the majestic island of Arran not far offshore, became a popular holiday resort for folk desperate to exchange the smoke and grime of the inland towns and cities for the sweeping, sandy bays and invigorating sea air of the Firth of Clyde.

They flocked to the coast in their thousands every year by bus and rail, and during July and August many of the local families living in two crowded rooms somehow managed to cram themselves into just one room in order to let out the other to holidaymakers arriving for a week, or two weeks if they could afford it.

The oldest dwellings, little more than slums by 1909, were all close to the sea that in earlier days had provided the local people with their livelihoods, while the well-to-do built fine houses on the outskirts of the town. It was in one of those handsome grey stone homes in Argyle Road that the Forsyths lived. It was an area where the genteel inhabitants liked to keep themselves to themselves. Gossip, in their view, was for the lower orders and those who lived in the poorer area, where rumours spread as fast as head lice and outbreaks of scarlet fever.

Even so, news of Hamilton Forsyth's sudden departure from Saltcoats was known up and down the length of Argyle Road and even further afield by the end of the morning.

Walter returned to the shop in Dockhead Street just before noon. Belle had been waiting for him with growing impatience in the tiny office where she sat taking in money and doling out change. Normally it suited her to be stationed there, where she could keep an eye on the shop through the glass window, but today far too many of the customers seemed over-interested in staring in at her as though she were some strange specimen in a zoo. She emerged now and again to hurry to the door so that she could peer up the street in the hope of seeing her brother's sturdy figure striding in her direction, but when he finally arrived she was at her desk, dealing with a customer paying his monthly account.

The man, a regular client, took his money with a brusque nod before turning away to find himself face to face with Walter.

'Good morning, Mr McCormack, I trust you are well?'

The man gave a loud harrumphing cough and

looked Walter up and down as though unsure as to just who he was, then muttered something and brushed past.

'It's been like that all morning,' Belle hissed through the slot left at the base of the window to allow money to pass between herself and the customers. 'Folk giving me strange looks, and some even behaving as if they don't know me! I thought you were never going to get here. Walter, what's...?'

'Not here.' Her brother cast a swift look around the premises. 'Come into my office.' He snapped his fingers. 'Mr Stoddart, kindly take charge of the shop for a few minutes. Miss Campbell, to the cash desk, if you please.'

'Walter, I have had a dreadful morning!' Belle burst out as soon as she and her brother were in the back office with the door closed against any would-be listeners. 'People have been behaving so strangely. Some have wandered round the shop, peering at me when they thought I wasn't looking and then going out without buying anything. Those who did come in to buy have either cut me off as if I were a total stranger or asked after me with such sympathy that you would think that I'm the one who was ill, and not Mother. Even the staff are behaving strangely.'

'That's because everyone knows.' Walter threw himself into the swivel chair before his desk.

'About Father?'

'Of course about Papa, who else? I've had to put up with stares and smirks everywhere I went, even in the bank while I was waiting to see Mr Pinkerton. I've seen people whispering in the streets behind their hands, and watching me. God knows how they know, but they do! Even Mr Pinkerton knew why I wanted to see him.'

'The money...' Belle suddenly remembered.

'It's all there, just as Papa said. He must have been taking a wage from the place and investing it somewhere else all these years. But at least he's not left us destitute. Mr Pinkerton was sympathetic, I'll say that for him. He's as dumbfounded as we are over what has happened.'

'Did Father say nothing to him about his plans?'

'Not a word, as far as I can make out. But good riddance to him!' Walter spat the words out savagely. 'He's gone from our lives, Belle, and we must forget him.'

'How can we forget our own father?'

'From what he said last night, he has forgotten us already. What's good for the goose is good for the gander.'

'Did Mr Pinkerton mention Clarissa? Does she know?'

'Not as yet, he says. But fortunately he does not blame me, or any of us, for our father's sins. He still gives his blessing to our marriage.'

'Well, that's something,' Belle said with relief. Clarissa Pinkerton was her best friend, and both families had looked on her engagement to Walter six months earlier as an ideal match. For her part, Belle felt that Clarissa would be more of a sister to her than Morna had ever been.

'He's coming to the house this evening to go over some business with me and he will bring Clarissa with him. He says she is eager to spend some time with you and Morna. At least we have his support,' Walter said. 'As to the rest of the town, we must just ride out the storm.'

'You don't think it could have been Sarah, do you? Could she have realised what was going on and mentioned it to … no, of course not,' Belle corrected herself at once, 'she's only a servant, without the wit to work such things out. But she might have overheard us talking. If she's gossiped to any of the other servants in the road I shall have her out of the house, bag and baggage, before the day is over!'

'It's not Sarah,' Walter said swiftly. 'I spoke to her last night, quite severely, and made her promise that she would not utter a word of what had happened.'

'You think that a servant girl can keep promises?'

'She would not dare to disobey a direct order from me, Belle, I can assure you of that. In any case, the damage is done and can't be undone. It's up to us now. If we can behave calmly and with dignity, folk will get tired of tittle-tattling soon enough. But for the moment,' Walter sighed heavily and got to his feet, 'we must go out into the shop and face them all.'

'It came as a terrible shock when Father broke the news to us, but after some consideration, all of us agreed that we stand united in our support for you poor souls. The wicked thing that your father has just done should not reflect upon you, my dearest friends.' Clarissa Pinkerton's voice was firm, and her large dark eyes were steady as she surveyed Belle and Morna. Everything about Clarissa was

41

firm, even to her sturdy body, encased in a well-boned corset. 'Naturally, as soon as I heard the dreadful news I resolved to stand by Walter. We are pledged to each other for the rest of our lives and beyond, and so my place must always be by his side!' She paused to draw breath, patting her bodice lightly and beaming at her audience. 'My goodness, I feel almost like the heroine in one of those delightful romantic novels! Now you must not concern yourselves, my dears, for together we shall win through this adversity.'

'It's easy for you, Clarissa,' Belle said miserably. 'You didn't have to sit in the shop and watch people staring and whispering and ... thinking things about you.'

'Oh, fiddle! No doubt there are those who will say that I should turn my back on my poor innocent Walter in his hour of need, but I do not intend to pay any heed to them, and neither should you. Sticks and stones may break our bones, but whispers and stares can never hurt us or turn us from doing our duty. Hold your head high and pull your shoulders back,' Clarissa said briskly, following her own advice. She and the Forsyth sisters had known each other all their lives; even although Clarissa was six months younger than Walter, and therefore two and a half years younger than Belle, the three Forsyths had always been in the habit, during childhood, of deferring to her in the choice of games and activities. When she decided, in her mid-teens, to fall in love with Walter, their engagement had become inevitable, partly because Clarissa wanted Walter as a husband, and partly because they were eminently suited and both sets of parents desired the union as much as she did.

As she stood before them with her chin up, shoulders squared and head thrown back defiantly, she looked, Belle thought, like the pictures she had seen of a female singer dressed as Britannia. If Clarissa had suddenly seized the brass toasting fork from its place on the hearth and burst into 'Land of Hope and Glory' she would not have been in the least bit surprised.

Morna, for her part, glanced down at her own small, softly rounded chest and wished that her bosom was as magnificent as Clarissa's.

'Walter says that folk will soon get tired of talking about us,' Belle said.

'Of course they will! And we'll always stand by you.' Clarissa sat on the sofa beside her, taking Belle's hand in both of hers. 'Father has already said so, and Mama agrees. She would have come with us this evening if the shock of what has happened hadn't brought on one of her headaches. As for me,' she added, her voice deepening and ringing out as though proclaiming an oath in public, 'I would marry Walter tomorrow if I could. I said as much to Papa on our way here, but he says we must observe a proper period of mourning for dear Aunt Frances.'

'What she would say about all this, I don't know,' Belle wailed.

'If she was still here it wouldn't have happened,' Morna pointed out. 'You heard Papa say that once the marriage was over there was no reason for him to stay.'

'I suppose,' Clarissa's voice was thoughtful,

'that when we marry, we will live here, since the house will now be Walter's.'

'Oh yes. He said to me only last night that he intends to have the main bedroom redecorated to your taste.'

'Really? I must have a good look at it ... in a month or so, I mean,' Clarissa added swiftly. 'Or perhaps a week or so. In the meantime, I suppose the three of you will go on living here as before?'

'I'll certainly continue to run the household as I have done since Mother fell ill,' Belle agreed. 'And work in the shop. But once you and Walter marry...' her voice trailed away.

'You must both continue to look on this house as your own home, even after I become its mistress,' Clarissa said kindly. 'After all, we're more like sisters than friends and I would never seek to turn either of you out.'

'I may well have a home of my own by then,' Morna said swiftly.

'Indeed?' Clarissa's eyes widened and she gave an arch little giggle. 'Are you thinking by any chance of a certain Mr MacAdam?'

'Arthur would make a suitable husband,' Morna acknowledged coyly, 'and I have good reason to believe that he is more than ready to settle down.'

'But that's grand news,' Clarissa gushed, smiling warmly at the younger girl. She had no objection to sharing her marital home with Belle, who would be more than willing to act as housekeeper as well as being very useful to Walter in the shop, but the prospect of sheltering *two* unmarried sisters-in-law under her roof was not attractive. 'You'll make an enchanting hostess in the home of the right man,

Morna, and just think what fun you and I will have, setting up our new lives together!'

'I had no idea that Arthur MacAdam was on the verge of proposing marriage, Morna,' Belle said after the Pinkertons had gone home.

'What's that?' Walter asked.

'Morna has just told me and Clarissa that she is about to become engaged to Arthur MacAdam.'

'Indeed? That *is* good news, Morna. He's a fine young man.'

'Father seemed unsure of his suitability,' Belle pointed out, and her brother shrugged.

'I scarcely think that Father is a fit judge. For my own part, I have always liked Arthur.'

'But isn't it rather soon for Morna to be speaking of an engagement?'

'In view of Mother's passing, Belle,' Morna protested, 'we will of course wait a respectable length of time before making anything official.'

'No, I meant that you and he have only been walking out together for a few weeks at the most. He hasn't even come to tea yet. I had no idea that his feelings for you were so strong.'

'How often did Mother tell us that she fell passionately in love with Papa from almost the first moment she laid eyes on him?' Morna asked irritably.

'I know, but I always thought she was romanticising. Do people really fall in love at first sight?' Belle wondered. 'Did you, Walter, with Clarissa?'

'What a thing to ask! And considering that I've known Clarissa almost all my life, what a daft idea! Children don't fall in love. Should I perhaps have a word with Arthur?' Walter asked his sister, suddenly reminded of his new role as head of the household.

'Certainly not. D'you want to frighten the man away? Let him declare himself to me first.'

'*If* he does. It still seems to me to be too early for you to be so certain of his feelings, let alone yours.'

'I have no doubt as to his feelings, *or* mine,' Morna snapped at her sister. She was already upset over Walter's suggestion that she should start thinking of ways to earn her keep, and Clarissa's reminder that once she married Walter she would be mistress of the house, and her somewhat condescending, 'I would never seek to turn either of you out,' had chilled Morna to the marrow. The prospect of being little more than an unwanted lodger in the house that had always been her home was frightening. Until that day she had had no desire to rush into marriage, but now, it seemed, she must give the idea serious thought. It would certainly be a much more attractive alternative to earning her own living.

Later, in her bedroom, she sat down by her dressing table to think the matter over carefully. Arthur MacAdam came from a respectable Saltcoats family. He was pleasing enough to look at, and he had always been both courteous and attentive towards her. In fact, now that she came to think of it, he had been most attentive at her mother's funeral, taking her arm as they walked from the cemetery, and proffering a snowy white handkerchief during the reception afterwards, when solicitous murmurings from the mourners had caused her cheeks to dampen with tears. She still had the handkerchief, washed and ironed by Sarah and put away carefully in one of the dressing-table drawers.

She took it out now and unfolded it carefully. It was made of stiff linen, and had his initials, A. MacA, in one corner. Morna ran a fingertip over the letters. Morna MacAdam. It had a certain ring to it. 'Mrs Morna MacAdam,' she said aloud, to her reflection, and then tried, 'Mrs MacAdam.' And then, extending a gracious hand towards the glass, 'How do you do? I am Mrs Arthur MacAdam.'

She tipped her head to one side and smiled prettily, pleased with the good solid sound of the name. No doubt, if she worked hard at it, she could come to love and respect Arthur. And she would far rather be mistress of her own house than become a poor relation in her brother's.

She and Arthur had arranged to go together to a musical concert in Saltcoats Town Hall at the end of the month; because she was in mourning she would not, of course, be able to go. She would send Sarah to his home in the morning to deliver the handkerchief, together with a nicely written note regretting that she must miss the concert, but suggesting that he might care to call at the house one day soon to take tea with her.

She folded the handkerchief carefully along the creases that had been ironed into it, and put it aside. She would write the note in the morning. And on second thoughts, she would not mention the handkerchief in her letter, but would keep it and give it to him in person.

She smiled again at her reflection, and decided that marriage might, after all, be quite pleasant.

4

The corset sprang joyously open as soon as the laces were loosened, and Sarah sucked air into her starving lungs in a great gusty sigh of relief. Glancing down, she saw that her white skin was covered with crimson weals where the corset, drawn as tight as she could manage, had bitten into tender flesh. She ran a hand over her belly, which had never been flat but had at least been soft. Now it was hard to the touch, a sure sign that the child within was growing. As she began to clamber into the washtub she had filled laboriously from water brought to boil in pots on the range she wondered how much longer she could manage to hide her condition from her employers.

It was almost midnight and the three Forsyths, who usually went to bed at around ten o'clock, were all sound asleep in their comfortable bedrooms two floors above the kitchen. Sarah had allowed plenty of time in order to be sure of that, and to be sure, too, that Mr Walter didn't take it into his head to come creeping down the stairs in search of her. Not that he had done so since the death of his mother.

The washtub was high sided and difficult to get into, but Sarah was desperate and, after a struggle, she managed to lower her bare backside into the water, which was hot enough to make her moan softly, bite her bottom lip and squeeze her eyelids tightly shut. Even so, the pain was enough to force a few tears into her eyes. The tub was not meant to be used as a bath and she was wedged into it uncomfortably, her white thighs pressed against her belly and breasts, her knees almost beneath her chin. She had poured too much water into it, and some of it slopped over the sides. It was just as well that she had thought to spread newspapers over the kitchen floor.

The stinging sensation eased as her skin got used to the heat, and, reaching out to the bottle on the nearby stool, she uncorked it and took a sip. Liquid fire raced down her throat, burning everything in its path, and Sarah choked, a hand flying to her mouth as her stomach heaved and threatened to empty itself into the steaming water. How could anyone want to drink such stuff for pleasure? She had only been able to afford the cheapest gin; perhaps that was why it tasted so vile. She nerved herself to take another mouthful and then decided, as the neat alcohol threatened once again to come spouting back out of her, that perhaps it might be easier to have the baby.

But that was out of the question, so gin it had to be. She forced down some more and this time, thank the Lord, it seemed to go down more easily.

'Out of the question,' she whispered to herself, for soon, before the child she carried grew much larger, she would have to leave this house, the only home she knew. If Samuel refused to marry her and accept responsibility for the baby he had fathered on her, where could she go? She had nobody in the world but Samuel.

She said his name aloud, and the mere sound of it gave her the courage to take another gulp of gin. She admired Samuel not only for his looks but also for his intelligence. He could talk about any subject under the sun. He was well read and subscribed to the local library. *And* he was ambitious.

'I'll not always be a delivery boy,' he often said, sitting at the kitchen table enjoying a cup of strong tea, a home-baked scone and Sarah's adoration. 'One day I'll find a way to rise in the world, you wait and see if I don't.'

It had been a dream come true when he started courting her, taking her out walking on her evenings off and teaching her something of the town she lived in, but seldom saw, since the Forsyth house was where she spent almost all her time. The first time he kissed her, his warm tongue slipping beguilingly into her mouth, his breath mingling with hers and his strong young body crushing her breasts against his chest, she had floated on air for the next three days. There had been more kisses, and then came the soft summer evening when they had become lovers. Sarah's body tingled even now, thinking of that first time below a hedge in a field near the town – the springy grass prickling against her naked back, the delicious warm weight of Samuel's body on top of her, the silkiness of his skin against hers, the strength of his arms and the sweet strong curve of his backside beneath her eager fingers.

There had been other times too, some of them right here in the Forsyth house, when the two of

50

them wrestled passionately in her narrow little bed, mouths locked together to prevent them from giving voice to their pleasure lest they got carried away and were heard by the Forsyths who slumbered above them, safe in the knowledge that their servant, a good, well-behaved lassie, was snoring demurely in her chaste cot.

The thought of those night-time adventures set Sarah to giggling, and again she pressed a hand against her mouth, peeping up at the cracked, smoke-grimed ceiling.

Suddenly remembering that she was still wedged in the tub, she peered down into the water, not quite sure of what she might see. She had heard the other servant lassies talk of gin and a hot bath as a good way of getting rid of an unwanted pregnancy, but she was unsure as to what actually happened, and she had not dared to ask anyone for fear of her secret being found out.

The water was cooling and the gin almost finished. With a struggle and much slopping of water, over the side of the tub, she managed to wriggle out, staggering slightly as she straightened her cramped body. After drying herself and pulling her nightgown on, she used a pail to empty the tub before mopping it and putting it away in its cupboard. Lastly, she gathered up the soggy newspapers and took them out into the back yard.

Back in the warmth of the kitchen she yawned and scratched her head, feeling pleasantly relaxed and sleepy. For some strange reason she felt as though the kitchen was circling slowly around her. She reeled into the room that was only large enough to hold her bed and a three-drawer dresser and blew out the candle before crawling beneath the blanket and folding her hands together under her chin, as her aunt had taught her.

'Dear God...' she mumbled, 'please...'

And then she fell asleep.

Morna spent most of the next day planning the scene that would greet Arthur MacAdam when he arrived to take tea with her. She would be in full mourning, of course, but the black clothing would contrast well with her fair hair and ashen cheeks.

Glancing into her dressing-table mirror she was annoyed to see that her cheeks were in fact flushed with excitement at the thought of the forthcoming meeting and the outcome she had planned for it. It was true that she looked very pretty, but ashen was the effect she needed. She would have to use face powder every day, just in case he arrived unannounced. She would be in the parlour, playing something sad on the piano – or perhaps she should be caught at her easel. She decided to start work right away on a likeness of her mother, painted from the family portrait on the parlour mantelpiece. She hurried downstairs and was annoyed, when she went into the room, to see that it was no longer in its usual place.

Sarah, working at the sink, jumped as Morna burst into the kitchen. 'Where have you put the family likeness that should be on the mantelshelf in the parlour?'

Sarah whipped round, wiping the back of her hand across her mouth. 'I didn't touch it, Miss Morna. It hasn't been there since the mornin' after the master ... the mornin' after the mistress's funeral.'

'If you didn't move it, then who did?'

'I don't know, miss.'

'Oh, for goodness' sake!' Morna turned to flounce out, then turned back. 'Did you deliver that letter to Mr MacAdam's house?'

'Yes, Miss Morna.'

'Into his hands, as I said?'

'The maid took it from me. She said that Mr Arthur MacAdam was out, but she would see that he got it.'

'Oh. Very well. I'll have a cup of tea, Sarah, in the parlour.' Morna returned to the front room and stared at the various surfaces, wondering where the photograph could be. Walter must have put it away after their father's sudden departure. She started to search, and had just found it face down in a drawer in the writing table when Sarah brought a tray in.

'Put it down there,' Morna ordered, and then, as Sarah bent to obey and a shaft of sunlight fell on her unusually pale face, 'You're not ill, are you?'

'No miss, I'm fine.' Sarah's head felt woolly and her stomach was uneasy, but that was all. She was beginning to suspect that the scalding bath and the gin she had forced down had not had the desired effect after all.

'You can go now,' Morna said sharply as the maid stood before her, her brown eyes vacant. Honestly, she thought crossly when she was alone, there was no reason for Sarah to look so wan, and to have those shadows beneath her eyes.

It wasn't as though it was *her* mother who had just died!

She looked into the mirror on the wall and ran a hand over her own cheeks, as though trying to smooth the colour out of them, then turned her attention back to the portrait. Perhaps it would be best not to attempt a painting of Mother, since faces were not her strong point.

Pouring tea, she decided that she would paint a nice vase of flowers instead. She would bring her easel down to the parlour and when Arthur arrived he would find her working on a pretty floral picture, her face suitably pale, with perhaps just a suggestion of delicate but becoming shadows beneath her eyes.

She smiled, thinking of his reaction. If their meeting went as she hoped, she and Clarissa might well have a double wedding once the period of mourning for her mother had ended. And there was no doubt that she would be the more beautiful bride.

'Two letters, both delivered by hand, sir,' Sarah said. 'One for you and one for Miss Morna.'

'To me, Sarah,' Walter said as Morna held out her hand. He took the envelopes from the little silver tray. 'Thank you, Sarah. That will be all.'

'I believe that one has my name on it,' Morna reminded him, stretching an arm across the breakfast table. Her brother leaned back in his chair so that the envelope was out of her reach.

'All in good time.'

'You're enjoying this, aren't you? You're enjoying being the head of the family, master of the house.'

'It has its rewards,' he acknowledged with a barely concealed smirk.

'My letter, if you please!'

'Walter...' Belle interceded. 'Give it to her. I don't want to start a headache before I've even reached the shop.'

'Oh, very well.' He handed the envelope over and Morna tore it open eagerly. Belle took the last piece of toast from the rack as the other two read their letters.

Walter finished first, groaning. 'I've been summoned to Aunt Beatrice's house to tell her what's happening with the shop.'

'When?'

'This morning, she says. As if I've not got enough to do!'

'I'll be in the shop, and Mr Stoddart is reliable,' Belle said calmly, spreading marmalade thickly on her toast. 'We'll see that everything runs smoothly.'

'But it's none of her business! When did she ever take an interest in the shop?'

'I expect she just feels that since Papa has gone, she is the senior member of the family...'

'She is the oldest by far, but not the head of this family,' Walter said haughtily. 'I am perfectly capable of seeing to the shop and to our financial affairs, and the sooner she understands that, the better.'

'Are you going to tell her so?' Belle's eyes were bright with interest and amusement.

'Of course!'

'I wish I could go there with you.' There was just a touch of malice in Belle's calm voice, and a smile tugged at the corners of her mouth. 'I doubt if anyone has defied Aunt Beatrice since Uncle Hector died. Perhaps not even before that.'

'Are you saying that I'm afraid to stand up to an interfering old woman?'

'I believe I am. What do you think, Morna?'

'What?' Morna dragged her eyes from the note in her hand.

'Don't you think that it's time Walter stood up to Aunt Beatrice? After all, it's not as if we're asking her to support us. We're not poor little orphans,' Belle said. Then, as Morna's gaze returned again to her letter, 'What's wrong? Is it bad news?'

'It's not from Papa, is it?' Walter chimed in. 'He's not thinking of coming back, is he? Because if he is, I shall forbid it.'

Morna pushed her chair back and got up. 'It's from Arthur MacAdam, saying how sorry he is that I won't be able to attend the concert with him next week. But he hopes to call on me soon.'

'That's good, isn't it?' Walter said encouragingly.

'Yes, it is. If you'll excuse me...' Morna made for the door.

'You haven't finished your breakfast.'

'I've had sufficient,' Morna said over her shoulder as she fled from the room.

'Do you think she's pining for Mother?' Walter wondered.

'More likely to be pining for Arthur MacAdam and the social life she's going to have to give up for the time being. I must get to the shop,' Belle said briskly, 'and you must call on Aunt Beatrice.'

'I hope she doesn't expect to be consulted on every aspect of our lives from now on. I have no desire to be ordered about as if I was one of her precious dogs.'

'They live more comfortable lives than a lot of humans,' Belle reminded him.

In the privacy of the small bedroom she had opted to move into a year earlier rather than continue sharing with Belle, Morna read Arthur's brief note for the tenth time. 'While I too regret that you will not be able to accompany me to next week's concert, and I thank you for your kind invitation to tea, I feel that it would be best that you and your family have ample time to mourn your recent bereavement before entertaining again. In the meantime, Miss Forsyth, may I wish you continued good health. Yours sincerely, Arthur MacAdam.'

Tears stung her eyes and blurred the handwriting before her. He had referred to her as Miss Forsyth, and signed the letter – if such a brief epistle could be graced with the word – with his full name, as though they were nothing more to each other than acquaintances. When she thought of all the times they had stepped around a dance floor together, the tennis games they had played, the solicitous way he had taken her arm when they spun together around the roller skating rink, the conversations they had had...

She crushed the note up and threw it into the wastebasket. How dare he treat her so coldly? How dare he desert her like this, and leave her to the tender mercies of her brother and, eventually, his new wife? She would not tolerate such behaviour!

As soon as she heard the front door close behind Belle and Walter she flounced downstairs to the parlour, where she opened the roll-top writing desk and found a sheet of notepaper and a pen.

'Dear Mr MacAdam,' she wrote. Let him see how hurtful it was to be addressed so formally by one thought to be a close and dear friend. 'While I appreciate your consideration, let me assure you that your friendship and your company at this sad time would be of consolation to me, and not a burden in any way. Indeed, it would be such a pleasure to be able to talk to someone as understanding as yourself, and...'

She stopped, read over the words she had just written, and decided that she sounded too desperate. She tore the page in half and started again, just as the door opened.

'Yes, Sarah, what is it?'

'I was going to start doing this room, miss.'

'Can't you see that I'm busy?' Morna snapped. 'Find something else to do. I'm sure there's plenty.' As the door closed she started on another letter, then stopped again, feeling that this time she was being too cold. It might be best to wait until she felt calmer. She picked up the two letters and carried them into the kitchen, where she threw them on the range and watched as they burst into flames and then became ash. After that, deciding that a cup of tea might calm her nerves, she went in search of Sarah.

'Tomorrow, Sarah, you must start to clean the house from top to bottom.'

'You mean like spring-cleaning, Miss Belle?

But we've only just come into October.'

'I'm well aware of that, but since the big front bedroom's been stripped, you might as well start there and then do the rest of the house. You may tell Annie McCall to help with the heavier work,' Belle added.

The few possessions left behind by Hamilton Forsyth had been removed – Belle had no idea where they had gone and no intention of asking Walter what he had done with them. The feeling that with so many drastic changes in their lives, the house itself must be thoroughly cleared, cleaned and reclaimed had seized her.

'And be thorough, mind,' she added. The girl needn't think that she could slack just because her mistress had died.

Life had to go on, but sometimes, Belle thought as she took off the blouse and skirt she had worn to the shop and sluiced her face, arms and throat with cool water, going on was quite a struggle. The shop had been hot and busy, and she felt tired and dispirited. She longed for the days when her mother ran the house and she herself had only the shop to think of. When her mother fell ill Belle had been more than willing to take over the domestic duties, and she would have gone on working between house and shop for her father, but now everything had changed. If the clock could just be turned back – but it never could. No doubt they would all settle down again and get used to being three where there had always been five, but by that time Walter would be preparing for marriage, and Clarissa's arrival would cause yet another upheaval. Although she and Clarissa were fond of each other, Belle was not altogether sure that she would enjoy seeing someone else in charge of the family home.

Perhaps it was time she considered taking up some new interests and meeting different people; possibly even some presentable young man intelligent enough to value strength of character and a good mind over a pretty face and slim waist.

She smiled tentatively at her reflection in the dressing-table mirror. She had good teeth and her skin was as soft as the skin described in the romantic novels she and Clarissa had often giggled over together. She was not so very unattractive.

The small bronze gong in the hall sounded, summoning her to dinner. As she went downstairs Belle wished, not for the first time in her life, that she had been born as pretty as Morna.

Lucky, lucky Morna!

5

Morna only picked at her food that evening, pushing the rest around her plate until Walter snapped at her to eat it or stop tormenting it.

She pushed the plate away. 'I don't like mackerel!'

'You always have before,' Belle said reasonably.

'Then I don't like it now!'

'You're not sickening for something, are you?' The doctor had said that their mother had a weak heart; what if it were hereditary, Belle wondered in sudden panic. What if Morna had it, too?

'I'm in mourning, that's all. Grief causes some of us to lose our appetites,' Morna said, eyeing Walter's clean plate in a pointed manner. 'You've almost taken the pattern off that – nobody would know *you're* in mourning.'

'Sarah's a good cook, and in any case, I work hard and I need nourishment.' He leaned back in his seat, pushing the plate away. 'Something substantial for pudding, I hope, Belle?'

'Jam roly-poly.'

'Good,' he said with relish, and then, as an afterthought, 'I saw Arthur MacAdam heading for the tennis courts on my way home, talking with a pretty little thing – not someone I've seen before. They were both carrying rackets.'

'Arthur MacAdam? With a young lady?' Belle's eyes were bright with curiosity. 'But I thought that...'

'If you don't mind,' Morna said, 'I'm going to my room. I have a headache.'

'I'll tell Sarah to take your pudding up, shall I?'

'I don't want any pudding, Belle. I don't want anything, except to be left in peace.'

'Perhaps you should go after her,' Walter suggested as the door closed behind their younger sister.

'Best to leave her in peace, as she asks. If you want my opinion,' Belle said, 'poor Arthur MacAdam has no idea that he and Morna are more or less betrothed. I don't even know if she likes him very much. She only came out with the story when Clarissa told us that we were both welcome to stay on in this house once you and she were married.'

'Did she, indeed?'

'Indeed. And Morna promptly said that she would probably have her own home by then, with Arthur. I believe that she just wanted to be upsides with Clarissa. To think that just a few weeks ago everything was normal, apart from poor Mother's health. Now I'm wondering when this household will ever feel normal again. Surely nothing else can happen to upset us?'

'An upset is to be expected, after Mother's death.'

'And Papa's desertion.'

'That hasn't helped.' A steely note crept into Walter's voice and he reached across the table to pat her hand. 'We're going through a very difficult time, but together we shall overcome it, Belle, have no fear of that.'

'To be honest, that's of little comfort right now.' She drew her hand from beneath his and put it to her forehead. 'I do believe that I also feel a head-ache coming on. I'd best go to my room and lie down. Ring for Sarah, will you, and tell her that Morna and I don't feel like eating any pudding tonight.'

Alone in the room, Walter Forsyth went towards the tasselled bell pull hanging by the fireplace, then changed his mind and went into the hall and along to the kitchen.

'I was just about to bring them through, sir,' Sarah said hurriedly, nodding at the table, where three portions of jam sponge sat on a tray.

'Then let me save you the walk.' Walter closed

the door quietly and came towards her. 'My sisters both have headaches, and no appetite. I shall have my pudding in here, Sarah, and you shall have some with me.'

'Oh no, sir, I couldn't.'

'Indeed you could.' He pulled out two chairs as he spoke, setting a plate before each place. 'Sit down, Sarah, and eat with me.'

'But Miss Belle...'

'Is upstairs in her bedroom with the door shut. In any case, I am the master of the house now, and if I say that we eat pudding together, then you must do as I say, mustn't you?' He playfully caught her hand and pulled her towards one of the chairs. 'Won't you sit down, milady?'

He ushered her into the seat as though she were royalty, and when she would have drawn her hand from his, he retained it, kissing her fingers one by one. 'What pretty hands you have, Sarah.'

'They're all rough with work, sir,' she protested, her cheeks as red as her fingers.

'True, but they are pretty nonetheless.' He released her hand, only to move behind her seat so that he could bend to nuzzle at the curve of her neck. Sarah closed her eyes, knowing what would come next. And sure enough, within a few seconds Walter was smothering her ears with tickly, annoying kisses.

'So pretty,' he whispered. 'Delicate little shells. You have the ears of a lady, Sarah Neilson.'

'Do I, sir?' She set her teeth and stared with a nauseous fascination at the creamy yellow sponge and bright red jam on the plate before her, while Walter nibbled and kissed. The hot bath and the gin had done nothing for her; she was still with child, and feeling tired and nauseous all the time.

Finally, tiring of her ears for the time being, Walter asked, 'Where are the spoons, Sarah? No, don't get up, let me serve you for once.'

'Left-hand drawer of that dresser, sir.' She watched as he rummaged in the drawer, wondering if Samuel might look in this evening and hoping that if so, Mr Walter might be back in his own part of the house by then. The thought of the two of them coming face to face made her feel sick again. She pressed her hands against her rib cage and took a deep breath as Walter seated himself by her side and put the spoons down on the table.

Sarah watched as he dug deep into the pale yellow sponge, scooping up a great mound. He lifted the laden spoon to his mouth and a red cavity opened beneath his dark moustache to receive it.

'Mmmm, it's good. My sisters don't know what they're missing.' He scooped up another spoonful and began to chew it with relish, his eyes twinkling at her while the lower half of his face worked busily. He looked, Sarah thought, the nausea threatening to go out of control, like an oversized, moustached child devouring a hitherto forbidden treat.

'Go on, eat up,' he urged through the third mouthful.

'I don't like to, sir, not with you sitting here in the kitchen. It doesn't seem right...'

'Nonsense!' Walter sprayed crumbs over the table. 'It feels very right to me.'

'What would Miss Belle say, sir? And Miss Morna?'

'Don't you bother your pretty little head over what they might say.' He filled his spoon again. 'I'm the master in this house, and if I choose to eat my pudding in your company then that is my business and nobody else's. And I do choose.' He swallowed before continuing. 'I like being with you, Sarah. You're real, and decent, and warm and comforting. Here...'

He used his own spoon to dig a scoop of sponge and jam from the untouched plate before her. 'Open up,' he demanded, almost coyly, and she had no option but to obey. The spoon was immediately thrust between her parted lips, scraping against her lower teeth in a way that made her flesh crawl, then it withdrew, leaving what seemed like a great mass of soft, raspberry-tasting stuff in her mouth. She jerked away without thinking, and the bowl of the spoon trailed over her lower lip and chin, leaving them sticky.

'Good, eh?'

She mumbled through the food, nodding her head and praying that when she swallowed, it would stay down.

Walter was scraping his plate now. 'You make an excellent jam roly-poly, Sarah,' he was saying when the front doorbell jangled. Sarah jumped to her feet.

'I'll have to answer the door, sir,' she gabbled, and fled through the hall, her hands automatically straightening her apron and then her hair. She remembered, just before opening the door, to rub hard at her lips and chin with one fist.

Mr Pinkerton stood on the step, a bulky envelope beneath his arm. 'Is Mr Forsyth at home?'

Sarah almost said that Mr Forsyth had gone away, before remembering that the bank manager must be referring to the son and not the father.

'Yes, sir, he is. Come in please, sir.' She closed the door behind him and took his hat and stick, then showed him into the front parlour before hurrying to the kitchen, where Walter scowled when he heard about his visitor.

'Why did he have to come pushing in at this time of night?' he said crossly, straightening his cuffs. 'Follow me, Sarah, he may well want some tea.'

But Allan Pinkerton was in the mood for something stronger than tea.

'I'm here on business, with a pile of papers for you to sign, Walter, but since it's after business hours and we've both had our dinners, a drop of that fine port that your father always kept in there would not be out of place,' he said, nodding at the handsomely carved corner cupboard.

'Of course. Sarah, you can go now.'

'Yes, sir.' She closed the door and went swiftly through the kitchen and out to the water closet in the back yard, where she emptied her stomach of the unwanted jam roly-poly and her entire evening meal.

Samuel didn't come tapping at the door that night, which was just as well, since Walter's visitor stayed until late. Sarah, mindful of the spring-cleaning on the following morning, was almost dropping with tiredness when the parlour bell finally summoned her to fetch Mr Pinkerton's hat and stick and open the door for him.

As soon as it closed behind the banker's broad,

straight back, Walter let out his breath in a great sigh of irritation. 'Damn the man, why did he have to choose tonight to see to business that could have easily been dealt with in his bank by day?' he grumbled, taking a step towards Sarah.

One hand was reaching out for her when Belle enquired from the stair landing, 'Who on earth was that, Walter?'

'Only Clarissa's father with papers for me to sign.'

'Do you know what time it is?'

'Yes, but he got well settled with Papa's best port and I thought he was going to stay for the night and take his breakfast with us in the morning. Go back to bed, Belle.'

'I won't settle for ages now,' she complained, coming down a step or two, her dressing gown pulled tightly around her uncorseted body. 'Sarah, bring me a cup of hot chocolate, will you? And Walter, get to your bed or you'll be fit for nothing tomorrow.'

'Just coming,' he called back, then muttered a curse beneath his breath. As Sarah went to make his sister's drink he followed her and managed a quick, clumsy fumble by the kitchen door before turning reluctantly towards the stairs.

Morna decided on the following morning to forgo her plan to write again to Arthur. Instead, she would take the handkerchief to his home that afternoon and hand it over to his mother. Mrs MacAdam had always been very kind to her, and would clearly look on her as a suitable daughter-in-law. She would be sure to be understanding, especially if Morna looked pale and wan and quite overcome by the distress of her mother's death and her father's cruel desertion.

Although she was quite hungry when she woke, she forced herself to pick at her breakfast, scarcely eating a morsel. Unfortunately Belle was too busy organising the spring-cleaning that Sarah was to start on that day and Walter too lost in his own thoughts to notice their sister's lack of appetite.

She kept to her room all morning and punished herself further by refusing to eat any lunch. At two o'clock she dressed in the clothes she had bought for her mother's funeral before surveying herself critically in the full-length mirror in one corner of the room. It was most fortunate that black made the most of her fair looks, she thought, and a lavish application of face powder had worked well, making her look suitably pale; while the slightest touch of blue eye-shadow smoothed into the skin beneath each eye added to the delicate look. She smiled at her reflection as she arranged her fair hair so that a few curls were allowed to peep prettily from beneath her hat. Mrs MacAdam would be sure to take pity on her now, and even Arthur's heart, should he chance to come home while she was still there, sipping at a cup of weak tea and refusing as much as a biscuit, would melt at the sight of her.

'I'm going out for a while, Sarah,' she said, running the maidservant to ground in the room that had belonged to her parents. The curtains had been taken down and Annie McCall had carried the rugs down to the back garden, where she was beating dust out of them. The room, with its stripped bed, bare floor and air of desertion, was no longer her parents' domain. 'I should be home by five o'clock.'

'Yes, miss.' Sarah was on her hands and knees, scrubbing the skirting board.

The Three Towns, as they were known locally, consisted of Ardrossan, Saltcoats and Stevenson, strung along the coast and more or less blending with each other. The MacAdams lived in Caledonia Road, an extension of Argyle Road, leading almost to the border with Ardrossan.

The heels of Morna's black shiny boots tapped briskly along the pavement. It was grand to be out of the house and walking in the fresh air – so grand that she had to keep reminding herself that she was in mourning and must keep her head lowered and her eyes on the ground. It would never do to seem happy at such a time.

She resorted to the childhood game of counting the cracks between the flagstones, allowing herself to glance up only when she happened to be passing someone. She met several neighbours on her way to the MacAdams' house, greeting them with a subdued smile and a quiet voice. Much to her surprise, she was mainly greeted in return with inquisitive stares. Some wished her good day, but in the briefest of words, and one or two hurried past with eyes averted, pretending that they had not recognised her.

Unlike her brother and sister, Morna had not as yet experienced the local reaction to her father's sudden disappearance. She had heard Walter and Belle talking about the way people in the streets and customers in the shop were behaving, but it had never occurred to her that she, too, might be cold-shouldered by people she had known all her life. Morna was the most sociable member of her family, and was used to being liked and admired by everyone.

She had almost reached the house where Arthur MacAdam lived with his two younger sisters and his parents when the door opened and Mrs MacAdam, dressed to go out, paused on the top step to survey the blue sky, and then to glance first up the road, and then down, in Morna's direction. Just as Morna hastened her steps the woman turned swiftly and disappeared back into the house as though she had forgotten something. When Morna arrived at the door, it was shut.

A maidservant wearing a snowy white apron answered her knock. 'I'm sorry, Miss Forsyth,' she said when Morna asked for Mrs MacAdam, 'the mistress is not at home.'

'But I just saw her on the doorstep, turning back into the house. Of course she's at home!'

'I'm sorry, miss,' the woman repeated, for all the world as though she was a wind-up toy, 'the mistress is not at home.' Her small dark eyes were fixed on a spot just above and beyond Morna's right shoulder, and one big-knuckled, work-reddened hand smoothed her skirt over and over again in a nervous gesture.

'Is Mr Arthur at home?'

'None of the family is in, miss.'

'But...' Morna began, and then as the woman took a tiny step back from the door, gazing at her imploringly, clearly desperate for her to leave, she

70

squared her shoulders and said in a clear, ringing voice, 'I see. Please tell Mrs MacAdam and her son that Miss Morna Forsyth called.'

It seemed to her that as she spoke her name, the girl's mouth twitched in the beginnings of a sardonic smile, and a gleam came into her sharp little eyes. Morna stood her ground, giving the servant her very best stony glare, and the smirk vanished as swiftly as it had arrived.

'Yes, miss – Miss Forsyth,' the maidservant said, and Morna, satisfied that she had put the impertinent minx in her place, turned and walked away, wincing as she heard the door close before she had taken the few steps to the garden gate.

She kept her head high as she walked along the pavement, biting her lip hard and resisting the desire to turn around to see if anyone was watching her retreat from the lace-curtained windows. She reached a corner, rounded it into a side street, and slowed to a standstill, remembering that Mrs MacAdam had been on the point of going out when she'd arrived.

She strolled on for a few yards before turning and sauntering back, trying to look as though she was merely taking the air and perhaps waiting for a friend. When she reached the corner she peered carefully round it, just in time to see Arthur's mother reappear on the top step. The older woman's glance swept down to the far corner, giving Morna time to duck back out of sight before Mrs MacAdam turned to look in her direction. She giggled, reminded of childhood games with her brother and sister and Clarissa Pinkerton and Arthur himself. If only, she thought, she could return to those happy, carefree days! Then as she heard approaching footsteps she ran a few swift steps on tiptoe before turning, drawing a deep breath, and strolling back to the corner just in time to step out in front of Arthur's mother. The woman came to a sudden stop, biting her lower lip.

'Mrs MacAdam!' Morna said sweetly, 'How fortunate! I was on my way to call on you.'

She watched a series of expressions flit over the older woman's face as she recognised the blatant untruth, realised that she could say nothing without admitting that she had made her servant lie on her behalf, then decided to go along with Morna's story.

'Indeed?' she said at last, fidgeting with the basket looped over her arm. Then, rallying a little, 'I'm surprised, my dear, to see you calling on people so soon after your poor mother's funeral and...' she paused, then said carefully, '...and everything.'

'To tell the truth, Mrs MacAdam, my brother and sister have had to see to the shop, and staying at home with reminders of poor Mother everywhere I looked was breaking my heart.' Morna had put a small lacy handkerchief into her pocket before leaving the house; now she took it out and put it to her lips. 'I had to get into the fresh air, and as I had a handkerchief of Arthur's to return, I thought that...'

'Arthur is away on business, but I can give it to him.' Mrs MacAdam, a small cold smile pinned to her lips, held out one gloved hand. 'I will see that he gets it.'

'Are you going to the shops? If so, we could walk together. There are a few items I need.'

'I am calling on a friend who lives nearby. We have arranged to go in to the town together,' Mrs MacAdam said.

'Oh. Then perhaps I might call on you tomorrow instead. The thing is,' Morna coaxed a tremor into her voice and applied her handkerchief to the corner of an eye, 'I miss Mother so very much, Mrs MacAdam, and with Belle and Walter out of the house most of the time I feel very alone. I would so appreciate the friendship and guidance of another woman, and since you and Mother were friends, I...'

'Miss Forsyth.' There was no warmth in Mrs MacAdam's voice, nor, when Morna ventured to look up, in her expression, 'You may well feel alone and even ostracised, but that has nothing to do with your poor mother's death. It is due to your father's disgraceful behaviour in deserting his family, friends and duties in such a cavalier way. I can only say that those of us who cared for Frances Forsyth are grateful that she, at least, has been spared the humiliation felt by the rest of us.'

'But you can't blame me for what Papa has done!'

'I don't blame you, I pity you,' Arthur's mother said flatly. 'But even so, you and your brother and sister must realise that in a small and close community such as Saltcoats you will find few doors open to you for some time.'

'But Arthur and I...!'

'Were childhood friends,' Mrs MacAdam said firmly, 'and nothing more than that. There is no

73

point in trying to gain his sympathy, Miss Forsyth; I am confident that if you persist in your rather foolish endeavours you will quickly find that he is in complete agreement with his father and myself on this matter. You mentioned a handkerchief? I will return it to him.' She held her hand out again, and Morna had no option but to take the wrapped handkerchief from her bag and hand it over.

Mrs MacAdam acknowledged receipt with a faint nod of the head, then with a curt, 'Good day, Miss Forsyth,' she stepped around Morna and continued on her way.

Suddenly the street seemed to dissolve in a shimmer of tears, and Morna had to lean against some house railings while she dabbed at her eyes with the little handkerchief. When she could see again, she realised that a maidservant sweeping the steps of a house across the road was watching her. Morna tried to retaliate with her haughty stare, but just then an errand boy came along the pavement, a laden basket over his arm. As the girl put her brush aside and accepted a wrapped bundle from the basket she said something and the boy turned and gaped at Morna. She walked briskly around the corner, out of their sight. By the time she was halfway along the next road, she had begun to walk faster, and then to run.

All she wanted to do now was to get home and stay there for ever, and never have to see anyone else again in her entire life.

6

As soon as the front door closed behind Morna, Sarah clambered painfully to her feet and went to the window to watch the girl's slender, black-clad figure go down the garden path. As Morna turned to latch the gate, Sarah pulled back, in case she happened to glance up at the window. When she looked out again, Morna was walking briskly along the pavement.

Sarah rubbed both hands over her stomach and tried in vain to draw a decent breath. In an attempt to hide her swelling waistline she was lacing her corset so tightly these days that she could scarcely breathe even when upright. Bending down, or kneeling, made her feel as though a very strong man had wrapped his arms around her from behind, and was squeezing and crushing the life out of her.

She went into the bathroom and splashed cold water on her flushed face, then drank some from her cupped hands before returning, reluctantly, to the skirting board. When it was finished the pictures had to be taken down from the walls and dusted, then the wallpaper wiped before they were put back on their hooks. The tops of the wardrobes would have to be cleaned, the grate polished, and every curve and angle of the ornate metal bed frame gone over with a duster. No doubt Miss Belle would check everything when she got home.

When the room was finally finished and she and Annie had carried the heavy rugs back upstairs and laid them on the polished floor, Sarah straightened her aching back and ran a forearm over her sweating face.

'That'll do for today. We'll do the master's room tomorrow, and Miss Belle's too, if we can manage it. You can get off home now, Annie.'

'Are you sure? I can stay a bit longer if you need me. You look awful tired.' The woman's eyes were sharp, and without thinking Sarah folded her arms in an automatic attempt to hide her growing bulk from the other's gimlet gaze.

'Of course I'm tired, and who wouldn't be, with the funeral and all, then having to do the spring-cleaning out of season as well.'

'They never stop tae think of the folk that have tae do all the work, do they?' Annie said sympathetically.

Back in the kitchen, Sarah paid the woman, then once Annie had gone she sank into a chair by the kitchen and laid her head on her folded arms for a few precious minutes. It would have been so easy to close her eyes and drift into sleep, she realised, and dragged herself to her feet, terrified in case she did just that.

Instead, she stepped outside the back door in search of some fresh cool air, but her corset, biting into her cruelly now, made it impossible to catch a decent breath. If she didn't get some ease from the discomfort, she thought miserably, she would go mad. Returning to the kitchen, she glanced at the clock. Miss Belle would not be due home for an hour, at least.

Swiftly, Sarah shed her blouse and skirt and petticoats, then unfastened the corset and pulled it off. The relief, as the laces loosened and she was finally free of the instrument of torture, was indescribable. She sucked in a great lungful of air, and let it out again in a sigh of sheer animal pleasure, her nails scratching busily at her hot, itchy torso.

Belle hated quiet days in the shop because the minutes dragged by when there was nothing to do. The few customers who came in bought little, and as Walter said, it was depressing to think of wages being paid to the employees who, with nobody to attend to, were standing around doing nothing.

'All I can think of,' Belle told her brother, 'is the spring-cleaning at home. I could just as well be there, making sure it's done properly and giving Sarah a hand, than sitting here.'

She had to say it twice more before Walter agreed to release her. She almost skipped out of the shop and set off at a brisk pace for the house, free at last to get on with some worthwhile work.

She used her door key rather than ring the bell and take Sarah away from whatever work she was doing, but as soon as she stepped into the hall she realised that the place was unnaturally silent, with none of the bustle to be associated with spring-cleaning – no footsteps, voices, or sounds of furniture being moved. She stood for a moment, head cocked to one side, frowning, and then without stopping to take off her hat or coat, she went straight to the kitchen and threw open the door.

Sarah, luxuriating in the relief of being free of

the corset, stretched her arms high above her head, fingers spread as far as they could go, and took in great deep breaths, letting them out again very slowly. With each breath, a little of the hot tiredness that had plagued her all day eased away. When the kitchen door opened she spun round, startled, trying at the same time to cover herself with her arms.

'Sarah?' Belle Forsyth said. 'Sarah, what do you think you are doing?' And then, as the maidservant swung round to face her, and she took in the heaviness of the girl's normally trimly corseted body, and the full curves of her white-skinned, blue-veined breasts and belly, Belle's eyes widened in sudden, shocked realisation.

'Sarah Neilson!' she said. 'You wicked, wicked girl!'

Belle's furious tirade finally ended with, 'You may prepare the dinner, but I will serve it. I will not have you coming into the dining room, do you understand?'

'Yes, ma'am.' Sarah's voice was a whisper, her eyes lowered. All Belle could see were the reddened, puffy lids.

'And you will leave at the end of the week, do you understand *that?*'

'Leave? But where will I go, miss?'

'That,' Belle said icily, 'is not my concern.' And then, giving in to a hint of natural curiosity, 'What about the – the man? I take it that you know who's responsible for – for this?' She indicated Sarah's thickened body with a wave of one hand and a disgusted curl of her lip.

'I can't … he doesn't…' Sarah said, and began to weep again.

'He's married?' Belle asked, horrified. 'You wicked girl, have you destroyed the sanctity of some poor woman's marriage with your loose morals?'

'Oh no, Miss Belle, I would never do that!'

'Then he is surely free to marry you. You must make certain that he does his duty by you, Sarah.'

'He can't marry me!' Sarah sobbed.

'Why not?'

'He just can't, miss. I know he can't.'

'Then you should have thought of that sooner, you foolish girl. You had a good home here, didn't you? We've been kind to you, and paid you well enough, haven't we? My mother spent many an hour teaching you how to be a good maidservant, and what thanks do we get? I will give you until Saturday night,' Belle said magnanimously, 'so that you can finish the spring-cleaning. After that, you're out of here. In the meantime, I don't want you to step beyond that door while my brother and sister are in the house, do you understand? You can do the housework and complete the spring-cleaning when we are all out. For the moment, since we are alone, you may make tea and serve it to me in the parlour.'

Her final salvo as she marched off to the parlour to start writing an advertisement for the *Ardrossan & Saltcoats Herald,* was, 'And for goodness' sake get dressed. There's no need to look like the slut you are!'

Sarah, still weeping, did as she was told,

squeezing herself back into the corset and buttoning her blouse up to the throat. She made the tea and took it into the parlour, where Belle greeted her with a stony stare. Sarah slunk back to the kitchen, where tears splashed on to the potatoes as she began to peel them.

Her mind raced around as frantically as a rat she had once seen trapped in a metal cage. The Forsyths' house was the only home she had. Where was she to go? Perhaps she *should* find some woman who could get rid of the bairn in her belly. Plenty used their special skills, and not all died from the experience.

But that would cost money, and she only just had enough saved from her meagre wages to pay for a bed for a few nights while she looked for work. If she spent what little she had on an abortion she would have to sleep out on the streets. But on the other hand, if she allowed the child to be born there would be little chance of finding work then. She and her bairn, always assuming that the little mite was born alive, would both starve in the gutter.

She sobbed aloud as the thoughts, like the trapped rat, banged frantically against the bony, constricting walls of her skull.

In the parlour Belle was near to tears herself. Didn't she have enough to worry about with Mother dying and Papa deserting them and half the town, the half that mattered, at least, pointing and whispering and sniggering, without having to start interviewing applicants for the post of servant? How could Sarah do this to her?

She rubbed at her forehead and then pressed the palms of her hands tightly against her closed eyes, but the headache refused to go away. She longed to lie down in her darkened room with a cloth soaked in cool water on her forehead, but now that she was, to all intents and purposes, mistress of the house, she could not afford such luxuries. Life was so unkind!

She drained her cup and had only just started work on the advertisement when Morna came home, slamming the front door behind her and sweeping into the room like a sudden thunderstorm.

'I hate this town!' she announced, pulling her hat off and throwing it across the room. It landed on the arm of a chair and bounced off again, on to the floor. 'I hate everyone in it. And I hate Mother for dying, and Papa for leaving us just when we needed him most!' First one glove, and then the other, was removed and hurled to the carpet.

Belle paused, pen in hand, and gave her sister a look of pure loathing. 'Please be good enough to hate everyone and everything in the privacy of your own room, Morna. I am very busy at the moment.'

'Mrs MacAdam had the impudence to tell me that she doesn't want Arthur to have any more to do with me – with us!' Morna kicked her hat across the room and threw herself into a chair. 'And all because of Papa! He's ruined my life! How could he do this to me? What harm have I ever done to him – or to Mrs MacAdam, for that matter?'

'Morna, go to your room and lie down for half

an hour. You need to compose yourself.'

'How can I compose myself when I've just been insulted by one of Mother's closest friends?'

'If you had to work in the shop as Walter and I do, you would have become accustomed to such treatment. It will pass; people will soon forget.'

'I won't. I won't ever forget! That – that woman,' Morna said scathingly, 'will live to regret the day she slighted me. She'll soon be begging me to marry her precious son, and then see how *I* treat *her!*' Then, as her sister merely looked at her before returning to her writing, she got up again and announced with dignity, 'I am going to lie down. I need to rest.'

'Pick up your hat and gloves and take them with you,' Belle said without turning round.

'Sarah can do it. That's what we pay her for, isn't it?'

'Sarah is ... busy with the spring-cleaning at the moment. Take them upstairs,' Belle repeated with a note of steel in her voice. Morna hesitated, and almost defied her sister, but after a glance at Belle's set mouth and determined eyes, she did as she was told before flouncing out of the room.

The three Forsyths ate a cold supper, helping themselves from serving dishes laid out on the dining-room sideboard to sliced beef and salad and cold boiled potatoes, followed by the rest of the previous day's jam sponge, also cold and with no custard. When Walter complained that this was scarcely a meal fit for a man who had been working all day, Belle informed him that Sarah had enough to do with the spring-cleaning. Each word was posted through set lips and, like his younger sister, Walter decided against an argument.

Instead, he swallowed a mouthful of roast beef and nodded at Morna's plate, where the food was being cut into very small pieces and then pushed around with a fork. 'That food costs money – my money. If you're going to waste it you might at least leave it in a fit state to be returned to the kitchen.'

'I'm not hungry.'

'No need to take it out on the beef. I doubt if Arthur MacAdam will be pleased once it's his food you're spoiling,' Walter said, and then, as his sister dropped her fork and burst into tears, 'What's the matter now?'

'Could you not have just kept your mouth shut?' Belle hissed at him.

'I only said that I was concerned for Arthur's housekeeping money if she's going to play around with good food like that once they're married.'

'We're not getting married,' Morna sobbed.

'Not right away, of course. You'll have to wait for a suitable period of mourning, like Clarissa and me, but...'

'Don't you ever listen to a word I say? We are not – getting – *married!*' Morna spaced the words out, throwing each one across the table at him. 'Not after a suitable period of mourning, not ever, because Arthur's family disapproves of the way Papa has abandoned us.' She dabbed at her face with her linen napkin. 'We've done nothing wrong – nothing, and yet we're all three of us being treated as outcasts because of that man!'

'You mean the engagement's been called off?

When did this happen? Nobody's spoken to me about it. Am I or am I not,' Walter demanded, laying down his own knife and fork, 'the head of this house? Here I am, waiting for Arthur to come and ask me for your hand in marriage, and the next thing I hear is that this engagement of yours is off before it was on! Who decided that?'

'Mrs MacAdam,' Morna sniffled. 'I went calling on her this afternoon, and the maidservant said that she wasn't in, though I knew that she was, for I had seen her about to go out...'

'You went calling less than a week after Mother's funeral? For goodness' sake, Morna, have you no grasp of simple etiquette?'

'I was returning a handkerchief Arthur had loaned me. And I was in need of company. It's been very lonely here, without Mother.'

'You could have called on Aunt Beatrice. It's acceptable to call on relations.'

'I wanted comfort, not ordering about and dog-talk,' Morna snapped. 'But it seems that Mrs MacAdam was not at home to me.'

'The weather was pleasant,' Walter pointed out. 'She may well have been taking the air, or visiting a friend.'

'I saw her! She came out on to the top step as I was walking towards the house, and then rushed inside when she saw me. When I asked for her the maid said that she wasn't in, although I knew full well that she was. So then I waited around the corner until Mrs MacAdam came out again...'

'And accosted her in the street?' Belle said, shocked.

'I only wanted to explain how lonely I was and

84

how much I would appreciate her company to help me through this very difficult time.'

'Yes, yes, but what did she say?' Walter was growing impatient. It was difficult enough to make out what his sister was saying because of her sniffling, without having to listen to more than was necessary.

'She made it clear to me that she and her family no longer cared to have any social connection with us, because of what P-Papa had done. And when I sent a friendly note inviting Arthur to tea, he wrote back to say that it was best to leave things for now.'

'What were you doing, inviting a young man to tea so soon after Mother's funeral?' Belle wanted to know.

'It's acceptable, I suppose, since Morna and Arthur have an understanding,' Walter pointed out.

'So Morna has said,' Belle said, adding sweetly, 'but perhaps Arthur was not of the same mind as she was.'

'Are you saying that I made it up?' her sister demanded hotly.

'No, but you might have been a little – presumptuous?'

'How dare you! I've been jilted, and I can't bear it!' Morna wailed, and fled from the room, sobbing.

'That girl,' Walter observed when he and Belle were alone, 'seems to have forgotten how to leave a room with dignity.'

'She's very upset, with all that's happened.'

'Belle, we are all very upset, but all of us,

Morna included, have to make the best of our unfortunate situation.' Walter sighed and pushed his plate away. 'I myself feel as though I have aged several years in the past few days.'

'You haven't finished your beef. I thought you were very fond of cold beef.'

'On occasion, perhaps, but cold food lies heavily on my stomach at the end of a busy day.'

'The weather's mild enough – very mild for October. Cold meat can be quite refreshing on a mild day.'

'Possibly, but not today.' Walter glanced at the bell pull and pushed his chair back. 'I think I would like some tea. I'll ring for Sarah.'

'I'll make it,' Belle said swiftly. 'I've set Sarah to polishing the silver and it will keep her busy for the rest of the evening.' She began to gather the plates and stack them on a tray. 'I'll just take these things to the kitchen while I'm at it.'

7

Morna did not reappear, and her brother and sister, after working on the shop accounts for an hour, both decided that they, too, were ready for an early night.

'Not that I'm likely to sleep,' Belle said as they parted in the upstairs hall. 'Between the heat and everything else, I've scarcely slept these past few nights. I waken at every creak the house makes.'

Walter had planned to creep downstairs to visit

Sarah once the house had quietened down for the night, but after his sister's parting remark he decided that he dare not risk it. Instead, he tossed and turned in his comfortable bed, his mind dwelling longingly on Sarah's narrow cot with its thin, lumpy mattress, rough sheets and threadbare blankets. None of those discomforts meant anything to him because they were well compensated for by Sarah's presence. The fact that she smelled of grease and harsh soap bothered him not a bit. Her hands might be work-roughened, but the creamy-skinned body hidden by day beneath drab clothing was soft and warm and her hair, when he loosened it and let it tumble across his face and throat, felt like a silken curtain. As for her small, neat ears...

Walter groaned and turned over for the twentieth time in a vain search for peace and rest. It was those pretty ears, peeping demurely from beneath the two smooth, neat wings of her chestnut brown hair, which had caught his attention when Sarah first came to work for his mother. Walter, who had never noticed anyone's ears before, loved to stroke them and kiss them and feel them against his face. Clarissa's ears were larger and quite ordinary, and on the only occasion he had tried to fondle them he had been rebuked so severely that anyone would have thought he had attempted to unfasten her blouse.

He would miss being able to spend time with Sarah once Clarissa became his wife and mistress of the house; but on the other hand, he thought, brightening, he could probably persuade Clarissa to continue to employ the young servant rather than find a replacement of her own choosing.

Walter's last thought, as sleep finally reached out to draw him into its soft, warm embrace, was that he must make quite sure that Sarah did everything she could to impress Clarissa on her visits to the house.

While Morna dreamed of meeting and marrying a rich man, becoming a respected and sought-after local hostess and snubbing Arthur Mac-Adam and his mother at every opportunity, Walter yearned to be in Sarah's bed rather than his own and Belle's mind was full of worries about how she could best cope with the shop, the house and her younger sister's turbulent romantic life, Sarah was weeping softly in the kitchen.

'Ah, now, why d'ye want to go on like that?' Samuel Gilmartin protested. 'Most girls would be happy to get rid of an unwanted bairn, so's they could get on with their own lives.'

'But I'd have to pay one of those women that help girls out and I don't have enough money, not now that Miss Belle's goin' to turn me out with nowhere to live!'

'She'll not do that if ye get rid of it.'

'She will.' Sarah cringed at the memory of the things Belle had said to her. 'She'll say that she can never trust me again. Can we not find a room to rent, Samuel? That's all we need,' she begged, 'a tiny little room that doesn't cost much. We could pay the rent from our wages.'

'How can you pay rent if you've no work and a bairn on the way?'

'I can find somethin' to do – I could be like

Annie, doin' washin' and heavy work. I don't need tae be a housemaid.'

'You'd have tae stop work when the bairn arrived.'

'Only for a little while, and when I start again I could wrap it in a shawl and take it with me. Plenty of women do that. I'd not let you down, Samuel, honest!'

He glowered at her, chewing his lower lip. He had arrived late, his breath heavy with cheap beer and his body eager for hers. Heedless of her worries about one of the family finding them together, he had taken her to bed at once. Now he was drinking tea, since she had nothing stronger to offer him, before returning to his lodgings.

'How do I know that?' he asked sulkily. 'How do I know ye haven't already let me down?'

'What d'you mean?' She scrubbed the back of her hand across her face, smearing the tears she was trying to mop up.

'How do I know it's mine, that's what I mean. I don't want tae spend the rest of my life raisin' another man's bastard, do I?'

'Of course it's yours! How could you say such a thing?'

He had the grace to look a little ashamed of himself. 'I've known plenty of men who've been tricked intae marriage,' he muttered, 'and then found themselves raisin' bairns that look nothin' like them.'

'This one'll look like you, you needn't worry about that.' For a fleeting moment, Walter Forsyth swam into Sarah's mind, but she dismissed him at once. Samuel was a strong and exciting lover,

89

while Walter's attentions – and that's all they were – were quite pathetic. Sarah only put up with them because her job depended on keeping him happy; besides, for some reason she felt sorry for him.

There was no possibility that Walter could have fathered the child she carried, she thought, and leaned forwards, holding Samuel's gaze with her own. 'It's yours,' she said, 'yours and nob'dy else's, you can take my word on that.'

He finished off the last of his tea and got to his feet. 'I'm goin' now.'

'Samuel, please.' She flew round the table to clutch at his arm. 'What am I to do? I have to leave here at the end of the week!'

'Ye know what ye have tae do, lassie, for I've told ye often enough. Get rid of it and get yerself another position, then ye can let me know where tae find you.'

'Samuel...!'

'There's no sense in any more talkin',' he said roughly, pushing her away and making for the back door. 'I've had enough of it.'

Then he had gone and she was left alone in the kitchen. Not quite alone, though, for there was still the baby. Sarah clutched at her belly, frantic with worry.

'Now that Morna's marriage plans have come to nothing, Belle, we must find some other occupation for her. A live-in companion perhaps – she has some experience of that, since she kept Mother company.'

'I doubt if she would be in favour of that suggestion.'

90

'I doubt if she would be in favour of any suggestion,' Walter sighed. Now that it was near to closing time the steady flow of customers had eased, leaving the two of them free to count the day's takings in the office behind the shop. 'But I will not support her as Papa did! I shall tell her that if she refuses to find a position for herself, she must come in to the shop with us.'

'D'you really see Morna as a shop assistant?' Belle asked nervously. The thought of her younger sister flouncing around the shop with her airs and graces and no doubt finding ways to insult or upset the handpicked, carefully trained staff, was unnerving.

'Not for a minute. She would look on it as lowering herself.' Her brother stacked a pile of coins neatly and started counting out more. 'She's not daft – she'll find her own salvation rather than work for us. She has no choice. You and I have earned our way since we left school – why shouldn't she?'

'She wasn't brought up to it, while we were.' Now that the threat of having to work with Morna was abating, Belle found herself pitying her younger sister. 'It's not her fault, Walter. Mother greatly appreciated her company, while Papa was quite content to support her.'

'*He* may have been content, but *I* most certainly am not going to follow his example. Morna would be well advised to seek a position as companion to some elderly person; she plays the piano and has a pleasing voice, should anyone need to be read to.' Walter counted the piles of coins, noted the sum on a sheet of paper, and began to stow the money away in canvas bags. 'We'll give her two weeks,' he decided, 'and then she will have to accept whatever we find for her, like it or not.'

A thought struck Belle. 'If she's really determined to continue living at home, perhaps we can ease the burden on me by suggesting that she take over the running of the house?'

'There's no need for that.' Walter had been flipping swiftly through the notes taken from the till. Now, scribbling down another figure, he murmured absently, 'Sarah's perfectly capable of working on her own, and she can be trusted. She doesn't need supervision.'

'I mean when Sarah's gone – we could suggest to Morna that she should take on the duty of interviewing for a new servant and then supervise the girl until she learns to do things properly. That would keep her busy and...'

'What do you mean, when Sarah's gone?' Walter asked sharply. 'She's not found another position, has she?'

'Not as far as I know – nor will she find a position with a respectable family in her condition.' Disgust thickened Belle's voice.

'Condition? What condition?'

'Really, Walter, do I have to say it? Surely you must know what I mean.'

'Yes, you do have to say it.'

Belle coloured, looking away from him, fiddling with the ledger lying on the sloping desk. 'She's – going to have a child.'

'What?'

'No need to sound so surprised. It happens

quite frequently to women of Sarah's class –
though I thought that she would have shown
more sense.'

'Are you sure of this, Belle?'

'Of course I'm sure. I went home early
yesterday and found her – well, I realised as soon
as I set eyes on her. I can't think why I didn't
notice it earlier, but with all that's been going on,
that's understandable. Poor Mother would turn
in her grave if she knew about it,' Belle swept on,
not even noticing that the colour was draining
from her brother's face. 'To think of the years she
spent training that girl, and this is the way she
rewards us – just when we most need her!'

'What about the – the father?'

'What indeed? I asked, of course, but I got
nothing out of her, except that they can't marry.
It sounds to me as though the man is already
married, but she claims that he is not. You would
think, if that is true, that there can be nothing in
the way of him making an honest woman of her
and accepting responsibility for his own child.
Not that it's any concern of ours,' Belle finished
briskly, 'so don't fret about it, Walter. I've already
put a notice in the *Ardrossan & Saltcoats Herald*.
I wonder if Aunt Beatrice would be willing to
send her housemaid round to us for part of each
day until we're settled again? I shall ask her.'

'Sarah...'

'She will be out of the house at the end of the
week – once the spring-cleaning is finished. It
would be useful, of course, to keep her on until I
find someone else, but best to get rid of her as
soon as possible. Now then, how much are you

taking to the bank?'

She opened the ledger and dipped her pen into the inkwell, waiting. Then, as no reply came, she turned to look at her brother. 'Walter?'

'What?'

'I asked you how much you're taking to the bank. Are you all right?' Belle asked with sudden concern. 'You look quite pale.'

'I just... I felt a sudden twinge of indigestion,' Walter said, and forced his mind back to business.

It seemed to Walter that the evening dragged on forever. He and his sisters had been invited to the Pinkertons' home for supper, and he had been looking forward to a hot, cooked meal instead of the cold food they were getting at home because of the spring-cleaning. But when it came to it, the excellent supper prepared by Mrs Pinkerton's efficient cook/housekeeper seemed to have no taste to it. Nor did the glass of port or the cigars that he and Mr Pinkerton shared in the older man's comfortable study after the meal. Walter, who had never taken to cigars, sucked hard at his and then blew the smoke out at once, surrounding himself with a thick blue-grey cloud.

Afterwards, the two men joined the ladies for an evening of card games and music, with Morna playing the piano and Clarissa singing. Then finally he and his sisters were free to walk back home through the cool night air.

'Tea, I think,' he said as they were taking their coats off in the long narrow hallway. 'I'll go and tell Sarah.'

He turned eagerly towards the kitchen, but

Belle put a restraining hand on his arm. 'I told her to go to bed early in order to make an early start tomorrow morning – there's a lot to be done by the end of the week. I'll make the tea,' she said, and brushed past him.

Sarah was down on her knees, clearing the night's ashes out of the kitchen range, when Walter came downstairs in the morning. The noise made by the poker as she wielded it fiercely between the bars drowned out the sounds of the door opening and his slippered feet crossing the linoleum. When he put a hand on her shoulder she jumped and squealed, dropping the poker.

'It's all right, it's only me.'

She gaped up at him, struggling to collect her wits. 'What are you doing up at this hour, sir? Are you ill?'

'Not a bit of it.'

'You want your shaving water; I can have it ready in no time at all, sir.'

'You'll not bother yourself, Sarah. Here...' He drew her to her feet, regardless of the fact that her hands were filthy with coal dust and ashes, and led her to the table. 'Sit here,' he said, drawing out a chair. 'I want to talk to you.'

'But the range...!'

'The range can wait.'

'It can't, sir. If it's not riddled out first thing in the morning it gets choked up and then it won't heat the water, and then I'll be in trouble,' she protested as he pushed her down on to the chair.

'Just you sit where you are and let me see to the range.' His eyes still on Sarah, he picked up the

95

poker by the wrong end and then yelped and dropped it. It clattered back on to the hearth while Sarah jumped up from the chair.

'Oh, sir, you've burned yourself! Here.' She caught his hand and examined it, then pulled him across to the sink and turned the tap on. 'Hold your hand beneath the cold water to soothe it,' she instructed, then flew to fetch the tub of bicarbonate of soda and a clean cloth.

'There,' she said when the hand had been patted dry and the burned fingers liberally scattered with soda before being carefully wrapped up. 'Does that feel better?'

'Much better. Sarah...' he began, but she was already back at the range, grasping the poker by the handle instead of the poking end, as Walter had done, and rattling it between the bars.

'I must just do this first, sir,' she said breathlessly as she worked. 'Then I'll build the fire up again before fetching your shaving water to your room.'

She had hoped that he would go back upstairs and leave her in peace to get on with her work, but when she had finished with the range and got to her feet, rubbing her hands together to remove the worst of the coal dust, he was still sitting at the table, staring at her.

'Sarah, your eyes are all red.'

'It's the heat from the range.' She rubbed at her eyes, not realising that she was only transferring what was left of the coal dust to her face.

'Why didn't you tell me?'

'Tell you what, sir?'

'About the child you're carrying. How long have you known about it?'

96

Sarah's heart, already low, dropped into her shabby, much-mended boots. 'Only a few weeks, sir,' she mumbled, staring down at her hands as they plucked nervously at her apron.

'Why didn't you tell me?'

Astonishment brought Sarah's eyes up to meet his. She had expected him to be as outraged as his sister, but instead he was looking at her kindly.

'Tell you about something like that? I couldn't, sir! I'm going at the end of the week,' she added hurriedly. 'Miss Belle said I could stay until I'd finished the spring-cleaning, if that's all right with you, sir.'

'It most certainly is not all right with me,' he said firmly, and her aching heart gave an added twinge. She had counted on a few more days under the Forsyths' roof – a little extra time in which she might come up with a solution to her problem.

'You want me to go now, sir?'

'Of course I don't want you to go now, or at the end of the week, or at any time. Do you really think so little of me, Sarah?'

'Sir?'

'Do you think,' Walter said, 'that I would treat the mother of my unborn child so harshly?'

Sarah fumbled blindly for a chair and sank into it. She knew that it was wrong of her to sit in the presence of one of her employers, but between worry, lack of sleep and shock at what he had just said, her knees suddenly felt so weak that her only alternative was to fall to the floor at his feet. 'Your child?' she whispered.

'You're staying here, Sarah. You and I will be married as soon as it can be arranged. A quiet

97

affair, of course, given my mother's recent passing, but essential under the circumstances.'

'But you're already promised to Miss Pinkerton...'

'How in the name of honour can I go through with that arrangement while you're carrying my child, Sarah? I may have behaved badly towards both of you, but at least I know now where my duty lies. We shall be married,' Walter said firmly, 'as soon as possible.'

'Sir, I cannae marry you!'

'Why not?'

'Because it's not your...'

Walter reached out and took one of Sarah's work-roughened, ash-streaked hands in his. 'Not my responsibility? I think it is, Sarah. I'm not one of those men who look on girls of your position as mere vessels on which to slake their desires. You know that I've always cared for you, and I want to do right by you and acknowledge our child as mine. Sarah Neilson...' He dropped to one knee, still clutching her hand in his. 'Will you do me the honour of consenting to become my wife?'

8

Sarah's head teemed with more thoughts than it could safely hold as she gazed down at Walter Forsyth's uplifted face, suddenly realising that if he wanted to do right by the child he believed that he had fathered on her, the bleak future stretching before her might be turned around.

But the flash of hope was fleeting. She knew in her blood and her bones and in the very womb where the foetus nestled, that the child was Samuel's. Walter's fumbling, clumsy lovemaking could surely never result in the creation of another human being. Only Samuel's lusty coupling could have brought about this burden she carried within her, and she could not deny it, even to save herself and the unborn infant.

'You cannae marry me!' She jumped from the chair and fled across the kitchen towards the back door. It was still bolted and Walter caught up with her as she fumbled desperately to open it.

'Why not?'

'It wouldnae be right – I'm a servant lassie, and you're...'

'Sarah, I'm a man and you're a woman, and in there...' his free hand touched the soft roundness of her belly as he turned her to face him, '...is our child. My child. I have a right to claim my own child, surely?'

'But what'll the townsfolk say? What'll Miss Belle say, and Miss Pinkerton?'

'I don't care what any of them have to say. Be damned to the lot of them,' Walter said passionately. 'This is our concern, Sarah, and nobody else's. Say you'll marry me and the whole world can go to hell as far as...'

'What's going on?' Belle said from the kitchen doorway. She was still wearing her nightclothes, and her brown hair, normally knotted on top of her head, hung over one shoulder in a thick plait. 'What's all the noise about?' Then, as she saw the two of them together, her brother's hand gripping the maidservant's arm, her puzzled expression turned to anger. 'What's the slut been up to now? She's not trying to steal from us, is she? Sarah Neilson, you wicked girl – you can just leave today, and never mind waiting until the end of the week!'

'That's enough, Belle. Sarah's done nothing wrong.'

'Nothing wrong? What about the child she's carrying, and her not married?'

'That's why I'm here – to make amends for my wrongdoing.'

'What wrongdoing? You're not making any sense, Walter,' his sister said impatiently. 'For goodness' sake, man, get out of the kitchen and let the girl get on with her work. Sarah, the range must be choked, for there's no hot water upstairs. You'll have to boil kettles and bring them up to the bedrooms. And hurry!'

'Sarah,' Walter said, 'will do nothing of the sort. You and Morna can wash in cold water for once, or see to your own kettles. Sarah's not in a fit condition to fetch and carry for you.'

'That is not my concern. While she's under our roof she'll…'

'It may not be your concern, Belle, but it's mine. You might as well know that I have just asked Sarah to marry me.'

'Mar…' Belle swayed slightly, then leaned against the door frame, one hand clutching at her throat. 'You? Marry with her? Have you gone clean out of your senses?'

'On the contrary, Belle, I think I've just found them.'

For a moment Belle's mouth worked soundlessly, and then, as she looked from the maidservant's flushed, tearful face to Walter's smug smile, understanding dawned. 'You mean that you're...?'

'I am the father of Sarah's child,' Walter confirmed proudly. 'And you, my dear Belle, are soon to become an aunt.'

Morna, awakened from sleep by the noise, arrived in the kitchen to find Belle standing in the middle of the room, both arms flailing about and scream after scream pouring from her throat. Walter was trying to wrestle her into a chair while Sarah filled a cup with water from the tap.

'What's happened? Has she had a seizure?'

Walter yelped as one of Belle's flailing hands caught him on the nose. With difficulty, he captured both wrists and managed to force her down on to the chair. 'She's just being daft,' he said breathlessly. 'Sarah, where's that water?'

'Here, sir.'

The maidservant arrived by his side with the cup just as Belle, with a roar of 'Don't you touch me!' ducked her head and sank her teeth into one of the hands imprisoning her. Walter yelped again and released her at once. She bounced to her feet just as he snatched the cup from Sarah, and instead of holding it to his sister's lips as he had first intended, he dashed its contents into her face.

The screams stopped at once, to be replaced by strangled gasps as the shock of the cold water took what little breath was left in Belle's lungs. She sank back down on to the chair, wiping her incredulous eyes.

'I'm wet!' she said, stunned.

'Well, at least you're quiet, too.' Walter examined his bitten hand, rubbing at the marks her teeth had left on the skin. 'It's a wonder you didn't draw blood!'

'It's a pity I didn't!' Belle snapped back at him, while Morna asked, bewildered, 'What's going on here?' She, too, was still dressed for sleep, her soft fair hair caught back by a narrow ribbon.

'Ask him,' Belle snarled, and then, with a glare at her brother, 'Murderer!'

'Walter? Who's he murdered?'

'Nobody, she's havering. I'm no murderer – I'm bringing new life into the world, and what's wrong with that?'

'What's wrong with it?' Belle's voice began to rise again. 'What's wrong with getting the servant lassie with child and then announcing that you're going to marry her? What's Clarissa going to say about that? What'll her father say, and Aunt Beatrice, and all the folk that come into the shop?'

'Sarah's having a baby?' Morna asked. And then, as neither her brother nor her sister seemed interested in replying, 'Is this true, Sarah? Are you having a child?'

Sarah had been trying to bury herself in a corner; now, addressed directly, she hung her head and whispered, 'Yes, miss.'

'And it's yours, Walter? But how can it be yours when you're promised to Clarissa?'

'Don't be so childish, Morna,' her brother snapped. 'This is 1909, not the nineteenth century. I'm sure that all those novelettes you've

102

been reading must have taught you something of the facts of life.'

'And you're going to marry Sarah, and not Clarissa?' Morna went on, and Belle let out a pathetic bleat reminiscent of a lost lamb searching the fields for its mother.

'I am going to marry the mother of my child, yes. Would you expect your brother to do otherwise under the circumstances?'

'I think that Clarissa might expect you to do otherwise,' Morna said. 'Does she know yet?'

Which was enough to send her sister into another fit of hysteria.

'Ye've lost the few wits God gave ye, Walter Forsyth,' Beatrice McCallum said flatly. 'And betrayed poor Clarissa Pinkerton intae the bargain.'

'On the contrary, Aunt Beatrice, I have found my wits. Surely you can see that as a man of honour I have no choice but to marry Sarah Neilson and acknowledge her child as my own.' Walter's eyes were bright, his voice exultant. After years of living in his father's shadow, constantly assessed and found wanting, he felt that he had at last come into his manhood. He had behaved stupidly but he was going to accept full responsibility for his own actions. He was going to become a father, master of his own fate at last.

'Of course ye've got another choice, man! Find somewhere for the lassie to stay and settle some money on her – Meggie Chapman that used tae be your nurse has a lodgin' house down by the water, has she no'? I'm sure she would offer Sarah and the bairn room and board in return for help in the house.'

'But I care for Sarah.'

'Care for her? She's a servant, Walter. If I'd a sovereign for every servant my Hector bedded – though mostly in his mind, I'll tell ye, for I saw tae it that he got little chance tae do it in the flesh – I'd be a wealthy woman,' said Beatrice, ignoring the fact that thanks to Hector's prudent thriftiness and knack for investment, she was already a wealthy woman.

'I've already asked Sarah to become my wife.'

'And look what's come of it,' the old woman shot back at him. 'She's cryin' in the kitchen, your poor sister's havin' the vapours up in her bedroom and the shop's bein' left tae run itself. Romeo here's got more sense than you have.'

The dog she had brought with her today was stretched out on the parlour rug in a patch of sunlight. Now he lifted his head at the sound of his name, licked his owner's boot, and settled back down again with a contented sigh as Beatrice went on, 'You've caused more confusion in this household than your father did. And what about Mr Pinkerton? D'you think he's goin' tae stand idly by and watch his daughter bein' jilted? She could take ye tae court for breach of promise, d'ye realise that?'

'I suppose I should go and see her today.' Walter ran a hand over his chin and added, 'After I've shaved, that is. And broken my fast.'

'And who's tae make your breakfast and take up your shaving water?'

'Why, Sar...' Walter began, and then, as his aunt gave him a grim nod, he amended it to, 'I shall see to it myself.'

'I can't stay here,' Belle wailed, scrubbing at her eyes with a damp wad of handkerchief.

'Of course you can,' Beatrice told her, having left Walter to feed himself. 'Who's goin' tae run the house if you don't?'

'And who's going to interview the applicants for the post of serving lassie?' Morna broke in. 'I don't know how to do that sort of thing, Belle.'

'I don't care if the house goes to rack and ruin and falls down around Walter's stupid ears! Why should I look after things for him, when he's let us down so badly? I wish Mother were still here. I wish Papa hadn't gone away!'

'If you ask me, your father would have been no help at all, and your poor mother's been spared a terrible shame.' Beatrice glanced again at her elder niece's distraught, tear-stained face and began to soften a little. 'If you're so determined not to stay in this house you'd best come to me for a day or two, until you feel better. Morna, help your sister to get ready. I'm goin' downstairs to have another word with Walter before he goes runnin' off to Mr Pinkerton and makes things even worse than they are already.'

'Poor, poor Clarissa, what's she to do now? She might never speak to me again!'

'And her father might refuse to go on handlin' your accounts,' Beatrice said on her way out. 'That would be even worse.'

'You'll not be gone for long, will you?' Morna begged as she packed some clothes for her sister.

'You'll be back tomorrow?'

'How can I ever return to this house if Walter persists in this daft ploy of his?'

'But you must,' Morna protested, appalled. 'What's going to happen to me if you don't?'

'You can come to Aunt Beatrice's with me.'

'And live with those horrible little dogs?'

'Then stay here and take my place. It's time you learned to do something useful.'

Morna's lovely eyes filled with tears. 'Belle, how can you speak to me like that? I'm your sister – Mother always told you to look out for me.'

'She didn't mean all your life,' Belle said, almost out of her mind with misery. 'She didn't mean once you were old enough to look after yourself! Oh, Morna, I wish she were still here. None of this would have happened if she had still been here!'

'If Sarah's really carrying Walter's child then it surely must have happened before Mother died,' Morna pointed out, and then sighed as her sister burst into fresh tears.

After lecturing Walter on the need for approaching Mr Pinkerton with an air of humility and bitter regret, Beatrice McCallum went to the kitchen, where Sarah was polishing the silver as though her life depended on it.

'Well now, this is a pretty kettle of fish,' the older woman said, and then, as Sarah jumped to her feet, 'sit down, lassie, and get on with what you're doin'. Romeo, behave yourself,' she added sharply to the dog, which was nosing around. Romeo obediently flattened himself against the floor while his mistress hauled a chair out from under the table and sat down.

'It seems that my nephew's determined tae marry you, for all that I've tried tae explain tae him that he's bein' a fool.'

'It wasnae my doing, Mrs McCallum. I told him that we couldnae marry, what with him bein' who he is and me bein' who I am. But he'll no' listen.'

'He's got a bee in his bonnet about doin' the right thing by you, though if you ask me, he should have thought of that a good sight sooner than this. If he had, my niece wouldnae be havin' hysterics upstairs and poor Clarissa Pinkerton would still have a weddin' to look forward to.'

'She still can as far as I'm concerned,' Sarah said at once.

'No, she can't, for he's just gone off to speak to her father.'

'Already?' Sarah jumped up as though to run after him, then sank back into her chair when the older woman said, 'He'll be well along the road by now. You'll never catch him up.'

'I wish he hadn't done that!'

'What will you do if the Pinkertons talk him out of marryin' you?'

'I'll...' Sarah hesitated, then said lamely, 'I'll manage.'

'D'ye have any fam'ly to go to?'

'Not now.'

'Friends?' Beatrice probed, and then, as Sarah shook her head, 'So what are you plannin' to do? Birth your bairn in a ditch? You think that the two of you can live on grass like the cows in the fields?'

Sarah's eyes filled with ready tears. 'That might be better than marryin' Mr Walter and settin' the family against each other.'

'Lassie, this fam'ly began to fall apart the day Walter's father left. D'you care for him?' Beatrice asked, adding when the girl stared at her in bewilderment, 'Walter, I'm talkin' about, no' his father.'

'I like him well enough,' Sarah said evasively.

'Enough to let him get you intae the fam'ly way.'

'It was...' Sarah hesitated, then mumbled, '...he was always lonely, Mr Walter. I felt sorry for him. And he was kind to me.'

'Not many folk take the time tae be kind tae servant lassies,' Beatrice agreed. 'But when all's said and done he's a grown man with a mind of his own, and if he's willin' tae marry with ye and you're willin' tae pledge yerself tae him, then I suppose that that's goin' tae be the way of it.'

'You mean you'd give your blessing?' Sheer shock brought a squeak to Sarah's voice on the final word.

'It's no' for me to say aye or nay if ye're both set on it.'

'But you're his aunt!'

'No' by blood, though. Did ye not know that?' Beatrice asked. 'Then again, why should ye? McCallum's your late mistress's own name. Hector McCallum's wife died in childbirth, and the poor wee bairn with her, and he took me on as his housekeeper. I looked after him for years, then finally, since he was gettin' older and he'd never met anyone else he wanted tae marry, he settled on me.'

'You married your employer?' Sarah had forgotten her polishing and was leaning across the table.

'I did – though not for the same reason as you and Walter,' Beatrice added firmly. 'It caused a right stooshie in the town at the time, I can tell you, but folk got over it, just as they'll get over Walter marryin' you, given time.'

'Miss Pinkerton won't get over it.'

'She's no' daft, and I'm sure she'll realise soon enough that there's better fish in the sea and Walter wasnae the right one for her. Those two were thrown together by their parents when they were just bairns; they never had the chance to make their own minds up. You might even be doin' them both a blessin'. Now then, lassie,' Beatrice McCallum went on briskly, 'I know that your late mistress, rest her soul, thought well of ye, and from what I've seen and heard I think ye're a sensible enough girl, so I'm willin' tae teach ye the things ye need tae know if ye're tae be mistress of this house instead of just the servant lassie. First of all, there's another servant tae hire in your place. Belle's already put an advertisement in the newspaper, but she's comin' tae stay with me for a few days, just till she gets used tae the idea of what's happened, so I'll do the interviewin' along with ye. Then there's...'

She began to tick each item off on her large-knuckled fingers as she talked, and Sarah watched and listened, caught up in a situation that was carrying her helplessly along with it.

Between them, Walter and his aunt were offering her salvation. She still felt that she should refuse it and be honest with them both, but nobody was giving her the opportunity. At least Walter wanted her and her baby, which was more than could be said for Samuel. Despite the need to be honest with him, and with Mrs McCallum, she was beginning to think that it might be best for her and her unborn child if she just held her tongue and went along with what was being arranged for her.

9

Beatrice McCallum was a natural-born meddler, and it had been a while since she had enjoyed herself so much. Fortunately for Sarah, the woman considered her a decent, honest and hardworking lassie, and she secretly believed that with some careful tutoring from a mentor such as herself, the maidservant might even make a better wife for Walter than Clarissa.

Hector McCallum, Beatrice's husband, should by rights have inherited the ironmongery business set up by his father, but Hector's interests and ambitions had been with bricks and mortar, and dogs. His first wife had had money of her own, and Hector had put it to work, buying up old properties that could be renovated and rented out. Because he and his wife were both thrifty and had little interest in luxuries, and because he invested his profits sensibly, Hector soon became quite a wealthy man.

His private passion was breeding King Charles spaniels, and again, he did well financially selling the puppies. While he was alive the back garden of the Caledonia Road house was filled with kennels and runs.

As a result of his investments and his lucrative pastime, Beatrice found herself comfortably off when she was widowed. Since she had never shared her husband's business interests she promptly sold all of his properties, and with Allan Pinkerton as her adviser she invested the proceeds wisely. Most of the dogs were also sold, though she kept Romeo and Juliet, personal gifts from her husband.

Her first step in sorting out the pickle Walter had got himself into was to visit the banker and issue a carefully worded and most regretful reminder that if her nephew and nieces were forced to find another bank, then as their only blood relation she herself would have no option but to follow suit. Her wealth by then was sufficient to persuade the banker that it would be in his best interests to retain the Forsyth account and to forget about encouraging his daughter to sue Walter for breach of promise.

Beatrice then called on the Pinkerton household, where she commiserated warmly with Clarissa and her mother.

'I cannot understand what has got into that nephew of mine,' she said, sipping tea and accepting a sugar biscuit. 'I've tried to get him to see sense, but it's no use. To think that he's thrown away the chance of marryin' into this family – what his poor dear mother would say, I don't know.'

'I can only think,' Mrs Pinkerton said coldly,

111

'that Walter has taken after his father.'

Beatrice nodded sagely. 'Breedin' will tell,' she pronounced. 'Hamilton never would talk much about his background, and given the way he suddenly upped and left, without as much as an explanation, there was probably bad blood in his background. Gypsy blood, for all we know.'

'Gypsy blood?' Clarissa asked, horrified, while her mother shuddered visibly.

'Look at the way he just left, with no preparation and scarcely takin' anythin' with him,' Beatrice pointed out, breaking off a piece of biscuit and tossing it into the air. Juliet, the dog chosen to be her canine partner for the day, fielded it neatly before it could land on the thick carpet. 'Is that not the way of gypsies?'

'I'm beginning to think that Clarissa may have had a fortunate escape,' Mrs Pinkerton said faintly.

'Fortunate? I'm jilted in front of the whole town and you think that I'm fortunate?' Clarissa's voice began to tremble and she dabbed a small handkerchief at her eyes. 'I truly cared for Walter. I was looking forward to becoming his wife!'

Beatrice leaned over and patted her arm. 'I know how much you cared for him, my dear, and so did poor Frances. She went to her grave a happy woman, believin' that her beloved son's future lay with you. It's just a mercy that she didn't live to see where his foolishness has led him. But I've come here today to ask you to be compassionate, Clarissa. It's my belief that his father's cruel desertion, coming so soon after his mother's death, has confused poor Walter. He has sinned against you, of that there is no doubt, but he himself, poor youth, has been sinned against.'

'Not least of all by that hussy of a maidservant,' Mrs Pinkerton said heatedly. 'She ought to be whipped out of the town! How dare she aspire to marriage with someone of Walter's status!'

'My sentiments exactly,' Beatrice agreed. 'But the important thing now is to protect Clarissa's good name, is it not?'

'There's nothing wrong with Clarissa's good name. It's your nephew's name that'll be dragged through the mud!'

'That it will, and there's little that I can do about it,' Beatrice said sorrowfully, 'for he's brought it upon himself. But just think how folk will admire you and look up to you, Clarissa, once they see that you have the nobleness of spirit to rise above pettiness and thoughts of revenge. To forgive is divine, is it not?'

'I suppose it is,' Clarissa said slowly.

'It's what sets the naturally noble folk apart from the others. There is nothing more admirable than a woman who can forgive those daft enough to sin against her,' Beatrice said. 'And I'll tell you another thing, my lass. What's meant for you won't go past you. It seems clear to me that this engagement between you and Walter has come to an end because you're meant for someone better than him.'

'That's certainly true,' Clarissa's mother snapped. 'I'm grateful to you, Mrs McCallum, for your understanding. You're quite right, of course; Clarissa must remain aloof, and distance herself from Walter and his strange goings on.

That way, folk will realise that this disgraceful episode has nothing to do with her. More tea?'

'Thank you, but I must go. I have so many things to attend to.'

Beatrice rose, and was about to take her leave when Mrs Pinkerton said, 'Was there not a similar sort of scandal a good while ago within Walter's family? Some other relation who married his servant girl?'

'You'll be thinkin' of Frances's older brother Hector, a widower who married his housekeeper. I was the housekeeper,' Beatrice said sweetly. 'Good day to you.'

As she made her way to the hardware shop, Beatrice McCallum marvelled over how swiftly scandal died and folk forgot. Little more than a dozen years earlier she had been called an upstart to her face while walking along a street in Saltcoats, and her employer-turned-husband had been treated as a renegade for marrying his housekeeper. A more timid couple might have moved to start a new life elsewhere, and goodness knows there had been no shortage of people willing and ready to suggest it to them, some in anonymous letters, but they had both been made of sterner stuff. They knew that people forgot easily, and as time passed they began to be accepted back into society. Beatrice had no doubt that with careful planning the same thing would happen to Walter and Sarah.

On reaching the shop she marched straight through to the office, where Walter was trying to make sense of the books.

114

'You can stop worrying about being taken to court by Clarissa, for I've talked her out of it.'

'Her father almost threw me out of the bank,' he said glumly. He had never been good at figures, and his head was aching.

'Can you blame the man? But fortunately they've had the sense to realise that they'll only bring unwanted attention down on themselves if they pursue you over the way you've treated Clarissa. And Allan Pinkerton's agreed to keep you on as a client, though I think you should deal carefully with the man for a good long while. Be respectful when you speak to him.'

'How did you manage to get the Pinkertons to agree to all that?' Walter asked, astonished.

'I've got my ways,' Beatrice said with an enigmatic smile.

'You couldn't get Belle to come back to the shop, could you? I can't make head nor tail of all this bookwork. I've got enough to do trying to run the shop without having to see to this as well.'

'She'll be back on Monday, but you'd be advised to be on your best behaviour with her as well. You've upset a lot of folk round here, Walter.'

'I know, but I've got to do the right thing. Surely you see that, Aunt Beatrice?'

'I suppose I do. But remember this – once you've made your bed, you have to lie in it.'

'I'll do that with pleasure, Aunt Beatrice. I've spoken to the minister; he's agreed to marry Sarah and me a week next Tuesday morning, in the vestry. A very quiet wedding.'

'It'll have to be. I suppose you'll want me to sort out a new serving lassie for you?'

'If you would. There are some letters for Belle – I think they might be from women seeking the post,' Walter said vaguely.

'I'll go to the house now and have a look at them. Sarah can sit with me when I interview the women, for she needs to learn how to do that sort of thing. And she'll have to be taught how to run a house as its mistress instead of the servant. I'll see what I can do with her. Juliet, you naughty dog! Why couldn't you have waited until we got outside? Better get one of the shop lassies to bring a mop and bucket, Walter,' Beatrice said, and went on her way, leaving her nephew to contemplate the pool on his office floor.

'Is it true what I'm hearin'? Are you goin' tae marry Walter Forsyth?'

'Oh, Samuel, you've come at last!' Sarah pulled Samuel from the dark night and into the lamp-lit kitchen. 'I've been out of my mind with worry – desperate tae see you!'

'Not desperate enough tae come to the shop and ask for me.' His usual smile had been replaced by a scowl, and his eyes were hard and narrowed.

'You've no notion of what it's been like here, Samuel. Miss Belle's gone to stay with Mrs McCallum and Miss Morna's in a right sulk about it all. What with one thing and another I've scarcely had a minute to...'

'Ye've not answered my question,' he interrupted. 'Is it true that ye're goin' tae marry Walter Forsyth?'

'No!'

'Ye're lyin', Sarah.' He took her wrist in a painful grip. 'It's all round the town. They're sayin' that he's determined tae marry ye – and that you've accepted him.'

'It's true that he's asked me,' she admitted, and then, hurriedly, 'but I've not said yes to him. It's no' him I want, Samuel. You know that!'

He released his hold on her. 'What I want to know is, why should a man like Mr Walter Forsyth – a man with a fine house and plenty of money and a woman already promised to him – suddenly propose marriage tae his servant girl?'

Sarah swallowed hard, rubbing at her arm, and then as he loomed over her, waiting for a reply, she mumbled, 'It's – he's got some sort of daft notion in his head.'

'What sort of daft notion?' he asked, his voice suddenly quiet. She looked up to see that he was staring at her hands, which, without her realising it, had automatically moved to cover her stomach.

'Have you been lettin' Mr Walter Forsyth tumble ye, Sarah?' Samuel persisted. 'Have you been pleasurin' him as well as me?'

'No – it wasn't the way it was with you...'

'Was it no'?'

'It was just a few kisses. You know what masters can be like with their servants,' she gabbled. 'He meant no harm, Samuel.'

'It must have been more than a few kisses, since it seems tae me that he thinks ye're carryin' his babby. And you swearin' tae me that there was nob'dy else. I was right tae doubt ye, was I no'?'

'Samuel, it's yours, I swear it!' She ran after him as he made for the door, catching again at the sleeve of his shabby jacket. 'Samuel, please!'

'I tell ye what,' he said, shrugging her off as though she were no more than a troublesome fly, 'if it's mine then you'll do as I say and get rid of it so's we can go back to the way we were, with the cups of tea and the kisses and cuddles, and mebbe a wee tumble now and again for friendship's sake. But if it's his then ye can keep it an' marry the man, and the two of youse'll be welcome tae each other as far as I'm concerned. But I'll tell ye one thing – Samuel Gilmartin won't share a woman with any man.'

The door closed behind him, and by the time Sarah had torn it open again he was gone. She was taking her jacket from the nail where it hung, determined to follow Samuel and beg him, on her knees if need be, not to desert her, when Walter came into the kitchen.

'Sarah? Where are you going at this time of night?'

'For a walk,' she said swiftly. 'I thought I'd clear my head.'

'It's too cold for that. You could catch a chill, and that would be bad for you and the child.' He took the jacket from her and hung it up again, then led her to the fireside chair and tenderly settled her into it. 'My poor little love, it's been a bad time for you, hasn't it, with Belle being so silly about everything. But you mustn't worry your pretty little head about it. She'll come to love you just as I do, and so will Morna. And soon you'll take your rightful place upstairs as my wife and mistress of the house. I've already spoken to the minister, and it's to be in the vestry

118

next Tuesday morning,' he added cheerfully, and when Sarah burst into tears of misery and despair he knelt beside her, taking her into his arms and stroking her hair.

'There, there, my darling, there's nothing to worry about. I'll look after you from now on. You and our child,' he promised, 'for the rest of our lives.'

Sarah, utterly wretched, wept all the more.

'Here, lassie, this is your wedding gift from me.' Beatrice thumped the heavy volume on to the kitchen. 'You can read, I suppose?'

'Of course I can read!' During the night Sarah had cried until she could cry no more, and had then begun to face facts. She was pregnant with Samuel Gilmartin's child, but Samuel refused to accept responsibility whereas Walter Forsyth was not only willing but also eager to offer a home to both Sarah and the child. As the alternative was to starve in a ditch, she had come to realise in the cold, grey, morning light, that she had no option but to marry Walter.

Having accepted that, she had found an inner strength. Without Samuel she could never be truly happy again, but the next best thing was to make the most of being Walter's wife. Being condescended to by Mrs McCallum, who didn't even live in the house, was not part of being Walter's wife.

'Aye, I suppose you can, since you seem to be a sensible lassie,' the older woman conceded amiably. 'Well now, this book tells you all you need to know about how to run a house and how to treat servants, so keep it by you at all times and don't be shy about askin' me if there's anythin' frettin' you. I've arranged for some women to come here this afternoon to be interviewed for the post of servin' lassie ... don't worry now,' Beatrice added swiftly as the girl shrank back and turned pale. 'I'll see to them, for I'm used to it. All you have to do is sit with me and watch and listen. And ask any questions that come to you. And you can sit with us too, Morna,' she added as her younger niece came into the kitchen.

'Sit with you?' Morna cast a disdainful look at the table. 'I've come to say I want a cup of tea. I'll drink it in the front parlour.'

'If you want it you'll drink it here, then help me and Sarah to find another maidservant.'

'Why do we need another? Isn't one enough?'

Beatrice suppressed an exasperated sigh. 'With your brother taking Sarah here for his wife next week, they need a new servant in her place. You can help us tae find someone suitable.'

'What would I know about suitable servants?'

'One day you'll be interviewin' for your own home, no doubt. There's no harm in finding out how it's done.'

'But...'

'Sit down, Morna,' Beatrice said firmly. 'I'll make the tea and we'll just about manage a cup before the first one arrives.'

The middle-aged woman was very capable and would make a suitable housekeeper, Beatrice thought during the interviews, but she had the look and manner of someone who might ride roughshod over a timid mistress, and Sarah would have enough to cope with as it was. Mentally she crossed the woman off her list, together with the next applicant, a superior being who was more of a lady's maid and would almost certainly sneer at a young woman who, lady of the house or not, had until recently been the servant. Beatrice, remembering her own early experiences, refused to put Sarah through the unnecessary humiliation that she herself had suffered.

'Well, what d'you think?' she asked when the last applicant had gone and the three of them – Beatrice, Sarah and Morna – were alone in the kitchen. 'I favoured the grey-haired one myself. She's gettin' on but she seems willin' enough, and she's got experience.'

'The fourth one,' Morna said decisively. 'She's been employed in some large houses and she has a good sense of etiquette.'

'Etiquette doesnae bring up a shine on a table or clean out a grate well,' Beatrice said dryly.

'She would be very helpful in other ways.'

'If you want a personal maid that badly, lassie, you'd best hire your own and find the money to pay her, for I don't see Walter putting his hand in his pocket on your behalf. Now then, Sarah, what did you think of them?'

'Me?' Sarah said, startled at being consulted. 'Whatever you think best, Mrs McCallum. Or whatever Miss Morna thinks.'

'So it's to be the one I like,' Morna said triumphantly, rising to her feet.

'Hold on a wee minute, now. As from next week Sarah's goin' tae be the mistress of this house.

It'll be her job to train up the new servant, and so she must decide which one she wants to hire. Which is it to be, lass?' Beatrice asked her, ignoring Morna's flushed, angry face.

Sarah hesitated, then said shyly, 'I liked the young girl.'

'Her? She's not got any experience,' Morna sneered, 'and she's such a plain little creature. Did you not see the way she scuttled in and scuttled out again? It would be like having a mouse about the place. I'd be hard put to it not to set traps every time I saw her.'

Sarah almost caved in, but there was something about the encouraging glint in Beatrice McCallum's eyes and the lift of her strongly marked brows that urged her on. 'She's eager to learn, and she comes from a large family, so she's used to takin' on her share of hard work,' she said doggedly. 'If I was to choose, I'd choose her.'

'Then that's settled. You and I will visit her home tomorrow morning and tell her that she's engaged. It'll give us a chance to have a look at her mother and find out if she's from a dirty house or a clean one. And then,' Beatrice went on, paying no heed to Morna's outraged gasp, 'we'll catch the train to Irvine to buy your wedding outfit, Sarah.'

10

Standing by Walter's side in the church vestry, dressed in the bottle-green flannel skirt and three-quarter-length jacket that Beatrice McCallum had bought for her, Sarah Neilson felt as though she were locked in a dream. Even as she obediently repeated the minister's words all she could think of was that she should be back at the house doing the ironing, or the baking, or turning out one of the bedrooms.

When the brief ceremony was over and they emerged from the side door of the church into the cold, dull November day, Walter shook hands with the minister and the church organist, who had agreed to be one of their witnesses. Money changed hands discreetly and then, leaving minister and organist behind, he and Sarah left the vestry with Beatrice, their other witness.

'I think that went very well,' Walter said cheerfully, taking Sarah's hand and drawing it through his arm. When she flinched back, startled, he tightened his arm against his side so that her hand was trapped. 'You're my wife now,' he reminded her with a smile. 'You're Mrs Walter Forsyth. From now on, my dear, we walk through life together.'

At his insistence they went from the church to a photographer's studio where, once again, Sarah numbly followed instructions. First of all she sat in a chair, hands clasped on her lap, while Walter stood behind her, handsome in his black frock coat and striped trousers, high-collared white shirt and dark-blue patterned waistcoat and tie. His bowler hat was held in the curve of one arm while his free hand rested lightly but possessively on his new wife's shoulder.

After they were pictured standing together, it was Walter's turn to take the high-backed chair while Sarah stood by his side, her gloved hand on his shoulder. Waiting for the photographer to prepare his camera, she looked down at her new husband's crisp dark hair and his hands, long fingered and with clean, oval nails, resting on his knee, and wondered when she was going to wake up from this strange dream and find herself in her little room by the kitchen, tumbling sleepily from her narrow cot to clean out the grate and set the fire.

'Ready?' the photographer asked, and she glanced up just in time to be blinded by the phosphorus flash.

Again, Walter drew his bride's hand through the crook of his elbow as they continued their walk to the house, pinning her as firmly into place by his side as her hatpins secured the cream straw hat, trimmed with a great mass of flowers, on her head.

As they progressed along the pavement with Beatrice McCallum walking just ahead of them, they met a few people going the other way. The passers-by acknowledged Beatrice with smiles and nods of the head, but in every case, once they recognised the couple walking arm in arm behind her, the smiles froze and eyes swivelled away. Unperturbed, Walter tipped his grey bowler hat to each and every one of them, calling out a cheery greeting.

'Don't let them trouble you, my dear,' he said as Sarah's hand trembled against his sleeve. 'They will come round in time.'

They had just turned the corner into Argyle Road when, to her horror, Sarah saw Samuel Gilmartin's delivery cart standing by the kerb outside a house. Her heart lurched and she tried to hurry her step in order to get past before Samuel himself appeared, but with a firm nudge of the elbow Walter kept her to his own even pace.

They had almost drawn level with the gate when Samuel came along the path, whistling cheerfully. He paused at the gate to let them past, glancing at them without great interest, and then looking again, swiftly.

Sarah, unable to meet his gaze, ducked her head and stared down at the pavement.

'Chin up, my dear,' Walter said in a quiet but clear voice. 'Don't forget that you're my wife now. You can carry yourself with pride in this town.' He patted the fingers trembling against the crook of his arm, and said again, firmly, 'Chin up.'

Sarah did as she was told, just in time to see Samuel whip his cap off and clutch it to his broad chest in a gesture of mocking servility. Then they had passed him by and she could feel his eyes boring into her back.

'That man,' Beatrice said, 'was being impertinent.'

'Nonsense, Aunt Beatrice, he was merely paying his respects to his betters. My dear, you're shiver-

125

ing,' Walter added solicitously to his bride. 'I should have insisted on you wearing warmer clothes. Finery's all very well, but we must consider the child's welfare. Never mind, we're almost home.'

When they reached the house he rang the bell and then, after waiting for a few seconds, rapped the handle of his walking stick against the door's stained-glass panel. There was a flurry and a scurry along the narrow hall and then the door flew open to reveal Nellie, the new servant, peering around its edge and bobbing a series of little curtsies as the three of them entered.

'A little faster from now on, if you please,' Walter said as he passed by the maid. 'People do not care to be kept waiting, especially on their own doorsteps.'

Sarah would have given much to be able to take refuge in the familiar kitchen, but instead she had to go into the front parlour, where the round table had been covered with the late Mrs Forsyth's best lace tablecloth and set with plates of sandwiches, cakes and biscuits.

'Tea, please, Nellie,' Walter ordered, adding, as the little maid ducked into another curtsey before scurrying to the door, 'and not too strong, mind. We're not navvies!'

'I could show her...' Sarah began, but he put a hand on her arm as she tried to follow the girl to the kitchen.

'She has to learn, my dear, and in any case, this is where you belong now.' He indicated the room, adding, 'But where's Morna? She should have been waiting to greet us.'

126

'I'll go to her room and...'

'Sit down, Sarah, I'll go.'

'Yes, do sit down, my dear,' Beatrice said kindly when they were alone. 'You must be feeling tired.'

'Oh no, Mrs McCallum.'

'Confused, then. It must have been quite a confusing day for you. I will go and see how the maid's getting on. After all, the girl's still new to this house.'

Left on her own, Sarah nervously jumped to her feet again and moved around the room, restless and ill at ease. Pausing before the mirror above the sideboard, she looked at her own reflection and was startled to see herself dressed in clothes other than her usual work dress and apron and cap, and with a beautiful three-strand pearl choker encircling her neck.

On the previous evening Walter had presented her with the black velvet case that had previously stood on his mother's dressing table. Sarah gasped as the jewels within sparkled up at her.

'This,' Walter announced pompously, 'was my mother's jewellery, and now, my dear Sarah, it is yours.'

'Mine? Oh no,' she said in sudden panic. 'No, I can't!'

'Of course you can. She was the last Mrs Forsyth and from tomorrow you will be the new Mrs Forsyth.'

'But Miss – your sisters should surely inherit all this.'

'They have each chosen some pieces, but it is only right that most of it should go to my wife. Now then...' He dipped his fingers into the case, and Sarah's eyes were dazzled by flashes of brilliant light as he stirred the contents around. There was the blue of sapphires, the green of emeralds, and the rich crimson glow of rubies; but above all, the clear vivid gleam of diamonds. There was gold and silver, tiny stud earrings and elegant drop earrings, as well as bracelets, rings and necklaces. It must, she thought, be worth hundreds if not thousands of pounds, all contained in one box.

'Ah.' Walter drew out a ring set with diamonds and rubies. 'You don't have an engagement ring – will this do?' He seized her left hand, but to his disappointment the ring would not go beyond the knuckle.

'It's the housework,' she said apologetically. 'It swells the joints.'

'Never mind, I'll have it enlarged for you.'

'No, don't spoil it!'

'Nonsense, it won't damage the ring, and you should be able to wear it since it's yours. No sense in letting it lie in a box where nobody can see it or admire it.' He set the ring aside and brought out a triple string of pearls. 'This, I think, for tomorrow. They will be perfect for your wedding day. Allow me.'

Before she could protest he had looped the strands around her throat and was fastening the diamond clasp at the nape of her neck. 'There – look at yourself, Sarah.'

The pearls were like a cold hand encircling her neck and when she reluctantly lifted her chin and looked at her reflection she saw that they looked ridiculous above her plain blouse.

'They don't look right...'

'Of course they don't suit the clothes you're wearing now, but tomorrow you will be in the wedding finery that Aunt Beatrice helped you to buy The pearls will look splendid then. Turn around to face me,' he ordered, and when she obeyed, he clipped on the matching earrings before putting his hands on her shoulders and easing her back to face the mirror.

'There,' he said with satisfaction, standing close behind her, smiling at her reflected face. 'They suit you even better than they suited Mother. You have such beautiful little ears, Sarah. You have no idea how much I have wanted to decorate those perfect lobes with jewels – and now, my darling, the day has come!'

He bent and kissed one ear, then let his tongue trail around its outline, as he had done so often before. Sarah gave an involuntary shudder, and Walter, mistaking the tremor for a shiver of passion, murmured thickly, 'It won't be long, my dearest dear, before we are joined for ever as man and wife!'

Now, standing before the mirror on her wedding day, Sarah put a hand up to touch the pearl choker. It felt all wrong, wearing something that had once graced Frances Forsyth's elegant neck.

She wasn't used to wearing a hat for so long; it felt heavy, and her head itched. She reached up to scratch what she could reach of her scalp, and was drawing the first of the hatpins out when Beatrice returned.

'Tea will be brought in a moment. Keep your hat on, my dear,' she added swiftly. 'It's expected of a lady, though you may remove your gloves before eatin'.'

Sarah, crimson with embarrassment, immediately thrust the pin back in, wincing and biting her lip as it dug into her scalp. She blinked hard to hold back tears of pain as Walter ushered his younger sister into the room.

Morna's face was stiff with resentment and disapproval. 'Isn't the tea here yet?' she wanted to know.

'It's on its way. But before we have tea...' Walter went to stand by Sarah, putting an arm around her waist, '...I think you should congratulate us on our marriage, Morna, and welcome your new sister-in-law into the family.'

Morna looked for the first time at Sarah, and her beautiful hazel eyes widened as she recognised the pearls clasping Sarah's throat and on her ears. For a dreadful moment Sarah thought that the girl was going to make a scene, but just in time, Beatrice McCallum, who had been watching the three of them closely, said, 'Morna?' and after a swift glance at her aunt Morna forced a smile to her lips.

'Congratulations, Sarah, on making a very suitable marriage. And welcome to the family. Walter...' the smile began to slip as she looked up at her brother, '...I wish you whatever you may wish yourself.'

'In that case, my dear Morna, you have just wished me a very long and happy life with my dear wife and the family soon to be.'

'Not as graceful a speech as it might have been, Morna,' her aunt said dryly, 'but I suppose that it will suffice. Ah,' she went on as the door opened

130

and Nellie appeared, carefully balancing the silver tray, 'here's tea. And very welcome it is too.'

There was an awkward moment when they took their seats at the table. Morna would have seated herself at the end, opposite her brother, but he firmly moved her aside and nodded Sarah towards the chair.

'Would you pour for us, my dear?'

'Let me,' Beatrice said swiftly. 'Let Sarah be a guest in her own home just this once, since this is her weddin' day.'

'Of course. Morna, you may pass the sandwiches,' Walter said smoothly and his sister, white with anger, did as she was told while Beatrice poured tea skilfully. Sarah watched her every move, knowing that from now on she herself would be expected to undertake that task.

Like most people of her class, Sarah Neilson had lived with hunger. She was fortunate in that, while growing up in her aunt's household, and then working for the Forsyths, she had had enough food to keep her strong and active, but the luxury of eating until she could eat no more was alien to her. She had always looked forward eagerly to the next meal, and as soon as it was over she began to look forward all over again to the next. But today, her marriage day, her appetite had entirely deserted her, and she could scarcely manage a small sandwich and a piece of shop-bought sponge cake that was so dry that every crumb threatened to stick in her throat.

Walter insisted on staying away from the shop for the rest of the week, and it was a relief to the other three inhabitants of the house when he finally returned to work. As she had always done, Sarah accompanied him to the front door, helping him on with his coat before fetching his hat and stick from the hatstand. She ran a brush over his coat and then opened the door for him, settling so well into the routine she had followed every morning when her mistress was alive that she was taken aback when he stooped to kiss her cheek.

'I shall be home for lunch at one o'clock, my dear. You should go out for a short walk this morning. The fresh air will do you good.' And then, peering up into the grey early-November sky, 'But be sure to put on warm clothing.'

As the door closed behind him Morna came into the hall.

'I've finished breakfast, Sarah. Now I have some letters to write and I do not want to be disturbed. I would like tea brought to my room at eleven o'clock.'

'Yes, Miss Morna,' Sarah said automatically, and then hurried to the kitchen, where Nellie was washing the breakfast dishes.

The girl spun round nervously when her mistress entered. 'I didn't hear the bell, missus. Mebbe it's broken...'

Sarah smiled at her. 'I didn't ring it, and you're best to call your mistress "ma'am", not missus.'

'Ma'am,' the girl repeated obediently, and then, realising that water was dripping from the ends of her fingers on to the floor, 'Oh, mis – I mean, ma'am!'

'It's all right, water's easily mopped up.' Sarah fetched a cloth and knelt down to mop the drips.

'You shouldnae be doin' that!' Nellie said, scandalised. 'That's my job!'

'You get on with the dishes and let me deal with this. Then,' Sarah said firmly, 'I'll show you how to make the beds and put the bedrooms to rights.'

The new little maid was eager to learn, and Sarah more than happy to teach her, for otherwise her days would have been long and lonely. Morna kept herself to herself, though Beatrice Mc-Callum made a point of coming in every other day to have afternoon tea with Sarah. Under her kindly tutoring the girl learned to pour tea and pass the sandwiches that she and Nellie had made earlier, as well as the scones and cakes that she herself had baked, since Nellie had not yet mastered the art of managing the kitchen range. So far, her attempts at baking had resulted in items that were either pale or burned to a crisp.

'You're doing well,' Beatrice said, ten days after Sarah's marriage. 'You need have no concern if any of your neighbours should call on you.'

'They won't, Mrs McCallum. They pass me in the street with their noses in the air and look the other way when I go intae the shops. The assistants can scarce bring themselves tae serve me.' Sarah swallowed hard to deter the tears of self-pity threatening to thicken her voice. Even the other maidservants in the street, always ready with a friendly smile and wanting to chat, had taken to avoiding her when she went out. She was neither servant nor gentry now, and so both sections of the community had disowned her.

'Give them time and they'll come round.'

133

'Will they? Miss Belle hasnae called once, and this is her house.'

'My dear, you must remember that it's Walter's house now, and as his wife you have more right to be here than Belle.'

'But this is where she's always lived!'

'And where she can live again once she comes to acknowledge you as her sister-in-law and her equal.'

'That would be very hard for her, and for Miss Morna.'

'You really must stop thinking of them as Miss Belle and Miss Morna, Sarah. As for things being hard for *them*, I imagine,' Beatrice said shrewdly, 'that they have not been at all easy for you either, and yet you are doing your best and doing it well. My nieces could use some of your courage.'

Sarah smiled wanly, and Beatrice went on, 'I know that it can't be easy for you, Sarah. You look pale – are you getting enough fresh air?'

'Walter insists that I take a walk every morning, for the bairn's sake.'

'Then perhaps you need more rest. Are you sleeping well?'

'Well enough,' Sarah lied. To her great relief her new husband had announced on their wedding night that for the child's sake – his favourite phrase these days – he would not claim his conjugal rights until the baby had been safely delivered. But the nights were still a torment, for she was unable to get comfortable, being unused to sleeping in such a soft bed, never mind the fact that she, a mere servant, was in the bed that until fairly recently had been occupied by her master and mistress.

134

The night hours dragged by slowly while she lay listening to Walter snoring and huffing and snuffling only inches away, and all she could think of was Samuel. The pain of missing him was so bad that almost every night her pillow was dampened with her tears, and in the mornings, when Walter bounded out of bed refreshed, Sarah was as tired as she had been the night before.

'Hmmm.' Beatrice leaned forwards, peering into her face, and Sarah recoiled slightly, certain that the older woman's sharp eyes would penetrate into her mind, see her utter wretchedness and somehow guess the cause of it. But instead Beatrice said, 'Then perhaps you need to lie down for a little while each afternoon to keep your strength up. And take a glass of tonic wine every day. I will have some delivered. Come along, Romeo...' she nudged the sleeping spaniel with the tip of her boot, '...we must leave young Mrs Forsyth to rest.'

Today was the day that Samuel delivered the groceries. As soon as the door had closed behind her visitor Sarah hurried to the kitchen, intending to send Nellie off to some other part of house while she herself remained in the kitchen until he arrived. But Nellie was busy in the pantry, sorting out a pile of fresh vegetables.

'Oh – has the greengrocer's delivery arrived already?'

'He's just this minute away, ma'am. Did you want to speak to him?' The little maid wiped her hands on her work apron, smearing it with earth from the leeks she had been putting away. 'I can run and fetch him, he can't have gone far.'

'No, it's all right. I just thought I might give him next week's order, but it can wait.' Sarah's voice shook with disappointment, and she put a hand to her mouth and coughed in an effort to hide her sudden weakness.

'Are you all right, ma'am? You look awful upset. Are you ill? D'ye want me tae run for the master, or fetch Miss Morna from her room?'

'No, I'm fine. There's nothing wrong with me that can't be cured by a cup of tea.'

'You've just had tea, ma'am,' Nellie said, perplexed.

'I know, but I fancy some more. And I'm sure you'd like some too.'

Nellie's eyes rounded. 'Me, Mrs Forsyth? In the middle of the afternoon?'

'Why not? I'll finish the vegetables and you fetch the tray from the parlour, then make tea for the two of us in the tin pot,' Sarah said briskly. When the little maid had scurried off to do her bidding, she took on the task of storing the vegetables, thinking as she handled them of Samuel's hands packing them into the box in readiness for the delivery. She found herself caressing the cool green leeks, the rounded firm globes of the onions, the carrots with their green feathery tops, in much the same way as he had once caressed her. Her longing to be with him again burned afresh, and if Nellie hadn't staggered back into the kitchen just then, her thin legs buckling under the weight of the silver tray, Sarah might well have ended up in tears.

11

A month after his marriage Walter Forsyth let himself into the house in the early afternoon and was puzzled to find the place silent and seemingly empty.

'Sarah?' he called, and then, since there was no reply, 'Nellie?'

Again he was greeted with silence. Becoming alarmed, he looked first into the parlour, then the small dining room, before hurrying upstairs to find the marital bedroom empty. He ran back downstairs, by now convinced that Sarah had been taken seriously ill and conveyed to the hospital, and went into the kitchen. It was also empty, but the back door stood slightly ajar, and he could hear voices and laughter in the yard behind the house.

He went outside to be greeted by the sight of his wife beating a large carpet slung from a stretch of clothes line, while their maidservant unpegged and folded dried clothing from the other two ropes.

'Sarah? Sarah, what do you think you're doing?'

She spun round guiltily, the smile fading from her flushed face. 'Walter, I didn't expect you home so early.'

'Obviously.' His voice was grim. 'And it's as well that I did come back early. Goodness knows what harm you might be doing to yourself and the child.'

'I'm only beating the dust from the carpet from Miss Belle's room. We thought we would clean the room thoroughly to make it ready for when she...'

He stepped forwards and took the carpet beater from her unresisting fingers, thrusting it at the frightened maid, who stood with a half-folded towel clutched to her flat little chest by both fists. Mutely, she unclenched one in order to take the beater from him.

'Perhaps,' Walter said icily, 'you would be good enough to see to the carpet when you have dealt with the laundry. After all, that's what I pay you to do.' And then, ignoring the girl's whispered, 'Yes, sir,' he escorted his wife into the house.

'What,' he asked again when they were in the parlour, 'do you think you were doing?'

'I was only helping Helen.' A few strands of hair had been loosened by Sarah's exertions; she tried to capture them and tuck them back into the soft roll of hair.

'Helen?'

'It's Nellie's real name, only everyone insists on calling her Nellie.'

'And in this household,' Walter said, 'we will continue to call her Nellie. Helen is too fine a name for a maid of all work. I don't know what her parents were thinking of, giving her such a name. And I don't know what you were thinking of either, Sarah. Quite apart from your delicate condition, it's unseemly for the mistress of the house to be beating carpets. That's what I pay the maid for.'

'I was only showing her how to do it properly.'

'It didn't look like that to me. What if someone

138

had come to call on you? What would they think of me if they found my wife covered in dust and with a carpet beater in her hand?'

'There's no danger of that, Walter,' Sarah protested. 'Nobody has called here since our marriage. The neighbours won't even acknowledge me in the street or the shops. Hel – Nellie's the only companion I have when you're at the shop.'

'There's Morna,' Walter was saying when the door opened and his sister hurried in, her arms full of clothing. As Walter's angry pacing had taken him to the bay window, Sarah was the first and only person she saw.

'There you are, Sarah. There's a nasty stain on one of my blouses, I think it might be ink from when I was writing a letter. See if you can remove it, and while you're at it, these other things need washing and ironing as soon as...'

'What do you think you're doing, Morna?' Walter interrupted, and his sister spun round to face him.

'Walter – what brings you home at this time of day?'

'Never mind me, what makes you think that Sarah – my wife – should wash and iron your clothes?'

'Because she's...' Morna stopped suddenly, biting her lip, then finished lamely, '...she's much better at these things than I am.'

'That's because she had to learn how to do them. Just as you will have to learn to do them for yourself.'

'Me? Why should I? I never had to do that sort of thing when Mother and Papa were here. Sarah

139

always attended to my clothing – to all our laundry.'

'Because she was Mother's servant,' Walter acknowledged coldly, 'but now that she is the mistress of the house, how dare you presume to go on treating her like a servant?'

'I don't mind, Walter.' Sarah reached out to take the bundle from Morna. 'To tell the truth, time passes slowly these days and I welcome something to do.'

Walter moved to one side, blocking her way and making it impossible for her to take the clothes from Morna. 'Morna will see to her own possessions.'

'The new maid...'

'If you want your laundry done and your every whim obliged, Morna, then I will expect you to contribute from now on towards the girl's wages.'

'What?' Morna's flushed face suddenly went white with anger. 'Where would I get the money from, when you've cut my allowance?'

'As I have already suggested, you could find work.'

'If Mother and Papa heard you speak to me like that...' Morna's lower lip began to tremble.

'If they were here we would not be having this conversation. I am the master of the house now, and by God,' Walter's voice was tight with exasperation, 'I intend to make sure that everyone under my roof knows it. Everyone! In future, Morna, you will obey my rules or you will find somewhere else to live.'

His sister hurled the clothes at his feet, where they lay in a colourful heap. 'So you're throwing me out of my own home now, just as you threw poor Belle out!'

'Belle knows full well that she is welcome to come back any time she wishes, and you are also welcome to stay, but only on the understanding that you both accept Sarah as my wife and your equal.'

Sarah watched, appalled, as brother and sister faced each other, Morna with her fists clenched and Walter cold and aloof.

'Then you leave me with no option,' Morna said through gritted teeth. 'I am leaving this house, Walter, and I doubt if I will ever come back to it again.'

'That, my dear, is up to you. No, Sarah,' Walter said, putting a hand on her arm as she started to protest, 'Morna is a grown woman and it's time she behaved like one, instead of a spoiled child.'

'Oh!' Morna's fists opened into claws and for a moment Sarah thought that the girl was going to fly at her brother and tear her fingernails down his face. She could tell, by the way Walter tensed, that he thought the same.

Then Morna said, 'I shall leave this house now!'

'No – please!'

'As I said, Sarah, it's up to Morna. If she no longer wants to live here, she is free to go.'

'But where to?'

'Anywhere, as long as it's not here,' Morna said, turning to the door.

'Before you go, Morna, pick up your clothes.'

She turned back again, glared at Walter, then with a sudden, furious movement bent and scooped the blouses and skirts into her arms.

141

'Walter...' Sarah said as the door closed.

'Let her go. I will not have her treating you as though you were still the servant. I suppose,' he said angrily, 'that this monstrous behaviour of hers has been going on behind my back ever since we married?'

'I didn't mind helping her.'

'But I mind. I will not have my wife treated like a skivvy.'

'They're your sisters, Walter. Your family!'

He put an arm around her shoulders. 'You're my family now, Sarah; you and the child. As long as we have each other we have no need of anyone else,' he said.

Fine words, as Beatrice McCallum was wont to often say, do not fill stomachs. As the door of the house where she had enjoyed a comfortable life closed behind Morna she suddenly realised the enormity of what she had just done. It was one thing to fly into a rage with Walter, but quite another to let her anger leave her homeless.

The weather that morning had been clear and sunny, but without Morna noticing it had become overcast, with heavy sullen clouds coming in over the Firth of Clyde. As she stood on the path, wondering what to do next, a stray snowflake drifted down, followed by another, and then another. It was as though they had chosen her exit from the house to remind her that it was now early December, a bad time to make oneself homeless.

She almost turned back to ring the bell and announce that she had decided to forgive her brother and remain beneath his roof, but was halted by the prospect of humiliating herself in such a manner, not only before Walter's amused eyes and sneering grin, but before Sarah, who until recently had made Morna's bed, darned and washed her clothes and obeyed her every command.

A tear began to well up in Morna's eye, and was firmly blinked back. She would not, *could* not, beg to be taken back. She picked up her two small cases and walked firmly down the path and along the road without bothering to close the wrought iron gate behind her. Let Walter close it, or Sarah, or the useless, tongue-tied fool of a girl they had seen fit to employ.

She pulled her shoulders back and lifted her head high on her slender, elegant neck until she was out of sight of anyone who might have been watching from the parlour's bay window. Then she had to stop, lower her cases to the ground, and lean against a wall for a moment because her knees had suddenly become quite weak. Where could she go? Dependent as she was on Walter for an allowance, she had very little money in her purse, certainly not enough to pay for a room. Her small share of the profits from the shop were locked away in a bank account and could not be touched until she was twenty-one years old, or until she married. The first event was still some two and a half years away, and the second – her eyes filled with tears of self-pity – would probably never happen now. In any case, women of her station couldn't stay on their own in hotels or boarding houses. But she had to find somewhere to sleep while she decided what to do next.

She would have liked to confide in Belle, but

Belle would probably be in the shop, where the staff could, and no doubt would, spy and eavesdrop and store up even more gossip about the Forsyth family and their scandalous goings on. She could imagine the whispers already– 'Threw his sister out, him and that servant he's taken as his wife. Poor Miss Morna, what will become of her now? No skills at all, and who would want to marry her after all that's happened in that house?'

She could go to Aunt Beatrice's, where no doubt she could share Belle's room for the time being, but the thought of living under her aunt's roof made Morna shudder. And although she had never lacked for company among the town's young men and women, she realised now that the people she had been in the habit of referring to as 'friends' were in reality little more than acquaintances.

She flushed at the memory of Mrs MacAdam saying coldly, 'You will find few doors open to you until such time as your father's actions fade from people's minds.' No doubt most, if not all of the people she and her family had known and consorted with, would be of the same mind as Arthur's mother. And now, by marrying Sarah, Walter had made things much, much worse.

In that moment Morna hated her father and brother with such passion that she kicked one of the suitcases, causing it to fall over right in the path of a little boy running along with his face tilted to the sky and his chubby hands outstretched to catch the fat snowflakes still drifting down. The child recoiled, his face beginning to crumple, and the plainly dressed young woman

144

following close behind caught his arm and hustled him past, glaring at Morna as she skirted the suitcase.

'Naughty lady,' she heard the boy say as they hurried off, and the woman replied, 'Yes, a very rude lady!'

Morna glared at their retreating backs and then all at once the answer came to her. The child had been quite well dressed, and the woman was probably his nursemaid. Morna, Belle and Walter had had a nursemaid when they were children, a pleasant woman who had married and, with her husband, taken over a lodging house down by the shore. On several occasions Belle had taken Morna to visit Meggie who would surely be willing to offer her former charge a room for the night.

Morna smiled, picked up the suitcases, and set off with renewed confidence.

The lodging house owned by Billy and Meggie Chapman was down by the river, in Quay Street, largely inhabited by fisher folk and, in the nineteenth century, the legendary Betsy Miller, for many years captain of the brig *Clytus*. Once, Belle had insisted on reading a newspaper article about the redoubtable Betsy Miller to her disinterested brother and sister. It concerned an incident when the *Clytus*, caught in a storm, was in grave danger of being wrecked on the shore at the nearby town of Irvine. 'Lads,' said Betsy to her crew, 'I'll go below and put on a clean sark [chemise], for I wud like tae be flung up on the sands kind o' decent. Irvine folks are nasty, noticin' buddies.' While the lady was changing her clothes, the

145

Clytus had managed to struggle to deep water and safety. Betsy's crew claimed ever afterwards that her clean chemise had been the saving of them all.

'I'd like to grow up to be a strong, capable woman like that,' thirteen-year-old Belle had said, her eyes shining, while Morna wanted to know, 'Was it a pretty chemise, with blue ribbons?'

The memories fled as Morna stood looking down Quay Street. The buildings were old and the gutters choked; when it rained, as it did frequently, water tended to lie on the surface, where it became stagnant. The snow began falling faster. Soon it would cover the pavements, roofs and gardens in Argyle Road with a pretty white veil; but in Quay Street the delicate flakes seemed to melt as soon as they landed. If it snowed hard enough, and for long enough, the street would be covered with little more than a dirty grey slush.

Arriving at the door of the lodging house, Morna set her cases down with a sign of relief and, unable to find a bell pull, thumped on the scarred wooden panels with her fist.

The tenements on either side of the narrow lane were like cliffs dominating a dark ravine. A few people passed as she waited for someone to come to the door – pale-faced women in shabby clothes and one or two men, all hurrying to get into shelter and away from the thickening snowfall. The men eyed Morna in a way that made her shiver, and one, old and with a mop of grey hair matted with dirt, made a point of passing so close to her that she could smell his unwashed clothing and the nauseating reek of cheap whisky. He gave her an almost toothless grin, and she spun round

146

and hammered with desperation at the door, which finally opened.

'Meggie?'

The large woman in the doorway peered blankly at her visitor for a moment before recognising her. 'Miss Morna, is it you?' One hand, red and shiny and steaming from recent immersion in hot water, automatically went up to tidy the wisps of hair straggling around her flushed face.

Morna noticed that the old man had paused only yards away and was eyeing her from top to toe in a most impertinent fashion. 'Of course it's me, Meggie, let me in!' She thrust one of her suitcases into Meggie Chapman's hand and moved forwards. Meggie retreated before her, and then, as Morna slammed the door, the older woman led the way down a dark passage and into the kitchen at the back of the house.

The room was filled with the aroma of the soup simmering on top of the kitchen range. Meggie poured two cups of black tea and added generous spoonfuls of condensed milk that made it taste unbearably sweet but did nothing to relieve the harsh flavour. Morna's thick cup was chipped almost all round the rim. She took a cautious sip and then set the cup down, trying to hide her disgust.

Meggie picked up a knife that was lying on the table beside a tin basin half filled with peeled potatoes, then took a potato from the sack on the floor and began to work on it. 'Ye don't mind me gettin' on while we talk, do ye, Miss Morna? The men need a good dinner when they come back from their work and there's so much tae do. It's a while since you've been here, eh? Miss Belle looks in now and again, but she's not been for a wee while. Not since...' She stopped abruptly, then said, 'I was awful sorry tae hear about yer ma. She was a good employer tae me.'

'And you'll no doubt have heard about my father leaving us, and about my brother marrying our servant. Of course you have – gossip travels fast in Saltcoats.'

'Aye, I've heard, and I'm sorry about the troubles you and Miss Belle have been goin' through. The mistress would be sore upset if she knew what had happened after her passin'.'

'Meggie, she must be turning in her grave right now. And I know she'd say that I'm doing the right thing by coming to you for help. As you said yourself, she was a good employer and she'd want you to do all you can for me. The thing is,' Morna swept on before Meggie had a chance to speak, 'I need a room.'

The potato Meggie had been peeling slipped from her hand and splashed into the basin. She stared at her visitor. 'A room? Here?'

'It's what you and your husband do, isn't it? You run a lodging house, and I'm in sore need of lodgings. D'you think I make a habit of carrying these around with me when I go calling on folk?' Morna indicated the suitcases by the door.

'But this is a lodgin' house for workmen. It's no' good enough for a lady like you, Miss Morna!'

'If I had the money I would, of course, go to a hotel. But for the moment beggars can't be choosers. Now then, do you have a room for me?'

'But ... would ye not be better off stayin' in comfort in yer own home?'

'How can I possibly stay in a house where my brother's lost his wits and set up the servant girl in my mother's place? You've no idea what it's like, Meggie! Walter's quite beyond listening to reason, and now he's brought in a new servant who has no idea of what she's supposed to do.'

'What about Miss Belle? Is she managin'?'

'Obviously you haven't heard all the gossip. Belle's already left. She's living with our Aunt Beatrice.'

'There you are, then,' Meggie said, her face brightening. 'Mrs McCallum's got a fine big house; ye'd be more comfortable there with yer sister than in a place like this.'

'Mrs McCallum's got a fine big kennel,' Morna corrected the woman icily. 'It's overrun with dogs and she pays more attention to them than she does to people. I don't know how Belle can stomach it. I know that I couldn't. Do you have an empty room or don't you?'

'There's one – but it's not fit for the likes of you, Miss Morna,' Meggie repeated.

'Needs must.' Morna pushed the mug of tea away and got to her feet. 'Let me see it.'

12

Morna's heart plummeted when she saw the room. It was little more than a cupboard, with barely enough space for the single bed, a dresser with three drawers and an upright wooden chair.

The narrow window looked out over a small dreary backyard festooned with lines of washing.

'You see?' Meggie was almost in tears with embarrassment. 'It does fine for a man who's out at work all day and just wants somewhere tae sleep at night, but it's not nearly good enough for a lady like yersel', Miss Morna.'

Morna, almost in tears herself, swallowed hard, then said with forced firmness, 'It'll do until I find somewhere more suitable. All it needs is a bit of a clean out.'

'I've got the men's dinner tae see tae...'

'Then we'll work on the room together,' Morna said generously. 'Do you have an apron I can borrow?'

There was little that could be done to make the dark narrow room more attractive, but with Meggie doing most of the work, they dusted the few pieces of furniture, washed the window and swept the floor. Meggie stripped the thin blankets and sagging, stained mattress from the iron bedstead and found a slightly better mattress as well as some bedding from her own store. She also found patterned curtains. 'There,' she said when they were in place, 'that makes the room look much better.'

Privately, Morna thought that the red and blue curtains only made the rest of the room look even more sad and dingy than it had before, but reminding herself that she had nowhere else to lay her head that night, she held her tongue.

The lodging house had room for ten tenants altogether, she was told as she sat in the kitchen watching Meggie make the dinner. The ground floor was taken up with the kitchen and adjoining washhouse, with a communal dining room and a parlour for the use of the lodgers at the front of the building.

'Most of the lodgers sleep up in the attic, and me and Billy have a room at the front of the house on the same floor as you,' Meggie explained as she chopped onions. 'There's another two wee rooms there for folk that like their privacy and are willin' tae pay a wee bit extra. One of them's the room you're takin'; the man that had it died just last week.'

'In that room?' Morna asked, horrified.

'No, he was killed in an accident on the railway, poor soul. Buried in a pauper's grave, for he'd nob'dy in the world tae give him a proper send-off.

'The top floor's just one big room with eight cots in it.' Meggie tossed several double handfuls of the onions into a huge pot simmering on the range, wiped her stinging eyes with the back of a plump forearm, and scrubbed her hands against the sacking apron she wore. She disappeared into the small pantry and returned with a stained paper parcel which she unwrapped on the table to reveal a large slab of dark red meat mottled with strings and clumps of grey-white fat. Morna recoiled from the sight and smell of it.

'What's that?' It looked to her like something Aunt Beatrice would feed to her yapping dogs.

'Tonight's stew.' Meggie clamped one hand on the revolting mess and used the other to saw at it with a large carving knife. 'The men like a plate of stew after their day's work.'

Morna moved to a chair at the far end of the table, trying hard not to look at the meat being dissected at the other end, but even if she managed to avoid looking at it, she could still smell it. The thought of actually eating it was repellent, though once it had joined the vegetables in the pot and the whole concoction had been simmering for a good while the smell began to seem more tempting. It had been a long day and she had eaten nothing since breakfast.

When the town's sirens began to signal the end of the working day Meggie carried cutlery and plates to the dingy room where her lodgers ate and then returned to the kitchen to cut a loaf into thick slices.

'Billy and me eat here, for there's not room for all of us in the other room when the house is full. You'll eat with us, of course,' she said, and then, as the front door opened and a man's voice called her name, she went on, 'That's Billy now; he's usually first in.'

There was something about the woman's voice, and the tension in her face as she watched for the kitchen door opening, that made Morna uneasy. She had never met Meggie's husband and had no idea what sort of man he was.

'He'll not mind me being here, will he?'

'No, no,' Meggie assured her without much conviction as the door swung open and Billy Chapman walked in.

For some reason, possibly because Meggie was quite tall for a woman and well-built into the bargain, Morna had expected her husband to be

152

large, but the man who marched into the kitchen and tossed the canvas sack he carried into one corner was at least half a head smaller than Meggie and only about half her girth. His movements and his manner were those of a larger man and his voice, when he barked, 'Is the dinner ready?' was deep and powerful.

'Aye. I'll put yours out now, Billy.'

'Dae that. I'm bloody famished.' He grabbed the back of a wooden chair and hauled it out from the table. Meggie flinched at the obscenity and looked apologetically at Morna.

'Billy...' she began, but her husband had noticed their visitor.

'Who's this?' Instead of sitting down, he stayed where he was, his dirty hands gripping the chair back as though ready to use it as a weapon.

'It's Miss Morna, Billy.' Meggie was ladling soup into a bowl as she spoke. 'Ye've heard me speakin' about Miss Morna that I used tae look after afore we got married.' She set the bowl before her husband.

'Oh aye. Just visitin', are ye? Callin' on a faithful old servant?' A faint sneer underlined the last three words.

'Not exactly,' Morna began as the street door opened again. Deep voices could be heard in the hallway, together with the clatter of boots on the wooden flooring.

'We'll tell you later, Billy. Best get the men's dinners first,' Meggie said hurriedly. Using both hands she hefted the heavy soup pot from the range and glanced at Morna, nodding towards the bread slices which she had piled on to a tin

153

tray. 'Bring them through for me, will ye?'

Morna was happy to oblige rather than be left alone with Billy Chapman.

The long table was crowded with men and the room rang with the sound of their loud rough voices, but when the two women entered the voices died away and Morna suddenly found herself the centre of interest.

'Who's this then, Meggie?' one of the men asked. 'Got yersel' a new servin' lassie, have ye?'

'Ye must be payin' her awful well, judgin' by her fine clothes,' someone else said, and Morna went crimson as a snigger ran all round the table.

'Now you behave yerselves, lads. This is Miss Morna Forsyth that I used tae look after when she was a bairn, and she's come tae call on me.' Meggie dumped the pot of soup down on the table. 'Put the bread down there, pet.'

Morna did as she was told and then stood close to Meggie as the woman ladled soup into the bowls stacked on the table. As each bowl was filled it was passed to the nearest man, who passed it on round the table. They were all dressed in heavy working clothes, and some still wore their cloth caps. Their clothes were shabby, and their hands, Morna noted with a shiver of disgust, were filthy, the nails black. She winced as she watched dirty fingers seizing slices of bread and cramming them into mouths.

'They haven't even washed,' she whispered as she and Meggie left the men to their meal and returned to the kitchen. 'You always made us wash our hands before we ate.'

'They're too hungry tae wash first. It'd be more

154

than my life was worth tae tell that lot they were-nae goin' tae be fed until they wash their hands.' Meggie's hearty laugh boomed out and her large bosom shook with mirth.

'But think of the filth they're putting into their mouths with the food! They'll make themselves ill!'

'Not them. They've eaten dirt all their lives and it's not done them any harm. It's the way they are,' Meggie said, and Morna shivered again.

'Come tae live with us?' Billy Chapman's mouth fell open in astonishment and Morna, catching a glimpse of half-chewed stew and potatoes behind a ragged wall of yellow teeth, looked away hastily. Despite her earlier misgivings the stew was edible, but now she suddenly realised that she had lost her appetite.

'Why wid gentry like her want tae live with us?'

'I told you, Billy, she doesn't get on with the lassie her brother's married tae, and she's got nowhere else tae stay.'

'What about yer friends? Surely a fine lady like yersel' has plenty o' them?'

'Not the sort of friends who would welcome me into their homes,' Morna said bleakly.

'And you thought *we* would? Well, I suppose this is a lodgin' house,' the man said, scraping up the last of the stew and mopping the gravy with a wedge of bread. 'But it's for workin' men. Women cause trouble.'

'I can assure you that I have no intention of "causing trouble", as you put it,' she snapped, deeply offended by the accusation. The man

155

must be mad to think that she could be interested in any of the loud, dirty creatures who were wolfing their food down in the other room.

'Women always cause trouble.'

'Billy, it's not for long,' Meggie pleaded. 'Just until she finds somewhere else.'

'If she's lodgin' here then she'll have to pay for the room. Two shillin' a week.'

'Two shillings?' Morna asked incredulously, and only just managed to stop herself from going on with, 'For that nasty little cupboard?'

'It's an awful lot, Billy. More than we would charge a man.'

'A workin' man,' he pointed out. 'You and me know how much every penny matters tae folk that have tae slave till they drop for no more than a pittance. Wealthy folk can afford tae pay a bit more.'

'I can't. I've scarcely got any money at all.'

'So ye're expectin' me and my wife tae feed and house ye for nothin', are ye? Just because she was once your nursemaid?'

'No, but – you'll have to give me time. I'll find some sort of work.'

'Doin' what?' he asked derisively, and then, as she fell silent, he shrugged his muscular shoulders. 'All right, ye can stay, but until ye can pay yer way ye'll have tae work for yer keep. That means helpin' Meggie here tae see tae the house. And she'll have tae do her fair share, Meggie. You're not her servant any longer. Now that that's settled...' Billy Chapman pushed himself back from the table and began to unfasten the thick leather belt around his waist, '...I'll have a cup o' tea. And ye can let the lassie pour it, Meggie. She's had her

156

dinner – she might as well start earnin' it.'

Only pride kept Morna from running back home or begging her Aunt Beatrice for help. While Billy Chapman sat by the range on that first evening reading his paper and smoking his foul-smelling pipe, she and Meggie cleared the table in the dining room and washed and dried the dishes. They brought in a great pile of washing from the backyard and spent the rest of the evening ironing and folding, sewing on buttons and mending tears. Then, after Billy had gone to his bed, they steeped oatmeal for breakfast and set the long table in readiness for the next morning.

When she was finally free to escape to her narrow little room she stripped and washed herself as best she could in water so cold that it might have been lying out in the yard all day, drying herself with a threadbare towel that, as Aunt Beatrice might say, was worn enough to spit peas through. She was pulling her nightdress over her head when she heard a floorboard creak just outside the door.

'Meggie?' she asked tremulously There was no reply, so she crept over to press her ear against the crack between the door and the frame. All was silent but she was certain that there was someone in the darkness outside; someone breathing and listening – and waiting.

'Go away!' Morna said fiercely. 'Go away or I'll scream for Mr Chapman!'

Again, there was no sound, but as she looked down she thought that she saw the door handle moving very slightly. There was no lock or bolt on the door, but she snatched up the little wooden chair and wedged its back firmly beneath the door handle. 'Go away!' she said again, and after a moment she heard another board creak, but further away this time, as though whoever had been hovering on the other side of the door panels had realised that he was not going to get into the room, and had retreated.

She stood listening for a long time, one hand pressed against her fast-beating heart, but all was quiet.

Before getting into the bed she hauled the blanket and sheet off and examined the mattress, but although Meggie Chapman's home might be shabby, it was clean, and there was no sign of bedbugs. Reassured, Morna blew out her candle.

The mattress was thin and lumpy and the blanket inadequate on such a cold night. She curled into a tight ball, convinced that she would never manage to sleep, exhausted though she was, but even as the thought went through her mind her eyes closed. Before she knew she had slept, Meggie was tapping on the door and whispering to her that it was time to start making the men's breakfasts.

With no time to brush her hair out or pin it up properly, only a splash of icy water for her face and little more than a minute to pull her clothes on, Morna felt as though she had been dragged through a hedge backwards, but even so, the men eyed her appreciatively as they gathered to break their fasts. She looked back at each one of them stonily, trying to work out which of the noisy, grimy lot had been creeping around outside her door the night before.

It was clear from the way Meggie treated them and the way they behaved towards her, that the woman looked on her lodgers as the children she had never borne. She treated each one of them with the same cheerful affection she had shown to Morna, Walter and Belle years before. To Morna, it was like watching a lion tamer working confidently within a cage full of dangerous and unpredictable beasts.

One lodger stood out from the others; a younger man, less rough and rowdy than his companions. Once or twice Morna happened to catch his eye and each time he gave her a warm smile, but she looked away at once. She stayed close to Meggie at all times and every time the older woman left the room Morna followed close on her heels.

'Ye've no need tae worry about the men,' Meggie assured her when they were back in the kitchen. 'They're just a bunch of grown laddies – loud and daft, mebbe, but not a bad bone between them. We'd not let them stay here if they were out tae cause trouble.'

'Are you sure about that? Someone was outside my room last night.'

'Ach, he'd just be goin' tae the privy out in the backyard. We don't let them use the one by the kitchen; Billy likes to keep it just for the two of us – and you, now.'

'Whoever it was tried the handle of my door.'

'Did he now?' Meggie said, a sudden glint in her eye.

'I had to push the back of the chair under the handle before I felt safe enough to go to bed.'

159

'We'll see about that,' Meggie said, and before Morna could utter another word the woman had stormed out of the kitchen and along the passageway to the front room. Morna, cowering at her back, heard a sudden babble of male voices as the door was thrown open; a babble that stopped as though cut by a knife when Meggie said in a bellow that seemed to fill the entire house, 'Which one of youse was sniffin' around outside that lassie's door last night?'

She waited and then, as nobody spoke, swept on with, 'Right. I'll just say that I know he's no' speakin' up because he knows as well as the rest of ye that he'd be put out right this minute tae sleep in the streets. But there'll be no more warnin's. Miss Morna Forsyth's a lady and she'll be treated as such while she's livin' under my roof. Is that understood?'

There was an immediate rumbling chorus of agreement. 'That's better,' Meggie roared. 'This is a lodgin' house, no' a madhouse, and I'll thank the lot o' ye tae remember that!'

She slammed the door and came back along the passage, sweeping Morna before her into the kitchen. 'That's them told. Lucky Billy's already gone off tae work, for he'd have made the man speak up all right, and then kicked him out intae the street. We'll say nothin' of this tae him.'

'Whoever it is'll be angry with me,' Morna whimpered. 'I wish I'd never said anything to you.'

'Away ye go, lassie, nob'dy's goin' tae bother ye, let alone be angry with ye, for they all want tae keep a roof over their heads and food in their bellies and they know well enough that I'll no' have any badness in this house. Now then,' Meggie said briskly, 'we can sit down and have our own breakfast while they finish theirs and get off tae work.'

Morna had thought, when she ventured from the kitchen to collect the breakfast dishes, that all the lodgers had gone out into the still-dark morning and the coast was clear, but when she went into the stuffy front room one man remained at the table, a newspaper held up before him.

'Oh...!' she said in dismay, and was backing out hurriedly when the newspaper was lowered and the young man she had noticed earlier said, 'Don't leave on my account, miss.'

'I thought everyone had gone.'

'I start work later than the others, for I work in a shop, not the dockyard or the railway,' he said in a soft, pleasing Irish accent. And then, nodding towards the newspaper, 'I like to take advantage of the peace once they've all gone. It's the only time I have for a quiet read.'

Morna moved back into the room. This one was safe enough; she was quite certain that he was not the man who had silently tried her door handle the previous night. 'Go on reading, I won't be a minute,' she said, but he had already put the newspaper aside and leaped to his feet.

'I've finished it. Let me help you.'

'You don't have to.'

'Sure, and it's no bother at all. I like to be useful.' He smiled down at her, a dazzling smile that seemed to light up his entire face, and began to stack the plates and mugs, making good use of every inch of the tray.

'You're better at this than I am,' Morna said ruefully, watching his deft movements.

'That's because I'm probably more used to this sort of work than you are. My parents had a large family and we were all expected to turn our hands to whatever needed doin'. Now a lady like yourself would leave this sort of work to her servants, am I not right?'

'You are, but now I'm going to have to learn to do these things for myself.' She reached out to lift the full tray, but he had already picked it up as though it weighed next to nothing.

'I'll take it; it's too heavy for you,' he said, and then, with a mock bow, 'Lead on, my lady, and I shall follow, though it may be to the ends of the earth.'

'The kitchen will do,' Morna said primly, and was glad, as she went ahead of him, that he could not see the smile spreading across her face. It had been a long time since she had had cause to smile.

Meggie was up to her elbows in dishwater. 'Doin' your good deed for the day, Sam?' she asked as the two young people came into the kitchen.

'Aye, Meggie, I am, and it's a pleasure to help such a lovely young lady. Two lovely young ladies,' he added, setting the tray down.

'It's well seen that you've kissed the Blarney Stone,' the woman said amiably. 'Away tae yer work now and let us get on with ours.'

'He's a nice lad, but ye have tae take everythin' he says with a pinch of salt,' she went on when the lodger had gone, with one final sparkling smile for Morna. 'Irishmen are given to flattery.

162

It's nice, mind. Scotsmen can be awful slow with the compliments and a woman likes a wee bit of attention now and again.'

'He's cleaner than the rest; he said he doesn't work in the dockyard or on the railway.'

'Sam Gilmartin works for Mrs Smith that runs the greengrocer's in Hamilton Street. It's handy to have a lodger in that sort of work,' Meggie said as she plunged a pile of plates into the sink, splashing water everywhere, 'because some days Mrs Smith lets him bring back a box of greens that havenae sold. Use that cloth hangin' on the nail, Miss Morna, tae dry the dishes. Then we'll give the house a clean. We can leave the washin' till this afternoon.'

'But we ironed the laundry last night!'

'That was yesterday's washin'. The men pay a few pence extra every week tae get their clothes seen tae,' Meggie explained. 'And with so many of them in dirty work I have tae use the washtub every day Ye'll find that there's never a spare minute in this place!' She gave a rusty chuckle, while Morna felt her heart sink.

13

By the time Meggie was satisfied with their labours that morning Morna was aching all over, and would have given the very clothes off her back for the chance to wash in hot water and then crawl into her narrow, lumpy bed to sleep for at least twelve hours. But there was still the shopping to do.

'Those men work hard and they need a lot of food to keep their strength up.' Meggie pushed her feet, lumpy with bunions, into shoes well worn down at the heel and wrapped a woollen shawl around her shoulders. 'And if we don't get to the shops in good time we'll have missed all the bargains. Here…' She thrust a huge shopping basket at Morna, '…you can carry that.'

'But people will see me!'

'Aye, lassie, they will, and they'll mebbe stare and whisper, but ye made yer choice when ye knocked on my door, and ye cannae hide away for the rest of yer life. Best tae face them all and get it over with.'

There were stares aplenty. Even folk who didn't know who Morna was gaped as the two of them went from shop to shop, for she and Meggie, one in clothes that had seen better days and the other smartly dressed, made an ill-assorted pair. But Meggie was right – she couldn't hide away in the lodging house for ever, so she lifted her chin high and stared past the curious faces instead of full at them. But when she realised that they were in Dockhead Street, and that Meggie was guiding her towards the entrance to Forsyth's shop, she faltered.

'I can't go in there!'

'I need gas mantles and that's where I always buy them.' The older woman gripped Morna's arm with a large firm hand and marched the girl into the shop. 'Besides, I think you owe it to yer brother and sister tae let them know ye're safe,

164

and bidin' with me.'

As it happened, Belle had emerged from her small cubby-hole in order to show one of the assistants how to set up a display. When she saw the newcomers she immediately left the girl and came hurrying over. 'Morna, I've been so worried! Where have you been?'

'With me, Miss Belle, and she's quite safe.'

'Meggie?' Belle stared, then rallied. 'She's staying with you? But you run a lodging house, don't you – for workmen?' She said the final word with a faint shudder of distaste.

'Aye, Miss Belle, I do, and glad the poor souls are for somewhere tae lay their heads and fill their bellies after a hard day's work. Miss Morna's earnin' her keep by helpin' me until she can find somewhere more suited. I'll just go and see about they gas mantles,' Meggie said tactfully.

'You can't stay in that lodging house!' Belle said as soon as the sisters were alone.

'Why not?'

'Because it's completely unsuitable! Come with me,' Belle demanded when her sister pursed her lips and glared at her. She caught Morna's arm and dragged her into the back office where Walter was working on a ledger. 'Walter, Morna's gone to stay with Meggie Chapman in that lodging house down by the shore. Tell her that she must go back home at once!'

'It seems to me, Belle, that nobody can tell Morna anything these days. But I am sure she knows that any time she cares to return to Argyle Road my wife and I will be pleased to see her.'

Every fibre of Morna's being longed to be back

in her comfortable room with a servant down in the kitchen to minister to her needs, but her pride would not let her admit it. So she drew herself up, stiffening her spine until she could almost hear it creaking under the strain, and said coldly, 'I am very well suited where I am.'

'What's got into you, Morna? If Mother only knew the worry you've caused us!'

'The worry *I've* caused? What about—'

'That's enough, Morna,' Walter thundered, and then, at an agitated gesture from Belle, who could see through the observation window behind her brother that some of the people in the shop were turning to stare, he lowered his voice and went on, 'As I said, you are welcome to return to the house at any time. Your room is still there, waiting for you, but whether you like it or not, Morna, it is my house now, presided over by my wife, and you must accept that.'

'Accept that the house I was born in, the house I grew up in, is now the domain of our kitchen maid? How can you ask me to accept such a situation?'

Colour stained Walter's cheekbones. 'Sarah stopped being our kitchen maid the day she married me,' he said stiffly. 'Are you going to see reason and come back to Argyle Road or are you not?'

'I am not!'

'In that case I shall tell Sarah that she may look on your room as the new nursery,' he said, and left the office.

'Morna, see sense!' Belle begged, almost in tears. 'We can't let this business tear the family apart.'

'Walter seems to have done that already. I will not go back to that house under his terms.'

'Then come to Aunt Beatrice's. She has room for us both.'

'And let her start telling me what to do? She'd be just as bad as Walter. Belle, I left most of my clothes and all of my jewellery in my room. Could you arrange to have it packed up and taken to Aunt Beatrice's for safe keeping?'

'But you'll need your clothes, surely?'

Morna, thinking of the tiny cold room where she had spent the night, with its shaky dresser and the nail hammered into the door to act as a hanger, gave her sister a smile with more bitterness in it than amusement. 'I've got all I need for the moment. You'll make sure that the rest of my things are kept for me?'

'Of course, but Morna, you can't stay in a place like that. It's not seemly.'

'It will do for the moment.'

'And then where will you go? What will you do? How will you support yourself?'

'I'll think of something,' Morna said. But as she and Meggie left the shop she had to swallow hard to halt the tears pressing against the backs of her eyes. Only a month or two earlier her life had been comfortable and safe, but now the future, which had once consisted of marriage to some as yet unknown man who adored her and was willing to give her everything she might want, had become an unknown journey And she had no way of knowing what might lie at the end of it.

'Perhaps,' Clarissa Pinkerton said thoughtfully,

'the maidservant will die in childbirth. Do you think that's likely?'

'I don't know,' Belle said, startled.

'It does happen, you know.' Clarissa paced around Beatrice's parlour, which, unlike most homes of the era, was quite sparsely furnished and allowed room for pacing. 'But then again, servants tend to be strong.'

'You surely don't want the girl to die, do you?'

'I was thinking that if she did die, Walter would be left a widower with a small child. He would require comforting and the child would need a mother.'

'You would consider marrying Walter after what he's done to you?'

'I'm a foolish girl, I know, but to tell you the truth, Belle, I have never in my life considered marriage to anyone but your brother. Even when we played together as children I always saw Walter as the father of my dolls.'

'Oh, Clarissa!'

'I know – it's a foolish weakness of mine, but I can't seem to shake it off.'

'You would even raise Sarah's baby as your own?'

'I admit that if the child also died during the birth that would make life easier. But if it were to survive I could perhaps come to look on it as my own and be a good mother to it. A better mother, I am sure, than that girl could ever be,' Clarissa said, wrinkling her nose. 'And it would be a very unselfish act, don't you think? Forgiving the man who had so grievously wronged me, in order to care for him and for his motherless child.' She paused in her pacing, thinking, and then added cheerfully, 'And of course, there are always nursemaids. We rarely saw my mama all through the years of our childhood. We were in the nursery with the nursemaids and she was busy with the house, and visiting friends and entertaining. That's as it should be. Yes, I am convinced that I would be willing to marry Walter if he were to become free of that dreadful girl. And just think...' she came to where Belle was sitting, taking both hands and pulling her friend to her feet, '...you and I would be sisters-in-law, just as we have always wanted. Now wouldn't that be a lovely, happy ending to all this unpleasantness?'

At that moment, if Clarissa had only known it, Sarah would almost have been willing to look favourably on the other girl's plans for her early demise. She was bent over a basin in the front bedroom, relieving her queasy stomach of the lunch that Walter had insisted on her eating, while Nellie stood by, wringing her hands.

When the paroxysm was over, Sarah wiped her mouth and smiled faintly at the little maid. 'There now, all over. No need to look so worried; women can have upset bellies when they're carrying bairns.'

'But not all the time, surely.'

'It's not all the time, Nellie, it's only now and again.' Sarah picked up the basin and carried it out of the bedroom and along the passage to the bathroom as the maid hurried after her.

'Let me do that for you, ma'am. You should be havin' a rest, like the master says ye have tae do every afternoon. You look so pale!'

'I don't want to lie down; I want a cup of tea to take the bad taste from my mouth. And I can manage the basin fine,' she added firmly as Nellie tried to take it. 'You go and make tea for the two of us and I'll be down in a minute.'

Alone in the bathroom she splashed cold water on to her face and then dried herself slowly, staring into the mirror. As Nellie had said, her normally pink cheeks were pale, and quite sunken, as though the child within her was drawing flesh from her face and using it to swell her belly. She emptied and rinsed the basin listlessly before taking it down to the kitchen.

The tea was welcome, but the smell of mutton boiling on the range for that evening's dinner made her stomach twinge uneasily again. She stepped out of the back door and took several deep breaths of air before returning to the kitchen table. 'While we're drinking our tea I'll show you how to polish Mrs Forsyth's silver,' she said briskly.

'You mean your silver, ma'am. You're Mrs Forsyth,' the maid said, perplexed.

'I was speaking of the master's mother. She was my mistress up until she died and Mr Forsyth went away and Mr Wal – my husband became the master,' Sarah was trying to explain when there was a swift, familiar rat-a-tat on the back door. Before Nellie could scramble to her feet it swung open and Samuel Gilmartin walked in, a basket over one arm.

'Delivery, Nellie,' he said cheerfully, then stopped as he saw Sarah.

'Mornin', madam.' He put a faint emphasis on the second word.

Sarah's heart, as always happened when she saw him, gave a jump and then began to beat faster.

'You're early on your rounds today.'

'Mrs Smith wants me back at the shop to help with shiftin' things around.' One hand swept aside the cutlery they had been about to clean, so that he could set the basket on the table. 'Hope that's not inconveniencin' you – madam.'

'Of course not. Nellie, put the vegetables away. Would you like a cup of tea, Mr Gilmartin?' Sarah jumped up and went to fetch another cup from the dresser.

'Are ye sure that's allowed, *madam?*' Again, he sneered out the final word with mock servility, and Sarah felt heat rise to colour her pale cheeks. When she turned, clutching the cup in both hands, she saw that he was standing by the table, chin jutting out, his gaze sweeping slowly down from her face to the firm swell of her stomach.

'It's allowed if I say it is,' she shot back at him and poured the tea with shaking hands while Nellie, quite unaware of the tension between her two companions, unpacked the basket, darting like a busy little field mouse between the table and the pantry until Samuel stopped her with a hand on her arm.

'Save yer legs, lass,' he said. 'Take the basket tae the shelves, like this.' He picked it up and went into the pantry, closely followed by Nellie.

Left alone in the kitchen, Sarah sat back down again and waited, listening to Samuel's musical voice rising and falling. The door was almost completely closed and she couldn't make out what he was saying, but judging by Nellie's frequent giggles and the occasional squeal of shocked amusement, he was charming her the way he had once charmed Sarah. The way, she thought, sick with longing for him, he probably charmed all the maidservants on his rounds.

It seemed to take a long time before the two of them emerged from the pantry, the basket empty, Nellie glowing, and Samuel smiling lazily at her as he slid on to a chair opposite Sarah and picked up the cup waiting for him. He took a deep drink and then gave a sigh of pleasure and ran a hand over his mouth. She watched, mesmerised.

'Well now, you make a lovely cup of tea, madam. Or is it you that makes it?' he added, turning to Nellie. When she nodded, beaming, he said in his soft, seductive Irish brogue, 'Perfect, it is. Hot and strong, just the way I like it.'

He emptied the cup with a second swallow, and when Nellie asked eagerly, 'Would you like some more?' said, 'Lass, I'd like fine tae stop and drink more tea with ye, but I've got the rest of my deliveries to make, and your mistress here'll be givin' the both of us the edge of her tongue if I keep ye from yer work any longer.' He stood up, grinning down at the little maid. 'But there'll be other days,' he added, then picked up his basket and turned to go.

'Wait...' Sarah said swiftly. 'I'll pay you the money owed.'

He raised his eyebrows at her. 'You can pay Mrs Smith at the end of the week. Is that not what the last mistress of this house always did?'

'The money's here, and I know how much is due. I might as well give it to you now.' She got up and went to the inner door. 'Follow me,' she said, and saw him wink at Nellie before doing as he was bid.

In the front parlour he stared at the pictures and the flock wallpaper, the ornaments, heavy window hangings and comfortable chairs, and then gave a long, low whistle. 'Well, Sarah, ye've landed on yer feet, have ye no'?'

'I'd as soon be livin' in one room with you.' The words were out before she could stop them. She put a hand on his arm, but he freed himself with a shrug.

'Then you're a fool.'

'No, I'm just a lassie who wants to be with the right man.'

'Is that me ye're talkin' about? Did I not tell ye that I'm no' the marryin' kind?' he said, then went over to the mantelshelf and picked up a china ornament, turning it over in his big hands. 'Though mebbe I should start thinkin' the way you did, for I'd not mind livin' in this sort of comfort for a change. Tell me,' he went on, putting the ornament back exactly where he had found it, 'who else lives in this house now, besides you and yer fine new husband and that bonny wee maid-servant?'

Her heart twisted in her breast at his description of Nellie, who was quite plain, but who had looked almost pretty earlier as she glowed beneath Samuel's admiring attention. The girl was clearly smitten and would be a ripe plum for his plucking if he so minded.

'Only the three of us.'

'What happened tae the rest of the Forsyth fam'ly, then?'

'Miss Belle's stayin' with her aunt just now.'

'There's another one, is there not? A pretty lass with hair the colour of a cornfield under the summer sun, and bonny eyes that would charm the soul out of a man.'

Sarah's heart twisted again. 'Miss Morna? You've seen her?'

'Only comin' out of the front door now and again when I've been deliverin' vegetables round the back,' he said casually. 'So – is she not livin' at home any more?'

'She's...' Sarah didn't have the faintest idea where Morna had gone to; Walter, when asked, had merely snapped that his sister had made her bed and now she must lie in it as best she could. 'She's with friends,' she finished lamely.

'Is that right, now? With friends? Well, it's been nice seein' ye, Sarah, and seein' how well ye've done for yersel', but I'll have tae go on my way, so if ye want tae pay me for the vegetables ye'd best be gettin' on with it.'

'Samuel...'

'I've got work tae do. Some of us still have tae earn our keep.'

Defeated, she went to the writing bureau where, she knew, Walter kept some money. There was enough, and she carefully counted out the right number of coins and then handed them over to Samuel, who pocketed them before pulling his cap down over his head.

'Can you not stay and talk for a few minutes?

174

I've missed you these past weeks.'

His eyes laughed at her, but not in a friendly way. 'And why would a fine lady like you want tae talk tae a message lad like me?'

'Samuel, please,' she begged, but he had already moved out into the hallway and was heading for the front door. Sarah caught up with him and put a restraining hand on his arm just as the door opened and Walter came in, halting at the sight of the two of them standing close together in the narrow hallway.

14

'What's this?'

Sarah stared at her husband in dumb dismay, and it was left to Samuel to say easily, 'I've just been deliverin' the vegetables, sir, and the mistress here was payin' me what's due.'

'Paying you? You gave this man money?' Walter turned to his wife.

'I – I thought it was the right thing to do...'

'My dear, we never give money to the delivery people. For all we know they might just run off with it.'

Sarah dared not look at Samuel, but she was keenly aware of the way his big body tensed with anger at the accusation.

'I'd never do that, *sir*,' he said with just enough emphasis on the final word to make it sound like an insult. 'Bein' poor doesnae mean that I'm dishonest as well.'

Walter ignored him. 'How much did you pay him?' he asked, and when Sarah named the sum, he swung round to Samuel, his hand outstretched. 'Give me the money.'

When it had been placed in his palm he counted it out carefully, then nodded. 'It's the correct sum. Did you make him sign a receipt for it?'

'There was no need. I knew that...'

'Never pay money without getting a receipt. Wait here,' Walter ordered Samuel, then took Sarah's arm and drew her with him into the parlour, where he found a sheet of paper in the bureau. As he dipped a pen in the inkwell and wrote a few brief words, Sarah looked towards the open door. She could see Samuel in the hall, standing where he had been left, his back to her and his fists tightly clenched by his sides.

'You – fellow. Come in here,' Walter called when he had finished writing, and when Samuel appeared at the parlour door he said, 'Come over here and mark this paper with a cross.'

As Samuel passed Sarah, she could feel the waves of anger flowing from him, and was terrified in case his rage broke. There was no doubt at all that he was by far the stronger of the two men, and if provoked enough he could possibly kill Walter with one blow.

Dumbly, she watched as he picked the sheet of paper up, ran his eyes over it, then said, 'I don't need tae make a cross, Mr Forsyth. I can read and I can sign my name.'

'Oh? Then do so,' Walter said coldly, and when Samuel relinquished the pen and stepped back he lifted the paper and examined it closely. 'Hmmm. Very well, here's the money Make sure that every penny of it is put into Mrs Smith's hand.'

'I'd as soon leave it with you, Mr Forsyth, so that Mrs Smith can send in her account and be paid in the usual way.'

Samuel's voice was soft, yet it held a note that brought colour to the other man's cheeks and a snap to his voice when he retorted, 'And so would I, but apparently my wife would prefer to trust you to deliver it yourself. So take it.'

Samuel hesitated, swinging his head round to look at Sarah with eyes that burned with such cold anger that she was convinced his temper was about to break. She took a step towards the door, ready to run to the kitchen and scream for Nellie's help, but he turned back to Walter and held out his hand for the money. Once it had been transferred, Walter led the way out into the hall, stepping back so that he stood between Samuel and the front door.

'The servants' entrance is at the back of the house. The front entrance is for the family and their friends.'

Samuel hesitated, then shrugged and tugged at the peak of his cap. 'Aye, sir. Thank you, sir,' he said, and then as he turned to walk past Sarah, 'and thank ye, ma'am, for the tea. It was very welcome.'

As she pressed herself against the wall to let him by, Sarah was briefly aware of the familiar smell of him – a blend of sweat and sheer masculinity. She stayed where she was as Walter passed her in turn, aware of his entirely different smell of hair oil and

177

soap. When the door at the back of the hall closed behind the two men she sagged against the hatstand as her knees threatened to give way.

Samuel swaggered through the kitchen, picking up his empty basket and tossing a cheerful wink in Nellie's direction as he opened the back door. Even as he stepped into the backyard he heard the door slam violently behind him. The cocky grin immediately vanished, to be replaced with a snarl of rage and hatred. Turning, he lifted one hand in an obscene gesture in the direction of the closed door before walking around the side of the house.

The slam of the back door brought Sarah to her senses. Realising that she couldn't afford to be found swooning in the hall, she hurried into the parlour, where Walter found her tidying her hair with trembling fingers before the mirror.

'Sarah, my dear,' he began, in the voice he used for gentle chastisement, 'you must remember in future that I pay the household bills at the end of each week. You do not give money to errand boys. These people can't be trusted – for all we know they could pocket it and take to their heels.'

'But Samuel Gilmartin has been making deliveries here ever since Mrs Forsyth first employed me. I know that he would never steal money.'

'That's because he hasn't been tempted – until now. Where did you get the money?' Walter wanted to know, and when Sarah's pale face turned crimson and her eyes flew to the bureau drawer, he pulled it open and looked inside. 'I hope he didn't see you take it from here? He did, didn't he?' he rushed on as she opened her mouth to deny the charge. 'For goodness' sake, Sarah, you must learn to be more cautious! That man is taking advantage of your new position within this household, and I will not have it! Is it true that you allowed him to drink tea in my house?'

'He called when Nellie and I were making tea in the kitchen...' Sarah faltered.

'If Belle had any sense of duty she would be here, teaching you how the mistress of the house behaves,' he fumed. 'Nellie should have been making the tea and you should have been waiting for it in here, not in the kitchen where that man could worm his way into your favour! I shall complain to Mrs Smith and tell her that he is not to call here again.'

'Walter, no! You could lose him his place!'

'I have no intention of demanding his dismissal – but if Mrs Smith sees fit to turn him off I would not argue with her. He has a bold and insolent way of looking at his betters. When I ordered him to leave by the back door he strutted out like the cock of the walk. He'd be better employed in the dockyard or on the railways. A bit of hard work would do him no harm at all,' Walter said grimly, and then, as his wife's eyes filled with agitated tears, he relented and went to her, taking her hands in his and kissing her forehead. 'There, there, my dear, you mustn't get yourself upset, it's bad for the child. Come along now, I'm going to take you upstairs so that you can rest for an hour. You see what that lout has done?' he continued as he eased her into the hallway. 'He's upset you with his insolence. I promise you, my dear, that you will

179

never have to set eyes on him again.'

It was hard to believe, Morna thought, as she went out to the small, weed-choked backyard to hang out the last of the day's washing, that she had been living in the lodging house for three whole weeks. On her first night there, the night someone had tried to get into her room, she had not thought that she could stand another minute in the place, with its smells and damp walls and, above all, the big, dirty, frightening men who lodged there. But faced with the alternatives – either returning to Argyle Road to eat humble pie and become little more than the poor relation, subservient to the woman who had once fetched and carried for her, or going to live under Aunt Beatrice's thumb – she had gritted her teeth and stayed put.

It had not been easy. The house was bitterly cold, the food monotonous and the work hard. The men, with their loud deep voices and their hungry eyes and their big hands, still frightened her, but she had learned to pay them as little attention as possible, and never to look any of them in the eye. She still wedged the chair beneath her door handle every night, though as far as she knew there had been no further attempts to intrude on her privacy.

Meggie had a kind heart, and since she still saw Morna as one of her former little charges she had done her best, when the men were at work and the two of them were in the house on their own, to let Morna off her household duties. This suited Morna, but as soon as the bells and sirens around the town began to signal the end of the working day for the factories and the docks she had to rise from Billy Chapman's comfortable chair by the kitchen fire and busy herself at some task or other before the man came home. Billy believed firmly in the adage that a woman's work was never done – in his house, at least. Men were entitled to their time off because men did proper work, but women were different.

Today was Saturday, and on Saturday afternoons and Sundays, when Billy and the other men folk were around the house, Meggie and Morna worked without a pause. That afternoon the men were all out about their own business, most of them in the local public houses, but even so, the two women kept busy, never knowing when Billy might suddenly appear.

Morna had not yet decided what she should do next. She was beginning to think that she would have to settle for a position as companion to some elderly lady, if she were fortunate enough to find an elderly lady willing to take her on. And yet she still had the nagging sense that there was something better waiting for her. There *must* be something better waiting for her!

The tufts of grass straggling through cracks in the broken flagstones were stiff with frost. The wet clothes heaped in the old tin basin at her feet would soon be frozen into boards, but they would have to stay out overnight because the kitchen was already filled with washing hung from the overhead lines and heaped on the big wooden clothes horse in front of the fire. Cold though the air was, Morna took a moment to stretch her aching back and then studied her hands, roughened by work and reddened by frequent immersion in water. The nails, once neatly shaped ovals, now tended to break and split. She gave a heavy, self-pitying sigh and began to peg the first item – a work shirt as big and thick as her winter coat – on the sagging rope. Once it was in place she bent to take the next garment from the basin, then as she straightened and found herself looking into a man's face, she jumped and gave a little meowing sound of fright and surprise. The rough wooden clothes pegs fell from her hands.

'Sorry, miss, did I startle ye?'

'Of course you startled me,' she snapped, her heart pounding. 'What are you doing out here?'

'Enjoyin' a bit o' peace and quiet, just.' Samuel Gilmartin held up his open book as proof. 'I cannae sit and read in the house, for there's always someone willin' tae make a fool o' me, and that just leads tae a fight, an' Meggie throwin' us out intae the street tae cool down. D'ye want some help with that?'

He picked up the pegs and reached out for the shirt she was holding, but Morna twitched it out of the way. 'I don't need help.' She knew that out of all the lodgers she could consider herself safest with him, for he had never shown her anything but courtesy, but even so she was still on her guard. 'The clothes pegs, if you please?' she said, holding out a hand. And then, as he put them into her palm, 'Please go on with your book.'

As she worked her way along the line she kept darting little glances at him to make sure that he wasn't ogling her. He sat in a corner, sheltered from the worst of the wind by the wall, his auburn head, bright as a polished chestnut in the one stray shaft of sunlight that had found the courage to venture into the dreary little yard, bent and his eyes intent on his book. It seemed to be quite a large volume and on several occasions she caught him in the act of turning a page.

Finally her curiosity got the better of her. 'What are you reading?'

He looked up, his wide brown eyes unfocused for a few seconds, as though he were still in the world of the book; then they cleared and he said, '*Nicholas Nickleby*, by Charles Dickens. Have you read it?'

'I know of Charles Dickens, of course,' said Morna, who had never actually read any of his books. Her taste ran more to light romantic stories.

'The man had a fine understandin' of what life was like in his day for ordinary folk. It's no' changed all that much,' Gilmartin said. 'I've learned a lot from him.'

'Where do you get the books from?' Morna folded another shirt and dropped it into the basket, then tucked the clothes pegs into the big pocket of her apron.

He grinned at her. 'Ye're thinkin' that a man like me could never have the money tae buy books like this. An' ye're mebbe wonderin' if they're stolen. I get them from the lib'ry – the library,' he corrected himself before she had a chance to pretend that she had been thinking nothing of the sort.

'Isn't there a subscription to pay?'

'Aye, it costs me two shillin' an' sixpence a

month, but for that I get tae read all the books that I cannae afford tae buy. Though I sometimes buy a book from one of the second-hand shops or a pawnshop if it's one I'd want tae read again and again.'

Heavy clouds had begun to mass overhead and the bitter, salt-laden wind blowing in from the sea carried more than a threat of further snow on the way. Morna's nose began to run and she fumbled in her sleeve for a handkerchief. Her hands were turning numb, making it difficult to cope with the clothes pegs. 'It's not a day for sitting outside.'

Samuel shrugged his shoulders, clad in nothing more than a shirt and a thin jacket. 'Ach, I'm used tae the cold. And this corner's fairly sheltered.'

'You like reading?'

He nodded. 'My father was a great reader. We always had books in our house. He even had a fine set of encyclopedias that he'd saved for years tae buy when he was a young man, before he married my mother. Nearly everythin' I know I learned from his books. I brought them over from Ireland with me when I came here. He left them tae me when he died.' Then, with a faint shrug, 'Well, he didnae exactly leave them tae me because he died in an accident and he'd no way of knowin' his life was comin' tae a sudden end, God rest the man. But nob'dy else wanted them. If I'd not taken them they'd have been thrown out or sold for drink money. Here, let me.'

He put the book aside carefully and jumped up to help her as she struggled with a large bed sheet that was doing its best to entangle her in its chilly, wet, windblown folds. He liberated her deftly before subduing the sheet and pegging it securely to the rope, then he picked up the next item. When she tried to protest he said, 'Four hands can do the job in half the time.'

For a moment the two of them worked in silence, then Morna stopped, her head cocked to one side. 'What's that sound? Church bells on a Saturday?' And then, as realisation dawned, 'It's the twenty-fifth, isn't it? It's Christmas Day!'

'Aye, that's right. Not that it means anythin' tae the likes o' us – the likes o' me,' he added swiftly. 'You'll no doubt be visitin' with yer own folk later, though.'

'Where did you learn to hang up washing so quickly?' she asked, in an attempt to change the subject rather than come up with an answer. The attractive grin lit up his face again.

'From my mother – she brought us all up tae help around the house, lads as well as lassies. She thought that readin' was nothin' more than a waste of time and a luxury for the rich.'

'Perhaps she was right.'

'Not at all.' Gilmartin picked up the final item just as her own fingers were reaching for it. 'The way I see it, God gave every one of us brains and he'd never have done that if we werenae meant tae use them. I like tae find out all about anythin' and everythin'. I've got what ye might call an enquirin' mind.'

'And do you put your knowledge to good use?'

'I will, one day. For now, I'm just a delivery-man,' he said, and then, the smile fading from his face and his voice, 'at least, I was. I've just been turned off. That's why I'm readin' in the yard on

185

a Saturday instead o' bein' at work.'

'Why were you turned off?'

He shrugged. 'One of the customers said I was insolent.'

'Were you?'

'I didnae think so, but he's got money and a fine house while I've got nothin', so he won the argument, as ye might say.'

'What will you do now?'

'For one thing, I'll be sure tae get my own back on the man that got me turned off.'

The reply was so unexpected, and delivered in such a cold, malevolent voice, that Morna took an involuntary step back. All at once the usual carefree sparkle had left his eyes to be replaced by a cold, hard light. His eyelids had lowered until the eyes were little more than two glittering slits and his mouth hardened, pulling down at the corners, while the muscles stood out on his jawline and throat. Suddenly, she saw Samuel Gilmartin in a new light – a frightening light.

Then as swiftly as it had arrived the dark mood vanished and he was giving her an easy, rueful grin and a shrug of the shoulders. 'I'll be standin' at the dockyard gates on Monday with the other poor wretches desperate for work,' he said. 'All of us hopin' the foreman'll pick us out of the crowd.' And then, spreading his hands out and wriggling the fingers at her, 'So take a last look at my nice clean hands. After Monday I'll no' be able to get the dirt and grease out of them, no matter how hard I scrub. But I cannae live on fresh air and books, can I?'

'Can you not get another delivery job?'

'Not in this area. Who'd want tae hire a man that gives insolence tae the gentry?'

'But you said you weren't insolent.'

'I said it was my word against his. I'm poor and I'm nothin' and I'm Irish intae the bargain. Folk like me don't even need tae open our mouths tae be accused of impertinence tae our betters. "Dumb insolence" it's called when we keep our tongues still.' He leaned forward, holding her gaze with his. 'Tell me this – can you put yer hand on yer heart and say that ye've never accused a serv-ant lassie or a shop assistant of givin' offence when mebbe it's been you that's just been a wee bit quick tae take offence when none was intended?'

Morna drew herself up to her full height. 'How dare you question me like that? It's none of your business! You're being...'

She stopped short, flushing to the roots of her hair as he finished the sentence for her. 'I'm bein' insolent, am I no'? Now d'ye see how easy it is for the likes of you tae put the likes of me in the wrong? At least when I'm workin' in Ardrossan dockyard, Miss Morna Forsyth, I'll be with folk that don't take offence easily. Or if they do...' he curled one hand into a fist and chopped it sharply through the air '...they sort it out in their own way and then it's done with. Here, I'll carry that for ye.' He picked up the peg bag and the empty tin basin and went ahead of her into the house.

Morna lingered for a moment, listening to the faint sound of the church bells calling the faithful to Christmas worship. Most Scots celebrated Ne'erday – New Year's Day – rather than Christmas, but her mother had loved to decorate her home for Christmas. Now, shivering in the cold, shabby, overgrown, sunless backyard, Morna recalled Christmases when she and her brother and sister and parents had attended church in the morning before going home to unwrap their gifts from each other beside a tree hung with glittering baubles. Then – her mouth began to water – they would sit down to a huge Christmas dinner, followed by a lazy afternoon in front of the fire.

The longing for those lost days threatened to overwhelm her, but she managed, by biting her lower lip hard, to bring herself under control. She was about to follow Samuel Gilmartin into the house when she noticed that he had forgotten his book. Picking it up, she saw that the pages were covered by small, densely packed print, with not a single illustration to please the eye. What sort of working man would be interested in something that looked so dull?

She closed it and carried it indoors, puzzling over this ordinary man who enjoyed reading.

On the following Monday morning Samuel Gilmartin left the house early.

'So's I can be one of the first at the dockyard gates,' he explained briefly to Morna when they met in the dark narrow passageway. She, heavy-eyed and still half asleep, was on her way to the kitchen to help Meggie. 'I have tae make sure that I'm picked tae do a day's work, at least. I've got tae pay for my lodgin's.'

'Have you had something to eat?'

'Aye, and I've some bread and drippin' in my

pocket.' He gave her a brief grin, and as they passed each other she was aware of the clean soapy smell she had begun to identify with Samuel.

15

Samuel Gilmartin was taken on at Ardrossan dockyard as a labourer, but Morna could see the heart going out of the man as he returned to the lodging house at the end of each day with so much grease and dirt on him that he was scarcely recognisable from the other men. He tried his best to clean himself up, washing in a small tin basin that he kept in the room he shared with several others and then changing into the worn but clean garments that were all he had other than his work clothes; but it was almost impossible to shift the grease from under his fingernails and between his fingers.

'It seems a shame that he's having to find work as a labourer when he already had a decent enough job with Mrs Smith,' Morna said as she and Meggie worked in the lean-to washhouse. Meggie was stirring the clothes around in the big copper boiler while Morna, her sleeves rolled up to above the elbows, struggled to turn the handle of the old mangle. The floor was puddled with water that had poured from the clothes as they were transferred from the washtub to the big basin where they awaited their turn in the mangle, and the small dark space where they worked was steamy and airless – but at least it was warm. Sweat ran down Morna's beet-red face and her hair, pinned back that morning, hung in damp wisps around her cheeks and neck.

'It's a shame right enough, but that's the way it is for the likes of us, and there's nothin' we can dae about it.' Meggie deftly twisted the pole she was using and then heaved it up, leaning back to take the strain. The end of the pole rose from the steamy water, a soggy mass of material entwined around it. With a swing of her strong arms the woman delivered the soaking bundle, raining water all the way, to the battered tin basin.

The washhouse, damp and humid, was a haven for wood lice, and as Morna bent to lift the next garment from the basin she suddenly noticed one particularly large creature marching towards her. She jumped back with a squeal of disgust.

'What is it?' Meggie asked, and then, as Morna, shuddering, pointed at the floor, 'A slater? Ach, they're no harm tae ye, lassie. They're more scared of you than you are of them.' She slammed her shoe down on the insect, squashing it flat, then returned to her work.

'But I d-don't *like* them!' Morna whimpered. The house, like all its neighbours, was overrun with slaters, and every night she took her bedding apart and checked it before settling down to sleep. Twice, she had found one of the creatures in the bed, waggling its antennae at her.

'Life's full o' things we don't like, but we just have tae thole them,' Meggie was saying. 'Just as Samuel Gilmartin has tae take whatever job he can find. It's that or starvin' in the gutter for folk like him and me and Billy and the other lads. That's another thing that folk like us just have tae thole. But it's different for you, lassie; you were meant for a better life than we have. Ye shouldnae be workin' here like a skivvy.'

'Try telling that to my brother!' A pair of trousers was going through the mangle and Morna had to struggle to turn the handle as the folds of thick material jammed between the rollers.

'I'm tellin' it tae you, hen, for you're the one that can dae somethin' about it.'

'Such as what?' Morna asked through gritted teeth. She gave one last determined heave, putting so much effort into it that for a moment she thought the buttons on her blouse were going to tear themselves from their buttonholes, then at last the big rollers submitted and the trousers were forced through, shooting a jet of water in their wake. It spattered over her arms and she paused to catch her breath, snatching up a thin towel and using it to mop herself. 'A job as a washerwoman? Or perhaps,' she said wryly, 'I should go and stand at the dockyard gates. I'm sure that this mangle's given me enough muscle to do a man's work.'

Meggie held her own brawny arms up. 'Housework does that, lassie, but I was born tae earn my own livin' while you were born tae be a lady. A right bonny wee thing ye were too,' she recalled fondly. 'Pretty as a picture, sittin' up in yer perambulator like a princess. Folk were always stoppin' me when I took ye out, just so's they could have a look at ye in the beautiful clothes yer mother made for ye. She was a lovely lady, yer mother!'

191

'Yes,' Morna agreed, then, as memories of her happy childhood brought longing to her heart and a lump to her throat, she swallowed hard and went on briskly, 'but she didn't raise me to earn my own keep.'

'You were so bonny from the start that she thought ye'd marry a man able tae take care of ye. And so did I.'

Morna thought of Arthur MacAdam and again, the lump began to form. 'Who'd want to marry me now, looking the way I do?'

'That's what I mean. It frets me tae see ye workin' away like this, Miss Morna. Look at yer poor wee hands...' Meggie took one of them in her own hot, damp grip '...all roughened with the work. Ye'll be gettin' calluses next.'

Morna knew well enough that she would soon have to start thinking of her future, but hard though life was in the lodging house at least she had a roof over her head. Besides, she felt safe with Meggie. 'But what else can I do?' she said feebly. 'I've not been trained to any sort of work.'

'Could Mr Walter no' find a place for ye in the shop?'

'He's got Belle running things for him, and even if he did agree to employ me, I'd not want to work for him. And don't tell me that beggars can't be choosers, Meggie,' Morna added as the older woman began to speak. 'I'm fine where I am for the moment. Something's sure to turn up. Sure to,' she added, without much hope, and began to stuff a patched vest through the mangle.

Morna, who had never before cared about

anyone but herself, became quite concerned over the change in Samuel Gilmartin within a week of him starting work at the docks. He became quiet and morose; when she tried to strike up a conversation his replies were brief and usually bitter. One day he sat down to dinner sporting a black eye and split lip.

'What happened?' Morna asked, horrified.

'He walked intae a wall,' one of the other men said, and a roar of laughter went round the table, ebbing and then swelling again when another man asked slyly, 'Goin' tae kiss it better, lassie?'

'If that's the case, me and big Jamie here'll just nip oot the back an' gie each other a good punchin' so's ye can kiss us better an' all,' someone else leered.

'Mind yer manners!' Meggie said, catching the direction the talk was taking as she came through the door carrying a basin filled with boiled potatoes. Then, as Samuel looked up and her eyes fell on his bruised and battered face, 'Mercy me, laddie, ye've never been fightin', have ye?'

'Ach, it happens tae all of us when we start a new job,' one of the older men assured her. 'The lad had tae get blooded.' He snatched at Samuel's wrist and held his hand up to display skinned knuckles, 'An' he stood up for himsel' well. It was a bonny fight! Gonnae entertain us again tomorrow, Sammy?'

'Mind yer own business!' Samuel snarled, freeing himself and getting up from the table so swiftly that his chair toppled and crashed to the wooden floor.

'Here, what about yer dinner?' Meggie called

193

after him as he slammed out the room.

'I'll have it,' half a dozen voices chorused.

'Ye will not. That lad's put in a hard day's work and he needs his meat. Here, Morna...' Meggie shovelled a generous helping of potatoes on to Samuel's discarded plate of stew '...you can take that up tae him.'

'And make sure that you're no' the puddin', lass,' one of the men added, then yelped as the back of Meggie's large hand flicked painfully across his ear.

Samuel was sitting on the edge of his cot in the dreary, low-ceilinged dormitory. 'I don't want it,' he said as soon as Morna put the plate down on the bed beside him.

'Eat it,' she insisted, and after a moment he picked the plate up. His first mouthful was slow and reluctant, but once he had tasted the food, hunger overcame him and he began to shovel up large mouthfuls.

'What happened?'

'Ach, there's always someone who wants tae prove that he's cock of the walk,' he said indistinctly. Fragments of food sprayed out and he rubbed the back of his forearm across his mouth before taking another forkful.

'Could you not have ignored him?'

His brown eyes no longer sparkled and the look he gave her made her feel small enough to walk under a closed door. 'And be bullied by him and his like for the rest of my life?'

'It's not fair,' Morna burst out. 'You deserve better than that.'

'I deserve nothin', have ye no' realised that yet? I'm just a labourer ... a nob'dy with no rights.'

'You're an educated man.'

'I'm self-educated, an' that stands for nothin'. It's worse than nothin',' he added viciously, 'because it makes me different from the rest, an' that's the worst thing tae be when ye're with a gang of workin' men. Here,' he pushed the empty plate at her. 'Ye can take this back tae the kitchen.'

'Your face looks sore.'

'It'll mend. Then it'll get bust again.'

'Can I do something to help you? Iodine, or mebbe...'

'I'm goin' tae sleep,' he interrupted rudely, and turned over on his side, away from her.

Morna hesitated, then turned towards the door. She had reached it when he said, 'Mebbe there *is* somethin' ye can do for me.'

'What?'

He was sitting up again, the evening light from the small window she had cleaned only hours earlier making the bruising on his face stand out lividly.

'Ye could teach me figures.'

'Figures?'

'Aye, addin' and takin' away and the like. And workin' with money. I suppose you know about those things?'

'A little. Not enough to teach anyone.'

'All I'm askin' is for you tae show me what ye know It's the only way I can get away from the docks and intae somethin' better.' She had moved back towards him, close enough for him to reach out and take her wrist in an urgent grip.

195

'Will ye dae it?'

She looked down at the hand on her arm, with its torn knuckles and the black rims beneath broken, once carefully trimmed nails. 'I'll try, but I might not be any good.'

'Ye'll be better than nothin', an' nothin's all I've got at the minute. I cannae pay ye more than a few pence a week.'

'I don't want your money,' she said hurriedly, and he glared with his one good eye while his grip tightened painfully on her arm.

'An' *I* don't want your charity. Thruppence a week, right?'

'Right,' Morna agreed against her better judgement. How could she teach anything to anyone?

Samuel Gilmartin proved to be a quick learner, and thanks to his thirst for knowledge teaching him arithmetic proved to be easier than Morna had first thought. In the evenings, when Billy and the other men tended to be in the nearby public house, Meggie allowed the two of them to use the kitchen table while she sat in her chair by the range, knitting and darning and, as often as not, snoring with her head tipped uncomfortably back and her mouth gaping like a cave while Samuel mastered the intricacies of addition, subtraction, multiplication and division by moving groups of dried peas around the table.

To her surprise, Morna began to look forward to their evening classes. Her pupil's triumphant pleasure at each step forward and his appreciation of her help gave her a much-needed sense of achievement. On the evening when he soared through the multiplication tables from one-times-one to twelve-times-twelve with scarcely a moment's pause for thought she felt as though they had climbed a mountain together and arrived at the top to see beautiful scenery spread out far below.

'Bravo!' She clapped her hands, but quietly, mindful of Meggie's slow, heavy breathing. 'You go to the top of the class!'

'Ach, it was nothin',' he said modestly, though his face, still carrying faint smudges of bruising, glowed.

'I can't believe how quickly you've learned it.'

He shrugged, and then allowed a delighted grin to slip through. 'You're a good teacher, and I was desperate tae learn, for I'll go mad if I have tae stay in that dockyard much longer.'

'You're going to look for other work? Where?'

He glanced over his shoulder, saw that Meggie was sound asleep, then leaned forward and said in a low voice, 'Forsyth's are lookin' for a shop assistant.'

'My brother?'

'Aye, yer brother. That's why I asked you tae help me with my sums – I'd seen the notice in their window.'

'They've surely filled the post by now.'

'Aye, they did, for the notice disappeared. But today it was back again. They cannae have been pleased with whoever got the place. But *I'd* find ways tae please them if I could just get the chance. D'ye think I know enough about figurin' tae be able tae work in a shop?'

'Maybe – if folk use dried peas instead of money.'

'I've thought about that.' He got up and dipped deep into his pockets, then laid a handful of silver and copper coins on the table. 'I've been savin' up for this. You're a customer and you want tae buy...' he looked around and then pointed at the battered tin teapot on the range, '...that bonny china vase. It costs ninepence, madam.'

Morna hesitated, and then, as he nodded encouragingly at her, she selected a florin and pushed it towards him. 'There you are, my good man.'

'Thank you, madam.' He studied the coin for a moment, reminding her of the days when she had watched her father playing chess with Mr Pinkerton, then selected several coins and slid them along the table. 'One shillin' and thruppence change. Am I right?'

'You are. And while I'm here, I'll just have that elegant figurine as well.' Morna indicated Meggie, sprawled in her chair with her nose pointed ceilingwards. 'How much is that?'

It turned into a game, with the two of them giggling behind their hands like conspirators while Meggie's heavy breathing developed into soft snores.

'So will I do?' Samuel asked when the clock on the mantelshelf showed that Billy and the other men would soon be back.

'As far as the money's concerned, you'll do. But...' She stopped, reluctant to dim the pleasure he was taking in his success.

'But what? Go on, now, ye have tae tell me,' he coaxed. 'You're my friend, and who else but a friend would tell a man the truth?'

'You have a bonny accent, Samuel, but...'

'Ach, is that all that's frettin' ye?' He rose with one easy movement, stepped back from the table, gave her a deep bow, and said, 'Cock a doodle doo, my dame has lost her shoe, my master's lost his fiddle-stick, and knows not what to do. Mary, Mary, quite contrary, how does your garden grow? With silver bells and cockle shells, and pretty maids all in a row. How many miles to Babylon...'

'Stop, stop!' Morna protested through giggles.

He bowed again, and then asked as he sat down, 'How many marks out o' ten? I cannae rid myself of my Irish accent, but I've tried tae tone it down a bit.'

'The accent is pretty to listen to and I think that the ladies who go into the shop will be quite charmed by it. How did you learn to speak like that?'

'By listenin' to you, of course. And the money I've saved is for some decent clothes, so that I can look my best. D'you think I could persuade your brother to give me the position?'

'It's more likely you'll have to please my sister. Walter has never been as interested in the shop's affairs as Belle.'

'D'ye tell me?' Samuel's eyes narrowed slightly. 'So it's the ladies of your fam'ly that have all the brains?'

'No, just Belle. She's very good at figuring, while Walter's more interested in his new wife.'

'New wife? So you've a sister-in-law as well as a sister?'

'I wouldn't say that.' She spoke without thinking and then, as he raised his eyebrows, 'Walter married our servant lassie. That's why I'm lodging here.'

'So you don't approve of what your brother's done? I quite agree,' Samuel said earnestly. 'Different classes don't mix well. I mind a neighbour of ours at home who did much the same thing. It was a poor sort of marriage, and the woman soon ran off with someone of her own sort and left him countin' the cost of his foolishness.' Then, casually he asked, 'Your sister, the one that sees to the shop – does she approve of the marriage?'

'Belle? She does not. She left home before I did. She's staying with our aunt, Mrs Beatrice McCallum.'

'Would that be Mrs McCallum in Caledonia Road? I used tae deliver to her house when I worked for Mrs Smith,' Samuel said. 'I'm sorry there's trouble in yer family, Miss Morna, and I hope it will soon pass. Blood kin shouldnae fall out.' He reached over, and had taken possession of her hand and raised it to his lips before she knew what was happening. She let out a surprised squeak, which was answered by a sudden loud snore from Meggie.

On Meggie's advice, Samuel found a smart suit in a pawnshop. 'Some poor soul's misfortune has become my good luck,' he told Morna, adding blithely, 'Ach, but isn't that always the way of it?' And then, in a lower voice, 'There's just one last thing, Miss Morna, that ye could do for me, if only ye would.'

'What's that?'

'D'ye think ye could put in a good word for me

200

with yer sister?'

'I don't know...' Morna faltered. 'I've scarcely spoken to her since I came here.'

'Then she must be missin' ye. You could do two kindnesses with one visit – make her happy, and help me intae the bargain. Would it be that hard?' he added as she hesitated. 'Ye never know, I might be the one that brings the two of yez together again. And that would make me feel as if I've gone some way to repayin' ye for all yer kindness tae me.'

When Samuel coaxed in his lovely Irish accent, he was hard to resist, Morna thought, little realising that only months earlier her sister-in-law, then the Forsyth housemaid, had fallen under the spell of the same caressing voice and beseeching eyes.

16

Rather than warn Belle of her coming, and perhaps having to face a snub, Morna called at her aunt's house unannounced. The maid who answered the door left her standing on the step while she went to fetch Belle, who came bustling along the hallway almost at once.

'Oh, Morna, I'm so pleased to see you! Come in out of the cold...' She ushered her sister into the parlour. 'Are you well? Are you going back to stay with Walter and ... and Sarah?'

'This house,' Morna said, 'still smells of dog.

How can you bear it?'

'One becomes used to it, and Aunt Bea has been very kind.'

'Where is she?' Morna looked around, half-expecting her aunt to bounce up from behind an overstuffed chair. One never knew with Aunt Beatrice.

'In the kitchen. She may come through later. It's Romeo,' Belle explained, her voice suddenly sombre. 'Aunt Bea's favourite dog. He's very ill, and not expected to last much longer.'

'Oh?' Morna was inspecting a chair for dog hairs before sitting down.

'She's very upset. She's had a bad chill lately, mainly brought about by walking the dogs in the rain for too long, and her own health is not so good. But tell me about you.' Belle's eyes skimmed over her sister, noting the pale face and the casual hairstyle – much less elaborate than Morna's usual. 'Where have you been living?'

'With Meggie and her husband.'

'Still? In their lodging house!'

'I have nowhere else to go,' Morna said coldly. 'Has the child arrived yet?'

'No, but it won't be long now. Walter's so taken with being a husband and a prospective father...' Belle stopped suddenly as the maid brought in a tea tray.

'Mrs McCallum says she'll join ye in a wee while, Miss Belle, as soon as Romeo settles,' she reported as she set the tray down.

'What were you saying about Walter?' Morna prompted as soon as the woman had gone.

Belle scowled as she picked up the silver teapot.

'He's scarcely ever in the shop these days. Too busy preparing for fatherhood and teaching that new little wife of his how to be mistress of her own home. You'd think nobody had ever become a parent before!'

'Perhaps he's determined to prove that he can be a better parent than Papa was to us.'

'Perhaps,' Belle said without conviction.

'So you're left to run the place on your own?'

'It's hard work, but Walter was always more of a hindrance than a help where the shop's concerned; Papa knew that.'

'He should have left the shop to you.'

'If you recall, he didn't leave it to any one person, since it wasn't his to leave. It belongs to the three of us,' Belle said, and then, as Morna removed her gloves, revealing work-roughened hands, 'Don't tell me that Meggie has you doing menial work in that lodging house of hers?'

'I have to earn my keep.'

'Oh, Morna, what would Mother say?'

'If Mother were here to pass judgement on any of this, you and I would still be at home and Sarah would still be in the kitchen where she belongs. And tell me, pray, what work was I trained for? If I want to eat then I must help in the lodging house.' Morna went over to take her cup of tea, and then said as she returned to her chair, 'About the shop ... if it was left to the three of us, then surely I must have some say in the running of it?'

Belle, about to take a sip of tea, lowered the cup back down to its saucer, eyeing her younger sister warily. 'You want to work there?'

'With you and Walter? I doubt if that would be

a good idea for any of us. No, but I know of someone who would like to be interviewed for the post you're advertising. He stays in Meggie's lodging house...'

'Then he'd not be the right person for us,' Belle said immediately.

'You're wrong; he's ambitious and clever – he reads books, and he's good with figures and he's got a good brain.'

'What work does he do just now?'

'He's in Ardrossan dockyard – but only because he's not been able to find anything better. He hates being there, and I'm sure that he would be of great use to you. You might at least see him, Belle.'

'And if I don't consider him suitable?'

'Then he would accept your decision. He knows that you and Walter wouldn't consider hiring anyone just to please me. Will you agree to see Samuel Gilmartin?'

'Is that his name? Oh, very well, tell him to call tomorrow morning. But I'll make no promises,' Belle added as the door opened and her aunt came in.

'My dear Morna, how good of you to call.' Beatrice came to a standstill in the middle of the room and waited, head slightly tilted to one side. Morna, taking the hint, set her cup aside and rose to kiss her aunt on the cheek.

'Tea, Aunt Beatrice?' Belle asked, and Beatrice nodded, moving to the chair Morna had just vacated, leaving the girl with no option but to collect her cup and saucer from the small side table and find somewhere else to sit.

204

'How is Romeo?' she asked, catching Belle's silent signals.

'Not at all well. The poor old fellow has come to the end of his time.' Beatrice's normally strong voice shook, and she bit her lip, then rallied and turned her attention to Morna. 'Where have you been staying these past weeks, my dear?'

'With Meggie Chapman – our former nursemaid. Meggie Butcher as was,' Morna explained as her aunt looked puzzled.

Beatrice's frown cleared. 'Ah yes, I remember Meggie Butcher. A very able young woman; your dear mother thought the world of her. What happened to her?'

'She married, Aunt Beatrice, and now she and her husband have a...'

'A small hotel near the shore,' Belle interrupted smoothly. 'Morna is helping Meggie to run the place, but only until she finds work more suited.'

'Good,' Beatrice said absently. She got to her feet and picked up her untouched cup and saucer. 'I think, my dears, that I will go back to the kitchen to sit with Romeo. We have so little time left together.'

'But she'd only just arrived!' Morna burst out as soon as the door had closed behind their aunt. 'Anyone would think that Romeo was her husband or her sweetheart to hear her talk, instead of just an old dog!'

'He was a gift from Uncle Hector. She can't imagine life without poor old Romeo.'

'She doesn't look well.'

'She's been staying up at nights with the dog,

and as I told you, she recently suffered from a bad chill. She's not getting any younger.'

'I suppose not. Why didn't you let me tell Aunt Beatrice the truth about Meggie's lodging house?'

'I thought it would upset her to know that one of her nieces is living and working in a place like that.'

'I doubt if anything would upset Aunt Beatrice. I believe that you're ashamed of me, Belle,' Morna challenged, and her sister flushed.

'I'm not ashamed of you at all!'

'Good. I scarcely think,' Morna said with a return to her former haughtiness, 'that someone who works in trade has the right to look down on anyone else.'

'I may work in trade,' Belle pointed out, stung. 'But you do menial work. It must be quite a shock to your poor hands to have to wash and clean instead of holding a paintbrush or playing "The Blue Danube" on the piano. I take it that Meggie doesn't have a piano?'

It was Morna's turn to colour. Her mouth tightened and she was about to deliver another insult when she recalled that she had come to the house to ask Belle a favour. She picked up her gloves, and rose. 'I must go. Belle, you will give Samuel Gilmartin a fair hearing tomorrow, won't you?'

Belle, ashamed of her sudden anger, nodded. 'I said that I would.' At the door she added tentatively, 'Will you visit us again?'

'Perhaps,' Morna said, and walked swiftly down the path and out of the gate.

Beatrice, kneeling by the dog basket in the corner

of the kitchen, looked up as Belle went in. 'Is Morna gone? She looks tired,' she went on when Belle nodded.

'I wish she would go back home,' Belle fretted. 'But she's stubborn. Even when she was tiny she was stubborn. If you told her not to fall over a cliff she'd do it rather than pay heed to you.'

'You have to admire her determination to stand on her own two feet, hard though it must be after a lifetime of being cosseted. And it won't do her any harm to find out how other folk have tae live.' Beatrice stroked the little dog's head and murmured to him before lifting him carefully into her arms. 'Help me up, Belle,' she instructed, struggling to her feet. When Belle had done as she was told, her aunt went on, 'Ena, come and help Miss Belle tae carry the basket intae the parlour. Romeo and I will be more comfortable there.'

She refused to go to her room that night, so Belle and the maidservant brought pillows and blankets downstairs, so that Beatrice could stay with her sick pet.

When Belle went downstairs for breakfast in the morning, the table in the small dining room was set for one.

'The mistress is having somethin' on a tray in the parlour,' Ena said. 'She looks worn out, Miss Belle, could ye no' persuade her tae go tae her room for a lie down after?'

'I'll try, but you know what she can be like.'

'Aye,' said Ena, who had started working in the house when Beatrice was housekeeper. 'A right thrawn old – lady. She says ye've tae break yer fast and then go through tae her. I'm bein' sent out tae do the shoppin'. She's given me a list as long as my arm – it'll take me all mornin' tae do it!'

Beatrice's eyes, as she looked up at her niece, were pools of exhaustion and sorrow. She was sitting on the floor by Romeo's basket and looked as though she had been there all night.

'Aunt Bea, don't you think you should rest?'

'There'll be plenty of time for that later.' She stroked the dog's head. 'I think it's time to put him out of his misery, poor old man.'

'You want me to send Ena to fetch the veterinary?'

'Tuts, lassie, there's no need for that. I used tae help Hector with his dogs, and I know what tae do. There now, my lad,' Beatrice said gently as Romeo struggled to get up. 'Just you lie easy, son. I've given Ena a shoppin' list that should keep her out of our way for a while, so first of all, Belle, I want you to make certain that she's gone, then you can go to my bedroom and fetch the tin box that's pushed right to the back of the wardrobe. There's also a small key on a key ring in my jewellery box on the dressing table. Bring them both down here tae me.'

When Ena had stamped off along the pavement with the big shopping basket over her arm, Belle brought the battered box and the key downstairs.

'Now go and heat some milk and put it into Romeo's bowl – warm but not too hot, just right for him to drink. And bring a teaspoon too,' Beatrice ordered before returning her attention to her dying pet.

When Belle did as she was told, her aunt

unlocked the tin box and took out a brown glass medicine bottle. 'Ten drops should do it.' She added them to the milk with a steady hand and then she helped the old dog to sit up before feeding the milk to him spoonful by spoonful. He drank it trustingly, his eyes, no longer as bright as Juliet's, fixed on her face the whole time.

'There now – good lad,' Beatrice said when the bowl was empty. 'You can rest in your basket now. Belle, mind you wash the bowl out well, then you can fasten the bottle tightly and put it back in the box. Lock the box and put it and the key away where you found them. Then go and sit in the dinin' room until I call for you.'

'What was in the bottle?'

'Just somethin' that Hector used tae give his dogs when life got too much for them. It's a kind endin' with no pain. Romeo'll just go off tae sleep, but this time he'll not wake up,' Beatrice said with a tremor in her voice.

Banished to the dining room, Belle glanced anxiously at the clock. There was no knowing these days if Walter was going to grace the shop with his presence or not, and there were two people to interview that morning for the assistant's post – three, she suddenly remembered, including the man that Morna had come to see her about. She bit her lip and then decided that if Walter didn't turn up they would just have to wait until she arrived, for she could not leave her aunt in her time of need. Come to think of it, she would prefer to interview them herself, for she had a better idea of the sort of assistant they required.

Just then she heard Beatrice call and went into the parlour to find her aunt standing by the basket, damp-eyed but calm.

'It's over.'

'So soon?' Belle could scarcely believe it, and yet there was a strange stillness in the room; a sense of empty space, as though something that had been alive was no longer there. She glanced at the basket where Romeo looked as though he was in a peaceful sleep and might waken at any moment, eyes bright and tail wagging.

'Aye, he's gone to his Maker. I've got no truck,' Beatrice said with a flash of her usual spirit, 'with this nonsense about dogs not bein' allowed intae heaven. They were made the same way we were and by the same personage, and tae my mind what comes from the Creator returns tae the Creator. I've said that tae the minister time and again but the man'll just not listen tae me. Fetch the blanket I left ready in the kitchen and we'll take Romeo tae the garden shed. The gardener's comin' in later and he can lay him tae rest beneath the trees at the end of the garden.'

The thought of carrying the dead dog filled Belle with horror, but she had no option but to do as she was told. The neatly folded blanket waited on the kitchen table and she had just lifted it and was nerving herself to return to the parlour when she heard Juliet barking and someone knocked at the back door.

The gardener has come early, Belle thought with relief, but the young man standing on the doorstep, though strongly built and with the healthy complexion of someone used to being out of doors, was obviously wearing his best clothes.

'Yes?'

'Would you be Miss Forsyth?' He had a soft voice with a pleasing accent.

'I am.'

'Good mornin', ma'am, I've come about the position.'

'The position?' Belle echoed foolishly, her mind filled with the scene she had just left in the parlour.

'The position of shop assistant, ma'am. I believe your sister, Miss Morna Forsyth, mentioned my name to you.' He had taken his bowler hat off to reveal a head of auburn hair, well slicked down with hair cream. 'Samuel Gilmartin, at your service, ma'am.'

'Oh – you were supposed to call at the shop, not here.'

'At the shop, you say?' He took a step back. 'My apologies, ma'am, I must have misunderstood; I thought I was expected to call here. I'll go to the shop, then?'

'Yes you should, and wait there for me,' Belle said, and was about to close the door when Beatrice said from behind her, 'Who is it?'

'Nobody,' Belle said shortly, but Beatrice was already by her side.

'You – what is it you want?'

'It seems that I made a mistake, ma'am. I was told to attend Miss Belle Forsyth to be interviewed for the post of shop assistant, but I should have gone to the shop and not come here. I'm very sorry, ma'am,' he said humbly, and then, nodding towards the wire run, where Juliet was

211

going hysterical at sight of her beloved mistress, 'I see that ye're a dog lover like myself, ma'am?'

'Quiet!' Beatrice roared, and Juliet paused and then sat down, whining. 'Come in, young man, I have some work for you.' She swept Belle aside and opened the door wide. 'My other dog has just died...' Her voice broke slightly, but she shook off the hand that Belle laid on her arm, drew herself to her full height, and went on, 'He's in the parlour. I wonder if you would mind carrying him to the garden shed for me? I can't let Juliet into the house until he's gone. My gardener will bury him this afternoon.'

'Of course I will. Anythin' I can do to help, ma'am,' Samuel Gilmartin said eagerly, wiping his feet vigorously on the mat before venturing into the kitchen.

Once in the parlour, he dropped to his knees beside the basket, running a gentle hand over Romeo's still, small body. 'Ah, would ye look at the poor old soul, he's so peaceful. Here, give me the blanket...' He wrapped the dead dog as gently as a mother swaddling her firstborn, then straightened, Romeo cradled in his arms. 'There now,' he said, and smiled at Beatrice, who smiled back.

As the three of them went into the back garden Juliet burst into delighted barks at sight of her mistress.

'That wee one's wantin' fed by the sound of it,' Samuel Gilmartin said as he laid Romeo's body down in the shed. 'I tell you what, ma'am, why don't I dig a grave for this little fella while you see tae the other? Then you can have a decent wee burial whenever you're ready.'

'I couldn't ask you to do that. The gardener will be here later.'

'I'd count it as a privilege, ma'am. I love dogs myself, and I'd like to help you in your time of suffering,' he said earnestly.

'But you'll spoil your clothes,' Belle pointed out, and he turned his warm smile on her.

'I'll be careful.' He began to remove his jacket. 'You'll want him settled as soon as possible, ma'am. Just show me where you keep your spade and where you want me tae dig, and then you go off and see tae the other wee dog. It sounds upset, so it does,' he added as Juliet began to howl.

17

'That young man is both charming and understanding,' Beatrice said as she and her niece took Juliet into the house.

'Too charming, perhaps.'

'Nonsense. He's willing, and he likes dogs. What more can you ask for in a shop assistant?'

'Someone who's good with figures and able to deal with customers?'

'As to the customers, you need have no worries on that score. So that just leaves the ability to work with figures. Come along now, Juliet, your Auntie Belle shall help me to feed you and make a fuss of you. Did we leave you out in the garden all alone, then? Poor little lass.'

By the time Juliet had been fed and petted the

grave was ready. Samuel laid Romeo within it and stood back, head bowed and hands clasped before him, while Beatrice said a swift prayer.

'A very moving service, ma'am, if I may say so,' he said, and then, picking up the spade, 'Now then, I'll just finish the job and be on my way.'

'You'll come into the house and have some breakfast, young man. I owe you that, at least,' Beatrice said firmly when he tried to protest. 'Knock on the back door when you're done here.'

Ena was in the kitchen, unpacking her shopping basket with Juliet frisking around her ankles. 'Ena, make fresh tea,' her mistress instructed her, adding, 'there's a young man coming in soon to wash his hands, and he's going to be hungry. Make some breakfast for him and bring him through to the dining room when he's ready.'

'Yes, ma'am,' the maid said, used to her employer's whims.

'I should be getting off to the shop. I have folk to interview.'

'You can just stay here, Belle, and interview your first applicant while he's eating his breakfast,' Beatrice said, and went upstairs to brush her hair and wash her face and hands.

It was clear to see from Samuel Gilmartin's expression when the large, generously filled plate was set before him, that he was very hungry; Belle expected him to shovel the food into his mouth, but to her surprise he ate neatly, using his knife and fork to cut small portions and emptying his mouth before answering the questions Beatrice fired at him.

'So – where are you employed at the moment?'

214

'I've been workin' as a labourer at Ardrossan dockyard, ma'am, for the past week or so.'

'You're not of a mind to stay there?'

'I hate it,' the young man said flatly. 'It's not for me at all.'

'There's a big difference between labouring in the dockyard and serving customers in a shop,' Belle pointed out coolly, and his brown eyes caught and held hers.

'There is, Miss Forsyth, and I can understand you thinkin' that a man can't move easily from one tae – to – the other. But I can, I promise you. All I need,' he added earnestly, his gaze moving back to Beatrice, 'is the chance to prove it.'

'Are you any good with figures? Sums of money?' Belle persisted.

He had finished eating and not a crumb was left on the plate. He pushed it away and sat back in his chair. 'I like figurin',' he said, and went on to give correct answers to the imaginary purchases she set him.

'Well now,' Beatrice interrupted after five minutes, 'I think we have a good idea of your abilities, Mr Gilmartin, and it's my belief that you would make an excellent shop assistant.'

'Thank you, ma'am!' His face lit up, while Belle glared at her aunt.

'I have other people to interview,' she said swiftly.

'I could look in this afternoon to see if you've made a decision,' he offered, getting to his feet. 'But for now, I've taken up enough of your time. Thank you, ladies, for your kindness and hospitality, and my condolences, ma'am,' he added to Beatrice, 'for your sad loss. Just remember that you gave your wee dog a very happy life, and for that he'll bless you through eternity.'

'So you believe that animals can aspire to heaven and eternity, young man?'

'Of course – don't they have souls like the rest of us?' said Samuel.

'A most agreeable young man,' Beatrice said when she and her niece were alone. 'You must employ him, Belle!'

'I'm not sure that someone used to working in the dockyard could settle in a shop.'

'You heard him say that he's longing to improve his lot. He deserves a chance, surely?'

'We'll see,' Belle said, and left for the shop, her mind in turmoil. Part of her felt that Samuel Gilmartin had been too glib and her aunt too easily won over, while another part was interested in finding out if a silk purse could really be made from a sow's ear.

The day had started well, with grey skies but visibility clear enough to give sight of Ailsa Craig, a rocky, conical-shaped islet known to the Ayrshire folk as Paddy's Milestone, since it stood halfway between Scotland and Northern Ireland. But by mid-morning the clouds had thickened and lowered and the white-flecked sea was driving hard on to the shore. Paddy's Milestone had disappeared completely, as had most of Arran. Sleet had begun to fall and by the time Morna struggled to the shops it had turned to icy, driving rain. The old umbrella she had found in

216

the wash-house was torn and leaking, and it came as a great relief when she left the final shop and headed back to Quay Street to find that the rain had eased.

'Morna Forsyth? Is it really you?' The ringing tones caused several heads to turn, and Morna winced. The last thing she needed was to be recognised and sneered at. She turned reluctantly, weighed down by the heavy basket she carried, to find that the woman confronting her was smiling, pleased by the meeting.

'It is you – how lovely to meet up with you again.' Then, with a laugh, 'You don't remember me, do you? Ruth Durie – we were at school together.'

'Ruth, of course.' Now she was able to place the long thin face with its direct, deep blue eyes below strong black brows and thick black hair that used to escape with relentless regularity from its restraining ribbons but was now trapped beneath a straw hat.

'So, you're still living in Saltcoats. Come and have a cup of tea,' Ruth suggested. 'We have so much to catch up on.'

'I can't. I have to get back.'

'Still at home, or married with a house and husband of your own? As you can see...' Ruth drew her left glove off and waggled her long ringless fingers, '...I have no husband, and little wonder. Who would put up with me? But you were made for marriage, weren't you?'

'I'm not married, nor am I living at home. I'm helping a friend to run her lodging house,' Morna said stiffly.

217

'Indeed? Here, let me help.' Before Morna could protest the other girl had caught at the handle of the basket and turned to walk alongside her, the basket swinging between them. 'I've just moved back from Glasgow. My parents have both died and the family house belongs to my brother and me now. I've set up a small school there.'

'You're a teacher?'

'Oh yes, it's what I've always wanted to do,' Ruth said enthusiastically, stepping out so quickly that Morna was in danger of being tugged along by the basket. 'You must come to tea and hear all about it. And I want to hear all about what has been happening to you too.'

They were nearing Quay Street and Morna, reluctant to let the other girl see the lodging house, took a firm grip on the basket and slowed down, forcing Ruth to do the same. 'I'm kept very busy, Ruth, I have little time to spend on visiting.'

'Oh, please! I seem to spend most of my time with the wee ones, and delightful though they are, I'm longing for some adult conversation. Say you'll come, even for a little while. Next Thursday afternoon. Will you be free next Thursday afternoon?'

The rain returned, even harder than before. Morna was sure that she felt a dampness in her left shoe. 'I'm not sure – but I'll try,' she said, deciding that her best chance of escape was to agree to the meeting.

'Please do. You remember our house in Ardrossan Road? I'll expect you at three o'clock.'

'Goodbye, Ruth,' Morna said firmly, retrieving control of her basket. Why, she asked herself

218

grumpily as she hauled the heavy basket the rest of the way on her own, had she agreed to see Ruth again? They may have been classmates several years before, but they had never been friends. Indeed, their interests had been very different; Morna preferring the company of the more frivolous girls in the class, while Ruth, in constant pursuit of knowledge and enlightenment, never seemed to lift her head from a book. Morna vaguely recalled her, tall and angular, leaning against a wall during the playtimes, reading while all the other children played at hopscotch or skipping games or, like Morna and her cronies, gossiped and giggled in a corner of the playground. What could she and Ruth possibly find to talk about now, when Ruth was a teacher and Morna was...

She groaned as she reached the Chapmans' door and set the basket down in order to lift the latch. What would Ruth make of her former classmate living in a shabby lodging house and earning her keep as a skivvy?

Meggie was pinning on her hat when Morna went into the kitchen. 'I have tae go out, pet. Wee Mrs McKay along the road's birthin' her bairn an' she needs me. Can you peel the potatoes for tonight's dinner? An' the soup'll need a stir now and then.'

'Will you be back to see to the meat?' Morna quavered. She could eat the stuff – though only because the hard work made her hungry – but the thought of handling the great slabs of raw fat-laced meat made her feel sick.

'Aye, I will, if you dae the carrots and onions

219

beforehand. Now where's – here it is.' Meggie picked up a small coil of rope from the dresser, and Morna eyed it nervously.

'What do you need that for?' Her knowledge of childbirth was very sketchy, but she could not believe that ropes were necessary.

'Tae fasten tae the bedposts, of course, so's she's got somethin' tae pull on when the pain gets bad,' Meggie said briskly. 'There's a pile o' darnin' in that basket that could do with a good goin' over with a needle.' Then she was out of the door while Morna was still wrestling with the thought of the pain becoming so bad that the expectant mother was forced to pull on a length of rope. With just a few words, Meggie had turned childbirth into some sort of tug of war. Morna shuddered, then began to put the shopping into the cupboard.

She left the vegetables for as long as she could in the hope that Meggie would return and deal with them, but after almost an hour of sitting by the fire forcing a big darning needle through thick socks and yellowed vests she decided that peeling and dicing onions and carrots was preferable to feeling like Cinderella without any hope of a fairy godmother arriving to save her.

Ten minutes later, weeping over a pile of onions and wondering if she would have been better off with the darning, she heard the street door open. Her hope that Meggie had returned was dashed when the kitchen door was thrown open and Samuel Gilmartin swept in, grinning from ear to ear.

'I got the position,' he exulted. 'I start next Monday and it's all thanks tae – what's wrong?

220

Has Meggie been shoutin' at ye?' Then, as Morna gave a huge sniff and shook her head, holding out a half-peeled onion, 'Och, is that all it is? Here…' He took the onion and the knife from her and laid them down, then led her over to the kitchen sink, where he turned on the single tap and then pushed her hands beneath the flow of cold water. 'Hold them there for a minute,' he instructed.

Almost at once the unbearable stinging in her eyes began to ease and after another minute she was able to shake the water from her hands and turn the tap off. Being old and very stiff, it continued to dribble water until Samuel reached over her shoulder and turned it off completely with a swift twist of his wrist. Then he spun her around to face him.

'D'ye have a handkerchief?' When she produced one from the pocket of her sacking apron he took it from her and mopped her eyes. 'There now, is that not better? Have ye never heard o' takin' the sting of the onions away by puttin' yer hands under cold runnin' water? Take a good blow, now,' he went on, clamping the handkerchief to her nose. Enraged, she snatched it from him and turned away. When she had managed to sort herself out she whirled around to face him again.

'Of course I know that cold running water takes the sting away, but Meggie's out with a rope, helping some neighbour to have a baby, and that beastly tap's too stiff for me and – and…' she blinked up at him with eyes that were still painful.

'Poor wee lass,' he commiserated, and then, the huge smile breaking over his face again, 'but did ye not hear what I said? I got the position!'

221

'At the shop?'

'Aye, at the shop. No more getting meself filthy dirty in that dockyard!' he crowed, and before she knew what was happening Morna was being whirled around the kitchen with her feet several inches off the ground.

'Put me down,' she squeaked, and when he finally did so, 'Who interviewed you for the position?'

'Your sister, like you said she would.'

'And she took you on, just like that?'

'Ah well, your aunt put in a good word for me.'

'My Aunt Beatrice McCallum? She was interviewing along with Belle?' Aunt Beatrice seemed to be poking her nose in everywhere.

'Not exactly. Y'see, I went tae your aunt's house by error, thinkin' that Miss Forsyth was to interview me there.'

'But I told you to go to the shop.'

'I must have been so excited at gettin' the chance of an interview that I got myself confused,' Samuel said glibly 'And as it happens, one of your poor aunt's wee pet dogs had just died. So I helped her out by diggin' a grave and buryin' the poor wee thing, and she gave me breakfast in return.'

'I don't see how...'

'Never mind that; the thing is, I got the position on a month's trial. I'm on the first rung of the ladder and it's all thanks to you. I love you, Miss Morna Forsyth!' His arms were still linked loosely around her waist, and in order to look up at him she'd placed her hands lightly on his shoulders; with one of his sudden and unexpected moves Samuel ducked towards her and gave her a lusty kiss full on the lips.

'Samuel!' She pulled away, embarrassed and horrified.

'Sure and I just wanted to say thank you.'

'You could have found another way to say it.' Morna's face was hot and her hands fluttered like birds over her hair and clothing in an orgy of patting and tidying.

'What other way? You name it and I'll do it.'

'Finish off the onions and then do the carrots and the potatoes.'

'With pleasure,' he said, and whipped off his jacket before settling down to the task.

'Fraser Walter Forsyth,' Walter said in ringing tones.

'Where d'ye get the Fraser from?'

'Mother's mother was a Fraser, Aunt Beatrice. It's a proud name that should be kept in the family.'

'Hector's a proud name too. You could name him after yer uncle.'

'Hector doesn't have the same weight to it. No, it's to be Fraser Walter Forsyth.' Walter rolled the words around his tongue as though sucking a particularly pleasant-tasting sweet.

A shaft of weak February sunlight suddenly shone through the window on to the baby's face. His eyes immediately shut tightly and he gave a little snuffling sneeze. Walter turned so that his body was between the bright light and the baby, bouncing the shawled bundle lightly in his arms, 'Belle, first thing tomorrow you must arrange for a sign writer to paint the words "Forsyth and Son" over the shop front. Young Fraser here shall have a fresh new sign in his honour.'

'I doubt he'll be bothered,' Beatrice said dryly, easing a coin into the baby's tiny hand for luck. Then, as the perfect little fingers immediately curled around her offering, 'Would ye look at that, now? He knows the value of silver already, for all that his name's longer than he is.'

'He's only one day old; of course he's small,' Walter defended his firstborn, while Sarah's aching body felt as though it had given birth to a young bullock, hooves and all, rather than the little scrap that Walter was so proudly showing off to his sister and aunt.

'And how are you, Sarah?' Belatedly, Beatrice remembered that the new member of the Forsyth family had a mother.

'Tired, of course, but in good health, according to the doctor. She did very well, didn't you, Sarah?'

Beatrice surveyed the paper-white face on the pillow and said kindly, 'You look tired, my dear. We should leave her to rest, Walter. And the little one too.'

'Indeed.' Walter handed his son reluctantly to the nurse and ushered his sister and aunt from the room. 'Go to sleep, Sarah,' he ordered his wife as they went. 'I will be back later to see how you both are.'

Alone at last, Sarah held her arms out for the baby. 'Give him to me.'

The nurse frowned. 'He needs his rest as much as you do, Mrs Forsyth. Your husband has scarcely let the wee soul lie in his cradle since he was born.'

'Just for a moment,' Sarah begged, and the child, smelling sweetly of soap and powder, was placed carefully in the crook of her elbow.

'A moment only, while I get his cradle ready.'

Young Fraser Walter Forsyth was already half asleep, but as his mother peered at him, anxiously searching for signs of auburn hair, brown eyes, and neat handsome features, he opened his dark eyes wide and stared up at her. His hair was dark too, and the baby face, made for a snub button of a nose, bore instead an appendage that, like Walter's and his father's before him, was always going to be slightly too large for its surroundings. Without doubt this child was a Forsyth, not a Gilmartin.

The nurse finished fussing over the elaborate cradle that Walter had had made for his son and turned to the bed in time to see Sarah's eyes flood with weak tears. One of them splashed on to the baby's cheek, and he screwed up his own dark eyes and let out a mew of protest.

'There now, I knew that you were overtired,' the nurse scolded, hurrying to snatch her precious charge away from danger. 'You must think of the child's well-being, Mrs Forsyth. If you let yourself become fatigued then it will affect your milk and it's this poor wee thing who will suffer. Come along now, little man.' She gathered the baby into her capable arms and bore him off to his rest, while Sarah turned her face into the pillow and wept quietly for the child she had hoped to bear – Samuel's child.

18

'Poor wee mite,' Beatrice McCallum said as she and Belle walked away from the house an hour later. 'Imagine havin' Walter for a father.'

'I'm sure he'll be a very good father,' Belle said sharply. She herself had little love for her brother, but it offended her to hear someone else criticise him.

'Oh, there's no doubt o' that as far as the material things of life are concerned, but I'm talkin' about the adventurous side of growin' up. Hamilton was always pompous and Walter's taken after him – that's why he's the way he is. A boy needs a bit of adventure tae bring out the best in–' A bout of coughing cut her sentence short, and she stopped, fishing in her pocket for a handkerchief.

Belle supported her aunt until the paroxysm was over, then said, 'You shouldn't have come out of the house on a cold damp day like this – I told you that earlier.'

'Nonsense, I couldn't miss the chance to see Sarah and the wee laddie for myself. It was just a tickle in the throat – the remains of that cold I had last week.'

'Mebbe so, but you're going to have a hot poultice on your chest tonight, and a hot toddy to drink too.'

'Ach, you're nothin' but a fuss, Belle Forsyth,'

the old woman grumbled, although secretly she quite enjoyed being fussed over from time to time, and also appreciated her niece's company in the house. 'It's just as well that the tickle waited until now,' she said as she and Belle started walking again. 'If it had happened in the house, Walter would no doubt have had the whole place fumigated in case his son caught the smit from me.

'How's that young man gettin' on?'

Belle, thinking her aunt was still referring to the new baby, was confused. 'What young man?'

'The one that came tae my house lookin' for work in the shop.'

'Oh, Samuel Gilmartin.' Without realising it Belle raised one hand to her hat, checking that it was neatly settled on her head. 'He's doing very well. In fact, he's quite an asset, now that Walter's more interested in his child than his work.'

'Why don't you invite him for his supper tomorrow night? And I'm talkin' about Mr Gilmartin, not your brother,' Beatrice added as her niece looked at her, startled. She knew, from months of sharing the same house with her niece, that Belle's mind could not leap from one subject to another as easily as her own.

'Invite him for supper? But Aunt Beatrice, he's one of our employees!'

'What difference does that make? He was very helpful when he was here last, buryin' poor wee Romeo and bein' so kind and understandin'. I was very taken with him and I'd like fine tae see him again. Ask him, Belle; and you can tell him that I'll not take no for an answer.'

There was something about Samuel Gilmartin that had caught Belle's attention from the moment he began working in the shop. Even when she was not looking at him, or looking *for* him, she could somehow tell just where he was; and on the many occasions she was unable to resist the temptation to check her instinct, it was always proved right.

Samuel also had a knack of always being where he was most needed – opening the door for important and valued customers, stacking a shelf that was beginning to empty, offering help to one of his colleagues or assistance to someone who was not quite certain as to what they wanted to buy. Whatever he was doing and whoever he was with, he was unfailingly cheerful, and he seemed to be able to sense the customer's wishes in an instant. He could switch with ease from being subservient to quietly sympathetic. The rest of the staff liked him and even Walter, after his initial reluctance to approve of someone hired by Belle rather than himself, had acknowledged that he was an admirable assistant. As for Belle herself, although he had only been working in the shop for a matter of weeks she found herself becoming more and more dependent on the young Irishman, for he was reliable and never had to be told anything twice. She now knew that the dockyard work he had hated so much was completely wrong for him.

Now, sitting at Beatrice McCallum's table, she was taken aback by the sheer power of Samuel's presence. All through supper Beatrice had been busy drawing him out, and he had responded with his usual cheerful honesty, talking easily and warmly of his family and his life in Ireland. Since there was no need for Belle to make conversation she was content to keep her eyes on her plate, letting his soft pleasant voice flow around her ears like music. An occasional surreptitious glance from beneath lowered eyelids made it possible for her to see his deft hands, the fingernails cut short and well scrubbed, and when he laughed, as he did easily and often, the sound rippled through her like skilled fingers caressing the strings of a harp.

On the few occasions when she looked at him properly his auburn hair lit the room like the autumn bonfires she, Morna and Walter used to dance around in the back garden as children, and his laughing eyes sparkled at her.

Although Beatrice, in her high-backed chair at the head of the table, ate very little, Belle was pleased to see that she looked better than she had done for weeks. Tonight there was colour in her face and her grey eyes, which had become as dull as stones since her favourite dog's death, sparkled just as much as Samuel's – so much so that Belle felt like a crow in the presence of two exotic, beautiful birds.

'Have ye done?' Ena asked from the door. 'Are ye finished yer puddin's?'

'Mr Gilmartin?'

'There's nothin' left but the pattern and even that looks delicious, so ye'd best take it away before I disgrace myself.' Samuel turned his warm smile on the servant. 'Are you the cook as well? That was the best meal I have ever eaten.'

Ena flushed with pleasure, but her voice was as

dour as ever as she accused, 'You've been kissin' the Blarney Stone and no mistake.'

'I never have,' he protested. 'My mother, bless her, always insisted on her children showing their appreciation. "It's all very well thankin' the Lord before ye eat," she always said, "but don't forget the Lord's servant that saw tae the makin' of yer food. Thank Him afore ye settle tae eat, and thank her after ye're full." So...' He sprang up to open the door for her, 'I thank you, ma'am, from the bottom of my heart.'

'Are you sure about the Blarney Stone?' Ena asked dryly, but as she went out her smile deepened to a broad grin.

'And my thanks to you too, Mrs McCallum, and Miss Forsyth, for invitin' me into your lovely home and makin' me feel so welcome,' Samuel said earnestly as he closed the door and returned to the table. 'Ye've no idea what a pleasure it is tae eat a fine meal in such good company.'

'What are you used to, then?'

'Me? Oh, I live in a lodgin' house down by the shore. It's a good lodgin' house too, don't get me wrong, Mrs McCallum. The couple who own it are decent people, and the lodgers are all looked after as well as they can be.'

'It's owned by Meggie Butcher, Aunt Beatrice,' Belle explained. 'Her married name is Chapman.'

'Of course, I remember now. That's where Morna went when she left home.'

'That's right, Mrs McCallum. Fortunate for me that she did go there, for it's thanks to her that I ended up working where I am now. As I said, the lodgin' house is as good as any can be, but it's not like being in your own home. They feed us and house us, and we can expect no more. All the other lodgers work in the Ardrossan dockyard or on the railways.'

'Perhaps you should find somewhere more congenial now that you're working for the Forsyths,' Beatrice suggested.

'To tell ye the truth, I've been thinkin' that myself. I'd like fine tae have a wee room tae myself where I could keep my books and be able tae read without bein' laughed at. But...' he glanced quickly at Belle, '...I'm still workin' out my month's trial and I'd not want to make a move until I'm sure of the position.'

'You've been in the shop for the better part of a month, have you not? And from what my niece tells me you've been giving satisfaction. Belle?'

Belle's face warmed under the expectant gaze of two pairs of eyes. Why, she asked herself, did Aunt Beatrice always have to be poking her nose into everything? Aloud, she said, 'My aunt is right, Mr Gilmartin. Your first month is almost over and I think I can speak for my brother and myself when I say that you have been most satisfactory.'

'God bless you, Miss Forsyth! You'll not regret puttin' your trust in me,' he said warmly. And then, with one of his infectious laughs, 'Now here's me been talkin' and talkin' about my past and my ambitions and never thinkin' how tired you must be with the sound of my voice.'

'Not at all,' Beatrice assured him firmly. 'I asked you to tell me all about yourself, and it has been a most interestin' story.'

'You're very kind, Mrs McCallum. Didn't I

231

think, when I first started, that I had nothing much tae say? And now I find that I've talked all through our supper. In fact, I've taken up enough of your valuable time. I should be goin'.'

'It's early yet.' Beatrice put out a detaining hand as he began to get to his feet. 'Ena will be taking tea into the parlour and we can't let you go until you've had a cup. Can we, Belle?'

'That's very kind of you,' Samuel said, and then darted forwards as Beatrice put her hands on the arms of her chair and began to ease herself upright. 'Can I assist you, ma'am? Just lean on me, and let me know if I'm doing things the wrong way.'

'Tell me, Mr Gilmartin,' Belle heard her aunt say as she followed the couple, now arm in arm, across the hall to the parlour, 'do you play cribbage?'

'No, Mrs McCallum, but I'm a very quick learner.'

'Then I shall teach you, and then you can come and play cribbage with me every week. You would be doing Belle a favour, for I enjoy my games of cribbage, but she finds them tedious.'

'I don't, Aunt Beatrice. It's just that I have the shop accounts books to keep in order, and they take up so much time in the evenings.'

'I would be charmed, Mrs McCallum,' said Samuel, and then, with a slight bow in Belle's direction, 'particularly if it gave me the opportunity to help you as well, Miss Forsyth.'

'A most remarkable young man,' Beatrice McCallum said when their visitor had gone. 'Quite impressive, wouldn't you say?'

232

'It's hard to believe that he came from such lowly beginnings,' Belle admitted.

'Tush – that has nothing to do with it. I came from lowly beginnings myself, and I've done quite well.' Beatrice looked around the comfortable, well-furnished parlour. 'It's all a matter of smeddum, Belle. Do you know that word?'

'I can't say that I do, Aunt.'

'I thought not. It means having strong spirit, determination and the will to get somewhere. I have it and so does Samuel Gilmartin. He will go far, mark my words,' Beatrice said, and then, giving her niece a mischievous sidelong glance, 'I never looked for another husband after your Uncle Hector died, for it seemed to me that one husband is enough for any woman, but if I were twenty years younger I do believe that that young man might just have been able to change my mind.'

'Aunt Beatrice, how can you say such a thing?'

Beatrice leaned over and patted her niece's hand. 'Perhaps, my dear, I enjoy teasing you now and again. Pay no attention; it's just my way. But now I'm going to leave you in peace to work on your ledgers. Pleasant though this evening has been, I feel quite tired now. I do believe that I shall sleep well for a change.'

Meggie came back from the shops and hunted the house for Morna, finally running her to ground in the attic bedroom, where she was changing the grey sheets on one of the beds. 'I've just heard,' she said, still in her hat and coat.

'Heard what?' Morna stuffed a sheet into the

233

basket, trying to touch it with her fingertips only, and turned the thin, stained mattress over. It was just as stained on the other side.

'Mr Walter's wife's had a wee laddie. Ye're an auntie, Miss Morna.' The woman's heavy face was beaming.

'Am I, indeed?' Morna shook out a fresh sheet – patched, and already patterned with its own stains – and began to smooth it over the mattress.

'Ye'll be goin' tae see the wee one?'

'I don't see why I should.'

'But he's yer own flesh an' blood!'

'So Walter says.'

'Miss Morna! That's a cruel thing tae say.'

'Even if the child had Clarissa Pinkerton as its mother I doubt if I would be rushing to see it,' Morna said. 'I don't care for children, I don't care for Walter, and I most certainly do not care for his maidservant wife.' There was another reason, but it was not one that she could admit to Meggie – she did not have the money to buy a gift for the child, and nobody visited a newborn child without some sort of gift.

'But the wee thing's innocent of any wrongdoing, and a bairn's a bairn. Ye should go and pay yer respects.'

'I most certainly will not.' Morna moved on to the next bed, while Meggie stared at her, baffled, then remembered something else.

'Is this not the day ye're supposed tae be visitin' with that friend ye met in the town last week?'

'Yes, but I'm not going there either.'

'Why not?'

'For goodness' sake, Meggie – it's not as if we

234

were close at school. We barely exchanged half a dozen words, and no doubt she'll have heard by now all about the way my father walked out, and about Walter's behaviour. I have no doubt that once she finds out the truth about what has been happening she will be as reluctant to entertain me to tea as I am to go.' Morna still burned with shame at the memory of the way Mrs MacAdam, the woman who might so easily have been her mother-in-law, had looked at her and spoken to her on their last meeting; she had no wish to see that look on Ruth's face.

'But ye need tae be with yer own sort of folk again. If ye won't go tae see the newborn babbie, at least have tea with yer friend. Tae please me,' Meggie coaxed, and Morna, too tired to argue any further, gave in.

Ruth threw open the door before Morna had even had time to lift the heavy brass knocker. 'I was watching for you coming along the road. In you come – tea first, I think. This way.'

The entrance hall, Morna noticed as she followed her hostess, was wider than the Forsyths', and the stairway curving to the upper floor more grand. A telephone stood on a small ornate table, and there was even a brass gong on a stand. She had expected to be ushered into one of the two front rooms, but instead Ruth passed them and opened a door at the rear of the hall. They went through another short, narrower hall and arrived, to Morna's astonishment, in the large, cluttered kitchen.

'Sit down and we can talk while I make the tea.'

235

Ruth swept a pile of books from a chair by the table, deposited them on the floor, and bustled over to the range, where a large kettle was simmering.

Morna took a seat, looking around the place. It was as though Ruth spent most of her time in the kitchen. Dishes were stacked on the draining board and a large cast-iron pot and a pile of vegetables stood at one end of the big, well-scrubbed kitchen table she had been seated at, but judging by the papers and books scattered over the rest of the table, it was also used as a desk.

'You live here on your own?' she asked, wondering why, in a house with several rooms, Ruth should choose to live in only one.

'Most of the time. My brother Tom is assistant minister at a church in Glasgow, but he comes here occasionally, and always in the summer, of course.'

'You don't have a servant to look after you?'

Ruth had measured tea into a china pot and added boiling water; as she set the kettle back on the hob she turned and gave Morna a wide smile, 'Good gracious no. Why would I want another woman to cook for me and clean up after me when I've got two perfectly good hands of my own? I wouldn't demean any woman in that way.' She delved into a cupboard and produced a biscuit barrel and a plate. 'There's Anna, of course – she lives down by the river and she has a sick husband and five children to care for. She brings her youngest to my little school every morning and stays to help with the children. She does some housework too, but that's because she needs the money badly. It's a fair exchange of skills, since she's much better at housework than I am, and in return I teach her little one and give Anna a small wage, which helps to feed and clothe her family.'

She laid the plate of biscuits on the tray, then went back to the cupboard and produced more plates. 'I made sandwiches for this afternoon, and Anna very kindly made a jam sponge for us. Unfortunately, I was never taught to bake and I can never make the time to learn. Do you know how to bake?'

'I've never had the need to bake,' Morna said, surprised by the question.

'I know what you mean,' Ruth agreed sympathetically. 'Our education was sadly lacking in practical matters, wasn't it? That's why I have to rely on Anna. Once a week she teaches the children something of cooking and baking. They love it, and I must say that it has helped me too.'

She fell silent, concentrating on cutting the sponge cake into delicate sections. Morna picked up a magazine that lay close to her hand and gave it a casual glance. Then she looked again.

'Are you interested in the suffragette movement?'

'Of course, aren't you?'

'I don't know anything about it,' Morna admitted.

'Really? You must borrow some of my literature; I'm sure you would find it interesting,' Ruth said, and then as Morna, raised to believe that the suffragette movement was unfeminine, disruptive and unnecessary, struggled to think of some way to reject the offer without giving offence, 'Tea's ready. I thought we would have it in the little front parlour.'

19

'My mother would be happy to know that her special little room is occasionally used for its proper purpose,' Ruth said as she set the tray down on a polished circular wood table with curved legs. 'I tend to spend all my time in the kitchen because it's warmer and everything I need is near to hand.'

'It's a beautiful room,' Morna said in delight. The room was restful, with its soft, comfortable chairs and flowered wallpaper in pastel shades. The polished floor was covered with rugs and pale green leaves were woven into the fawn curtains. A piano stood against one wall, and a small writing desk in the corner. There was also a lacquered wood chest of drawers inlaid with exquisite flower and leaf patterns.

Morna ran her fingertips over it lightly. 'I have never seen anything so perfect!'

'It was a gift from my father to my mother. He brought it home after a trip to Japan. I lit the fire especially for your visit,' Ruth went on, 'and what we need now are crumpets to toast at the flames. I do believe I have some.' As she went towards the door she added, 'Father brought the prints from Japan too. Mother loved them dearly.'

The prints were of mountains and deep blue lakes, delicate trees and flowers, and graceful Japanese ladies in rich robes taking tea, playing musical instruments and writing at low desks. Morna studied each of them closely before turning back to look around the lovely room. Its comfort provoked a sudden flood of longing for the home she had left; the home now presided over by Walter's wife. Tears sprang to her eyes, and she only just had time to blink them away before her hostess reappeared, a plate of crumpets in one hand and a butter dish and two toasting forks in the other. She speared a crumpet on one of the forks and offered it to Morna, then did one for herself. 'Come and kneel on the hearthrug.'

'The prints are beautiful. I used to go to painting classes,' Morna said wistfully as they settled on the rug together, 'but if I tried every day for the rest of my life I could never produce such perfect work.'

'At least you're artistic. Poor Mother, I must have been a sore disappointment to her. Instead of appreciating beautiful things as she did, I followed my father into the academic world. She would have loved to have a daughter like you, Morna. Oh, we adored each other, but I couldn't help being me.' She turned her crumpet so that it could toast on the other side. 'I used to envy you when we were at school together.'

'Envy me? Why would you do that?'

'Because you were so pretty – and now you're quite beautiful. And you laughed a lot and had fun. I knew even then that you were the sort of daughter my mother would have enjoyed. I heard, after we left school, that you stayed at home as your mother's companion. And I also heard of her recent death. I am so sorry, Morna.'

'No doubt you've heard of what happened after Mother died.' Morna heard a harsh note creep into her voice. 'About my father going off to goodness knows where and abandoning us? And about my brother Walter breaking off his most suitable engagement to Clarissa Pinkerton and choosing to marry our maidservant instead?'

'Yes, I did hear all that,' Ruth said calmly. 'One cannot help hearing gossip in a small place like Saltcoats.'

'And yet you invited me to your house for tea.'

'I think they're both ready now. Why shouldn't I invite you for tea?' Ruth went on as butter melted into the hot crumpets.

'Nobody else cares to know me now,' Morna said bitterly. 'I'm an outcast in my own home town.'

'Then the loss is theirs, for they must all be behaving very childishly. They'll forget about those small scandals in time.'

'I doubt if I ever will.'

'What is there to fret over? Your father did his duty by his wife and children, and once he was widowed and his family grown he decided to seek out a new life for himself – and to give you and your brother and sister the chance to find yourselves as adults. As for Walter – I admire him for realising that just because a woman is in service, she is no less important than her mistress. Just think,' Ruth swept on, oblivious of Morna's shock at such blasphemy from one who should know better, 'of all those poor souls who are only raised in order to look after their parents and then find themselves alone in middle age, with no lives of their own.'

'I can't say that I have found myself as an adult,' Morna protested angrily. 'I'm living in a lodging house run by my former nursemaid and her husband and I'm expected to earn my keep by working as a servant. That's not what I had wanted out of life!'

'Why are you in this lodging house? Did your brother put you out of your home?'

'I went of my own accord. How could I stay there and see our servant take my mother's place as mistress of the house?'

Ruth used her napkin to wipe melted butter from her chin and then glanced pointedly at Morna's reddened fingers. 'So, in protest, you chose to become a servant yourself.'

'You do your own housework.'

'From choice, and in my own home. It must be difficult, I know, to suddenly see the woman who used to be your servant girl become your sister-in-law,' Ruth said gently, 'but she was your brother's own choice and surely you would prefer to see him content in a marriage of his choosing than unhappy in one that was probably arranged for him and for his fiancée by their parents? Is she so terrible, this new wife of his?'

'Not terrible, just...' Morna struggled to find the right words.

'Just not of our class? My dear, in the path I've chosen I meet a lot of women, many of them "not of our class". And it has made me feel that we

241

might all be better off blending our differing outlooks and talents. We can learn so much from each other. Talking of talent, I seem to recall that you were a proficient pianist. Do you remember that school concert when you were the star performer of the evening? You played a beautiful piece on the piano; my mother spoke of it for weeks afterwards.'

'To a Rose.' Morna recalled the concert as though it had been yesterday. 'It was one of my mother's favourite pieces.'

'Play it for me now,' Ruth said suddenly.

'I couldn't! I haven't played the piano for a long time and my fingers have become quite stiff and swollen.'

'Please try, Morna. Mother's piano has been neglected too, and I would so like to hear it being played again,' Ruth coaxed and Morna, who had been longing to go to the piano from the moment she had entered the room, needed no further encouragement.

It took several false starts before her fingers began to feel comfortable on the keys, but once that happened they began to work of their own accord and the music came, shakily at first and then confidently. She followed 'To a Rose' with 'The Blue Danube' waltz, and then stopped and turned on the piano stool. 'I'm very much out of practice.'

'And I am no judge. To me, it sounded delightful. Thank you. Now if you've finished your tea, you must come and see my classroom.'

They crossed the hall to a large, elegant room that must once have been a beautiful drawing room. Now it was furnished with three long low tables surrounded by small chairs. A desk stood in the corner and slates were laid out on the tables.

'This was our family drawing room, but as you can see, it makes a perfect classroom now. I had the carpets taken up as well and now the floor is well marked by the children's boots. I am leaving it as it is, for it's wrong to expect children to creep about like little mice.'

'Do you enjoy teaching?'

'I adore it,' Ruth said. 'Here, of course, my pupils are all very young. My aim is to start them off with a year's general tuition before they go to the public school. I always think of children's minds as hungry little mouths, open wide and desperate to be fed with information.'

'I don't remember feeling like that when I was at school.'

'Ah, but that was because our minds were force-fed with facts, and that,' Ruth said, her voice suddenly steely, 'is a terrible thing to do to any human being, especially a child. I can remember sitting in the classroom when I was only about seven years old, wondering if three and eight really did make eleven, or if the teacher was just teaching us a lot of lies to amuse herself. Children need to find things out by their own efforts. That's the way I teach, and it is so rewarding. I think that you would enjoy it, Morna.'

'Me? I couldn't teach! What do I know of academic things?'

'I wasn't thinking of reading and writing or grammar and arithmetic. I can deal with those subjects, but I know nothing of music and art.

243

My little pupils would love to learn something of those subjects, and you could teach them, if you were willing to come and work with me.'

'I couldn't!' Morna said again.

'I think you could. Remember what I said earlier about those hungry little minds? I want my pupils to enjoy learning, and I'm sure that you could find a way of making your subjects palatable.'

'You are offering me a position in your school?'

'I wouldn't be able to pay you much. I draw my pupils from the tenement buildings down by the shore and their parents can't afford to pay more than a few pence a week.'

This was yet another shock. 'I thought you were teaching children of – of our own class,' Morna said awkwardly.

'Parents of "our own class", as you put it, can afford to send their children to music and painting classes, as your parents did. I teach children who would otherwise have no hope of learning such subjects. I want to show them that there's more to life than poverty and drudgery. You would be welcome to live here rent-free as part of your remuneration.'

'But how could you afford to pay me at all, since the parents can't pay you much?'

Ruth's shrug indicated that to her, money was of little importance. 'As you already know, Tom and I own this house, which means that I have no rent to pay. My parents left me a small allowance and I have few needs of my own. I earn a little by writing articles for various publications.'

'You're a writer? How wonderful to have such an ability.'

244

Ruth laughed. 'If you care enough about any subject under the sun, Morna, you will find that you have the fire and the ability to work at it. This is quite a large house with plenty of space; it would be such fun to have your company and I think you would enjoy the work. And if a little extra learning early in life, and an appreciation of beautiful things like music and art – if you agree to join me – could give even one of those little ones the chance to do something different with their lives, then it will all be worthwhile. You could use the little parlour as your classroom, since the piano is already in there. We can easily set up an easel there too. Please consider my offer, Morna. I would like to have a friend to share this big place with me. I enjoy what I am doing, and so, I hope, do my children. And so would you!'

'Do it,' Meggie begged when Morna told her of Ruth's offer.

'You think I could?' Morna longed to take the chance that her former classmate offered, but at the same time the challenge terrified her.

'I know ye could, Miss Morna. And ye cannae stay here for ever; ye know that this house and this life's no' right for the likes of you.'

'I'll miss you, Meggie.' She reached across the table and took the woman's hands, still hot and damp from washing dishes in the sink, in her own. 'You've been so good to me, taking me in as you did when I had nowhere else to go.'

'And you've worked hard and never complained, though I know fine that it's not been easy. But at last ye've got somewhere else tae go, and I'm not far away,' Meggie coaxed. 'You'll still visit me, I hope, for I'll want tae know how ye're doin'.'

'Of course I'll visit you.'

'So ye're goin'?'

'I think I am,' Morna said slowly, and then, with dawning excitement, 'Oh, Meggie, I feel as if I'm setting out on such an adventure!'

During her stay in the lodging house Morna had often encountered local children running around the streets in gangs, so absorbed in their own noisy games that as often as not she had had to skip aside in order to avoid being mown down. Once, deep in thought and unaware of danger, she had been knocked off the pavement by a lad almost her own height, and had narrowly escaped falling headlong into a steaming pile of horse manure. The basket of messages had been sent spinning, with packages and paper bags streaming out of it.

'Out o' ma way,' the boy had roared at her, stopping only to stick his tongue out at her and then snatch up a dropped carrot before speeding off. Ever since, she had felt quite shaky each time she came across the street gangs, and her first sight of the half a dozen or so shabbily dressed children clattering into Ruth's house froze the blood in her veins. How she could possibly manage to control this lot of small savages, let alone teach them anything?

'I think you should assist me for the first week,' Ruth had said as she helped Morna to unpack her small suitcase in the comfortable bedroom that had been prepared for her, 'so that you and the children can get to know each other. And you can also observe my teaching methods.'

'What if I turn out to be hopeless?'

'Of course you won't be hopeless. If you know anything about music and drawing then you have knowledge that you can pass on to others. The important thing to remember is that the children want to learn, and that they want to enjoy learning. Just watch me.'

It was obvious from the first that the children, much younger than the youth who had frightened her, adored Ruth, who behaved towards them as though she were a mixture of older sister and mother. The schoolteacher element was there too, but in moderation; her rules, though firmly endorsed, were sensible rather than restrictive.

School, Morna thought, as she watched the first morning's class, had never been like this. By the time the children, all dressed in brightly coloured smocks that Ruth had had made for them, were sent scurrying along the hallway to the kitchen for their mid-morning break, Morna had begun to wish that her own schooldays had been half as interesting and rewarding.

In the kitchen, Anna, a thin, anxious-looking woman, was pouring milk into mugs from a huge jug while some of the children bustled importantly around, handing out biscuits from a box on the kitchen table. 'One each, mind,' one of them was saying sternly. 'Yous can all count tae one and that's the number of biscuits, mind!'

The three adults also had milk, though Morna would much rather have had a cup of tea. Afterwards, they all took part in an energetic ball game in the back garden for fifteen minutes before class began again.

'When it rains we do exercises in the classroom after milk and biscuits, because young children need to work off physical energy in order to get their minds to concentrate,' Ruth explained as they shepherded their young charges back to the house. 'But I like to get them outside as much as possible. We're going to do botany in the summer.'

'You know about botany?'

Ruth grinned. 'I know about gardening and I know that I haven't the time to keep this place as tidy as it was in my parents' day. I can't afford a gardener, so in the spring the children will learn how to plant flower seeds and grow vegetables, and how to weed. It will be good for them *and* for me. And if it works then they can take flowers and vegetables home to their mothers.' Then, as they waited for the little ones to settle themselves back into their small chairs, she said, 'I seem to remember that you were good at needlework too.'

'I know how to embroider,' Morna said cautiously.

'Admirable!'

'Do you mean that you want me to teach that as well?'

'What a good idea, if you can find the time – but let's not put too much on your shoulders at the start of your career. It was another project I had in mind. A group of friends meet here one evening a week to make a patchwork quilt. I would help them but unfortunately I'm no seamstress,' Ruth admitted ruefully. 'Put a threaded needle into my hands and I'm quite likely to

248

prick my fingers on it and get blood all over the material. Perhaps you could help them instead?'

'A sort of sewing bee?'

Frances Forsyth and several of her friends, including Clarissa Pinkerton and her mother, had been members of a sewing group, meeting in each other's houses and combining trite conversation with stitching. Morna had considered it boring, and had resisted her mother's attempts to get her to join in.

'I'm not sure they could be described as a sewing bee. We have some interesting meetings. They're coming on Wednesday evening and I know that they could do with some help. You wouldn't mind, would you?'

'Oh no,' said Morna, polite on the outside, but sighing inwardly.

20

Morna was dismayed when she received the invitation to Fraser Walter Forsyth's christening. She had been too busy settling into Ruth's home and way of life to give any thought to Walter and Sarah or their newborn child, and the invitation was a sudden, sharp reminder of their existence and her duty as the child's aunt.

It wasn't just a case of attending the ceremony – she would be expected to take a gift for the baby, and she was still as poor as a church mouse. The small monthly allowance she had received from her father, and then Walter, had ceased after she'd stormed out of the family home, and she had been too proud to ask her brother for money.

She was on the point of asking Ruth for a loan when she remembered the jewellery she and Belle had inherited from their mother.

'I took all of it, and your clothes, to Aunt Beatrice's,' Belle said when her younger sister called at the shop, 'not that there were many trinkets left once Walter had claimed the best of them for Sarah. You'll have received your invitation to wee Fraser's christening?'

'That's why I need my share of the jewellery,' Morna admitted. 'I'll have to buy him a christening gift, and I've not got much money.'

'I could lend—'

'No, Belle, I'll not be beholden to you. And I'd not want to wear Mother's jewellery either, so it won't be missed. When can I come to the house?'

'I'll tell you what – why don't I bring it to Ardrossan Road? Next Tuesday afternoon would suit me. It'll be no bother,' Belle rushed on before Morna could object. She was desperate to see what sort of place her sister was living in now, *and* keen to meet Ruth Durie.

A brisk March wind blew Belle up the path and in through the door as soon as Morna opened it.

'My goodness, what a day!' Belle puffed as she unbuttoned her coat. 'I took a wee walk down to the shore this morning to clear my head, and the sea's just covered with white horses as far as you can see. Spray's being thrown up the beach and halfway across the road. Oh, this is very nice,' she went on as Morna ushered her into the small parlour. 'A big difference from where you were staying last. It's such a relief to know that you're living in a respectable house again. I was worried about you when you were sharing that house with all those rough men, and nobody to look out for you.'

'Meggie looked out for me very well and I'm grateful to her for all she did for me. I'll just fetch the tea – you'll be ready for it on a day like this.'

Morna returned to the parlour, teapot in hand, to find her sister studying the tray, with its two cups and saucers, 'Is your employer not joining us for tea?'

'She's had to go to Greenock to – see some folk.'

'That's a pity. I've been looking forward to meeting her.'

'Did you bring the jewellery?'

'Of course I did.' Belle produced a small box and as soon as she had served the tea, Morna began to sift through the meagre contents. 'This ring, for instance, with the emeralds. I would never wear it. And there's this brooch too.'

'It was one of Mother's favourites.'

'But never one of mine. I remember scratching my face on it once, when she picked me up. It goes too,' Morna said decisively. 'Do you think that these two pieces could raise enough money for a suitable gift?'

'More than enough. How are you going to sell them?'

'I'm taking them to McKellar's the auctioneers. I've already spoken to them and I think they'll be fair.'

'If that's what you want to do.'

'It is. How's Aunt Beatrice?' Morna remembered to ask.

'I'm concerned about her,' Belle said. 'It sounds daft, but ever since Romeo died she seems to have lost all interest in life – apart from visiting Walter's child. She and Sarah have become quite friendly.'

'Like calling to like,' Morna said dryly.

'Don't be a cat, Morna. Sarah seems to be a good mother and there's no doubt that Walter's happier than he has ever been. That's why he's never in the shop these days. I do the work while he takes the lion's share of the profits.'

'You know that Papa always looked on Walter as a liability rather than a help. You should get him to make you a partner since you're the one who's holding it all together for him.'

Belle's mouth tightened. 'We've only just paid to have "Forsyth and Son" repainted above the window, if you please. I doubt Walter would think that "Forsyth and Sister" had the same grand look to it. So you're settling in to this teaching then?'

'I like it well enough.' Morna was surprised at how much she was enjoying herself. With Ruth's help she had managed to work out a basic lesson programme, and the children's enthusiastic response had helped her to gain confidence.

'It's surprising to think of you teaching bairns when you've not had any training.'

'I only teach music and painting, as I know enough about those subjects to get by. Ruth sees to everything else.'

'She must be very clever.'

'She is. How is Samuel Gilmartin doing in the

shop?' Morna asked, anxious to get the conversation away from Ruth and her little school. As yet, Belle had no idea that the pupils came from the poverty-stricken part of Saltcoats.

'He's doing very well. He has a very quick mind for a man of his background; he only has to be told a thing once and he's grasped it. He's even come up with some ideas of his own. He's very good with the customers too,' Belle went on. 'Especially with the ladies.' And then, as her sister raised an eyebrow, 'By that I mean he's patient with them, and good at advising them as to their purchases. Walter never had the patience for them.'

Belle glanced at her empty cup. 'I've got a real thirst this afternoon. Let's have a fresh pot of tea.'

Morna, who had been hoping to work on the following day's lessons once her sister had gone, suppressed a sigh. 'Of course. I'll not be a minute.'

'There's a bell pull by the fireplace.'

'There's little sense in pulling it since there's nobody in the kitchen to hear it.'

'Is it the maid's afternoon off?'

'Yes.' In an attempt to hide the fact that she and Ruth did their own housework, Morna had had the tea ready when Belle arrived. 'I won't be a moment,' she said.

'I'll come and help.'

'There's no need,' Morna protested, but her sister was determined and there was nothing Morna could do but lead the way to the kitchen, grateful that at least she had had the foresight to gather up all the suffragette literature and put it out of sight, just in case.

Belle's eyebrows rose as she looked around the

kitchen. 'Your maidservant could do with a bit of training. This place looks as if a hurricane has blown through it.'

'That's because the children were in here this morning, taking their mid-morning milk.'

'They sit in the kitchen? And I thought you said that the maid was having her afternoon off – she could at least have put the place to rights before she went,' Belle was saying when the door opened and Ruth swept in, rosy-cheeked from the March winds.

'Tea, Morna, for the love of God. I'm parched. Oh, good afternoon.' She dumped a pile of papers on the table and beamed at Belle. 'I didn't realise that you were entertaining.'

'This is my sister, Belle. She brought some of my things, now that I have more room for them. Belle, this is Ruth Durie.'

'How do you do?' Ruth peeled a glove off and held out her hand. Belle shook it.

'How do you do?' she replied faintly, and then, 'Did you know that you appear to have hurt your hand? And that there's a rip in your sleeve?'

'Sorry about that.' Ruth sucked at her torn knuckles. 'I'll put something on them later, and perhaps you'd be kind enough to mend the jacket for me, Morna? Your sister is a much better seamstress than I could ever be,' she added to Belle, who sank on to a chair.

'Have you been in an accident?'

'More planned than accidental. A meeting in Greenock,' Ruth said blithely, 'and some unin-vited, but not unexpected, arrivals. One of them tried to snatch at the placard I was carrying, and

254

when I did my best to prevent him my hand was banged rather hard against a wall. Then in the general mêlée someone caught at my sleeve and almost took it off. But even so, it was a worthwhile meeting,' she added, while Belle, who had happened to sit down just where Ruth had tossed the papers, caught sight of one of the headlines, and froze.

'We were having tea in the little parlour,' Morna said swiftly, 'we came through to make a fresh pot.'

'Lucky that I came in just when you were making it. Let's go back to the parlour.' Ruth, ignoring the china cups and saucers on the dresser, picked up one of the children's mugs from the draining board and led the way, asking Belle over her shoulder, 'Has Morna shown you the classroom yet? You must come and see it. We're very proud of our pupils, aren't we, Morna? And you should be very proud of your sister, Miss Forsyth, for the little ones are enjoying their piano lessons, and their singing and painting. I'm so pleased that I met up with her again.'

'You didn't tell me,' Belle hissed when Morna accompanied her to the garden gate half an hour later, 'that your friend was one of those suffragettes!'

'Why should I?'

'For goodness' sake, Morna, did you not see the state of the woman? She looked as if she'd been brawling in the street like a common fishwife.'

'It's not her fault if other folk interrupt meetings.'

'She's not tried to get you to go to one of them, has she?'

'No, but I was wondering,' Morna said to irritate her sister, 'if I should go with her one of these days, to see what it's all about.'

'Oh, Morna, you wouldn't! Here was me thinking that you'd managed to land on your feet at last, and now I find you're mixing with women who make exhibitions of themselves in public, and teaching slum children.'

'Just because the children are poor it doesn't mean that they have no right to enjoy singing or playing the piano or drawing pictures. And Ruth and her friends are all respectable women.'

'You've met some other suffragettes?' Belle almost shrieked.

'They come to the house for meetings and I've joined one of their sewing bees.'

'You're not helping to sew those banners about votes for women, are you?'

'No, it's a quilt, and it's very well done. I find their conversation extremely interesting,' lied Morna, who found that most of it went over her head. But she enjoyed the sewing, and when they weren't harping on about the need for female emancipation, Ruth's friends could be witty and interesting. 'Thanks to Ruth I'm meeting a lot of people.'

'Yes – raggedy street children and militant women. What Mother would say...'

'The children – most of them, at any rate – are bright and eager to learn. And Ruth's friends come from all walks of life – there's a minister's wife, a singer, and folk from tenements as well as big houses. You'd be surprised, Belle.'

'Anyone we know?'

'They come from all over.' Belle had probably met some of the women socially, but Morna was not about to start gossiping.

'What if you end up in prison? It happens to these suffragettes, you know.'

'Then I shan't expect you to visit me,' Morna said, 'but I'm more likely to end up in bed with a chill if I stand out in this wind for much longer. Goodbye, Belle. You must come and visit me again soon.'

'You can be sure that I will, for someone has to keep an eye on you,' Belle said, and stamped off, her back rigid with outrage.

Ruth was writing at the kitchen table when Morna went back indoors. The wind had strengthened; it moaned around the corner of the house, and as Morna repaired Ruth's jacket she could see the bare branches of trees in the garden whipping around under its onslaught. Across the table Ruth's hand travelled over page after page, pausing only to dip her pen in the inkwell. The words seemed to pour from the nib of their own accord, though occasionally she tutted or gave an annoyed hiss and ran a thick black line through a word or phrase before rushing on again.

Finally she set the pen down and sat back with a sigh of pleasure. 'Finished. I shall read it over later and put it in the post tomorrow.'

'How can you work so fast?'

'It's easy when you care enough about your subject.' Ruth got up from the table and stretched.

257

'When you care, the words and thoughts are burning you up inside, and you have to let them out.' She put her hands on her hips and moved into a series of the bending exercises she gave the children when rain or cold trapped them indoors. 'I like your sister,' she said, twisting the top half of her body first to one side and then the other like a gymnast.

'Do you?' To Morna's mind Belle had been rather terse and unfriendly.

'She's very real, isn't she? Don't you hate those women who only say what they think they ought to say, or what they think you want to hear?'

'I thought that she was rather impolite. It's not like Belle, but she was annoyed with me.'

Ruth flopped forwards from the hips like a rag doll, fingertips brushing the floor, and then began to draw herself upright, straightening her spine bit by bit. 'She was annoyed with you because you left her to find out for herself that I support the suffragette movement, and that the children we teach come from the wrong part of town. It came as a shock to her, for she had assumed, as you did when you first came here, that because I was raised in a large house I would teach children from this area.' Ruth used both hands to push back the thick black hair that had become dislodged from its hairpins during her energetic exercising. 'I see that my magazines have been tidied away, and I realise that I arrived home earlier than expected, thanks to the meeting being disrupted. Are you truly so ashamed of me and my beliefs, Morna?'

'No! It's just that – I knew that Belle would disapprove...'

'I think you should let your sister make her own mind up,' Ruth said mildly. 'And she can only do that if you tell her the truth instead of trying to hide things from her. I believe that that is the real reason why she was upset. Perhaps one day when we know each other better I might be able to explain my political beliefs to her, and tell her that working in Glasgow and seeing how women in large industrial communities tend to be treated as little more than child-bearing workhorses made me realise how much we females need to have the right to control our own bodies and our own lives. That means having some control over the way our country is run, and *that*, in turn, means having the right to vote. But...' she flung out her hands and smiled down at Morna, '...I made up my mind when I asked you to come here that I would not force my beliefs down your throat, so I think we should occupy our minds instead with the much more important matter of what we should have for our tea.'

The North Parish Church was cold on that chilly early-March day and Fraser Walter Forsyth, slumbering contentedly, woke with a shocked cry as water from the font was dripped on to his smooth forehead.

Mortified, Sarah noted some ladies in the congregation covering their ears with elegantly gloved hands. Fortunately, the short christening service was soon over and the wailing baby handed back to his mother. Recognising her arms he fell silent and started instead to butt his white-capped head impatiently against her new blue jacket in search of milk as Sarah and Walter began the long walk to the door.

Heedless of the silent criticism wafting like incense from the body of the kirk, Walter smiled to the left and right while Sarah was keenly aware that several members of the congregation made a deliberate point of ignoring the christening party.

Only two pairs of eyes bored into her so hard that they caught her attention. The first belonged to Clarissa Pinkerton who, when she caught Sarah's attention, stared coldly and deliberately for a long moment before tilting her chin and turning away her beautifully coiffed head, topped by a wide-brimmed hat smothered with artificial flowers.

Sarah, her face burning, looked swiftly to the other side of the church and then gasped. That couldn't be Samuel Gilmartin sitting in the back row! To the best of her knowledge he was not a churchgoer, and even if he were, why would he be in that particular church on that particular day, the day of her child's christening? It must have been her imagination, she thought as she and Walter reached the door, with no opportunity for her to look back.

Once out in the churchyard she would have liked the chance to watch the other worshippers emerging, but Beatrice McCallum was saying, 'I think Sarah and the wee one should go on home with me and Belle and Morna. You can't keep the bairn outside on a cold day like this with just a christening shawl around him.'

Walter peered at his son, now wrinkling his face against the stiff sea breeze, and drew a corner of the shawl more closely over the bald little head. 'You're right, Aunt Beatrice. You go on up the road, Sarah, and I'll wait here and issue folk with invitations to the house.'

'D'you think anyone will accept an invitation to the house?' Sarah asked as she and Beatrice went along Manse Street with Belle and Morna walking behind them. Walter was determined to behave as though there had been no estrangement between himself and the townsfolk and she could not bear the thought of him standing in the chilly churchyard, being spurned by everyone.

'They might, even if it's only out of nosiness. Thank goodness that's over; I can't be doin' with all that formality A lot of fuss that doesn't mean anythin'.' Beatrice, who used to stride briskly along the street, her dogs scurrying to keep up, now thumped a sturdy walking stick on the pavement with each step she took.

'Walter's heart's set on a proper christening with a party in the house afterwards for all his friends and neighbours. He's desperate for folk to accept him again, and if that's what he wants then it's what I want too.'

'You're a good wee wife, Sarah Forsyth. If you ask me, he's better off with you than with that snooty Clarissa Pinkerton. But don't let him get away with too much,' Beatrice counselled as they left Manse Street behind and crossed over to Caledonia Road. 'The way to treat husbands is to let them win the wee battles while you win the big ones – but still lettin' them think they're the winners, of course.' She let out a yelp of laughter that turned swiftly into a bout of coughing so bad that she had to stop and lean against a wall.

Sarah, alarmed at the way the old lady's face was purpling, used her free hand to rub Beatrice's back while Belle, who had caught up with them, offered her handkerchief and Morna stood back, chewing at her lip.

When the attack finally ended and Beatrice had got her breath back, albeit wheezily, Morna said, 'Mebbe you should just go into your own house and have a rest, Aunt Beatrice. We're almost outside it now.'

'Not a bit of it, lassie! I've got through the worst part of today and I'm not goin' tae miss the best part. Belle, take the bairn so's I can hold Sarah's arm.'

'Me?' Belle asked, horrified.

'Aye, you. Ye can surely carry a wee thing like Fraser the rest of the way?'

'Could you not take my arm and leave him with his mother?'

'I'm in the middle of talkin' to Sarah,' her aunt said blandly, and Belle had no option but to do as she was told.

'Would you not like to hold him?' she asked her sister as they followed the others up the hill.

'You're his godmother,' Morna pointed out just as Fraser realised that he had been given over to a stranger who was not used to holding babies. He peered up into his aunt's face for a long moment and then favoured her with a gummy smile.

'My goodness, Morna, would you look at that!'

Morna, craning to peer at the baby, was blessed not only with a smile, but a gurgle of approval.

'He's not too bad-looking when he smiles, is he?'

'He's Walter's double. Healthy-looking, though. She seems to be a good mother,' Belle said as they turned right into Argyle Road.

'Did you see Clarissa's face when we were walking out of the church? She looked as if she'd a strong lemon sweetie in her mouth.'

'Poor Clarissa, I'm going to have to call on her tomorrow. It must have been an ordeal for her, watching Walter's son being christened.'

Particularly, Belle thought as they followed their aunt and Sarah in to the Forsyth house, as poor Clarissa had pinned her hopes on Sarah dying in childbirth and leaving the way free for Clarissa to reclaim her husband.

Walter arrived five minutes later with the minister and Fraser's godfather, a town councillor and former school-friend of Walter's. 'Unfortunately the cold weather sent most of the congregation hurrying home before I had the opportunity to invite them to the house,' he said as he came in.

'There's far too much food then.' Beatrice, recovered from her coughing bout, peered at the loaded table. 'You seem tae have felt the need tae feed the entire town.'

'One must be prepared, Aunt Beatrice.'

'It's an awful waste of good food.'

'I'll take what's not wanted,' Morna said. 'The children that Ruth and I teach would enjoy a wee treat and I could hand some in to Meggie Chapman on my way home.'

Walter began to protest, but Beatrice said loudly, 'That's a very good idea, Morna. Good food is never wasted when someone can enjoy it. Now then...' she seized a glass of sherry from the tray on the table. 'A toast to Fraser Walter, and...' she paused, taking time to look at her young relations one by one, with a special, warm smile for Sarah, '...to the Forsyth family. Ye're all doin' very well, and I've no doubt that there are better times tae come.'

21

The nurse hired to look after the Forsyth baby was only in residence for four weeks before she and Walter quarrelled. He slammed the door behind her back.

'Good riddance to her. No woman is going to tell me when I am allowed to pick up my own child in my own house. I never cared for her in any case,' he said, regardless of the fact that he had chosen the woman personally and bragged constantly about her efficiency and excellent references.

As he went upstairs to the room that had once been Morna's, Sarah trailed along behind him, weak with relief. The nurse had more or less taken over the running of the entire household, completely intimidating her. 'Nellie and I can manage very well together,' she said as they reached the upper landing.

'Nonsense, my dear, you have more than enough to do looking after the house, and me, and entertaining.'

'The only people who visit are Belle and Mrs

McCallum, and they don't come often.'

'But folk will soon start visiting again,' he assured her.

Fraser, sound asleep in his bower of lace, muslin and ribbons, woke with a start as he was scooped up into his father's arms, and burst into panic-stricken wails.

'There, there, my little man.' Walter marched around the room, rocking his son. 'Did the nasty nurse frighten him, then? Never mind, we'll find a much nicer one for you, won't we, Mama?'

'I would really prefer to look after him myself, Walter...'

'Sarah, my dear, women of my station – our station in life do not look after their own children. My sisters and I always had nursemaids, and it did us no harm, did it? Besides,' he swept on while Sarah thought of the three Forsyths, now living in three different houses within the same small town, and having little to do with each other, 'I can't afford to be known as the man who couldn't even provide a proper nursemaid for his son. There, there,' he added to the baby, who was working himself into a frenzy.

'We must at least take the time to choose carefully,' Sarah said, raising her voice above Fraser's screams. 'We want to be sure that we get the right woman this time.'

'Indeed we do. Fraser, Fraser, this is not the way little men behave, is it?' Walter thrust his moustached face down towards the baby, and Fraser, who had paused to catch his breath, took one look and roared even louder.

'Could he be hungry?' Walter wondered.

'He was fed just before you came home.'

'But he's a growing boy. Go to your Mama, Fraser,' Walter said, and thrust the angry little bundle into his wife's arms before hurrying downstairs to read the evening paper.

The baby's face was dark red and his eyes scrunched up into a series of tight little lines, while screams poured from the perfect circle of his mouth. Sarah settled herself in the low nursing chair, rocking and crooning until the screaming finally subsided to sobs then hiccups. He stared up at her from drowned dark eyes and she covered his little wet face with kisses.

She fetched a clean cloth and dried his tears, but when she tried to put him back in his crib to continue his interrupted sleep he stiffened and began to fret. Sarah carried him back to the chair and unfastened her blouse. He wasn't hungry, but he fastened on her breast eagerly, in need of its comfort. After only a few sucks, he was asleep. She sat on, watching him. He might not be Samuel's, as she had hoped, but he was hers, and she loved him with all her heart.

'It's time,' Walter said on the following morning, 'that we showed Fraser the shop that he's going to inherit one day.'

'Isn't he a little young to appreciate that?'

'What I meant, my dear, is that I think it's time my employees met my son. We will walk down there together once he has been fed and bathed. The fresh air will do him good.'

'We could visit your aunt instead.'

Walter shook his head firmly. 'According to

Belle, Aunt Beatrice has come down with another of her chills – I don't know what's wrong with her this year, she's been poorly ever since the turn of the year and it's almost the end of March now.'

'She's bound to feel better when the weather improves.' Sarah herself felt as though she were trapped in the house by the howling winds and sudden heavy showers, although on the few occasions when she had managed to go out she had enjoyed standing by the shore, watching the foam-capped waves race in as though frantically trying to escape the Irish gales driving them like cattle on the way to market. She particularly liked the way the larger waves offshore smashed themselves against the small tower at the end of Saltcoats harbour and then exploded upwards in a froth of snowy foam that rose into the grey sky and hung for a breathtaking moment before giving up and falling back into the sea to start all over again.

'I don't want Fraser anywhere near her until she has made a complete recovery,' Walter was fussing on, oblivious of his wife's thoughts.

'It might cheer her up to see him, and he's a very healthy baby.'

'Exactly, and I intend to make sure that he remains healthy. I'm surprised at you, Sarah; don't you know that when a small child falls ill he remains sickly for the rest of his life? My sisters and I,' Walter said proudly, 'were always healthy, and my dear mother put it down to her custom of swabbing out our throats regularly to avoid diphtheria and tonsillitis. You should do the same with Fraser.'

He insisted on Sarah dressing in her wedding outfit – her best clothes – and then the handsome perambulator had to be carefully prepared before Fraser was tucked in. They paraded slowly along the pavement, Sarah pushing the perambulator, while Walter walked by her side, one gloved hand resting proudly and possessively on the side of the handle. He tipped his bowler hat to everyone they met; some nodded and murmured a greeting, and some did not, but they all looked curiously at Sarah and the baby carriage before their eyes slid away.

'Shoulders back, my dear, and head high,' Walter said every now and again. 'Remember that you are my wife now, and the mother of my son.'

When they reached the shop he proudly pointed out the new gilt lettering above the door. '"Forsyth and Son". That's me, Fraser, and you,' he told his heir, who was half asleep and sucking his fingers. Then he studied the two shop windows carefully before giving a quick, approving nod. 'Belle said that the new man she hired had dressed the windows – he seems to have done it quite well.' He stepped into the doorway, checking to make sure that it, and the stretch of pavement fronting the shop, had been well brushed, and waited there until someone inside the shop noticed him. There was a sudden flurry of activity before the door opened wide.

Walter stepped inside and then turned. 'Come along, my dear.'

'The perambulator...'

'Bring it in,' Walter commanded with just a shade of irritation creeping into his voice. 'The

268

doorway is wide enough, and our visit today is to introduce the new arrival to the staff, after all.'

Carefully, unused to the high perambulator since the formidable nurse had never allowed her to take it out, Sarah managed to steer it into the shop, and immediately found herself the centre of attention. All pretence at normality had ceased and employees and customers alike stood gaping at her.

'Close the door, man, we're all safely inside now and the draught is not good for the child. A chair for Mrs Forsyth,' Walter went on crisply.

'Certainly, Mr Forsyth.' Sarah had been so busy manoeuvring the perambulator into the shop that she had taken no notice of the person holding the door open. Now, as he passed her on the way to the back office, she became aware of the way he walked, and the set of his head above broad shoulders.

Her heart began to flutter. She stared after the man, scarcely aware of Walter easing her aside and taking charge of the baby carriage. He wheeled it into a corner, nodding to the staff to come forwards one by one to see the precious heir to the Forsyth emporium.

Samuel Gilmartin – for it was unmistakably Samuel Gilmartin, though his shabby working clothes had been replaced by a white shirt, pale blue cravat and dark blue jacket, waistcoat and trousers – reappeared, carrying a wooden chair. He glanced at the staff lining up to pay homage to the baby, and at Walter Forsyth, bending to ease the silk coverlet aside so that Fraser's tiny face could be seen more easily, and then set the chair down a little distance away. Removing a snowy handkerchief from the breast pocket of his jacket with a flourish, he made a great show of dusting the chair. 'Won't you sit down, Mrs Forsyth?'

'Samuel?'

'Samuel Gilmartin, at your service.' He gave her a brief bow, 'I don't believe we have met, ma'am.'

'You work here?'

'Did ye not know?' He moved between her and the others so that only she could see the mocking amusement in his eyes – eyes that still had the power to make her weak with longing. 'You're no' the only one who's managed tae come up in the world, Sarah. The difference is that I used my head and my wits, while you...' he took a moment to look her up and down with studied insolence, '...used yer body.'

She sat down, lacing her fingers tightly in her lap to prevent them from shaking – or, worse still, from reaching out to touch him. 'But how did you get him to hire you, after that time he found us together in the house?'

'I was a message lad then, and dressed like a message lad. He saw me that day, but he didnae *look* at me.' Samuel's top lip curled in a sneer. 'He's scarce looked at me or spoken tae me since I started workin' in here, for I'm still beneath his notice. In any case, it was Miss Belle who hired me, and I'd no trouble with her.' He leaned closer, his voice lowered to a murmur. 'So here I am with my feet under the Forsyths' table, just like you. I may not have your husband's money, and I may not have you, Sarah, but I still have a way with the ladies, and that's goin' tae take me further than you've got. Just you wait and see.'

'You're not goin' tae tell Walter about...?' They had both reverted to their normal speech, Samuel because he wasn't trying to impress, Sarah because she was agitated.

'About us? There's more than one way tae skin a cat,' Samuel said, then, jerking his head at the others, 'Would ye look at them? They're like fairy godmothers at a christenin', fallin' over each other tae wish yer bairn well, in the hope that it'll keep them in *that* one's good books.' He indicated Walter, who was beaming smugly. 'It must make ye proud tae know ye've birthed such an important wean. And tae think...' he smiled down on her; a smile that curved his mouth without touching his eyes '...that I wanted ye tae get rid of it. Ye'd have lost more than an unwanted bairn, eh?'

'Ah, good morning, Sarah.' Belle Forsyth had come to investigate the cause of the commotion among her staff. 'You've brought the child, I see.'

'Walter wanted everyone t-to see him,' Sarah stammered.

'And now that they have I hope that they will return to their work with added enthusiasm.' Belle indicated the few customers who were watching with ill-disguised curiosity from a distance. 'Samuel, perhaps you could...'

'Of course, Miss Forsyth. I'll get them back to work before you can dot an "i" or cross a "t".'

'Thank you.' Belle touched his arm briefly and watched him go for a moment before turning back to Sarah, the smile she had produced for Samuel disappearing. 'So how are you keeping,

271

Sarah?' she enquired politely.

'I'm – very well, thank you.'

'I'm glad to hear it.' Belle's attention was already back with Samuel, who was dropping a brief word in one ear and then another. In no time at all most of the staff had returned to their duties while he himself glanced over at Belle. Sarah, watching like a hawk, saw her sister-in-law incline her head just a fraction of an inch in the direction of a well-dressed woman examining an ornate teapot stand. Samuel responded with a similar imperceptible nod and went over to the woman. It was as though, Sarah thought with a stab of jealousy, he and Belle were equal partners rather than employee and employer.

'Belle,' Walter called out, 'come and see your nephew.'

'I have already seen him, Walter, several times.'

'But small babies change all the time. You haven't seen him today,' he insisted, and with a sigh so faint that Sarah only just heard it, his sister did as she was told. Rather than be left on her own, Sarah went with her.

'He looks well,' Belle said after a cursory glance into the perambulator, where Fraser was beginning to stir. 'Did you see the window dressing? What do you think of it?'

'It seems to be in order.'

'Mr Gilmartin is an asset, Walter, and a great help to me, with you being so preoccupied at home these days. You are not intending to return there at once, are you?' Belle swept on, 'There are several pressing matters that I must speak to you about.'

He frowned, then shrugged. 'Oh, very well. Sarah, can you manage to take the child home without my assistance?'

'Of course, Walter.'

'I will be home for lunch,' he assured her, and beckoned to the nearest employee, who happened to be Samuel. 'The door, if you please,' he instructed, and followed Belle into the back office.

As Sarah struggled to turn the perambulator in the shop's confined space, Samuel sprang forward. 'Allow me, Mrs Forsyth.'

'Samuel...' she began as soon as they were out in the street and away from listening ears.

'I almost forgot – I haven't paid homage tae the young master.' He leaned forwards to look into the perambulator. Fraser's dark eyes – his father's eyes – returned the stare with interest. He gurgled and smiled up at Samuel, but the smile was not returned. Instead, Samuel straightened very slowly before turning to look down into Sarah's white face. 'Well now,' he said, his voice so low that she could scarcely make it out against the background of street noises, 'isn't that one just the spit of his father? You must be quite relieved about that, Sarah.' And then, his voice suddenly lashing out at her, 'Or did ye already know, when ye were pesterin' me tae marry ye, who the true father was?'

'I swear that I thought he was yours!'

'Did ye? Or did ye think that I'd be more easily snared intae marriage than him? Is that it? Aren't you the lucky one, now, with yer mistress dyin' and yer master goin' off just at the right time? If they'd both been in the house ye'd never have coaxed Mr Walter Forsyth intae marryin' ye

273

when I refused.'

'I wanted him to be your child!'

Samuel's eyes were like chips of ice. 'You swore tae me that I was the only man in yer life, when all the time ye were beddin' the son of the house. Have we not both of us had a lucky escape? You've got what ye wanted – marriage with yer bairn's true father, and a rich man intae the bargain, and as for me – I've got what I want.' He jerked his head in the direction of the shop. 'And I'll have more besides. Oh, I can promise ye that, *Mrs* Sarah Forsyth.'

Sarah was trembling so badly on the walk back to the house that she could scarcely keep the perambulator on the pavement. Her heart was chilled by the look in Samuel's eyes at the sight of Walter's likeness stamped on her baby's features, and his final words rang through her head. She had no idea what he meant, but she was frightened.

Defying Walter's wishes, she went to Beatrice McCallum's house, where the old woman was resting on the sofa in her front parlour.

'Ye didnae bring the wee fellow with ye?' she asked, disappointed.

'He's in his perambulator at the back door. Walter says...' Sarah stopped, colouring.

'He's scared that his son'll catch whatever I've got?' Beatrice finished the sentence for her. 'Walter takes after his father – Hamilton always flew intae a right fret whenever one of his bairns fell ill, in case it was passed on tae him. You fetch the laddie in, m'dear – what I've got won't ail him for many a long year yet. If it makes you feel

274

easier in your mind you neednae bring him too close. I just want tae see his bonny wee face.'

'When Sarah carried the baby into the parlour and sat down, Juliet, who had been lying at Beatrice's feet, came over to investigate, tail wagging. The baby beamed and reached out a little starfish hand.

Beatrice's eyes locked on to his bright face. 'It does me good just tae look at him. He's at the beginnin' of his life and I'm at the end of mine.'

'You're nowhere near that!'

'Lassie, there comes a day when ye just know that it's time tae go home. It's as if ye're beginnin' tae outstay yer welcome.'

'What does the doctor say?'

'Och, him!' Beatrice gave a wave of the hand. 'They always have tae put names on everythin'. The truth of the matter, Sarah, is that once Romeo went I knew that my turn was on its way. He was the last gift I had from my husband and I suppose that in a way he took Hector's place. Losin' him was like bein' widowed all over again.'

'But what would I do without you?' Sarah burst out without thinking.

'You'll do very well, for you're a sensible lass, Sarah Forsyth, and you'll put more strength intae my nephew's spine than that young woman he nearly wed. All you need now is tae have more faith in yerself, and tae stand up tae Walter a bit more for he needs tae be led, not followed.'

Sarah sighed, reminded of her latest problem. 'The nurse has left. She and Walter didn't get on.'

'D'ye tell me?' Beatrice McCallum said with a touch of irony in her voice and just a hint of a smile on her lips. 'I suppose they had words over which of them knew best for the wee laddie there?' And then, as Sarah nodded, 'I was never blessed with bairns of my own, but I always thought that it's the mother who knows her own bairn best. If there's times when you and Walter don't agree on the way things are bein' done for yer son you'll have tae be ready tae speak up. Walter's soft – he'll give in once he sees that you're determined.'

'What do I know about nursery nurses?'

'I'm not so far gone that I cannae help ye there,' Beatrice said just as the door opened and Ena brought in the tea. 'The very person. Pour the tea, will ye, Ena? My hands are shaky today and Mrs Forsyth's busy with the bairn. And tell me if ye know of any good child nurses in the town that might be lookin' for work.'

'There's Leez Drummond that was married ontae my cousin's man's brother Jockie,' Ena said as she poured tea.

'Jockie that was a fisherman?'

'Aye, that's him. Drowned at sea less than a year after him and poor Leez wed. She was the eldest o' a big fam'ly,' Ena said, taking a cup of tea over to her mistress, 'so she grew up knowin' how tae look after bairns. She worked as a nursemaid afore she married Jockie and she went back tae the same work when she was widowed. I heard the other day that she wasnae very well pleased with where she is. She's been thinkin' of movin' out of Saltcoats tae some place where there's more folk with the money tae pay tae have their children cared for.'

'Ask her tae come here at ten o'clock tomorrow

morning,' Beatrice said. 'You come along too, Sarah, and bring the wee one with you. We'll interview the woman together.'

'What should I tell Walter?'

'Tell him nothin' at all. If the woman doesnae suit us, or we don't suit her, there's no harm done.'

22

The postman brought a lot of letters for Ruth every morning. She usually glanced briefly at the envelopes during breakfast, then waited until after the morning class before settling down at the kitchen table to open them, but on this particular morning she pulled one out of the pile and slit it open with her butter knife. After scanning the contents swiftly she pushed her half-eaten breakfast away and jumped to her feet.

'I must go to Glasgow at once.'

'Glasgow? But it's a school day!'

'Nevertheless, I must go at once, if I want to catch the next train. A friend needs my help.' Ruth was already on her way to the hall, where Morna, hurriedly swallowing down a mouthful of toast, found her pushing her arms into her coat sleeves.

'But what...'

'Have I got enough money for the train?' Ruth delved into the large bag she took with her whenever she went out, and checked the contents of her shabby purse. 'Yes, I have.' She tugged her coat straight, buttoned it, and took her hat from its hook on the coat stand.

'Ruth, the children will be here soon.'

'You must see to them, Morna. I should be back by mid-afternoon.' Ruth fastened her hat to her head with long, sharp hatpins, thrusting each one in with the speed and skill of a magician pushing swords through a box containing his female assistant.

'But I can't teach them anything except painting and music!' Morna wailed, wringing her hands.

'Then let it be a painting and music day.' Ruth opened the door and glanced up at the sky. 'The weather seems to have taken a turn for the better. You can take them into the back garden,' she said, and as she hurried down the steps the next few sentences floated back over her shoulder. 'Anna will help you. You'll manage splendidly, I know. Back in the afternoon.'

Then she was gone, out of the gate and along the road, leaving Morna trembling on the top step.

To Sarah's horror, Walter had shillied and shallied about going to the shop. 'Now that you don't have a nursemaid, it might be best if I stayed here to help you with the child.'

'I can manage very well, Walter, truly I can,' Sarah protested, and he smiled at her, a kindly, patronising smile.

'But you're still very new to motherhood, my dear. Perhaps I should...' he began, and then as Fraser, lying in his mother's arms, turned a deep red colour, frowned massively, and held his breath, concentrating on something important that was going on out of sight of his parents, he asked, 'What's the matter with him? Is he ailing?'

'No, not at all,' Sarah said, and then, as her son gave a satisfied sigh and the deep flush began to ebb, 'but I think I must take him upstairs at once and change his napkin.'

Evidence of the soiled napkin was already beginning to taint the air in the parlour. Walter gave a grimace of distaste. 'On second thoughts, Sarah, I am needed in the shop today. Are you sure you can manage?'

'Quite sure.'

'Send the girl for me, if necessary.'

'I will, Walter,' she said, carrying her smelly bundle out of the door.

'They're in the front parlour, ma'am,' Ena said as she opened the door to Sarah.

'Thank you.' Sarah hesitated as she heard a burst of laughter from behind the varnished panels. She had assumed that by 'they' the maid meant that the woman to be interviewed for the post of nursemaid had already arrived, but mingled with Beatrice McCallum's familiar cackle was the deeper laughter of a man. She turned back to question Ena, but the maid had already bustled off to her kitchen, leaving Sarah with no option but to open the door.

'Ah, there you are, Sarah,' Beatrice greeted her. 'Do you know Mr Gilmartin, who works in Forsyth's shop?'

'We met yesterday, when Mr and Mrs Forsyth brought their son in,' Samuel said as he rose to his feet. 'The image of his father.'

279

'With good fortune he may grow out of that,' Beatrice said dryly, and then, to Sarah, 'Samuel brought me some items from the shop. I would ask you to join us, Samuel, but Mrs Forsyth and I have business to attend to.'

'I must be off in any case. Miss Belle will be wondering where I've got to.'

'Blame me for keeping you back, if you must. Oh – and it would be best if you didn't mention meeting Sarah here this morning.'

'My lips are sealed.' Samuel beamed down at Beatrice. 'Don't trouble your maidservant, Mrs McCallum, I should know my own way out by now. Good morning to you – and to you, Mrs Forsyth.'

'A most agreeable young man,' Beatrice said when they were alone.

'He comes here often?'

'Once a week, for supper. He plays cribbage very well and he has such a cheerful nature. He does me the world of good,' answered Beatrice, who did indeed look more like her former energetic self. 'Tae tell the truth, my dear – and you're the only one who'll understand what I'm sayin', he's a breath of fresh air after dealin' with Hamilton and Walter and Allan Pinkerton. They're all decent upstandin' men, but not one of them with an ounce of humour. Even my own Hector had tae have the stiffness teased out of his soul, bless him. But Samuel's got such an easy manner. Belle's become very dependent on him; she says that he's an efficient assistant.' And then, as the doorknocker was thumped and the little clock on the mantelshelf chimed the hour, 'Ah, that must be Mrs Drummond, exactly on time.'

Leez Drummond was a tall, slender woman, grey haired and neatly dressed.

'So, is this the wee one that's in need of a nursemaid?' she said as soon as she came into the room. 'Come to Leez, my mannie, and let's see what we think of each other.'

Fraser gave an astonished little gasp as the stranger plucked him from his mother's arms without so much as a by-your-leave. He was about to turn his still-bald head in search of Sarah when Leez made a strange clucking, crooning noise in the back of her throat. Curiosity overcoming panic, Fraser looked up at her and was met by a beaming smile. He smiled back and gave a little chuckle, nestling closer to her.

'Well then,' Leez sat herself down, 'that's us introduced and pleased with each other. Now I must meet your mother and find out what she thinks of me.' And giving Fraser a finger to clutch, she turned her warm smile on Sarah. 'Forgive me, Mrs Forsyth, but I've found that if the bairn doesnae care for me there's no sense in wasting the parents' time. You've got a fine wee lad here.'

'I've asked you tae my house, Leez,' Beatrice said, 'because wee Fraser's a firstborn, and Mr Forsyth's no' quite grasped what the bairn and his mother are lookin' for. He's no' very sure what he's looking for himsel', but he doesn't know that.'

'Men folk like tae think that they're in charge,' said Leez, rocking Fraser in the crook of her arm, 'that doesnae worry me.'

'I thought not. Do you have any questions, Sarah?'

'Why are you leaving the people you work for now, Mrs Drummond?'

'My present employer's youngest has just started school and I prefer tae care for younger bairns. They're more interestin'.'

Five minutes later Beatrice said, 'Well I think that's it settled, don't you, Sarah? We'll have a cup of tea to celebrate, if you'll be good enough to ring for Ena.'

'Walter...'

'Leave Walter to me,' Beatrice said blithely. 'I'll write to him this very mornin', tellin' him that I've arranged for a suitable nursemaid to call at the house tomorrow mornin'. Will eleven o'clock suit you, Leez? We'll let him think that he's the one who's hired you, so you and Sarah had best behave as if you've not set eyes on each other before.'

When Leez Drummond had gone Beatrice beamed at Sarah. 'That was a good mornin's work, was it not? You couldnae find a better nurse, Sarah. Be sure to let me know what happens.'

'I will.' Sarah got up and went to lift Fraser, who had fallen asleep in a chair, packed in snugly with cushions. He was sleeping so soundly that he hung bonelessly in her arms, his mouth gaping open. He even slept the same way as Walter, she thought. Aloud, she said, 'I hope we haven't tired you out, Mrs McCallum.'

'On the contrary, you've done me good. Mebbe I should have more visitors,' Beatrice said.

'We'll just have to turn today intae a bit of a

holiday,' Anna said once she'd been told that she and Morna were on their own.

'Send them all home, you mean?'

'No, no,' the woman said, and Morna's heart, which had begun to lift, sank again. 'They'll have tae stay here, but we'll no' be able tae teach the things Miss Dune teaches. Unless you...?'

'I don't know about anything except music and painting.'

'Then we'll spend the first half of the mornin' playin' games in the garden – it's a cold day, but if we keep them runnin' about they'll stay warm enough. And one of the farmers delivered a sack of early Ayrshire potatoes here the other day – I'll boil up a big pot and the bairns can eat them nice and hot for the mornin' break, instead of milk and biscuits. Then before they go home they can all crowd intae your room for some singin'.'

'I don't think I know enough songs.' They were standing in the entrance hall, thigh-deep in a sea of small children, all talking at once; every now and again one of the more exuberant youngsters thumped against an adult leg, causing the owner to sway and stagger slightly.

'Nursery rhymes'll do, and there's always music hall songs. I like the music hall,' Anna said with enthusiasm. 'I can teach them the words if you can thump the tunes out on the piano. I think there's some music in the piano stool; you look while I get them intae the back garden. The games'll help tae wear them out.'

Personally, Morna doubted if anything could tire her small pupils out. She and Anna organised three-legged races, tying stick-thin little ankles together with the children's threadbare scarves and anything else they could find in the house. After that they brought chairs out and set up obstacle races, then played Blind Man's Buff. Then they all trooped into the kitchen, where each child was given a hot potato wrapped in newspaper.

'What can we do next?' Morna whispered to Anna as the children bit into the tasty potatoes.

'Egg and spoon race – there's plenty of spoons in the kitchen.'

'You can't use real eggs!'

'Golf balls,' said the inventive Anna. 'I mind Miss Ruth showin' me a whole drawer full of them and tellin' me that her father was a great golfer. You keep them happy while I fetch the balls and the spoons.'

Morna, digging back into her own childhood, introduced her small pupils to Statues, which they loved. They were all stealing up on her from behind, smothering excited giggles and ready to freeze the instant she turned to face them, when Anna appeared from the back door carrying a large tray laden with spoons of all shapes and sizes, together with a bowlful of golf balls.

'Right, then, the wee-est weans get the biggest spoons and the rest of ye get the small spoons. That'll make it more fair.'

After the race they went into the parlour where Anna led the singing, acting out each song to make the children laugh. Many of the songs were new to Morna, but she did her best to follow them on the piano – although the way the youngsters bawled them out in various keys while spluttering with laughter at Anna's antics, nobody would have noticed if Morna had been playing something entirely different.

'"Onward Christian Soldiers"!' Anna suddenly cried out, and while Morna was thinking how grateful she was to be given a song she could play, the older woman went on, 'Come on, everyone, follow me. You too, Miss Forsyth. The music hall always has a grand finale, and this is ours.'

Singing lustily, she led her little band out of the parlour, along the hall, and into the kitchen. Still singing, she managed to supply every child with a spoon and something to hit with it – pots, kettles, roasting trays, cake trays, pot lids and enamelled bowls – and then led them out to circle the garden like a conga line, bawling the hymn at the top of their voices and beating time on their improvised instruments. Following along, hitting a pot lid with a wooden ladle, Morna glanced up and saw one or two curtains twitching in the adjoining houses. The neighbours would not be best pleased at the din, she thought with a trace of guilt, but she was enjoying herself so much that she dismissed the thought almost at once.

Back in the main classroom the children, flushed with excitement, chattered like a flock of sparrows as Morna and Anna got them into their outdoor clothes. Anna was just saying, 'An orderly line, if you please, two by two,' when the sound of a motor car stopping outside the gate sent the little ones scurrying to the bay window.

Anna followed them, and her hand flew to her mouth. 'It's Miss Durie, and she's got someone with her.'

Morna reached the window in time to see Ruth alighting on to the pavement and then reaching back into the cab. Slowly, carefully, she eased the other passenger out, then as the cab drove off she helped the woman in through the gate.

'I'll put a hot-water bottle in the spare room bed,' Anna said. 'Thank goodness it's kept ready and aired. You go and help, Miss Morna, and you lot,' she added firmly to the children, 'stay in this room and wait for me. Sing "Old MacDonald Had a Farm" – and remember that I'll be listenin', so none of your nonsense.' Starting off the first line of the song as she went, she rushed to the kitchen while Morna went to the front door.

Ruth had managed to half-carry her companion halfway up the path by the time Morna reached them.

'Let me help. Anna's putting a hot-water bottle in the spare bed.'

The woman Ruth had brought back with her was thin, with bowed shoulders. Each step seemed to be too much for her, but with Ruth on one side and Morna on the other they were soon in the hall, which rang with 'Old MacDonald Had a Farm' sung in more keys than Morna had ever thought possible.

'How lovely,' the newcomer said in a thin, exhausted voice, 'to hear bairns sing again.'

'That's our pupils. Into the parlour, I think,' Ruth said. 'You can rest there, Christina, while we get your room ready and the bed warmed.'

'Thank you.' The woman sank gratefully into the depths of a comfortable armchair and smiled up at the two of them. While helping her into the

286

house, Morna had got the impression that she was elderly, but the pale, drawn face looking up at her was quite young.

'Now just you sit there quietly,' Ruth instructed. 'Morna, come and help me, if you will. How did you and Anna get on?' she asked as the two of them went to the kitchen.

'Very well. Anna was so good with them.'

'She always is, bless her. She's been a real tower of strength to me on several occasions. Brandy, I think, with an egg beaten into it, for the moment. Then,' she said over her shoulder as she fetched a glass and the brandy bottle, 'we'll get her upstairs and try her with some soup.'

There were quick heavy steps on the stairs and Anna appeared. 'The bottle's in the bed and I've put a match to the fire. The room should warm up quickly. If you don't need me for anything else, Miss Durie, I'll get that noisy lot home and leave you tae see tae your guest.'

'Thank you, Anna!' Ruth swept her into a warm hug. 'You're a wonder.'

'Och, away wi' ye,' Anna protested, blushing with embarrassment and pleasure. 'I'll see ye both tomorrow, eh?'

Walter insisted on taking time off from the shop to interview the applicant for the post of nurse-maid. 'I don't doubt that you could manage very well on your own, my dear,' he said indulgently, 'but I have no wish to see a nursemaid like the last woman looking after our child. It's better that we interview her together.'

Sarah grew nervous as the time set for Leez

Drummond's arrival came closer. She had set her heart on employing the woman – what if Walter took a dislike to her and the search had to go on?

She jumped when the doorbell jangled and made an instinctive move to answer the summons, but Walter held up an admonishing hand. 'It is no longer your job, Sarah. Let the girl do it, since that's what I pay her for.' And then, drawing his watch from its pocket in his waistcoat, 'She's very prompt – a good beginning.'

Today, Leez had an air of humility and deference. She sat on an upright chair, hands clasped in her lap, meekly answering the questions he fired at her.

'I had to ask our last nursemaid to leave because she insisted on deciding on the way my son was raised,' he said when he had run out of questions. 'I will not be dictated to in my own home with regard to my own child, Mrs Drummond.'

'Indeed, sir, I agreed wholeheartedly. With me, the child's well-being comes first, with the wishes of the parents following closely behind,' Leez said sweetly.

'Well said, Mrs Drummond. You mentioned references?'

'I have references from all my previous employers, including the lady I am working for at present.' Leez delved into her bag and produced some envelopes, tied with a ribbon. 'Not many, as you see, but I tend to stay in each place for a number of years. This creates a stable background for the little ones.' And then, as Walter reached out a hand for the references, 'I wonder – might I see your little boy?'

Sarah, glancing across at her husband and receiving a slight nod, jumped to her feet. 'I'll bring him down.'

When she returned with Fraser in her arms, Walter was still studying the written references, while Leez waited serenely. Her face lit up when the baby was carried into the room. 'May I, Mrs Forsyth?' She held out her arms, and Sarah put the child into them. As she had done before, Leez summoned the clucking, crooning noise from the back of her throat – almost like a contented hen, Sarah thought in wonderment – and as before, Fraser beamed and gave a little chuckle as he nestled against her.

'Now aren't you just the bonniest wee man?' Leez said, and as he cooed his complete agreement with the statement, 'And so like your Papa. You're going to grow up to be very handsome.'

Watching her husband's reaction to the woman's comments, Sarah thought for a moment that he too was going to break into chuckles and crooning, just like his son. But he managed to contain himself, saying only as he put the last of the references back into its envelope, 'You seem to have won his confidence already, Mrs Drummond.'

'He's a lovely little boy, sir, and I would consider it an honour to be entrusted with his care.'

'Then I think the matter is settled, since your references are all excellent. What do you think, my dear?' Walter turned to her wife, as though suddenly remembering her.

'I don't think that Fraser could be in better hands.'

'Then all we need to discuss,' Walter said briskly,

'are your wages and the date on which you can commence employment here, Mrs Drummond.'

'I believe that that woman will do very well as our nursemaid,' he said when Leez had gone. 'She seems biddable and sensible, not like the last nurse at all. She impressed me greatly.'

'And me. Your aunt will be pleased to hear that you approve of her recommendation.' Sarah, who had been practising the long word, said it slowly and carefully.

'Oh, it has little to do with Aunt Beatrice's recommendation – I would certainly not entrust my son to anyone merely because my elderly aunt approves of her.'

'Of course not, Walter.' Sarah smiled down at Fraser, who was now slumbering in her arms and quite unaware of the careful deception that had been played out over his little head.

23

The brandy and raw egg revived Ruth's visitor and enabled her, with help, to go up to the bedroom prepared for her.

'She must have been very ill,' Morna said as she and Ruth went to the kitchen to heat up some soup. 'Has she been in hospital for long?'

'Not hospital, prison.' Ruth gave an amused snort. 'No need to look so shocked, my dear, we're not harbouring a vicious criminal, though most of the members of our learned and respected legal fraternity would have it so.' She began to ladle soup from the large pot into a smaller one, then said in a puzzled tone, 'This little pan has a dent that I haven't seen before.'

'One of the children must have hit it too hard. We were marching around the garden singing "Onward Christian Soldiers" and marking time with spoons and pots.'

'Ah, I see. Would you set that tray for me, please? I think there's a pretty little tray cloth in that drawer, and a napkin.' Ruth indicated the drawer with a jerk of her chin. 'Did the children enjoy themselves?'

'Very much.'

'Good,' Ruth said, stirring the soup.

'What did she – Christina – do?'

'Broke some windows, I think. And no doubt resisted arrest – and why not? Once sentenced and imprisoned in Duke Street she went on a hunger strike as part of her continuing protest, so they began to force-feed her.'

'How do they do that?'

'Several strong warders hold the woman immobile while a tube is forced down her throat and into her stomach. Then food is sent down the tube.'

Morna swallowed hard. 'I would be sick if that happened to me.'

'Being sick is not allowed. They merely pinch your nose and cover your mouth and...' Ruth glanced at her assistant's growing pallor and ended with, 'But enough of that. Our job is to help her to regain her health – beef tea and soups and coddled eggs and jellies. We're going to be busy over the next week or two.' She dipped a spoon into the now-simmering soup, blew lightly on its contents, and then tasted it. 'Ready. Why don't you tidy the classroom in readiness for tomorrow, while I take this up to Christina?'

And, Morna suddenly remembered with a rush of guilt, she must go out to the back garden and hunt for the golf balls that had belonged to Ruth's late father, and were now scattered all over the place.

A week later Christina Baird was well enough to come downstairs. Most of her time for the first few days was spent enjoying the April sun, but after that she began to help Ruth in the classroom. The children took to her at once, the girls describing her as a princess from a fairy story. Morna could understand why, for now that Christina was eating properly and sleeping well, her sky-blue eyes took on a lively sparkle and her small, neat mouth was always ready to curve into an infectious smile. Her thick hair was almost golden and it was easy to believe that should she choose to release it from the hairpins it could tumble down in a shimmering ladder for a prince to climb in order to rescue her from the tower where she was held prisoner.

While she was there, women visited almost every afternoon to sit in the kitchen, discussing meetings past and planning meetings in the future. The entire house seemed to throb and crackle with their energy and enthusiasm, and Morna, awed into shyness by this strong sisterhood, tended to retire to the parlour. But whenever the patchwork quilt was brought out and spread over the table there was no question of her hiding away; for the first time in her life she was singled out for special praise because, the others insisted, she was undeniably the best needlewoman in the group.

It was when she was working with the other quilters that Morna felt that she was part of the sisterhood. The silk quilt, now nearing completion, was made up of squares, oblongs, triangles and diamonds, in all the colours of the rainbow. It seemed to Morna that all the seasons were represented, from autumn's soft browns, golds and beige, through winter's cool strong blues and crisp snowy white and into the greens, fresh blues, pinks, reds and orange of spring and summer, all radiating out from the centre towards the beautifully embroidered silver-beige of the broad border.

The centre itself fascinated her; it consisted of a large diamond bordered in grey and black, broken into four smaller diamonds, two green and two white. Each of the smaller diamonds contained a wheel set against a violet background, and each wheel had a square centre and four triangular spokes, two wheels with green spokes and two with white.

'It's the symbol of the suffragette movement,' one of the needlewomen explained when Morna asked about the central emblem. 'The colours represent our purpose – the G of green also stands for the first letter of Give, the W of white stands for the first letter of Women, and the V of violet shares its first letter with Votes.'

'Some say,' said Christina, stitching a section of

the border, 'that green represents hope, purple – rather than violet – represents dignity, and white stands, of course, for purity in both public and private life.' She smiled warmly at Morna. 'These virtues are what all women, including suffragettes, aim for. Why don't you come to Paisley with us at the end of the month to hear Mrs Pankhurst speak? It's going to be a wonderful event!'

And to her own surprise, Morna agreed.

The sun, just beginning to disappear over Arran, the largest of the offshore islands in the Firth of Clyde, was an iridescent orange ball. As it dipped further, the island's mountain range, known because of its shape as the Sleeping Warrior, was outlined against it in sharp black. The final rays painted the clouds above the island dusky pink and then all at once the sun was gone completely.

The placid stretch of sea between the island and the mainland lost the last of the sun's glittering reflections and adopted instead a mantle of soft grey, broken here and there by black streaks where islets, hidden at high tide, poked their inquisitive heads above the surface.

'This,' Christina said, 'must be one of the most beautiful places on God's earth.'

'Maybe, but if you turn around you'll see the oldest buildings in the town. They should have been pulled down long ago.'

Christina held up an elegant hand in protest. 'My dear Morna, the houses are man's work. Look out over the water – see God's work and let your soul absorb the peace of it. A sight like this just confirms my earnest belief that folk should be like nature – free to grow as they will, and not constrained by man-made laws.'

'But surely we must have laws. Without them we would be little more than heathens.'

'Oh yes, we need some, but only the sensible laws that benefit folk, not those passed by shallow, greedy people who think to protect their own freedom by withholding it from everyone else.'

'I believe that I have as much freedom as I could wish,' Morna protested, and the older woman laughed, slipping a hand through her companion's arm.

'Then I am pleased for you – but there are so many different freedoms, and some folk who should have a fair slice of the cake are fortunate to be thrown a handful of crumbs now and again. Come on, Ruth will be wondering where we are, and it's turning cold now that the sun has gone.'

They were walking towards the Durie house when a man shouted, 'Miss Morna!' and she looked up to see Samuel Gilmartin running down Caledonia Road. The two women paused as he crossed over to where they stood, beaming.

'It's a while since we last met, miss. How are ye?'

'Very well, thank you, Samuel. You look extremely well yourself.'

'I am, thanks to you. Did ye know that I've moved tae new lodgings in Melbourne Terrace? Miss Morna taught me how to count money and give change so that I could obtain work in her family's shop,' he explained to Christina, who was studying him with interest. 'It's because of her that I've gone up in the world, and I'll never forget her for it.'

Morna, astonished at the change in him – the smart suit, the air of confidence where there had once been such despair and bitterness – suddenly remembered her manners. 'This is Samuel Gilmartin,' she told Christina. 'Samuel, this is Mrs Baird, who is staying with us at the moment.'

'How do you do, ma'am.' Samuel whipped off his bowler hat. 'I hope you're enjoyin' your stay in Saltcoats?'

'I am. We've just been down to the shore to watch the sun set,' Christina told him.

'I've been callin' on your aunt, Miss Morna. The two of us enjoy a game of cribbage once a week. I don't know if you've seen her recently?'

'Not recently.' Morna immediately felt guilty; she was so busy these days that she tended to forget that Aunt Beatrice's house was only a few minutes' walk from Ruth's.

'If I could be so bold as to suggest a wee visit...' Samuel's face and voice were solemn now. 'The lady's not been too well this winter and tonight she was coughin' and wheezin' so much that I didnae – didn't,' he corrected himself carefully, 'stay as long as usual. I think she'd a bit of a fever on her too.'

'A personable young man with his fair share of Irish charm,' Christina said when they had parted from Samuel and were continuing their walk to Ruth's house, 'and he's to be admired for making the effort to better himself. But at the same time, there's something about him...'

'What sort of something?'

'If I were you, my dear, I'd not put my full trust

296

in him.'

'You think he might take money from the shop?'

'I doubt if he would be so foolish as to bite the hand that feeds him. When I warned you not to put too much trust in him I meant in other ways,' Christina said, and then, with a quick laugh, 'but perhaps I'm just suspicious of all men these days!'

Women were converging from all directions on Paisley's Clark Town Hall when Morna, Ruth and Christina arrived from the nearby railway station. A large number of women had got off their train when it reached Paisley, all bound for the same destination.

The hall was packed, and when Morna commented on the smattering of men among the ranked women, Ruth said, 'There are many men sympathetic to our cause and interested in attending meetings.' Then, with a slight hardening to her voice, 'But our gatherings also attract men opposed to us getting the vote for some reason they have yet to explain.'

'Perhaps that's because they can't. Come along...' Christina drew her companions over to one of the tables set to the side. They were stacked with literature as well as lapel badges, and judging from the queues at every table, they were doing brisk business.

'Don't you already have a badge?' Morna whispered to Ruth.

'Yes, but this one belongs to the night Mrs Pankhurst came to talk to us. In any case, the movement needs all the money it can get.'

'The badge is certainly pretty,' Morna conceded as she pinned hers to the lapel of her jacket. It was in the suffragette colours – green, white and violet – and she felt quite proud to be wearing it in the company of women from all walks of life. The entire hall, and the front of the stage, was draped with banners and ribbons in the same three colours.

Just as they took their seats four neatly dressed women walked on to the platform and a wave of applause from the front rows was quickly taken up by row after row until the entire hall was filled with it. One of them stepped up to the lectern and waited calmly for the applause to end.

'Is that Mrs Pankhurst?' Morna whispered to Ruth.

'No, it's Dr Katharine Chapman; she's in the chair for tonight.'

Dr Chapman opened the meeting. When she began to speak there was none of the shouting and lectern-thumping that Morna had expected; instead, her audience listened intently as, in a clear, carrying voice, she spoke of the aims of the Women's Social and Political Union, organisers of that evening's meeting. The next speaker was both witty and perceptive; Morna found herself following and agreeing with every word, and she joined in the delighted howl of laughter when, in answer to a male voice shouting from the back of the hall, 'What you women need's a man!' the speaker said sweetly, 'If you find one, sir, you might be gracious enough to introduce him to me.'

When she sat down there was a sudden, excited

hush as the chairwoman stepped forward to introduce Mrs Emmeline Pankhurst on her first visit to Paisley. As the main speaker, a straight-backed woman with great elegance in the way she moved and spoke, took her place the applause rose to the very rafters.

When Mrs Pankhurst sat down after a rousing and impassioned speech Morna joined in the applause, clapping so hard that her hands glowed as though she had been nursing hot coals all evening. Even so, they could not match the glow in her heart and mind as she went from the hall to the street, determined to pick up the cause of the suffragette movement and make it her own. She vowed to read all the literature piled on Ruth's kitchen table, and to march proudly through the streets, proclaiming her belief in votes for women in ringing tones.

She also resolved to visit Aunt Beatrice the very next day to tell her all about the meeting. At last, she thought as she, Ruth and Christina were swept towards the railway station in a tide of excited, chattering women, Aunt Beatrice would be proud of her, instead of looking on her as a silly young girl fit only for marriage.

'I am going to join the Union,' she was announcing to her friends when suddenly they found themselves surrounded by a group of men who had been lying in wait. Morna was buffeted here and there, then a hand snatched the hat from her head, the pins pulling cruelly at the roots of her hair as they were wrenched free.

'Give it back!' She reached for her hat and the man who had taken it held it high above his head, laughing at her. 'Give it back, give it back,' he mocked. 'If ye think ye're good enough tae vote like a man ye should surely be ready tae fight like one. Come and get yer bunnet, hen!'

Just then someone fell violently against her back, sending her forwards into her tormentor's arms. He, too, was caught off balance, but grabbed at her outstretched arm and swung her round against a nearby wall. Pain burned through her cheek as it was scraped along the stonework and then she was grabbed again. This time her back thumped into the wall. Hair loosened by her struggles fell into her eyes but through its curtain she could see her captor's face and his triumphant grin, revealing several gaps where he had lost front teeth. His breath smelled of beer and his hands dug into her shoulders, pinning her helplessly against the wall.

Morna, aware that she was in real danger, kicked out at the man but felt the side of her booted heel slide harmlessly past his leg. His grin broadened and then gave way to an expression of astonishment as his body shuddered violently. Releasing Morna, he let out a bellow of rage and began to turn away from her; then she saw him toppling to one side, his arms windmilling in a futile effort to keep his balance. One of them flailed across her midriff, winding her, but as she doubled over, a hand caught her elbow and Ruth's voice said in her ear, 'Come on – quickly!'

Morna was dragged through the struggling crowd and then she and Ruth had broken free. Christina appeared from nowhere and took Morna's other arm. 'Straighten up,' she said with quiet urgency. 'Walk quickly, but as though there's nothing wrong.'

Whistles were shrilling behind them, and Morna could still hear the clamour of voices. 'My hat…'

'I have it here. We'll stop when we get to the railway station and make ourselves respectable,' Ruth said. 'But for now, we must hurry!'

Once the noise of battle faded behind them they withdrew up a dank close where they smoothed their hair as best they could and tidied their clothing. Morna made a valiant attempt to put her hat back on, but her hands were shaking so badly that Christina had to do it for her.

While the train rattled through the night and the other two discussed the meeting, declaring it to be a resounding success, Morna stared out of the window, though there was nothing to see now apart from her own pale smudge of a face reflected in the glass. Her mind, which had been filled with such feelings of excitement and exhilaration as she left the meeting, rang with the noise of feet scuffling, women gasping with pain and deep voices grunting filthy accusations. Her cheek, red and scraped, with a dank bruise beginning to form along the cheekbone, was throbbing and so was her head. She felt as though she were in the grip of a fever.

Even when she was back in Saltcoats Morna did not feel safe. She doubted that she would ever feel safe again.

'Why were those men so vicious?' she asked when they were back in Ruth's cluttered kitchen, drinking cocoa. 'Why did they attack us when we had done nothing to hurt them?'

'Some men only feel like men when they have someone to dominate,' Christina said calmly. 'They think we threaten their very existence because we ask for a right that has until now been theirs and not ours. The men you met tonight are frightened because they think we are invading their world.'

Morna felt that she was far more frightened than the men could ever be. 'I don't know what would have happened if you hadn't helped me, Ruth. How did you do it?'

'I jabbed him in the rump with a hatpin. Always have more pins in your hat than you need when you go to a meeting. When he turned to see what was happening I pulled on his arm while he was off-balance then put my foot against his ankle and down he went. It's a useful trick that my brother Tom taught me when we were children.'

'As you see, Morna,' Christina chimed in, 'we have in our midst a woman who can defeat a man with a mere hatpin.'

She and Ruth started to laugh and Morna joined in. It seemed like the most amusing thing she had ever heard, but when the others stopped laughing she went on and on until all at once her laughter turned into sobs, with tears pouring down her face and dripping off her chin.

'Brandy, I think,' she heard Ruth say crisply, and then someone thrust a handkerchief into her hand, while a mug held by Ruth clattered slightly against her teeth. 'Take a sip,' she was ordered, and while she was still grimacing over the fiery liquid's invasion, 'and another – go on, now.'

When the sobs had slowed to a series of hiccups

Ruth said, 'And now, my dear Morna, you're going to your bed. You've had more than enough excitement for today.'

24

Morna fell asleep as soon as her head touched her pillow and woke in the morning to hear Ruth and Christina going down to the kitchen. She peered into the mirror above her chest of drawers and saw that her hair was tangled, her face bruised and her eyes still swollen from the previous night's fit of weeping.

It all came back to her, more like a nightmare than a real happening, as she rinsed her face again and again in cold water, brushed her hair ruthlessly until she had managed to straighten out all the knots, and dressed.

'I am so sorry,' she said as she joined the other two at the table.

'About what?' Ruth wanted to know. She and Christina looked as fresh as daisies.

'About the way I behaved last night. Why can't I be more like you?' Morna wailed, tears beginning to well up in her eyes again.

'Because you're not us and we're not you, and thank the Lord for that. It would be a very drab world indeed if we were all alike. Morna, my dear,' said Ruth gently, 'your heart is in the right place but the rough and tumble of the movement is not for you. Not yet, at any rate. There are other ways in which you can help us if you so wish, and one of them is to eat your breakfast, for Anna and the children will be here soon.'

'But what will I tell the children when they ask about my face? You know how inquisitive they can be.'

'Tell them that you walked into a door,' Christina advised, and then, her voice suddenly flat, 'it is what women with bruised faces always say – and they are always believed, for there are times when nobody wants to know the truth.'

She got up to answer a knocking at the door.

'Did her husband...?'

'We all have our private lives, and friends never intrude into each other's,' Ruth was saying when Christina came back into the kitchen.

'It was a wee ragamuffin of a lad with a letter for you, Morna.'

'For me?' Morna unfolded the sheet of paper and scanned the few lines; when she looked up at the other two the bruise stood out sharply against her paper-white skin.

'It's from my sister Belle. I must go at once to my aunt's house,' she said, and then, unable to believe what she was saying, even though she heard the words being uttered aloud, 'Aunt Beatrice is dead.'

'I can't imagine a world without Aunt Beatrice in it,' Morna said an hour later. She and her brother and sister were in Beatrice's parlour; Ena, red-eyed, had retired to her kitchen. 'I always thought she would go on for ever.'

'It's as if the life has gone out of the place,' Walter said uneasily, running a finger round the inside of his collar to ease the choking sensation he had had since arriving at his aunt's house.

'It has.' Belle's voice was bleak. 'Only yesterday morning she seemed to be getting better. Ena says that that often happens to folk. One last surge of energy before the... Morna,' Belle said sharply, as her sister leaned forwards to put her untasted tea down and what little light was allowed into the curtained room fell on her bruised cheek, 'what has happened to your face?'

'I walked into a door. Is that Juliet I can hear upstairs?' The faint keening was so desolate that it sent shivers down her spine.

'She's outside Aunt Beatrice's door and nothing we do will coax her to come away.'

'Was it... Was Aunt Beatrice...?' Morna paused, and Belle said reassuringly, 'She just slipped away early this morning.'

'I'm glad of that.'

'Did she say anything about the house?' Walter wanted to know

'Only that it was too warm, so we opened the window a little at the top. That was around two o'clock. We set a screen between the window and the bed, so the little bit of fresh air can't have harmed–'

'I meant, Belle, did she say anything about who was to get the house?'

'For goodness' sake, Walter, do you think that I sat by her sickbed chatting to her about her will?'

'She did make one, I suppose?'

'That,' Belle said coldly, 'is a matter for her lawyer, not for us.'

'As her nearest kin–'

'Surely the first thing to be done is to arrange the funeral and then put a notice in the newspapers.'

'I will see to that.' He got up and started to pace the floor, stopping now and again to examine an ornament or a painting. 'It will take me away from the shop, of course, and so I would be grateful, Belle, if you would look after it.'

'I have been doing that since your marriage, Walter,' she said dryly, but the faint sarcasm was lost on him.

'Who is looking after it now, with you and I both here?'

'Samuel Gilmartin. I sent a message to his lodgings first thing this morning to tell him what had happened, and to entrust the running of Forsyth's to him for the time being.'

'But Mr Stoddart is the senior shop assistant!'

'Mr Stoddart has not been at work for almost a week. He has a bad chill.'

'There are others – Gilmartin has only been with us for a matter of months.'

'Walter, he already knows more about the running of the place than...' Belle, grieving for the aunt she had come to care for and tired after a night spent watching over Beatrice, only just managed to bite back the words 'than you do' and said instead, '...than any of the others. He learns very quickly and never forgets anything. And he is entirely trustworthy, I can assure you.'

'I certainly hope so. Can't you do anything about that noise?' Walter asked as the keening from above rose to a long drawn-out howl of anguish. 'It's sending shivers down my spine.'

'I'll try to coax her out into the back garden.'

'And I,' Walter said briskly, anxious to get out of this house of death, 'will start seeing to my duties.'

'Aunt Beatrice had already attended to most of the arrangements.' Belle unlocked a drawer in the desk and handed him a sheaf of papers. 'Here is the notice she wants put into the local papers, and the order of service for her funeral, the list of people to be notified and the list of mourners to be invited back to the house, together with instructions as to the refreshments to be served. Ena and I will see to that – with your assistance, I hope, Morna? And she has also left instructions as to the disposal of her clothing and personal belongings.'

'Oh,' Walter said. Even in death, it seemed that Aunt Beatrice was still head of the Forsyth family.

'I shall miss Aunt Beatrice,' Morna said again when Walter had gone and the sisters were alone.

'So will I. Since Father left us she has become my family.'

'You still have me – and Walter.'

'Walter,' Belle pointed out, 'has got Sarah and their child.'

'Indeed, but he is still our brother, and we still have each other. Perhaps,' Morna said, 'it is time for us to become a family again.'

Beatrice McCallum had been a well-known Salt-coats resident and on the day of her funeral the North Parish Church was filled to capacity. The Forsyth shop had been closed so that the staff could pay their last respects, but only one of them – Samuel Gilmartin – had been included on Beatrice's list of mourners to be invited back to the house.

'What is he doing here?' Walter muttered to Belle as the parlour rapidly filled.

'He's been very attentive towards Aunt Beatrice in the past few months. She taught him to play cribbage and they played every week. Do you know how to play cribbage, Walter?'

'If he thinks that he can go ingratiating himself into my family he must be made to think again!'

'Mr Gilmartin has been of considerable assistance to me, particularly over the past week,' Belle retorted sharply.

Sarah, who had opted to help Ena rather than be left standing in a corner, was carrying a large tray of sandwiches into the parlour when Samuel appeared before her.

'Allow me, Mrs Forsyth.' If he had not taken the tray from her, she would almost certainly have dropped it.

'What are you doing here?'

'I'm here by invitation. Mrs McCallum was a charming lady who will be greatly missed.' He put the tray on the table and turned to smile down at her. 'If I may be permitted to say so, Mrs Forsyth, you look very elegant. Mourning becomes you, which is more than can be said for many of the ladies in our company.' His voice was low and intimate, but even so Sarah found herself glancing round guiltily to make sure that they were not overheard before she replied, her voice trembling, 'And you look very fine, Samuel.'

'The clothes maketh the man.' He raised an eyebrow at her. 'Who'd have thought, in the old days, that the two of us would end up like this?'

'Do you ever think of those days, Samuel?' she asked with sudden yearning. 'Do you ever think of what we meant to each other?'

'Now what sort of a question is that for a respectable married woman to be askin' of one of her husband's employees?' he enquired silkily. 'It would be improper of me to allow myself tae think of my employer's wife in such a way. And improper of you to give a thought to a man who's not your husband.'

'I *do* think of you, though, and I wish–'

'Samuel,' Belle Forsyth called at that moment, and he looked over at her before turning back to Sarah. 'The thing is,' he said, lowering his voice to a whisper, 'Miss Belle keeps me so busy that I scarce have time to think of any thing or any one else. Is that not a mercy for both of us?'

Then he had gone, and in the space left by his body Sarah saw her husband watching her. He beckoned her over with an imperceptible tilt of the head.

'What did Gilmartin want with you?' he asked as she reached his side.

'He was expressing his condolences to the family.'

'Hmmm. I don't know why Belle allowed his name to be added to the list of invited guests. She should never have let Aunt Beatrice make such a pet of the man,' he said, and then paused. She could tell what was happening by his sudden, slight wince and the small movements of his mouth.

'Is that tooth troubling you again?'

'Just a little. These biscuits Belle is serving are

309

too sweet. The sugar is not good for anyone's teeth.'

'You should go to the dentist, Walter.'

'Nonsense, there's nothing wrong that a little oil of cloves can't...' he had begun when a slender, black-gloved hand landed on his arm and Clarissa Pinkerton said, 'Walter, my dear, I would have come to you as soon as I heard the sad news, but Mama felt that it was best to leave the family to themselves until the funeral.'

'You were always considerate, Clarissa. You know my wife, don't you?'

'Of course. How are you, Mrs Forsyth?' Clarissa asked sweetly, her grey eyes, which had been looking warmly into Walter's face, suddenly as cold as pebbles on the bed of a winter stream.

'I am very well, thank you, Miss Pinkerton. I trust that you are well yourself?'

'I am always well. Walter, I hope that you intend to take up tennis again this summer...' Clarissa turned towards him so that Sarah was excluded. Sarah hesitated for a moment, uncertain as to what to do; then Morna, who had been watching, came over.

'Sarah, come and tell me how my nephew is doing.' She linked her hand through the crook of Sarah's elbow and drew her to one side. 'My aunt told me when I last saw her that you have a new nursemaid. I hope that she is suitable.'

'Very suitable, thank you, Miss Morna.'

'I think you should call me Morna, since we are sisters now. I may not have behaved like a sister since your marriage,' Morna forged on as Sarah stared at her, open-mouthed, 'but I have changed, truly I have. You mustn't let Clarissa hurt you; she can be quite a cat when the mood takes her. To tell you the truth, I have come to believe that Walter is better off with you for his wife, since Clarissa's ambitions might've made his life quite miserable.'

'You must miss your aunt very much,' Ruth was saying to Belle.

'I had come to treasure her company, and now she has gone. Life will be quite lonely without Aunt Beatrice.'

'I hope that you will come to visit Morna and me whenever you feel lonely. My house is only a short distance away, and I know that she would be happy to see you. So would I – it's time we got to know each other.'

Belle looked doubtfully into Ruth's piercing blue eyes and decided that the woman was not just being courteous for Morna's sake. She was not the type to say what she did not mean.

'Thank you,' she said, 'I would like that very much.'

'This,' Beatrice McCallum's lawyer said as he settled himself at the dining-room table, 'is a particularly sad time.' He smoothed his black tie and then glanced down at the black band on his sleeve. 'First Mrs McCallum, a well-respected client for many years, and then this morning's tragic news of the death of our beloved king.'

'Yes indeed.' Walter, who also sported a black tie and band, bowed his head for a moment, then lifted it to glare at Morna when she remarked, 'The king is dead, long live the king.'

311

'Morna!'

'Isn't that what they say? Surely I am only wishing King George a long and healthy reign,' she protested.

The lawyer coughed behind his hand and then rustled the papers before him. 'Yes indeed, Miss Forsyth, a laudable comment. Now then, as to your aunt's will...'

Beatrice had left one thousand pounds each to Walter and Morna, five hundred pounds each to her housekeeper Ena, Sarah, her great-nephew Fraser Walter Forsyth and to an organisation for homeless animals. Her house and contents, together with the remainder of her estate, went to Belle, along with the request that she continue to provide a comfortable and loving home for Juliet.

'How much is the rest of the estate?' Walter wanted to know as the lawyer finished reading out the will and folded his podgy hands together on the table.

'Miss Forsyth?' the man asked Belle, and then, when she gave a dazed nod, 'Approximately four thousand and nine hundred pounds.'

Walter's mouth opened and shut, making him look like a fish cast up on a riverbank and gasping for air, then he managed to say, 'Almost five thousand pounds? All for Belle? Are you quite sure?'

'Mrs McCallum brought her will up to date two months ago, Mr Forsyth, and she was most definite about every part of it.' The man smiled at Belle, who looked as stunned as her brother. 'I understand that she appreciated Miss Forsyth's companionship and was anxious that her niece would not be left homeless after her death.'

'Well,' Walter said when the lawyer had left them, 'you've landed on your feet, Belle.'

'I can assure you that I had no idea that Aunt Beatrice had left me anything.'

'She's been very generous towards you. I suppose that I should be grateful that she left me anything at all,' Walter's voice was sour. 'And at least she remembered my son – though why on earth she should include you, Sarah, I cannot imagine.'

'You have the business, Walter, and the family house,' Morna pointed out. 'It's true that Belle might have been left homeless if Aunt Beatrice had left her house to anyone else, or directed that it should be sold.'

'You have no home of your own either, but she didn't think of that, did she?'

'She left me a considerable sum of money, and I am grateful because I have done nothing to deserve it, while Belle has been a good companion and comfort to Aunt Beatrice for the past six months or more. And I know that Ruth will allow me to share her home for as long as I please. I am very happy there.'

Belle had supplied tea for herself and her sister and sister-in-law. Walter had opted for a glass of Beatrice's malt whisky– 'Though now, Belle, it is your whisky,' he had said with a cutting edge to his voice. He now drained the final drops from the glass, tilting his head in order to allow the spirits to bathe his bad tooth, which had begun to ache again, then set the empty glass down, saying, 'Come, Sarah, we must go home. Will you be in the shop tomorrow, Belle, or are you too grand to be involved in anything as mundane as trade now?'

'You know perfectly well that I will be there tomorrow morning as usual,' Belle said calmly, but once he and Sarah had left, she sank into a chair and pressed a handkerchief to her mouth.

'Oh, Morna,' she said in a muffled voice, 'it seems so unfair that Aunt Beatrice should leave me more than you and Walter!'

'Nonsense, you've been a great comfort to her since you moved here. You are more than entitled to your inheritance.'

'But Walter–'

'Bother Walter! You know what he's like – what he has always been like. Even when we were children Walter expected the lion's share of everything, and he usually got it, being the only boy. It's time he grew up.'

'I could always share out the money between the three of us.'

'And have Aunt Beatrice coming back to haunt you because you went against her express wishes? Certainly not,' Morna said briskly. 'I for one would not thank you for it – I don't know what I'll do with the thousand I have now. Consult Mr Pinkerton, I suppose, then put it into a bank account and forget it until such time as I might have need of it. Don't you realise, Belle, that this is the first time you have ever gained anything for yourself? Walter was given preference because he was the only son, while our parents made a lot of fuss over me just because I happen to be the baby of the family – and I'm not going to pretend that I didn't like it, for I did, but you were always expected to be sensible and undemanding

314

because you were the oldest. You're the one who runs the shop – if it were dependent on Walter we would have gone bankrupt by now. Aunt Beatrice has probably known the truth all along – and known that her money is safer in your hands than in Walter's, or mine.'

'You've changed so much since Papa left, Morna.'

'I have, haven't I?' Morna agreed, with a pleased smile. 'A year ago I would have rushed off to Glasgow and spent that thousand pounds on clothes and jewellery. Now these things don't seem to matter nearly as much as they once did. Let's ask Ena for a fresh pot of tea, shall we?'

As his sisters settled down to more tea, Walter was saying to his wife, 'I shall look after your inheritance, my dear, since you know nothing about money other than the housekeeping allowance. My aunt has been most generous towards you.'

'Most generous,' Sarah agreed, still unable to believe her inheritance. Suddenly, she was rich beyond her wildest dreams. If only, she thought as Walter held the gate open for her, and then followed her up the garden path, she had had that sum a year earlier. Samuel would have been happy to marry her and they could have afforded a nice place to stay. But on the other hand, she reminded herself as Nellie opened the door, she had only been left the money because she was Walter's wife. And she would far, far rather have Mrs McCallum, with her kindness and her words of reassurance and wisdom, than all the money in the kingdom.

25

That evening, while Morna listened to the spirited talk of the women gathered around Ruth's kitchen table and stitched at her section of the almost-completed suffragette quilt, and Walter sat at his desk in Argyle Road, chin on hand, trying to look as though he was lost in thought when in actual fact he was nursing his throbbing back tooth, Ena showed Samuel Gilmartin into the parlour where Belle Forsyth awaited him.

'You wanted to see me, Miss Forsyth?'

'Yes, Mr Gilmartin. Please sit down.' Belle indicated one of the two chairs drawn up before the fire. He moved towards it, but remained standing, one hand resting on the back of the chair. 'Ena is bringing tea, but perhaps you would prefer a glass of whisky?'

'Tea would be very pleasant, thank you.' Samuel waited until his hostess had seated herself before taking his own seat opposite her. 'How are you, Miss Forsyth?'

'Very well, thank you – considering the circumstances.'

His brown eyes, soft and warm, met and held hers, and she was soothed by their concern. 'It's a sad time for you – for all of us,' he said as Ena brought in the tea tray and set it on a small table close to Belle's chair. Juliet had come in with the maid; she hurried over to Samuel, who made a

316

fuss of her and her little body squirmed with pleasure.

'Behave yourself, Juliet,' Belle told her.

'She's missing her mistress.'

'I know she is, but even so – take her back into the kitchen, Ena, or we shall get no peace to take our tea.'

'I wonder,' Samuel said as Belle poured tea, 'if I might be permitted to wash my hands in the kitchen?'

'Use the bathroom upstairs. The first door at the top of the stairs.'

'The kitchen will do me fine, Miss Forsyth.'

'The bathroom,' Belle said sweetly but firmly, 'is for the use of guests, and you are a guest. The first door at the top of the stairs.'

'Thank you.' He went out and all at once Belle felt as though the room had changed. It lacked the warmth that had been there only a moment before. She shivered slightly, wondering if she had caught a chill, and wrapped both hands around her teacup for comfort.

Samuel took his time as he went up the flight of stairs so thickly carpeted that it was like walking on soft moss. The bathroom door stood half-open while the other doors around the landing were firmly closed. He knew what lay behind only one of them – Beatrice McCallum's bedroom, where he had visited the old lady in the final weeks of her life.

The water was hot and the soap smelled of flowers. He washed his hands several times, revelling in the unaccustomed comfort, before drying them on a thick, absorbent towel. Then he looked into the oval, wood-framed mirror on the wall to make sure that not a hair was out of place. On his way back downstairs he dared to touch the raised flock wallpaper with the back of one finger.

'Will you take a rock cake?' Belle asked as he sat down opposite her.

'Thank you.' The cake was home-made, crisp on the outside and soft inside, but Samuel scarcely tasted it. He was hungry for more than rock cakes; he was hungry for a life that included soft carpets and chairs, hot water and scented soap and flock wallpaper. He was hungry for a life far better than any he had ever known.

'I will miss your aunt,' he said. 'She was very good to me.'

'To all of us. How are things at the shop?'

'Going smoothly. You have a good, loyal staff.'

'I'll be in tomorrow.'

'Are you sure, Miss Forsyth?' Samuel stirred his tea carefully, so as not to spill any into the pretty saucer. 'Should you not take a wee while off to recover from your loss? I can keep an eye on things and visit regularly to report on how business is doing.'

'It's kind of you, but I would rather keep myself occupied.' She put her cup down and picked up an envelope from the small table by her chair. 'My aunt asked me to give this to you.'

'To me?' He took the envelope and turned it over, studying his name printed in strong, bold characters. 'What is it?'

'It's for you, not me. I know nothing about the contents.' Belle had placed a silver paperknife beside the envelope; now she held it out to him. 'You can open it now, if you wish.'

'Thank you.' He accepted the knife, beautifully made in the form of a tiny sword with an enamelled handle, and slit the envelope open neatly. Then he gave a soft exclamation as several notes slid out into his palm. 'It's – fifty pounds! Miss Forsyth, I can't accept this!'

'If my aunt meant it for you, then it's yours, Mr Gilmartin.' Belle was smiling now, flushed with pleasure at his almost childlike astonishment. 'Is there nothing else?'

Carefully laying the notes aside, he dipped a finger into the envelope and withdrew a folded sheet of paper. 'With your permission...?'

'Of course.' Belle made a display of selecting a biscuit and taking another sip of tea, watching him over the rim of her cup as he read the letter. After a moment, he glanced up at her.

'It's – it is a very kind letter. Would you like to read it?' He held it out, and she recoiled as though he had offered her a poisonous snake.

'It's your letter, Mr Gilmartin. I would not dream of reading it.'

'Oh. Well, she says that she appreciated my visits and my company, and she asks...' he hesitated and bit his lip before carrying on almost shyly, '...and she asks that I continue to be your friend as I was hers, and to assist you if you ever need my help. As of course I will, with all my heart.'

Belle coloured slightly. 'I certainly hope that we will continue to be friends and that you will call on me again.'

'I would be honoured.' He gathered up the

notes, folded them, and then paused. 'Are you quite sure that it's in order for me to accept this?'

'Of course. I know that my aunt would want you to gain some enjoyment from it,' Belle said, and was taken aback when his eyes grew moist.

'Mrs McCallum was an angel of a woman,' he said with a tremor in his voice, 'and I consider myself blessed among men for having known her.' Then, getting to his feet, 'If you'll forgive me, Miss Forsyth, I must be on my way now.'

She had hoped that he would stay a little longer, but she could not possibly say so. 'Of course.' She got to her feet and took his proffered hand; then was taken aback for the second time as he lifted her fingers to his lips. 'I hope you're not offended, Miss Forsyth,' he said when he had released her hand, 'but since I can no longer salute your aunt it gives me great comfort to be able to thank her niece, who has also shown me such trust and kindness.'

When he had gone Belle sat on in the parlour for some time, smiling at the curtains drawn across the windows and occasionally stroking the back of her hand, where the skin still tingled from the soft but firm touch of his lips.

Outside the house, Samuel put his bowler hat on his head at a jaunty angle, patted the pocket that held the envelope and all its contents, and set off towards his new lodgings in Melbourne Terrace at a fast pace.

Once in his snug little room he took Beatrice McCallum's envelope from his breast pocket and opened it. Inviting Belle Forsyth to read it had been a gamble that had paid off. The combination of luck and quick thinking that had stood him in good stead so far had not let him down; he had been right when he guessed that women of Belle's social standing would never read other people's letters. He smoothed the single page out lovingly, then read it aloud slowly, line by line.

Dear Mr Gilmartin,
I hope that you'll accept the enclosed sum in appreciation of our enjoyable meetings and our games of cribbage. You are a swift learner, as I already knew from the way you have settled in at the family shop. One of the reasons why I've enjoyed your company so much is that to my mind, Mr Gilmartin, you are a bit of a rogue and a rebel, and I have always had a soft spot for men like yourself. My own late husband was certainly a rebel, though never to my knowledge a rogue.
I trust that as well as showing my appreciation, the money enclosed will assist you to travel further afield than Saltcoats, so that you may begin to seek the fortune that you will surely find one day. But you should not seek it here, and not at the expense of my nephew or, especially, my niece Belle. She trusts too easily, and as she is content in her own quiet way I would not want to see her life disrupted. I am sure that you understand my meaning, and believe me when I say that my best wishes go on your travels with you.
Beatrice McCallum.

'You were a grand woman, Beatrice McCallum,' Samuel said aloud, 'and I'm grateful for the money. You're quite right when you say that it will take me to better things. But I've no need tae

321

leave Saltcoats tae find my future. It's right here, and almost ripe for the takin'.'

He crumpled up the letter and held it to the gas fire until it caught alight, waiting until it was burned almost to the corner gripped between his thumb and forefinger before allowing the ashes to drop on to the hearth. Then he took the notes from the envelope and counted them slowly several times. Finally, he folded them over and clenched his fist around them.

Fifty pounds was a fortune, more money than he had ever dreamed of possessing in his lifetime. He could almost feel the notes glowing against his palm, clamouring to be spent. But Samuel Gilmartin was not going to give in to temptation. Everything he needed and wanted was now within his reach, and soon it would be grasped as closely as the money in his fist.

Morning classes were halfway through and the children were enjoying their milk and biscuits out in the sun-splashed back garden when the police came for Christina Baird.

'I'll go,' Morna said when a thunderous knocking was heard from the front of the house, but Ruth put a hand on her arm.

'Best if I go, Morna.' Her voice was quiet, and she and Christina exchanged glances. Christina nodded, and went quickly into the kitchen. Another volley of blows on the front door almost drowned out the sound of her footsteps going up the staircase.

'Ruth...' Morna stared at her friend, a chill beginning to trickle down her spine.

'It's all right, just leave it to me.' Ruth left the garden and Morna followed her as far as the kitchen door, where she hesitated, unwilling to go any further and yet not knowing what she feared.

The door opened to reveal two large policemen silhouetted against the brightness of the day. 'I believe that Mrs Christina Baird resides here, ma'am,' Morna heard one of them say.

'Yes, she's been unwell and I have been nursing her back to health.'

'I have a warrant here for her arrest. She must come with us to serve the rest of a sentence imposed on her by the Glasgow magistrates.'

'She is still not strong enough...' Ruth began, while Morna became aware of a soft murmuring and realised that small bodies were pressing against her legs. Some stared at the policemen in silence, grubby little fingers stuffed into their mouths, while others hid their faces in her skirt. One of the littlest children began to whimper, and Morna picked her up and held her close.

'The magistrates say that she *is* strong enough, ma'am. It is understood that Mrs Baird attended a meeting in Paisley recently.'

'Yes, she did, but that–'

'If you do not ask Mrs Baird to come to the door, ma'am, then we have been empowered under the terms of the warrant to enter these premises and–'

'That will not be necessary, Constable,' Christina said quietly from the foot of the stairs. She was dressed in her outdoor clothes and carried a bag that must have been packed earlier, in readiness. 'I am prepared to accompany you,' she said, then turned and smiled at Morna and the children. 'Be good, little ones,' she said, and then, to Morna more than the others, 'and be happy.'

She walked to the doorway where she and Ruth embraced briefly before Christina went out onto the top step. The police officers immediately moved to either side of her.

'Morna, take the children into your room, if you please,' Ruth ordered, 'and let them sing.'

'Come along, quickly.' Morna swept the little ones into the room and closed the door before hurrying to the bay window. A police van stood at the kerb, with yet another policeman waiting at the open back doors. A few passers-by had stopped to stare as Christina, as straight as a ramrod and tiny between the burly uniformed men, walked down the garden path.

'"Onward Christian Soldiers",' Morna said, setting down her tearful burden and opening one of the windows wide. 'We don't need the piano, do we? And we must sing it as loud as we can, so that Mrs Baird hears every word! One, two, three...'

She started singing, clapping time, and the children quickly joined in, their voices struggling at first and then gaining in power. They all stood by the window, watching as Christina reached the back of the van. She turned and smiled towards the front door, where Ruth must still be standing, and gave a little wave of the hand. Then she looked at the window, and this time her smile was broad and her wave a triumphant, farewell flourish. They all waved back, the song swelling, bursting out through the open window and pouring down the path to where, with fairly gentle assistance from the policemen, Christina Baird was clambering into the back of the van. As the doors closed one of the older children yelped, 'Sing louder, you lot, so's she can hear us!' and the children, abandoning their efforts to keep in tune, yelled the last verse at the top of their young lungs, some of them leaning out of the window to screech the final words as the van drove off.

Ruth clapped loudly from the back of the room as they finished. 'Well done, everyone,' she said, her mouth smiling and unshed tears sparkling like diamonds in her lovely dark blue eyes. 'The best singing I have ever heard. But now it's time to get back to our lessons.'

'Walter, you must have that tooth seen to.' Sarah picked up the current edition of the *Ardrossan & Saltcoats Herald,* which she had folded open at a prominent advertisement. 'Mr James Walker of Dockhead Street sounds very good. It says here, "It Don't Hurt a Bit".'

'It wouldn't hurt him, would it? He's the dentist, not the patient.'

'I doubt if he would claim not to hurt you if he intended to hurt you,' Sarah said, thrusting the paper at Walter, who had no option but to take it and read the advertisement. 'I have decided that I will call on him this morning to make an appointment for you.'

'But it's just the occasional twinge. All it needs is oil of cloves now and again.'

'Walter, your face is swollen and you and I are both suffering from lack of sleep. And so is poor Nellie, after being dragged from her bed at all

325

hours to make up hot poultices.' Sarah had never spoken so firmly to her husband before, but five nights of being wakened by Walter tossing and turning or pacing the floor and moaning quietly to himself had driven her to distraction. In any case, although she had no idea where he had invested her inheritance from Beatrice, and indeed, had never even seen the money, just knowing that she was now a woman of means had given her new strength and determination.

'I am not a child, Sarah. I will see the dentist when I need to see the dentist!'

'Since you mention the word "child",' she forged on, 'even poor little Fraser is being affected. Look at yesterday, when you were holding him and he threw his head up and accidentally hit your jaw. You shouted at him and reduced him to tears.'

'It was a moment's irritation, nothing more,' her husband mumbled, avoiding her gaze.

'It frightened him, Walter. If you remember, he was hesitant about being handed to you the next time Mrs Drummond brought him downstairs. He hid his little face in her shoulder. Do you want your own son to think of you as an ogre? Look at the advertisement again, Walter,' she pressed on as he began to weaken. 'You can have the tooth attended to under gas – you'll just go to sleep and you won't feel a thing.'

'Not gas! The last time I had that I thought I was suffocating. I won't take gas, Sarah!'

'Then try this cocaine he mentions. "Harmless, and with no side effects",' Sarah read out. 'And it only costs one shilling. I'll come with you, if you want.'

A few hours later she sat fidgeting in the dentist's waiting room, trying not to study the coloured pictures of damaged teeth and diseased gums that were hanging on the wall. Her ears strained for sounds of suffering from behind the closed door of Mr Walker's surgery, while at the same time she thanked her own good fortune in having strong teeth that rarely required medical attention.

When the door finally opened and the dentist ushered Walter out she sprang to her feet. 'How are you?'

'Absolutely very well,' her husband beamed. 'No trouble at all. It don't – didn't hurt a bit. This is a grand fellow,' he informed the entire waiting room, shaking the dentist's hand vigorously. A trickle of blood ran unnoticed down his chin and Sarah mopped at it with her handkerchief.

'Just rinse the cavity with warm water and salt, and get him to lie down for an hour or two,' Mr Walker advised. 'Bland food until tomorrow.'

'Fine man,' Walter called after him as he retreated back into his surgery. 'Salt of the earth. Wonderful stuff, cocaine,' he rambled on as Sarah, having paid the bill, escorted him out to the street. 'Everyone should try it. No pain at all.'

He pulled away from the hand she had slipped through the crook of his elbow and stepped out into the street, causing a butcher's van to halt abruptly and toot its horn. Walter waved benignly at the angry driver as he wove his way across the street and on to the opposite pavement.

'Where are you going?' Sarah asked when she caught up with him.

'To the shop, where else?'

'Mr Walker said you have to go home and rest, Walter. Your mouth is bleeding.'

He touched his mouth and then looked in surprise at the red smear on his fingers. 'So it is, by George. You go home, my dear, and attend to young Fraser. I must get to work. No knowing what they might be up to without my hand on the whatever-it–is.'

26

'Walter!' Sarah appealed, but her husband marched on, and there was nothing for it but to follow him to the shop, where the young female assistant rearranging shelves by the door dropped a swift curtsey when her employer entered and then reeled back, aghast, as he gave her a wide, bloody smile.

'Good morning, Walter – and Sarah too.' Belle came from her small cubbyhole. She also recoiled at sight of her brother's face. 'What on earth has happened? Did someone hit you?'

'Tooth out, no problem at all. Wonderful dentist, Walker. I may decide to get all my teeth out,' Walter said briskly. 'Save pain later. Now then, how is business?'

The door opened and a well-dressed gentleman came in. Walter tried to swing round to greet him, but halfway there he lost his balance and had to lean on Sarah's shoulder in order to steady himself. Her knees buckled under the sudden weight, and she threw a desperate, beseeching look at her sister-in-law.

'Mr Gilmartin...' Belle said, '...could you attend to Mr Harrison?' And then, to Walter, 'Business is doing very well, but I would like you to look at the books, since you are here.' Taking his arm she led him into the office while Sarah followed, keenly aware of the inquisitive stares from staff and customers alike.

'He should be at home,' Belle murmured once they had managed to get Walter into a chair.

'He insisted on coming here. What am I to do with him?' Sarah was almost in tears. Belle glanced at Walter, who was now doing his best to make sense of the neat rows of figures in the ledger before him.

'I'll ask Samuel to assist Walter home.'

'He's busy with a customer. Perhaps one of the others...?'

'Samuel can be very discreet, and we don't want the whole of Saltcoats to know about this, do we? Wait here,' Belle said, and left the office.

When Samuel's customer had gone she drew him aside. 'My brother has had a tooth removed and he is not feeling very well. I would be grateful if you could fetch a cab and escort him and Mrs Forsyth home.'

'Of course, Miss Forsyth, it would be my pleasure.'

Ten minutes later Sarah was hurrying up the path while Samuel helped Walter from the cab. 'Nellie, the master has had his tooth removed and now he needs to rest,' she said as soon as the maid opened the door. 'Please go and turn the bed down.'

'Yes, ma'am.' The girl scurried upstairs, passing Leez Drummond on her way down, the baby in her arms.

'We're just off for our walk, Mrs Forsyth,' the woman said as she arrived in the hall. And then, as Samuel eased Walter in through the front door, 'Is Mr Forsyth unwell?'

'He's had a tooth removed and he...' Sarah was beginning when Walter, catching sight of the little boy, pulled free of Samuel.

'And here's my son! Come to Papa, Fraser.' He plucked the child from Leez's arms.

'Mr Forsyth...'

'Grand wee fellow, aren't you?' Walter beamed bloodily and before anyone could stop him he tossed the baby into the air. Sarah, Leez and Fraser all screamed, and Walter, turning to find out what the pandemonium was about, staggered off balance. For a terrible, heart-stopping moment Sarah thought that her precious little son was going to fall to the floor, or against the nearby banisters, then Fraser, eyes and mouth wide with terror, was caught by Samuel's outstretched hands.

'Good man,' Walter said heartily. 'Ever played cricket?'

Leez snatched her charge from Samuel and held him close while she fixed her employer with a gimlet eye. 'I think, Mr Forsyth, that you would be the better of a wee lie down,' she said in a firm voice.

The tone, and the look, caused Walter to deflate suddenly. 'You're right.' He ran the back of his hand over his mouth and then studied the red smear, surprised. 'Where did that come from?'

'Let me help you, sir,' Samuel said, and began to ease his employer upstairs.

'Get him to rinse his mouth with warm salty water, Mrs Forsyth,' Leez advised, then bore her precious charge out of the house and away from danger.

By the time Sarah took the water and some clean cloths up to the bedroom, Walter was in bed, his clothes neatly folded and laid on a chair. Between them Sarah and Samuel persuaded him to rinse his mouth out, and then settled him against the pillows. He fell asleep almost at once.

Samuel tucked one of the cloths between his cheek and the pillow. 'To catch any blood that might still be there,' he said. 'And now I'd best get back to the shop.'

'Would you like a cup of tea before you go?' Sarah offered when they were in the hall. 'Or something stronger, perhaps?'

'Miss Forsyth will be looking for me.'

She watched him walk down the path and along the pavement without a single backward glance, then hurried upstairs to the bedroom where she went straight to the window. She was too late; Samuel Gilmartin was already out of sight.

Behind her, Walter began to snore. She rested her forehead on the cool glass pane and thought longingly of what might have been.

'I was wondering,' Walter said a few days later, 'when you intend to sell Aunt Beatrice's house.'

'Why would I sell it?'

'Because it's too large for you.'

'I don't think so.'

'Of course it is. You should sell it and buy something smaller and more suited to your needs. Then you can invest the profits. I am more than willing to advise you.'

It was the end of the week and they were in the parlour of the house that had been Beatrice McCallum's, going over the shop orders and invoices. Now Belle laid down her pen and stared at her brother. 'Aunt Beatrice left it to me because she expected me to live here.'

'But Aunt Beatrice is no longer here. The house is yours, Belle, to sell as you wish.'

Belle looked around the comfortable parlour and realised that she had developed a great fondness for this house – more than she had ever known for the house where she had been raised. That had been her parents' home, and it was now Walter's, whereas this was her home.

'Aunt Beatrice didn't seem to find it too large.'

'That's because she came to it as a married woman. It is an ideal house for a married couple, but you, Belle, are a maiden lady.'

'I may yet marry, Walter.'

'My dear girl, there has been no sign of a suitor as yet, has there?'

'So you consider me too old for marriage – or too ugly, perhaps?' Belle asked icily.

'There is nothing wrong with your looks – though we both know that when it comes to beauty Morna was blessed with the looks while you have a good brain. And there is certainly no doubt that thanks to Aunt Beatrice's generosity towards you in her will you would be a good catch for any man. But even so...'

'Walter, I believe that I have a headache coming on.' Belle put a shaking hand to her forehead. 'I really must go and lie down in a darkened room at once.'

When her brother had gone, completely unaware of how close he had come to being physically assaulted, she paced the parlour floor, her hands doubled into fists. Then she did something that she would not have dreamed of doing a year earlier – she went to seek advice from Morna, who was working with Ruth on the next week's lessons. Belle sat down and poured out the whole story.

'Aunt Beatrice left the house to you,' her sister said at once, 'and you are the only person who can decide whether to keep it or move somewhere else.'

'Do you like the house?' Ruth asked. She put her pen down and concentrated her full attention on Belle.

'I like it very much.'

'Then you should keep it. Look at this place...' Ruth indicated the kitchen with a wave of ink-stained fingers. 'Your brother would no doubt say that it is too large for me, but I feel comfortable in it.'

'But you need the space for your little school. I've no wish to do anything like that.'

'Why should you? We all have different needs and interests. You're a woman of property now, and dependent on no one. You can do whatever you please.'

333

She gave the visitor a warm smile and an encouraging pat on the hand before returning to her work.

Belle, soothed by the atmosphere of the cluttered house, stayed for longer than she had intended. When she returned home she went upstairs at once. Juliet, who had accepted Belle as her new mistress, scurried at her heels, but to the little dog's disappointment she was shut out of the bedroom that had always been Belle's. After snuffling along the narrow space at the bottom of the closed door she settled down on the hall carpet, head on paws.

In the privacy of her room, Belle examined her face closely in the mirror above her dressing table. Walter had only spoken the truth when he'd pointed out that Morna was by far the prettier of his two sisters. Belle's jaw was a little too strong, her brown eyes heavy-lidded and her hair mousy brown, while Morna had a heart-shaped little face, soft fair hair and wide hazel eyes with thick, curving lashes.

Belle pulled out the pins skewering her hair to the top of her head in her usual style; after brushing it until it crackled she tied it back loosely at the nape of her neck. This look softened the lines of her serious face. She then moved to the standing mirror to study her figure. She had a reasonable bosom – not as noble as Clarissa Pinkerton's or as sweetly curvaceous as Morna's, but reasonable – and although her waist was not hourglass slender, it too was adequate.

She spent some time posturing and primping before the glass and by the time she let Juliet in, her mind was made up.

'How would you like to have a master as well as a mistress?' she asked, gathering the little dog into her arms. Juliet licked her chin enthusiastically as Belle went on, 'I think that we need a man about this house. That would stop Walter's interfering once and for all.'

She returned to the long mirror and decided that it now reflected a handsome woman in her prime, posing with her little pet dog.

As Morna had done months before, she had decided that it was time to marry. But unlike Morna, Belle was determined to succeed. As Ruth had said, she was a woman of property. She was a good catch for any man she set her heart on.

And she had already set her heart on one in particular.

Samuel Gilmartin took some time over his appearance on the evening he was invited to have supper with Belle Forsyth. His landlady, easily won over with a little Irish charm, pressed his one and only suit and ironed and starched his shirt. His fingernails were well scrubbed, and his normally curly hair oiled into place.

He inspected himself carefully in the flyblown mirror on his bedroom wall and nodded approval before going downstairs to snip a particularly handsome yellow rosebud from his landlady's back garden while she was chatting to someone at the front door.

'Froggy went a-wooing...' he whistled softly as he walked to Caledonia Road. Samuel Gilmartin was also going a-wooing and tonight, he had decided when Belle invited him to the house, would see the first step in his carefully thought-out plan.

But even carefully thought-out plans can go awry, and the one thing that Samuel had not anticipated was that the proposal would be that very night. Nor had he anticipated that it would come from Belle and not from him.

The supper, beautifully laid out in the small dining room, with snowy tablecloth, silver cutlery and delicate bone china hand-painted plates, had been delicious. After rising from the table they moved into the parlour, where Ena had left a tray by Belle's usual chair.

'I've discovered a fondness for coffee,' she said. 'Would you care for some? Or there's whisky if you would prefer it.'

'I'm not much of a drinker, Miss Forsyth.'

'It's a particularly good malt, my brother tells me.' She nodded to where the bottle stood on a side table, two crystal glasses by its side. 'In fact, I believe that I will try it myself.'

'You – drink whisky?'

'I believe that some ladies do.'

'I'm not sure,' Samuel said cautiously, 'if you would care for it.'

'How will I know if I never taste it?'

'Well – if you wish...'

'I do. Just a little for me,' she said as he opened the bottle. 'There's a box of cigars there as well; my father used to enjoy a good cigar after dinner. I like the smell of them.'

He handed her the glass and took his own. 'To your very good health, Miss Forsyth.'

'To the future, Mr Gilmartin,' Belle said, and took a sip of whisky. Samuel watched, amused, as her eyes widened and her nose wrinkled. She swallowed and then took a deep breath.

'Would you rather have coffee?' he asked gently, but she shook her head.

'I believe that this is an acquired taste,' she said, and took another sip.

Samuel tasted his own whisky, which was superb, then lit the cigar and sat back in the comfortable chair which felt like soft arms cradling his entire body. Belle Forsyth had freed her hair from its usual severe style and drawn it back to the nape of her neck, where it was twisted into a knot finished off with a pretty pale-blue bow that matched her blouse. The style made her look younger, he thought, just as she said, 'You're the first proper guest to be entertained in my very own house.'

'I'm honoured, but why me? You must have many friends just longing to spend time in your company.'

Belle flushed slightly. 'You really think that I still have friends after the way my father behaved, and after my brother married our servant? You know little about society, Mr Gilmartin.'

'No I don't, never having moved in social circles. Are you telling me that the sins of the brothers are visited on poor defenceless women?' he asked in mock horror, and then, when she laughed, 'If you'll forgive me for being forward, Miss Forsyth, you have a lovely smile.'

The flush became her as well; it warmed her normally sallow skin and brought a glow to her eyes. 'You think so?' Her pleasure was clear; this woman, he thought to himself, had not known many compliments.

'I do indeed. You should use it more often.'

'Perhaps I will – now.'

A companionable silence fell between them. The cigar was enjoyable and the malt slipped down Samuel's throat like silk. The room was peaceful and he could smell the delicate scent of the yellow rosebud, which had been received with delight and now rested in a tiny china vase on the mantelshelf. This, he thought dreamily, was the life he had always wanted, the life he was born to.

His mind flitted over the next few months; while giving Belle time to get over her aunt's death he would work at making himself indispensable, not only in the shop but as a friend and confidant. In three months' time, say September or October, he would begin to make her aware of his growing affection, testing the water carefully as he went.

'My brother,' Belle said, 'thinks that I should sell this house.'

'Sell it?' Samuel stared at her, dismayed. This house was part of his future. 'But why should you do that?'

She took another sip from her glass. 'He thinks that it's too large for a woman on her own.'

'That's nonsense – if you'll pardon me for saying so. It's a lovely house and it's just right for you.'

'That's what I thought.'

'And anyway, you might not be on your own for long.'

Once again a soft pink wash touched her cheekbones. 'I thought that too.'

'You have a suitor?'

'I plan to have one.' She drank again, her eyes sparkling at him over the rim of the crystal glass. 'That would annoy my brother,' she said gleefully.

'It would indeed.' Not only her idiot of a brother, Samuel thought. All at once the whisky lost its mellow tang and the cigar its fragrance. He shifted uneasily in the chair and then shot bolt upright as she went on, 'And the sooner the better.' She took another drink, a larger gulp this time, then said, 'So, Mr Gilmartin – will you marry me?'

'What?' He put the cigar on to its ashtray so abruptly that his sleeve brushed the whisky glass and almost toppled it.

'I asked...' Belle put her empty glass aside and sat up in her chair, hands folded primly on her lap and her gaze fixed on his, '...if you would consent to become my husband?'

'But ... how can you ... how can we...?'

'Quite easily. We are both free to marry, unless you already have a wife or a sweetheart I know nothing about? So...' she said when he shook his head, '...we are both free to marry, as I said. We get on together and I admire your abilities and your head for business. I believe that we could suit each other very well.'

Samuel felt as though someone had just punched him in the stomach. 'You're asking me to be your husband just so that you can defy your brother and keep this house?'

'That would not be a good reason for matrimony. I am twenty-three years of age, Mr Gilmartin, and you are...?'

'A year younger,' he said huskily, still in shock.

'Oh. But no matter, our ages are close enough.

You see, Mr Gilmartin, people such as my brother believe that a woman who reaches my age without receiving a single proposal of marriage is doomed to be a spinster for ever. I intend to prove him wrong. Thanks to my aunt I am now a woman of property and means; all I need to make my life complete is a husband.'

'There must be others of your own class…'

She inclined her head. 'Indeed, and some of them would no doubt be delighted to marry a woman of independent means. But I do not choose them, I choose you. Should you reject me,' Belle said calmly, although her heart was beginning to beat faster and faster, 'then I will accept your decision and no more will be said of the matter. I promise you, by the way, that your position in the family business will not be taken from you. I am not a vindictive woman; in fact, I have decided that if you accept me, my wedding gift to you will be a junior partnership in the shop.'

'Your brother would never agree to that!'

'My brother,' Belle said, 'is fond of money. I believe that he will agree.'

'Could I … a turn in the garden…' Samuel said. 'Some fresh air…'

'Of course. Perhaps you would take Juliet out with you. I will go upstairs for five minutes,' Belle said, and stood up. Samuel immediately got to his feet and was further astonished when she stepped swiftly towards him, took his face in her two hands, and kissed him on the mouth. Her lips were soft, and tasted of whisky.

'Five minutes,' she said, and left the room.

27

Samuel swallowed the rest of his whisky in one gulp and took his cigar with him.

'Is she finished with the coffee?' Ena wanted to know as he went through the kitchen.

'I believe so.' He hurried past her into the neat garden, and while Juliet disappeared on some ploy of her own, he walked down to the wall at the end, where only months before he had endeared himself to Beatrice McCallum by burying the body of her other dog, Romeo. The thought of her reminded him of the letter she had left for him. It had made it clear enough that she had wanted him to use her gift of £50 to leave Saltcoats, and Belle. And now Belle herself had just made it possible for him to stay, and to live in comfort for the rest of his life. And if Belle made good her promise to buy him a junior partnership in Forsyth's, then he would be on the first step to easing Walter from the business altogether and taking it over.

On the other hand, he was shocked by Belle's bold proposal. Respectable women did not proposition men; they allowed themselves to be wooed and won, and Samuel had been prepared to do exactly that. He felt winded, and even used. Part of him wanted to prove himself a man – his own man and nobody else's – by refusing her, but standing there in the early summer dusk, looking across the garden towards the house where light glowed from the windows, he began to think of what he could lose by refusing her, and gain by accepting her.

She was not a pretty woman, or even a handsome one in his eyes, but tonight, her face flushed by whisky as she smiled at him nervously and the lamplight shone on the hair lying softly about her cheeks and temples, she had looked quite presentable. He thought of her kiss, still imprinted on his lips, and of the home she offered him, with its thick carpets and its flock wallpaper, its deep soft chairs, bone china dishes and crystal glasses. He thought of the days spent delivering groceries to the back doors of fine houses like hers and the hard, dirty, labouring job he had hated in Ardrossan dockyard – and the shop, where he could wear decent clothes and keep his hands clean and charm the money out of the pockets of wealthy women, many of whom had begun to ask for him personally when they came in.

'To hell with it,' he said softly, dropping the butt of the cigar on the ground and treading the glow from it with the toe of his polished shoe. 'Sure I was about to travel along that same road in any case. It's just as if she came along in her fine motor car and offered me a lift to where I was goin'. And where's the sense in sayin' no to a lift, when it helps a man to get where he's going sooner?' And whistling for Juliet, he returned to the house.

Belle had hurried up to the bathroom, where she dipped the corner of a towel in water and used it to cool her hot face. Her heart was beating fast and she was half-delighted, half-shocked by her boldness. How could she have come right out like that and asked him to marry her? The whisky had helped; bitter though it tasted, she could not have managed to be so forward without it.

She dabbed her face dry and smoothed her hair with trembling fingers. All at once she felt sick with fear. What if he refused her and told her that she disgusted him, and that he never wanted to see her again?

She would have given anything to retire to her room and stay there until he had left the house, but she couldn't do that. She had to return downstairs to face him.

She took a deep breath and went down to the parlour, to find it empty. The tray and the glasses had been removed and the fire made up.

When she heard the door at the back of the hall open, and Juliet's claws skittering over the polished wooden floor, Belle rushed to sit in her chair, snatching up a magazine as she went. She was idly flicking through the pages when the door opened and Samuel came in.

'Is the air cool outside?' she asked calmly as he made for the fire. He turned so that he stood with his back to the flames – just as Papa had done, and Walter did now. Why was it that men always wanted to warm their trousers, she wondered?

'A little, but pleasant. I must apologise, Miss Forsyth, if I seemed discourteous earlier,' he went on, and her heart sank. It was going to be a rejection then. 'I was – taken by surprise.'

'Of course you were. I am the one who should apologise for being so presumptuous.'

'Please don't do that,' he said swiftly, 'for if you do I shall have to believe that you regret everything that you said, and I would not be able to tell you how honoured I would be to accept your – proposition.'

'Accept?'

The magazine fell from her lap as he took her hands in his, still cold from the night air, and drew her to her feet.

'With all my heart,' he said, looking deep into her eyes. 'Believe me, I want nothing more than to be your husband and to cherish and care for you for the rest of my life.'

He bent to kiss her as a formal seal of their pact, and was taken aback when she pressed herself to him, holding him so tightly that he was keenly aware of the firm curve of her breasts against his chest. Her mouth opened beneath his and to his surprise he realised that he was becoming aroused.

It was Belle who finally drew away. 'How soon can we marry?' she wanted to know.

'Your aunt's death, and your mother's...'

'Soon,' she interrupted. 'As soon as we can. We can't be married in the church itself, of course, while I am officially in mourning, but in the vestry. You have no objection to being married in the vestry of my church?'

'None at all,' said Samuel, who had been born a Roman Catholic but had long since forsaken any form of religion.

'Then we shall visit the manse tomorrow evening to see the minister about having the banns called. You must invite your family, Samuel.' It was

344

the first time she had used his Christian name.

'I will, of course, but I don't believe that any of them will be able to come over from Ireland. My grandmother's in very poor health and my mother can't leave her. As to my brothers and sisters, they're scattered all over, with families of their own to look after.'

'Write to them anyway, and tell them that if they can't manage to come to our wedding we shall certainly visit them as soon as we can. I've never been to Ireland,' Belle said. 'You can show it to me.'

'I will, I will. What will your brother and sister say about all this? And the others in the shop?'

'They may say whatever they choose,' Belle said blithely. 'I am my own woman and you are your own man. Let them chatter and disapprove if they wish, it need make no difference to us.'

She reached up to kiss him again, then took a small box from her pocket and held it out to him. 'This was my aunt's ring. She left it to me and I would like to wear it as a symbol of our betrothal.'

Diamonds and sapphires flashed as Samuel opened the box. He drew the ring out and slipped it on to the third finger of Belle's left hand. It fitted well.

'It's a beautiful ring.'

'Yes, it is. And now that's settled,' she said, then drew in a deep, shaky sigh, and smiled up at him, her face alight. 'What an evening it has been. I feel quite exhausted with excitement. Would you mind very much if we said goodnight now, Samuel?'

'Not at all...' He stopped short, then said, 'I don't even know your full name.'

'Isabelle, but nobody has ever called me that.'

'I will, and nothing else,' he said firmly. 'It's a name that suits you.'

'Isabelle.' She said the name slowly, with pleasure. 'Yes, I would like you to call me that.'

'Your brother…' Samuel said uneasily.

'I shall go to see him first thing tomorrow morning. That means that he and I will be late, so you must look after the shop until I get there.' She kissed him again, a quick, soft kiss this time. 'And now you must go. I have so much to think about.'

'You've lost your mind,' Walter said bluntly.

'On the contrary, I think I have just found it.'

'You? Marrying one of our employees? I won't have it!'

He and his sister were in the small dining room at Argyle Road, facing each other over a table still strewn with the remains of the breakfast that Belle had interrupted. As soon as she announced that she had something important to tell Walter, Sarah had excused herself and slid quietly from the room. Just as well, Belle thought now, looking at her brother's purpling face.

'Are you so determined to disgrace the Forsyth name by marrying beneath you?' he wanted to know now.

'Walter, have you forgotten that you married our servant?'

'So that's why you've come up with this preposterous suggestion? You just want to spite me for marrying Sarah. Stop that!' he raged as Belle burst out laughing.

'You really think that I would be so childish? My dear Walter, I can assure you that I have too much regard for myself, and for Samuel, to stoop to such a childish trick.'

'This has all come about because Aunt Beatrice made a pet of Gilmartin and invited him to visit her home. She filled his head with ideas above his station.'

'Samuel was very kind to Aunt Beatrice. He found the time to visit her more often than you did.'

'I am a family man. I have commitments. How far has this nonsense gone?'

Belle drew her glove off and held out her left hand to display the ring sparkling on her third finger.

'That's Aunt Beatrice's ring!'

'She left it to me and I choose to wear it as my engagement ring. Samuel was kind enough to fall in with my wishes.'

'This fanciful nonsense won't last, Belle. If I was a betting man I would wager that you'll have gone off the whole idea long before your time of mourning is over.'

'You would lose your wager, for we plan to marry quietly as soon as possible. We are going to call on the minister this evening.'

His eyes bulged. 'You're not even going to wait for a decent length of time before you commit yourself?'

'You didn't.'

'That was different,' he said again. 'You know full well that Sarah was – dear God, Belle, are you carrying that man's child? Because if so, I promise you that I will horsewhip Gilmartin to within an inch of his life!'

'I doubt if you would manage that, and in any case there's no need. Samuel and I, at least, know how to restrain our feelings for each other until after marriage.' Belle drew her glove on again and picked up her bag. 'I must go; one of us should be in the shop. And remember, Walter, that I will expect you to treat Samuel with respect. After all, he will soon be a member of the family.'

'You can't do this!' he bellowed at her in frustration as Sarah tapped on the door and then peered in.

'I brought some fresh tea,' she said timidly, easing herself and a laden tray through the half-opened door. And then, pausing uncertainly as she glanced from one to the other, 'Is something wrong?'

'Not at all, Sarah,' Belle said, but her voice was drowned out by Walter's furious, 'Yes, something is very wrong! My sister has just informed me that she is to marry Samuel Gilmartin!'

'Samuel...?' Sarah whispered, and then the tray slipped from her hands and crashed to the floor, sending tea and broken china all over the place. Slowly, as though she was being neatly folded up joint by joint, Sarah collapsed to lie in a dead faint in the middle of the mess. Belle and Walter stared at her in astonishment, then at each other.

'Now look what you've done,' Walter fumed at his sister. 'You've upset her with your nonsense!'

There was a noticeable stir in church on the Sunday morning when the banns proclaiming a marriage between Isabelle Forsyth and Samuel Gilmartin were first called. Belle straightened her shoulders and lifted her head higher; by her side, Samuel stared straight ahead, a slight smile on his lips.

Walter, on her other side, also stared ahead, but stonily. Sarah was not in church that morning, pleading the need to stay at home with the baby, who was teething. Morna, next to Walter, was grateful for Ruth's company, both in the church and on the day when Belle had called to tell her sister about her engagement.

At first, the news had taken her breath away. Belle – and Samuel Gilmartin? The thought was almost as shocking as Walter's decision to marry Sarah – more so, since Morna had always thought of Belle as the most sensible person she knew. Walter marrying with their servant was one thing – she had never thought of Walter as sensible, but how could Belle also choose a life partner from a lower class?

'Samuel?' she said feebly when she was able to speak. 'You really want to marry Samuel Gilmartin?'

'Yes, I do want to marry him, very much. And I intend to marry him whether you like the idea or not.' Belle was on the defensive, her cheeks pink and her hands fumbling nervously with one of her gloves. 'I hope you can be happy for me, Morna?'

'Of course she is, and so am I,' Ruth said warmly. 'Isn't that right, Morna?'

Morna was recalling the day Samuel had kissed her in Meggie Chapman's kitchen – the day he had obtained a post at the shop. Even though she carried no romantic notions about the man, her heart still fluttered slightly at the memory of his lips, firm and warm on hers. Lucky Belle, she thought, to be marrying such a man, regardless of class. Then, looking at her sister, seeing how Belle's eyes were pleading for her understanding and support, she smiled and said, 'If it's what you really want, then I'm happy for you and for Samuel. Have you told Walter?'

'Yes, and he's not pleased.'

'Then he must get used to the idea, just as you and I had to get used to his marriage to Sarah,' Morna said firmly.

'Well done,' Ruth told her when Belle had left. 'I thought at first that you were going to let your sister down, but you managed to rally.'

'It's just that when I first met Samuel he was living in a rundown hostel and earning a pittance as a delivery man. And now...'

'And now he has pulled himself up by his bootstraps, with your help, and if he makes your sister happy, then surely that is all that matters.'

'It's strange to think of Belle marrying before me. All the time I was growing up,' Morna explained, 'I was expected to be the first to marry. I had no abilities, while Belle was clever. Father always meant her to go into the shop, but nobody ever planned a future like that for me.'

'We never know what life has planned for us. I will go with you to the church to hear the banns called,' Ruth said, 'for moral support. We women must show a united front.'

Morna nodded, while deep inside, a small voice clamoured, 'But what about me? When am I going to find someone who cares about me more than anyone else in the world?'

Clarissa and her parents were also in church, but after the service they hurried away without speaking to any of the Forsyths. 'We are in disgrace,' Morna said as she watched the other members of the congregation avert their eyes.

'Again.' Walter's voice was grim, and his younger sister put a hand on his arm.

'Never mind, Walter, perhaps I'll marry well and save our reputation.'

'And perhaps not,' he said gloomily.

'You cannot seriously intend to go through with this marriage!' Clarissa flounced into Belle's parlour.

'You heard the banns being called in church this morning.'

'Belle, we have been closest friends for all of our lives – like sisters. That is why I urge you to stop this nonsense before it goes too far.'

'I don't see it as nonsense, Clarissa,' Belle said calmly. 'I look forward to becoming Samuel's wife.'

'But from what I hear in the town he was a common labourer, living in a lodging house down by the harbour!'

'And now he is a valued employee in our family business.'

'What do you know of his family?'

'I don't intend to marry his family.'

Clarissa glared, frustrated, and then tried another tack. 'Do you remember us promising to be bridesmaids to each other? I cannot agree to be your bridesmaid if you insist on going ahead with this marriage; nor can I ask you to stand by my side when it's my turn to marry, which may be quite soon. Arthur MacAdam is paying me a lot of attention these days.'

'Then I'm happy for you, Clarissa. Can you not be happy for me?'

'Not if you persist in going on as you are. Belle, Mama has asked me not to see you again.' Clarissa made it sound like a threat.

'Perhaps you should tell your mama that you are an adult now, and free to choose your own friends – as I am. And I choose Samuel.'

'You know that he's only marrying you for your money, and for this house?'

'You don't believe that Samuel could want to marry me because he loves me?'

'Men of his class,' Clarissa declared passionately, 'know nothing about love!'

'They have feelings, Clarissa. They are flesh and blood and although it might surprise you to know this, they have brains too. Would you like some tea?' Belle asked calmly.

'It would choke me!' Clarissa said, and marched from the house. Belle watched her go without one pang of regret. Thanks to Aunt Beatrice, she was in a position to make her own decisions for the first time in her life, and she relished her newfound freedom.

It was one of those fairly frequent occasions when the west coast of Scotland forgot that June had arrived and presented its inhabitants with a grey, wet, windy day much more suited to November. Out in the Firth the waves threw up white spume as they rolled over hidden reefs; when they reached the shore they hurled themselves against the harbour walls in great spouts of spray that rose high into the air and then fell back to soak anyone foolhardy enough to be standing on the harbour walls. The pleasure steamers from Glasgow fought their way along as a few adventurous passengers clung to the railings to avoid being blown away entirely. Others had long since retired below to the comparative safety of the saloons, where they grasped the arms of their chairs and wished that they had stayed on dry land. From ashore it was difficult to make out the horizon, since the sea and the sky were of the same grey colour.

Morna had called in on Meggie Chapman in the afternoon, as she did every few weeks, and then done some shopping on the way back to the house. She was battling her way along Hamilton Street, the basket of groceries over one arm and her head bent against a wind that was doing its best to wrench her umbrella from her grasp, when an unexpected gust pounced from a narrow passageway between two buildings. It tore the umbrella from her fingers and then set about doing its best to pull her hat off.

'Oh!' Without thinking, she swung round to look for the umbrella while at the same time snatching with both hands at her felt hat, which was flapping like a bird about to launch itself into the air. The basket, looped over one arm, swung wildly against the underside of her raised arm. It was full, and the sudden jerk sent potatoes and onions spilling out of it.

A step or two took Morna beyond the passageway and out of reach of the gusting wind, which was one mercy. She set the basket down in the shelter of a wall, realising, as she straightened and turned to look for the fallen vegetables, that strands of damp hair had fallen over her eyes and her hat was now clinging to the side of her face, having managed to free itself from all but one of its hatpins.

As she hauled it off someone thrust her umbrella, now closed, into her free hand. 'Hold on to that for a moment while I pick your things up. Won't take a moment,' the man who had come to her rescue said cheerfully. Taking advantage of his assistance, Morna leaned against the wall and tried as best she could to pin her hat back into place while he scooped the vegetables up and returned them to the basket.

'I think that's the lot. May I?' He eased the umbrella from beneath her arm and opened it cautiously. 'It seems to be in good order,' he said, and then, surveying her sympathetically, 'your hat has suffered more harm than anything else.'

'Thank you, you've been very kind.' Morna rammed the final hatpin into place and reached for her umbrella.

'Let me help you.'

'Really, there's no need. I haven't far to go – just to Ardrossan Road.'

'I'm going there too,' he said, tipping the umbrella so that it protected her from the rain.

'You're going to get wet,' Morna protested.

'I can assure you that my hat is sturdier than yours, though not as pretty.' He stooped to pick up the basket and then said, 'Come along,' in a voice that dismissed any further attempt at protest.

She walked meekly by his side as he talked about the unseasonal weather and the train journey he had just made from Glasgow, where the sea had hurled spray right into the carriages as they approached Saltcoats.

'This is me,' she interrupted when they got to Ruth's gate. As he glanced beyond her shoulder to the house she saw raindrops dripping from his chin and running down his neck beneath the scarf that was drawn up around his throat. The poor man was soaking. She was just wondering if she should invite him in for some hot tea when he leaned past her, opened the gate, and urged her ahead of him up the path, still protecting her with the umbrella.

'You live here?' he asked with interest, waiting on the doorstep as she fumbled for her key.

'Yes. I wonder – would you like to come in for a moment?'

'I would indeed. Thank you.' He followed her into the hallway just as Ruth, hearing the front door close, came from the kitchen.

'My dear Morna, I've been worried about you. What dreadful weath– Tom!'

'Look what the storm's blown up.' Morna's rescuer put the basket down and opened his arms. Ruth ran into them.

'I didn't expect you until next week – oh, Tom, you devil, you're soaking me!'

'Why should you stay dry when we're both wet?' He indicated Morna, laughing. 'I rescued a damsel in distress and then found that she lives here.'

'Morna, this is my brother, Tom.' Ruth was

flushed and glowing with pleasure.

'How do you do?' Tom Durie held out a large wet hand, then added as Morna put her own fingers, clothed in a sopping glove, into his, 'You should change into dry clothing before you catch a chill, Miss Morna. We both should,' he added, unfastening his coat and taking off his scarf to reveal the white collar of a minister of the Church of Scotland.

'Indeed you should, and the sooner the better. You're in your usual room, Tom.' Ruth picked up the basket, saying when her brother tried to take it from her, 'I can manage – I'm not helpless. Off you go, the pair of you, while I put these things away.'

28

Morna's bedroom mirror showed her that she looked like a scarecrow. Her hat, soaked and shapeless, sat askew on her head, while limp strands of hair drooped around a face wet with rain and red from the cold. Even her blouse was wet. She ended up stripping down to her petticoat before putting on a dry blouse and skirt. She unpinned her hair and towelled it vigorously before combing out the knots and pinning it up again, while outside the wind howled around the house and rain battered against the windows.

Below, someone began to play 'Claire de Lune' on the piano, and when Morna went downstairs

Ruth called, 'We're in mother's parlour, Morna. Actually, Tom, it's Morna's parlour now.' she added as Morna went into the room. 'This is where she teaches music and drawing.'

Tom Durie stopped playing and swung round on the piano stool to smile at Morna. 'Ruth's told me all about your talents and the way you've helped her.'

'Don't embarrass the poor girl. Tell me what's happening in Glasgow,' Ruth ordered, dispensing tea. As brother and sister talked, Morna took the opportunity to study the newcomer. Tom Durie had his sister's black hair, now damp and tousled, and her thin face and piercing dark blue eyes. His straight nose was just a little too long, like Ruth's, and he also had a firm, well-shaped mouth. The features that seemed striking and slightly masculine in Ruth made him look interesting, though not handsome.

'Morna, I told you about the camp Tom works in each summer, didn't I?' Ruth belatedly remembered that there was a third person in the room. 'The one at Portencross?'

Morna nodded. There had been talk of some summer activity that would bring Ruth's brother to the area but she hadn't paid much heed at the time. 'What sort of camp is it?' she asked cautiously.

'It's for families from Glasgow and Greenock or Paisley who can't afford to pay for holiday lodgings in places like Saltcoats,' Tom explained. 'For a few shillings they can rent part of a big field at Portencross and bring their own tents. It gives them the chance to get some sea air and is a change from the streets and tenements.'

'Tom takes time off from his church every summer to work there – they hold open air services on Sundays and organise concerts, and games for the children.'

'We can always do with extra help, and from what Ruth has said in her letters, you're musical and very good with youngsters.' Tom raised a dark eyebrow at Morna. 'Why don't you go along with me this year?'

'Oh – I don't think I would be of much use to you,' she stammered, taken by surprise. He shrugged, then moved from the piano stool to a comfortable chair.

'Think about it,' he said.

At the end of June Belle Forsyth and Samuel Gilmartin became man and wife in a brief ceremony held in the vestry of the North Parish Church, with Morna and Walter as their witnesses.

'I would rather not have been part of this particular wedding party, but when Belle asked me I decided that it would be better than letting Gilmartin ask one of those rough fellows from the lodging house he lived in,' Walter said for the umpteenth time as he and Sarah walked to Belle's house on the day of the wedding.

'Yes indeed,' she said listlessly.

He tried to peer down at her face but was defeated by the large bunch of artificial cherries pinned to the wide brim of her straw hat. 'Are you well, my dear? You've been very quiet for the past three weeks or so. Not sickening for anything, are you?'

'No, Walter. I'm just a little tired.'

He patted the hand that lay in the crook of his elbow. 'Once this ridiculous wedding is over and Gilmartin established as shop manager I intend to spend more time with you and Fraser. That should cheer you up. You're not cold, are you?' he added as he felt a shiver run through the arm pressed against his.

'Just for a moment – but it has passed,' said Sarah.

'Good.' They walked on in silence, Sarah trying hard to prepare herself for the ordeal of seeing Samuel become Belle's husband, and Walter thinking about the shock he had had when Belle insisted on making Samuel Gilmartin shop manager.

'What do we need with a manager?' he had protested. 'You and I manage the place perfectly well between us.'

'But as a married woman I will probably want to spend more time at home. We need a manager and Samuel is the obvious choice.'

'George Stoddart has been in our employment for much longer.'

'Mr Stoddart's health is failing and I suspect that he will soon give up work altogether. Samuel is capable and reliable, and since I am buying him a junior partnership as a wedding gift he must be given more responsibility. I would also like to train Miss Campbell to be promoted to the post of assistant cashier so that she can attend to the financial side of the business when I am away from the shop. She's good with figures and, like Samuel, she is trustworthy. I will still be in

359

charge of the books, but I have decided that I shall keep them at home where I can work on them in the evenings. There will be a separate set of books in the shop from now on. I will be paying one thousand pounds into the business in Samuel's name,' Belle reminded her brother as he opened his mouth to argue further.

'Belle, I have to point out how foolish it is to squander your inheritance like that!'

'I don't see it as squandering; I firmly believe that with Samuel and Miss Campbell given more responsibility, Forsyth's will do very well. And in any case, Walter, let me remind you that I can do whatever I please with the money Aunt Beatrice left me.' Then, caressing her engagement ring with the fingers of her right hand, she added slyly, 'And I think that it would be fitting if you, as head of the family, announced Samuel's promotion at our wedding celebration.'

The suggestion flattered Walter's vanity, and he had come to realise, in the week since their conversation, that Belle's generous investment would be of benefit to the business. If his sister chose to make this foolish marriage and to throw her money away, then it was no concern of his.

Belle herself opened the door to them. She was dressed in her wedding finery, a high-necked, pale-grey silk dress with a bolero jacket. The bodice inset consisted of broad horizontal bands of embroidered flowers on a white background. The same floral motif was repeated around the hem of the slightly gathered skirt. Her brimless hat was also of grey silk, its severity softened by a great cluster of white feathers pinned at one side.

'You look – splendid,' Sarah said tremulously. 'So elegant!'

'Thank you, Sarah. Will I do, Walter?' Belle asked her brother, who cleared his throat before saying, 'Very apt, Belle. Just right for a small wedding.'

'I thought so,' Belle was saying calmly as Morna, in a brown jacket and skirt over a cream blouse, hurried from the kitchen.

'There you are, Walter. If we don't get to the church soon we'll be late!' She took a small feathered hat from the hatstand and used the mirror to settle it in place, tilted becomingly over her forehead. 'Ena's in the kitchen, Sarah,' she rattled on as she jabbed pins into the hat to anchor it, 'and Ruth and Tom Durie will meet us at the bottom of the brae after the ceremony and walk back here with us. Come along, then, let's not keep the bridegroom waiting.'

She ushered her brother and sister out, and Sarah, after taking a moment to steady her trembling lower lip, went to the kitchen to help Ena.

There were eight people at the wedding breakfast: the bride and groom, Walter and Sarah, Morna, Ruth and Tom Durie, and the minister who had performed the wedding service. When they had eaten, Walter officially, if somewhat stiffly, welcomed Samuel into the family and announced his new position as junior partner and shop manager in Forsyth and Son. He managed to make it sound as though it was all his own idea.

'I'm overcome by your generosity, but very happy to accept.' Samuel rose to his feet and held his hand out to his new brother-in-law. Walter, taken by surprise, clasped it briefly and then released it in order to lift his wineglass and propose a toast to the newly-weds.

'And may I propose my own toast,' Belle added, with a radiant smile. 'To Samuel, my husband.'

'And to Isabelle, my beautiful life companion,' Samuel said swiftly, raising his own glass. Catching his gaze, Sarah saw that his eyes sparkled triumphantly.

'I do declare, Belle, that you have never looked so beautiful,' Morna whispered to her sister as the guests prepared to leave. 'You're glowing as though a lamp had been switched on inside you.' Morna wondered, as she spoke, if any man would ever be able to make her eyes as brilliant as her sister's were at that moment. 'You look so very happy.'

'I am,' Belle whispered, flushing like a young girl.

'It was your idea, wasn't it?' Samuel said as he and his new wife returned to the empty parlour. 'It was you who set me up as the manager.'

'You could scarcely continue as one of the shop assistants after today, and we need a manager we can trust.'

'So you trust me?'

'With my life,' Belle said simply, and he took her hand and kissed it. The warm pressure of his lips on her skin sent a tingle of excitement flaring through her entire body. 'My darling Isabelle,' he said huskily. 'I promise that you will never regret marrying me.'

'I already know that.' She gave a contented sigh as she unpinned her hat. 'It may have been a quiet wedding, but it was enjoyable. Though I thought that Sarah was very subdued.'

Samuel shrugged. 'She strikes me as a woman with nothing much to say. Just the right sort of wife for your brother.'

'I have to warn you that *I* don't intend to be a quiet, submissive wife.'

'I'd not want you to be,' he assured her as Ena came into the room.

'Is there anythin' else you're needin', Miss Belle?'

'I don't believe so, Ena. Where's Juliet?'

'Out in the back garden. Shall I fetch her in?'

'I'll see to her, my dear. I think I'd like a final cigar and a turn in the garden. You go upstairs and I'll join you soon,' Samuel said.

As he had done on the evening when Belle had proposed to him, he walked to the end of the garden and stood beneath the trees, savouring his cigar. There was one slight difference – this time, instead of studying the house before him with envy, he surveyed it with the satisfaction of an owner.

Juliet emerged from the shadows and sniffed at his shoes in her usual friendly fashion; she gave an astonished yelp as the toe of one shoe suddenly caught her in the ribs.

'Just to remind you that things are different now,' Samuel told her briskly before throwing his cigar away and scooping the bewildered little dog up under his arm. 'Bedtime, my lady, and from now on, I think – you sleep downstairs. No more pampering.'

Ena was still in the kitchen when he entered the

363

house, locking the back door as he came in.

'Will there be anything else?'

Samuel set the dog down. 'I'll be looking for shaving water in the morning, Ena, but there's nothing else for tonight. You may go to bed.'

He crossed to the inner door, and then turned. 'Just one other thing, now I come to think of it. It's not Miss Belle any more,' he said with a pleasant smile. 'It's Mrs Gilmartin, or if you prefer it, ma'am – and sir. Good night, Ena.'

Ruth's bicycle looked as though it had been well used before being abandoned right at the back of the garden shed. Morna eyed it uneasily before announcing, 'I shall take a bus, or perhaps the train to West Kilbride, and walk the rest of the way.'

'Nonsense.' Tom Durie ran a big hand over the machine to dislodge dust, grit and spiders' webs. 'Fetch a cloth and I'll give it a good rub down and then oil it. It'll be as good as new.'

'I'm not sure that I can still ride a bicycle.'

'You never forget,' Tom said heartily. 'Now run along and find a clean rag, there's a good girl.'

Morna trailed miserably into the kitchen, where Ruth was busy writing at the table. 'I'm sure I won't be of any use at this camp, and there must be a lot of things I could be doing around the house.'

Ruth looked up over the top of the glasses she used for close work. 'Tom needs your help more than I do now that our little school is finished for the summer. You could do with some fresh air and exercise.' She sounded just like her brother,

Morna thought resentfully as she found a clean cloth.

An hour later she wheeled the bicycle, its large basket loaded down with an assortment of items that Tom needed, to the pavement in front of the house. He was already waiting for her, one long leg slung over the crossbar of his own bicycle.

'Off we go,' he said encouragingly, 'and remember, it's all in the balance. In fact, don't even think about it, just push off and let the bicycle and your natural instincts do the rest.'

At first, the machine wobbled horribly all over the road, and at one point Morna narrowly missed running into the side of a delivery van parked by the kerb. A group of youngsters idling along the pavement stopped to watch, and to Morna's horror they actually began to run after her, whistling and jeering, as she swooped and swerved behind Tom, who tossed a grin at them over his shoulder.

It may have been the natural instinct that he claimed she would find again or it may simply have been a burning desire to get away from the children, who were drawing attention to her from everyone on the pavement, but all at once Morna felt the bicycle steady itself, and without knowing how it had happened, she caught up with Tom and then passed him, pedalling strongly.

'That's it!' she heard him whoop, and then the sound of the children's voices faded and they were off, the fresh sea wind in their faces and the bicycle wheels hissing pleasantly along the road surface.

With Tom now in the lead and Morna following, they cycled through the neighbouring town of Ardrossan and were soon on the coast road leading to the small community of Seamill, with its fine houses and its handsome Hydro. The sea sparkled and Arran was a soft purple outline so close to shore on that day that Morna felt as if she could almost reach out and touch it.

Beyond Seamill they came to the junction of three roads. The road ahead led to the large seaside town of Largs while the inland road headed for the village of West Kilbride. Tom took the third option, turning left towards the coast and the village of Portencross.

Portencross, Morna knew from infrequent visits in her childhood, consisted of a few houses, a shop and post office, as well as the dramatic ruins of a small watchtower, known as Portencross Castle, that had been built on the shore. Portencross was a fishing village, but its picturesque harbour was so small that the fishermen had to anchor their boats at an island known as the Wee Cumbrae and row their catches ashore in dinghies.

She spun down the long tree-lined road after Tom, now sufficiently comfortable with the bicycle to enjoy the sense of freedom that she remembered from cycling trips with her brother and sister. Before they reached the village itself Tom slowed and stopped at a five-barred gate.

'Here we are,' he announced when Morna drew up by his side.

'Goodness!' The large field stretching from the road to the beach was dotted with tents of all shapes and sizes. There were vans and a lorry – even, she noticed, an old bus parked in one

366

corner. Most of the tents were still in the process of being set up by people of all ages, and in others, clearly just erected, bags and boxes were being carried inside. Children raced around the place and a man clutching what looked like a large ledger seemed to be supervising operations from the middle of the field.

'Where do they all come from?'

'Greenock, Paisley, even from Glasgow, some of 'em. Most come back year after year,' Tom said with quiet satisfaction. 'I started to help out when I was studying for the ministry and now I come every summer. I wouldn't miss it for the world.'

'They stay here all summer?'

'Most of them do. The local farmers and tradesmen visit every day to supply them with everything they need...'

A horn sounded from the roadway behind them and they had to wheel their bicycles out of the way hurriedly to let a small open-bed lorry cluttered with bundles and cardboard boxes drive in through the gates. Several little faces peered out of the cab's nearside window, and as the lorry passed a hand shot out, index finger pointing, and a child yelled, 'Tom! It's Tom, Mam – Tom's here!'

Another four or five hands began to wave excitedly through the window and Tom waved back, grinning. 'See you in a minute,' he called, and then, as the lorry jolted past, bouncing over the grassy tussocks, 'That's the Kennaways from Paisley; they're here every year. Come and see where we'll be based.'

He set off at a brisk pace and Morna followed him with some difficulty. Not only were her legs

367

weak from the unaccustomed pedalling, but the bicycle, as its wheels bounced from one grassy clump to the next, seemed to be doing its best to break away from her hold on the handlebars. She was relieved and breathless when they finally reached the old bus and were able to prop the cycles against it. The seats had been cleared from the interior and replaced by some rickety tables and chairs that looked as though they had already had a long and difficult life.

To Morna's surprise she recognised the young woman poring over a fistful of papers at one of the tables as a regular visitor to Ruth's house.

'Tom, good to see you again.'

'And you, Charlotte. You two probably know each other already.'

'We do,' Charlotte agreed, and then, to Morna, 'So he's roped you in to help us? We can always do with an extra pair of hands.'

'Talking of hands, the Kennaways have just come in. Come on, Morna,' Tom headed for the door, 'we'll go and help them to get their tent up.'

29

Morna, who would have sold her soul for a cup of tea after the long bicycle ride, followed Tom outside and back across the field on legs that were finally beginning to get used to walking again.

'Charlotte stays on site, together with Eddie and Frank,' Tom explained, moderating his long strides in order to give her the chance to keep up with him. 'The upper deck of the bus has been divided into compartments where they sleep. That way, there's always someone available in the event of an emergency.'

As they passed tents already erected, people sitting outside on wooden crates shouted greetings to Tom, who waved back. 'They're a friendly bunch; you'll get to know everyone quickly,' he assured Morna.

The lorry that had brought the Kennaways had been emptied of all its cargo and was bumping off across the field. Two teenage boys were putting together sections of wooden panels. 'This family has everything organised,' Tom said as he and Morna approached. 'The father's a joiner and a year or two back he made some flooring for their tent. He doesn't come with them – he prefers to stay in Paisley. Let me do that, Jess,' he added, leaping forward to ease aside a woman struggling to unfasten ropes lashing together a large bundle of canvas. 'You sit down and have a rest.'

The woman straightened, her rounded belly pushing against her skirt as she put both hands on the small of her back. 'Thanks, Tom; it's nice tae see you again, lad.'

'You too – all of you.' He lifted a rickety kitchen chair from among the luggage, bedding and boxes piled on the ground and eased her on to it as though she were made of porcelain. 'Just rest here, now,' he instructed as two small children hurried over, one of them staggering beneath the weight of a shawl-wrapped baby.

'Mammy,' the first child whined, 'I'm hungry!'

'I know you are, hen.' Jess Kennaway took the baby. 'Stay here by me, both of you, until the older ones have got the tent up, then we'll have somethin' tae eat.' She smiled apologetically at Morna. 'Weans are aye hungry,' she said. 'It's been a long journey, and a while since they had much tae eat.' Then, glancing from Morna to Tom and back again, 'Are you Tom's sweetheart?'

'Not at all,' Morna felt herself redden, while Tom just laughed. 'He asked me to come here to help.'

'Oh.' The woman shifted the baby to her left arm and held out her right hand. 'Pleased tae meet you. I'm Jess Kennaway, and these...' a nod of her greying head included the baby and the two children sitting on the ground at her feet as well as the four children, two boys and two girls, busy unfolding yards of stiff canvas, '...are my weans.'

Morna took the work-roughened hand. 'How do you do, Mrs Kennaway. I'm Morna Forsyth.'

'Morna – that's a bonny name. Call me Jess, hen, everyone else does. Mrs Kennaway puts me in mind of *his* mother, and a right dragon of a woman she was!'

Tom was already helping the children and now he shouted, 'Lend a hand here, Morna. The more the merrier.'

Morna looked down at her skirt and jacket, which were plain, but clean, and then at the thick green canvas which looked as though it had been stored in a lean-to all winter. Then, realising that she was not going to get the tea that she craved for until she had earned it, she stepped forward and set to work.

As she, Tom and the children struggled with the stiff canvas, which seemed set on burying Morna beneath its folds, people arrived from other parts of the field to help. Within half an hour the large tent was in place and the mattresses, bedding and pieces of furniture had been stowed. Morna noted with surprise that there was even a cast iron stove.

'Oh, we know how tae turn this place intae a home from home.' Jess had lit the stove and set a kettle on it; now she was hewing thick slices from a loaf and scraping thin layers of margarine and jam over each one. 'We started with next tae nothin', me and him, but we've collected bits and pieces over the years. Collected the weans too,' she added with a wry smile, 'so now he stays behind in Paisley tae earn the money while we spend the summer down here. He'll mebbe come down for a day or two before we go back home.' She raised her voice, 'Come on, you weans, and get somethin' tae eat. You too, Tom, you've earned it.'

'And I'm ready for it.' Tom sank down on to the grass, running a hand across his brow and leaving a black smear, much to the amusement of the Kennaway children. 'There you are, Jess, a palace fit for a queen. You'll all sleep in comfort tonight.'

'You're a saint, Tom – and thank you too, Morna. This is Morna,' Jess informed her children as they gathered, eyes fixed on the slices of bread and jam.

'Let me,' Tom interrupted, and then, pointing at each child in order of height, 'George, Joe, Kate, Mima, wee Jessie and wee Rena...'

'You remembered!' the thin girl called Mima crowed, dancing up and down with excitement.

371

'You remembered all our names!'

'Elephants and Tom Duries never forget,' he told her solemnly, and then, pointing to the baby, now on an elder sister's knee and sucking at a crust, 'but this one's new to me, Jess.'

'That's our Robbie.'

'And there's another on the way, I see,' Tom remarked, and Morna blushed.

'Not for another two months. We'll be back home by then.'

'I hope you're going to call it Tom.'

'What if it's a lassie?' one of the younger children – Rena or Jessie? Morna wondered, her brain reeling with names – asked cheekily.

'Thomasina – even better than Tom,' the young minister was saying when a woman came over from a neighbouring tent bearing a huge tin tray set with mugs.

'Yer stove'll no' be hot enough tae bring the kettle tae the boil,' she said, and Jess smiled at her. 'God bless ye, hen. Here,' she added sharply to her brood as they reached grubby fingers towards the great pile of bread and jam, 'mind yer manners. Tom's no' said grace yet.'

Obediently they bowed their heads, waiting until the brief blessing was over and their mother nodded permission before grabbing and devouring the bread. The tea was black and well stewed, and came with an open tin of condensed milk, but even so, Morna had never tasted anything better.

'Good afternoon, Sarah,' Samuel Gilmartin said amiably. 'May I come in?'

'Walter's out.'

'I know that. He's busy with a sales representative.'

Sarah hesitated, clutching the door as though ready to slam it if need be. 'Did he ask you to call? Did he forget something?'

'No; I was making a delivery to one of our customers who's too posh to carry her own purchases.' Samuel removed his hat. 'Keeping my hand in, you might say, having been a delivery boy at one time, as you'll remember. And since the lady lives near here, I thought it would be discourteous to pass the door without paying my respects to my sister-in-law. Are you not going to invite me in?'

'The maidservant's gone to the shops and the nursemaid's taken the wee one for a walk.'

'So you're on your own, then?' Samuel, who had hovered at the corner to watch the maid and the nurse leave the house before strolling in at the gate, hesitated. 'In that case it might not be right for you to invite me in. But on the other hand, we're both respectable married people, and we're related now. For all anyone knows I could be bringing a message from Walter.'

'But you're not.' Sarah didn't know what to do for the best. Beatrice McCallum had never told her whether it was proper for a lady to entertain her sister-in-law's husband in an otherwise empty house, and she could scarcely ask Samuel to wait on the doorstep while she consulted her book on household etiquette.

'If you wish, I could think of some message he might have asked me to deliver to you,' Samuel said, and then, tiring of the game, 'or you could just invite me in, Sarah. It's been a while since you and me got the chance to speak to each other.' He moved forward and Sarah automatically stepped back to give him access.

'That's better.' He closed the door. 'Now then, do we go into your drawing room, or should we go to the kitchen, like the old days?'

'In here.' She led him into the drawing room and then asked uncertainly, 'Would you like some tea?'

Samuel dropped his hat on to a small table. 'Why must the Scots be so eager to offer tea to everyone? Do they have some obligation to support the producers in India and China all the year round? To tell the truth, Sarah, I'd prefer a wee glass of Walter's best whisky, but they'd smell it on my breath when I get back to the shop, so I'll settle for a few minutes of your company instead. Will you not take a seat?'

She perched on one of the fireside chairs and he took the other, leaning back and smiling at her. An onlooker might have thought that Sarah was the uncomfortable visitor and Samuel the host, at ease in his own drawing room.

'So – how is my young nephew today?'

'Fraser? He's very well, apart from trouble with teething.'

'And I know that Walter is well, since I saw him not half an hour ago. That only leaves you, Sarah. How are you?'

'I'm v-very well, thank you.'

'I'm glad to hear it. You look v-very well,' he imitated her nervous stammer, his eyes sparkling with amusement. 'Marriage suits you – or perhaps it's motherhood, or having proper meals and not having to rise at dawn and be at everyone's beck and call all day. Tell me, do you enjoy being the mistress of the house?'

'I find it strange at times.'

'Do you?' He flicked an imaginary piece of thread from his trouser leg. 'For my part, I enjoy being master of a house. Who would have thought just a year ago, when I was a delivery lad and you a skivvy, that we would both do so well? And it's all been down to you.'

'To me?'

'Of course. If you hadn't allowed the son of the house to put you in the family way, you'd still be in the kitchen, and as for me – if Walter hadn't married you, Miss Morna wouldn't have left this house in a temper. She wouldn't have taken refuge in the Chapmans' lodging house, and then I would never have met her. She was the one who helped me to obtain a post in Forsyth's. And it was there that I met my dear wife.' He smiled at her. 'All down to you, Sarah. I'll never be able to thank you enough.' Then after a pause, during which she stared into the empty fireplace, aware of his eyes travelling over every inch of her, 'Tell me, Sarah – are you as happy as I am?'

'I – I don't know.'

'I'm sure you must be. Walter is a fine man. A fair employer, a devoted husband and a loving father to the child you gave him.'

Sarah could bear it no longer. 'Samuel...' she leaped to her feet, hands clenched by her sides, '...please go back to the shop. You shouldn't be here, alone in the house with me. What would Miss Belle think if she knew?'

'*Miss* Belle?' A sharp edge came into his voice. 'You must never call her that now that you're married to her brother. We're as good as any of the Forsyths now, you and me. Never forget that. Why should Belle think anything of me calling in to ask after your health? What other reason could I possibly have for being here?'

'No other reason, but you should go.' Sarah went to the door and waited, then as Samuel continued to lounge in the chair, 'Please go, Samuel.'

'Why are you so concerned about being alone with me?' He got to his feet slowly and went to her, standing so close that she was trapped between his body and the door frame. She stared down at her feet, silently willing him to walk past her and into the hall.

'Can it be,' Samuel's voice said softly above her bent head, 'that you still have feelings for me?'

She shook her head violently, more in denial to herself than to him.

'Are you sure of that? I believe that you still care for me, Sarah. D'you mind the times I came to the kitchen, when those that thought themselves better than you and me were sound asleep in their beds?' His voice lowered and softened and took on the Irish accent that had always sent delicious shivers down her spine. 'D'you mind the way we talked and talked in that nice warm kitchen, tellin' each other all about our past lives and our hopes for the future? You were my only friend then, Sarah, and God help me, I've not found another to match you.'

'You have a wife now.' Her voice was a mere whisper.

'Aye, I've got a wife and you've got a husband, but we both married a Forsyth, and they're cold, arrogant folk. Belle can never be you, Sarah, and it's my belief that Walter can never be me. Am I right?'

He lifted his hand and let the tips of his fingers rest against the curve of her cheek, smiling as he felt her entire body quiver beneath his touch.

'Tell me this, Sarah – do you and Walter ever laugh together the way we laughed? D'you love with him the way you did with me?'

'We could have been together! That was always what I wanted, but you'd not agree to it!'

'Aye, we could.' He cupped his hand beneath her chin, forcing her to look up at him. 'We could have starved together in an attic, or died of the cold together in a ditch – us and the child that wasnae mine.'

'As God's my judge I thought he was yours. With all my heart, I wanted him to be yours!'

The memory of her betrayal, and of the child with Walter Forsyth's features stamped for all to see on his small face still made Samuel seethe with anger, but he forced the censure from his voice. He had not come here to quarrel with Sarah. 'Even if it had been mine, how could I have looked after you both? Look what marriage to Walter Forsyth has given you, Sarah...' He took her by the shoulders and turned her to face the well-furnished room. 'You made a better marriage with him than you could ever have made with me.'

'You think that livin' in comfort matters to me?' Sarah turned back to face him, her eyes filling with tears. 'Oh, Samuel, I've missed you so much!' She laid her face against his jacket, feeling the steady beat of his heart against her cheek. 'I've never stopped wishing that things could have been different. But it's too late now.'

'Is it? Why d'you think I married Belle Forsyth if it wasn't to be nearer to you, with the chance to see you from time to time?'

She looked up at him with sudden hope. 'D'you mean that?'

'Do you think I could stop loving you just because you belong to another man?' he said, and took her into his arms. She came willingly, clinging to him and lifting her face to receive his kiss. As her mouth softened and parted beneath his, he felt the tremor run through her again and knew that he had achieved his purpose.

'Sarah...' he breathed into her hair when the kiss finally ended, '...I've hungered for you for such a long time!'

'We mustn't,' she said in sudden fright as he swept her off her feet and into his arms.

'We must!' He laid her down on the chaise longue and knelt beside her, kissing and caressing her, his mouth and hands swiftly growing bolder. 'We have so little time, my love; we must make the most of it,' he whispered into her throat.

Sarah, swept away on a great wave of longing and need, had just begun to give in completely to her hunger for him when the doorbell jangled and she sat up so swiftly that she almost knocked Samuel to the floor.

'Who can that be? Please God, don't make it Walter,' she whimpered, struggling to her feet. Her fingers flew to her bodice, fumbling with the two buttons that had become unfastened.

'Walter would surely have his own key.' Samuel was on his feet, smoothing his hair and snatching up his bowler hat. 'You have a headache and you were resting. Wait,' he ordered as she hurried to the door, 'give me time to get out by the kitchen.'

He dropped a swift kiss on her lips and then slid out of the parlour and along the hallway. As he closed the kitchen door noiselessly Sarah opened the front door to find Leez Drummond on the doorstep, Fraser clutched in her arms. The baby's hat was tipped over one eye and he was grizzling in a low monotone that emerged damply around the fingers he had crammed into his mouth.

'I'm sorry, Mrs Forsyth, if I had known that you'd open the door, I would have gone round the back. I thought that Nellie would have been back by now.'

'It's all right,' Sarah said faintly, putting a hand to her dishevelled hair. 'I was sleeping in the parlour – a headache. Give him to me.' She took her son, and he swatted at her irritably as she tried to straighten his hat. 'You're home early, are you not?'

Leez began to pull the perambulator up the steps. 'He couldn't settle, poor wee lamb. It's another tooth coming through.' She left the perambulator in the hallway and reclaimed Fraser. 'Why don't you go upstairs and lie down, Mrs Forsyth? Once I've seen to this wee man I'll mix up something to help your headache.'

In her bedroom, Sarah sank down on to the bed, both hands pressed tightly against her heart, which was beating swiftly. What if Leez had brought the baby home a little later, and found – what she might have found did not bear thinking about. She should never have let Samuel into the house when she was on her own, and once he was in, she should have kept the conversation to everyday things instead of letting him break through her guard by reminding her of what had once been between the two of them.

She was a wicked, stupid woman, she told herself fiercely, but her heart continued to leap and her treacherous body to ache for him, while a voice in her head whispered that if only they had not been interrupted...

Samuel whistled cheerfully as he walked back to the shop. His plan had worked well enough, though it was a pity they had been interrupted. But there would surely be other chances, he thought with satisfaction, tipping his hat to a respected customer as he passed; other chances to repay Walter Forsyth for the day he had come home to find Samuel and Sarah together, and had thrown Samuel out of the house by the kitchen door – the tradesman's door. Cuckolding the man was the best thing Samuel could think of as a reprisal, and it would happen, he was sure of that.

Every man should have at least two wives, he thought as he strode down Hamilton Street: one with money and one, like Sarah, for enjoyment.

'You've been away for a good while,' Walter said when Samuel arrived.

Samuel beamed at him, 'Mrs McLennan was having a dress fitting so I had to wait until she was free so that she could make sure that the tea service was in perfect condition.'

'Was she satisfied?'

'Oh yes,' Samuel said breezily. 'Very satisfied indeed. The ladies always like personal attention.'

30

Morna enjoyed the camp more than she had ever enjoyed anything in her life. She never knew, as she and Tom cycled along the coast road to Portencross every morning, rain or sunshine, what the day would bring; she only knew that by the time they cycled back to Saltcoats that evening she would be exhausted, but exhilarated.

Each day became an adventure in a world she had never before inhabited. She looked after small children while their harassed mothers bought their daily groceries at the vans by the gate, held a sewing class for some of the older girls – and some of the mothers too – played rounders, organised games, helped Charlotte to bandage scraped knees and elbows and supervised anxiously as the older children scrambled over the rocks that formed that part of the shoreline. She also tucked up her skirts and waded in rock pools with the littlest children, finding unexpected pleasure in their excitement. When Tom held Sunday services in the large marquee she played hymns on the battered old piano that had arrived on the back of a small lorry while the congregation sang lustily, heedless of the fact that it, like them, was slightly out of tune.

The marquee was well filled for the Sunday services and also on Friday evenings, when the campers gathered for the weekly concert. Between them they could summon up a wide variety of talents – musicians played the accordion, the mouth organ, the spoons and the penny whistle, while others sang, danced or performed monologues. The closing event of every concert was a loud and lusty sing-song, with Morna thumping out all the popular tunes on the piano.

Her creamy skin reddened beneath the sun during those daily cycle rides, and within two weeks it had taken on a golden glow.

'You look like a farm worker,' Walter said disapprovingly when the family met round his table for Sunday dinner. Morna, arriving late after playing at a camp service, had just taken her seat. 'Anyone would think to look at you that you're a tinker woman who earned her food by working in the fields.'

'Tinkers are as brown and as tough as leather,' Belle protested, 'whereas Morna's skin has just taken on a little bit of sun.'

'I think it suits her,' Sarah ventured, and her sister-in-law took a moment from her meal to throw her a grateful smile.

'I don't,' Walter snapped. 'Don't you remember, Morna, how careful Mother was to shade her face from the heat of the sun? She always said that one could tell a lady by her pale, delicate skin.'

'I'm sure she was right, Walter, but it wouldn't be practical for me to go around the camp wearing wide-brimmed hats and trying to protect my face from the sunshine, even if I wanted to, which I don't. I like sunshine and I'm sure that it won't do me a bit of harm. I shall soon become pale again once the autumn arrives. Sarah, could I trouble you for another potato?'

'You'll put on weight,' Walter warned as his wife passed the bowl across the table.

'Better fat than hungry. In any case, I shall work it all off playing with the children during the week. Sometimes, Walter, you can sound like an old woman,' Morna said with exasperation, and her brother almost choked.

'Morna!' Belle remonstrated mildly.

'Speaking for myself, I think that a touch of sun makes the most of Morna's perfect skin. I am in complete agreement with you, Sarah.' Samuel smiled across the table at Sarah, who coloured and became busy passing the gravy boat. Since everyone else had finished the main course and Nellie was waiting to bring in the pudding, only Morna availed herself of the offer.

'I will never,' Belle had sworn fiercely to herself in the sweet dark hours of the night as she lay by her husband's side after he had made love to her, 'be a jealous wife.' She always, long after he had turned away from her and fallen asleep, lay awake listening to his even breathing and feeling happier than she had ever believed possible. Samuel was hers for evermore, and he deserved the best wife a man could have.

But gradually, in the cold light of day, suspicion and jealousy began to creep into her mind. Before they married she had approved of his easy, charming manner towards female customers in the shop, seeing it as good for business. Now that she wore his ring on her finger, his attentions seemed to her to be overdone, and she resented the way women of all ages glanced eagerly around the shop as soon as they entered, their faces lighting up when they spied her husband. She noted the pink flush that came to their cheeks as he made his way towards them, and the way that most of the women, if he was already busy with a customer, pretended to study the items on the shelves and display stands, waving away the other assistants and waiting until Samuel was free to attend to them.

During her entire life Belle had never known jealousy. As a child, she had been happy to share her toys with her brother and sister. When she was old enough to have a few pieces of jewellery Morna was always welcome to borrow a brooch or pendant necklace that might match whatever she was wearing, and any clothing Belle finished with was parcelled up and sent to those in need of such charity. But Samuel was different – he was her husband, and she resented every smile he bestowed on other women.

She tried hard to fight her feelings, telling herself that Samuel was as deeply in love with her as she was with him, and that he would never deceive her. But she could not help mentioning to him that at times, his attention towards some of the ladies who called in at the shop was a little too friendly.

'Isn't that what we're supposed to do?' he asked, eyebrows raised. 'I thought you approved of the way I deal with the customers.'

'Yes, I did in the past, but now that you're the manager and a member of the family a little more decorum may be in order.'

'So you'd like me to be more of a Walter now, would you? You'd like to see me going about the place like this...' He put his hands behind his back and stalked around the parlour, looking down his nose at the furniture and pausing at the elegant stand that held a pot plant to say stiffly, 'Good morning, Mrs McBain, the weather is damp for the time of year, is it not? How are you, apart from dripping rainwater all over my nice clean floor? And how are Mr McBain and all the little McBains? Mr Stoddart, kindly attend to Mrs McBain.' He snapped his fingers then asked his wife, 'Is that what you want me to do?'

His malicious impersonation of Walter was so accurate that Belle laughed until she almost cried. 'Of course not, you silly man,' she said when she was able to speak again. 'You've got a much better way with folk than Walter ever had; all I'm asking is that you be a little less – friendly – where the ladies are concerned.'

'You're never jealous, are you?'

Belle felt her face grow hot, 'Jealous? What a daft notion!'

'I do believe that you are, you silly little thing. You,' Samuel said, capturing her hand in both of his, 'are my adored wife, the woman who rescued me from a miserable existence and taught me the true meaning of love. You are the centre of my world.' He raised her hand to his lips and covered it with kisses before drawing her into his arms. 'You are my very own, adored Isabelle,' he said against her throat, 'and those other foolish women who come simpering into the shop are nothing more to me than profit for Forsyth's.'

Several minutes later, sprawled in an armchair and watching his wife tidy her dishevelled hair in front of the mirror, he said thoughtfully, 'Talking of the shop, what are we going to do with Walter?'

'What do you mean?' Belle peered at her reflection, noticing a red mark on her neck. It looked like an insect bite, but she had not been aware of it before, she thought, puzzled. Then her already flushed face went a deeper shade of red as she recalled Samuel's teeth nipping gently at her skin.

'He's rarely in the shop – he certainly never spends a full day there. All the work of running the place is left to you and me.'

'Walter has always been like that. It's a pity that he was the only son, and born to go into the shop whether he liked it or not.' The top three buttons of Belle's blouse had been unfastened; now she fastened them again, easing her collar up so that the red mark was hidden. 'Had he been left to make his own choice, he might have taken up some business that suited him better.'

'You think that any business would have suited him? It seems to me,' Samuel mused, 'that your brother has no great interest in work of any kind. It's odd that a man who could have married a wife wealthy enough to keep him in comfort should have chosen his penniless maidservant, while I, who had nothing, find myself married to a wealthy woman. I was merely making an observation, my dear,' he added swiftly as Belle swung round to stare at him.

386

'You have never taken advantage of my money and I will not allow anyone to say otherwise! You work very hard.'

'Which brings me to the point I was going to make. I think we should buy Walter out.'

'Buy him out of the shop? I couldn't do that!'

'Why not? You have a far better head for business than he has – even I have a better head for business than Walter. Between us, we could turn Forsyth's into even more of a success than it is already. We could open up branches in Stevenston and Ardrossan – perhaps further afield,' Samuel swept on, his eyes bright with enthusiasm.

'Buy him out?' Belle repeated, still stunned.

'You have enough in the bank to do it, thanks to your Aunt Beatrice.'

'But what would Walter do with himself then?'

'What he does best, my dear. He will lounge around at home all day, appreciating that little wife of his, and their son. We've both heard him express an interest in standing for the town council, and I'm sure he would enjoy that far more than pretending to run an ironmonger's business. But why should we care what he would do, my love? We'll be too busy pursuing our own dream – "Forsyth and Gilmartin".' The words rolled off his tongue and hung in the air between them, embossed in gold letters against a polished black background. 'It has a fine ring to it, d'you not think so?'

A faint scratching was heard from the other side of the closed door, 'That's poor Juliet,' Belle said. 'She wants some company.'

'Can she not do with Ena's company in the kitchen?'

'She's just a little dog looking for affection. Let her in, Samuel.'

'She should be taught not to damage the doors like that,' he grumbled, getting to his feet. Juliet was waiting out in the hall, head cocked to one side; as she saw Samuel standing at the opened door her ears flattened against her head and she backed away, a gentle rumbling starting up in her throat. Then she whined as Belle called her name from inside the room.

'Come along.' Samuel stood to one side, opening the door wider. 'Your mistress wants to see you and I'm not holding the door open for you all day.'

The little animal trotted by him, giving his polished shoes a wide berth. She had learned how the toes of those shoes could hurt when they connected with her ribs. Once inside the room she raced over to Belle, almost leaping into her arms.

'There's a good girl,' Belle crooned as Juliet licked her face.

'You shouldn't let her do that,' Samuel remonstrated, putting out a hand to restrain the dog. Then he pulled it back hastily as Juliet whirled round with a sudden snarl and lunged at his fingers.

'Juliet!' Belle sat down and settled the animal on her lap, stroking her ears. 'Naughty girl, you mustn't hurt Uncle Samuel.'

Juliet, the growl still rumbling in her chest and her top lip drawn back to reveal a glimpse of sharp white fangs, twisted her head round in order to keep watch on Samuel as he settled himself into his usual armchair. He smiled blandly into her bright black eyes before opening his newspaper and lifting it so that it formed a screen between him and the rest of the room.

That was at least one bitch who didn't find him in the least bit desirable.

Once, Sarah had done all she could to encourage Walter to go to the shop every day. When he stayed at home he tended to disrupt the daily household duties and annoy Leez Drummond by interrupting little Fraser's routine. But after the day that Samuel had found her at home on her own she did all she could to keep her husband close by.

On the days when Walter was out, Nellie was instructed to inform Mr Gilmartin, should he call, that the mistress was not at home.

'But why should I say you're out when I know you're in?' the girl protested, confused.

'Because I don't want to entertain Mr Gilmartin in this house.'

'Does Mr Forsyth know that Mr Gilmartin can't come into the house any more?'

'Of course he can visit when Mr Forsyth is at home, or if Mrs Gilmartin is with him,' Sarah tried to explain, then ended up with, 'Oh, for goodness' sake, girl, just do as I tell you!'

As it happened, Samuel only came to the house once when Walter was out, and on that occasion Sarah herself happened to see him striding along the pavement when she was taking down the net curtains in the nursery. She flew downstairs, almost missing the final step in her haste, and into the kitchen, where Nellie was sorting through the laundry.

'Nellie, Mr Gilmartin is on his way to the gate. Remember what I told you – I am out of the house and you don't know when I will return.'

'Are you sure, ma'am? It seems wrong to lie to such a pleasant gentleman, and Mr Forsy–'

'Yes, I'm sure! Just remember what I told you – I am out and you don't know when I will return.' Sarah sped back into the hall and had gained the upper landing by the time the doorknocker was lifted and dropped. She clutched at the banister, holding her breath and listening to Nellie plod through the hall.

'Good morning, Nellie, and isn't it a fine morning too? I've come to call on your mistress.'

'She's out, and so's the master and Leez Drummond and the bairn and I don't know when any of them's coming back, sir.' Nellie rattled the sentence off swiftly.

'Now that's a great pity, for I was hoping that Mrs Forsyth might offer me a refreshing cup of tea. So you're the only one at home, are you?' Sarah heard Samuel say, and all at once her blood ran cold. Surely he wouldn't stoop so low as to try to seduce her little maidservant?

'Only me, sir, and I'm busy sorting out the washing, since it's Monday. Mrs Forsyth–' Nellie stopped short, then said, 'Mrs Forsyth said that I had to have it all done by the time she got back, sir.'

'Are you going to manage it without help?'

'Mrs McCall should be here any time now, sir, to help me.'

'Ah. In that case, Nellie, I'll say goodbye. No need to mention that I called,' Sarah heard Samuel say, and then, to her relief, the door closed.

She hurried to the nursery window in time to see him walk along the path below, still carrying his bowler hat in his hand. Under the late July sun, his hair had a rich glow to it. He went through the gate, and as he turned to close it he glanced up at the house.

Sarah threw herself back from the window, coming up against the side of Fraser's cot. She clutched at it, closing her eyes tightly in a childish attempt to make herself completely invisible. He must have seen her, unless the sunlight on the glass had made it impossible for him to see anything. But he had guessed that she was at home, for why else would he have looked up at the windows? The thoughts flew around her head like fallen leaves scampering before autumn winds and she put a hand to her heart, which was racing. She had escaped this time, but what about the next visit? It was essential that she keep him outside the house, because if he came in again, and if she found herself alone with him, she knew that she would not be able to resist him. And if she gave in to him, what would become of–

'I sent him away, ma'am,' Nellie said from the doorway, and when Sarah, her nerves stretched to breaking point, screamed and whirled round, the servant also screamed and clutched at her flat chest. 'Oh ma'am, it's no' a mouse, is it?'

'It's just you, coming in without warning.' Sarah drew a deep, shaky breath. 'D'you think he believed you, Nellie?'

'I think so, ma'am. He wanted a cup of tea but I told him a lie. I said that Annie McCall was

391

coming to help with the washing.'

'That's all right, Nellie, it wasn't a wicked lie. Now then,' Sarah said as her heartbeat began to slow down, 'I think I could do with a cup of tea myself, and you deserve one for doing as you were told.'

31

'Miss, Miss, my mam's no' feelin' well. Could ye come and have a look at her?' Kate, the eldest of the Kennaway girls, tugged at Morna's skirt.

'What's wrong with her?'

'She's awful red in the face and she's breathin' heavy.' Kate's thin face was screwed up with worry. 'Could ye come now?'

Morna, who had been sorting through music for the concert at the end of the week, dumped the papers on top of the piano and followed the girl out of the marquee and across the busy field, winding their way around tents and wooden shacks.

The four youngest Kennaway children were huddled in a tight, frightened group outside their tent, the baby struggling and whimpering in Mima's arms.

'Give him to me.' Kate took him and propped him over one shoulder, her free hand patting his back. Robbie belched loudly and then settled down to study the camp from his new vantage point. 'Why aren't you lookin' after Mam like I told you?'

'Mrs Baxter came across and sent us outside,' Mima was explaining when the young neighbour who had brought tea over on the day the Kennaways had arrived emerged from the tent.

'Yer mammy's doin' fine,' she assured the children, 'it's just a wee belly–ache, that's all.'

'It's the new bairn, isn't it?' Kate said rather than asked. 'It's comin' too early.'

'It might be the bairn,' the woman admitted, and then to Morna, lowering her voice, 'Can you come in for a minute?'

'Wait here, I'll not be long.' She followed Mrs Baxter into the tent and saw Jess Kennaway sprawled on the bed like a beached whale. Her face was flushed and her breathing heavy.

'I think it's the bairn comin', pet,' she whispered when Morna went to her side. 'Will you look after the weans for me, just till it's all over? They'll behave themselves for ye.'

'Of course I will.' Morna patted the woman's hand and allowed Mrs Baxter to draw her back towards the door. 'Could ye find Charlotte, hen? I don't think this one's goin' tae be easy. I'm comin', pet,' she added as Jess let out a deep groan and clutched at the metal frame of the bed. 'Get Charlotte quick,' she added over her shoulder as she hurried back to the bed.

When Morna went out into the daylight the children were grouped slightly apart from the women who had begun to gather as news of the imminent birth spread. 'Kate, could you run to the bus and fetch Charlotte?'

'She's not there,' Kate said, 'that's why I

393

fetched you.'

'Charlotte's in the Kerrs' tent,' one of the women offered. 'Their wee one's got the bronchitis again.'

'Mima, run across there and tell Charlotte that Mam needs her,' Kate ordered, and then, as the little girl scampered off, 'I'm goin' in to see my mam.'

She thrust the baby into Morna's arms and disappeared inside the tent.

'She's too young to be in there!'

'She might be young, but she's got an old head on her shoulders, that one,' one of the women said. 'And she comes from the tenements; she's probably seen and heard things you've no knowledge of.' Another groan came from within the tent and wee Rena, the youngest Kennaway girl, started to cry. 'It's all right, pet,' the woman comforted her. 'Yer mammy'll be better soon.'

A few minutes later Charlotte arrived at a fast trot with Mima puffing along at her back. She hurried into the tent and a moment later Mrs Baxter ushered a protesting Kate out.

'I should stay with Mam! I know what to do, I was there when Robbie was born!'

'Mebbe so, hen, but Charlotte needs plenty of room, so the less folk in there the better. The wee ones need ye,' the neighbour coaxed.

'Where are the boys, Kate?' Morna asked.

'Down at the water.'

'Let's take the others there as well. We'll have a competition to see who can throw a stone furthest into the sea. Thruppence for the winner,' Morna suggested, wishing that Tom had not gone with Ruth to Glasgow for the day. Kate took the baby, casting several reluctant looks back at the tent as Morna ushered her and her sisters through the field and towards the shore.

'Look, miss – look!' Mima said as the others scattered to search for pebbles. 'Look at Arran – it's gone!'

Although the day was clear, there was no sun, and the island had indeed disappeared completely behind a bank of mist.

'It's a magic island, isn't it?' Mima's voice was a whisper, her grey eyes wide as she glanced up at Morna. 'I've been watching it, and sometimes it's there, sometimes it's not. Sometimes there's mist all round, so that it's floating, and sometimes it's got a white scarf wrapped round its neck.'

Morna, who had thought nothing before of Arran's mists and clouds or the days when it was not to be seen at all, was taken aback by the city child's vivid imagination.

'Where has it gone?' Mima wanted to know.

'Far away, to a place where the sea's blue and the sun shines all the time,' Morna improvised.

'Mebbe it'll like that place so much that it won't come back.' The child's voice was anxious.

'It always comes back – you'll see,' Morna promised. 'Now then, let's find some stones for you to throw into the water.'

The competition to see who could throw their pebbles farthest attracted several other children and grew into a complicated event with rules and handicaps. Finally, as the smell of food cooking began to waft from the field behind them, the children who had joined them on the beach began to disperse to their various tents and huts, until only Morna and the Kennaway children were left. Robbie was crying with hunger by now, so Morna took her charges to the bus, where a small store of tinned food was kept as emergency rations. With Kate's help, she managed to put together a meal, which the children fell on as though they hadn't eaten for days.

'Can we go and see Mam now?' Kate asked when they had finished.

'Best wait until Charlotte says it's all right.'

'But Robbie needs his afternoon sleep. He needs to go into his cot!'

Morna managed to borrow a well-worn perambulator from one of the tents, and Robbie was laid in it and covered with various coats and jackets, then trundled over the bumpy grass to the marquee, where Morna coaxed all the other children, including Kate, to start a game of musical chairs. Again, others straggled in to join them, and from musical chairs they moved to a game of Statues, then a sing-song. When it finally trickled to a close, Morna shut the piano lid, stretched her aching fingers and said with as much cheer as she could muster, 'What shall we do now?'

But Kate had had enough. 'We're goin' to see our mam,' she announced.

'But we should wait until Char–'

'It's been hours! We need tae see what's happenin',' Kate said. She burrowed into the pile of assorted jackets in the perambulator until she found Robbie, and gathered him, rosy and smiling despite being wakened from his sleep, into her arms. 'Come on,' she ordered the others.

'Wait – why don't you wait here and I'll go and see how your mother is?'

Kate's glare was suspicious. 'You'll come right back? Cross your heart and hope to die?'

'Cross my heart and hope to die.'

'You've got to do it, not just say it,' snapped Kate, and Morna obediently drew a cross across the area of her heart and chanted the oath once more.

'All right then, but mind and come right back.'

'I will,' Morna promised, and set off across the field, worn out by the day's events.

Several women were still by the Kennaway tent, talking in low voices. Their faces were sombre, and a cold hand clutched at Morna's heart as she approached. They watched silently as she lifted the canvas flap and went in.

The interior of the tent was oppressively hot and smelled of disinfectant with an undertone of something she did not recognise; something eerily frightening. In the few hours since Morna had last seen her, Jess Kennaway had shrunk to a small, waxen image of her former self, she lay on the bed, her body motionless beneath the single blanket that had been thrown over her and her face as pale in the greenish light as a snowy water lily glimpsed just beneath the surface of a scummy pond. Her eyes were closed.

'Is she...?' Morna whispered to Charlotte, who was unfolding a piece of towelling.

'She's fine, but she lost the baby and she's very tired. She needs her rest. Where are the other bairns?'

'I persuaded them to wait in the marquee while I came to see how their mother is.'

Charlotte picked up a bucket and covered it with the towelling, but not before Morna had glimpsed the water within, gleaming with a reddish shimmer. 'I'll tell them that she's sleeping and they can see her in a wee while. Mebbe you could give Mrs Baxter a hand.' She nodded to where the other woman was working in a corner, and then went outside.

Mrs Baxter was wrapping something carefully in a shawl. 'A wee laddie, it was,' she murmured as Morna joined her. 'Never even got tae draw his first breath, poor wee soul. We'll just...' A child started to howl outside, and her head lifted sharply. 'That's my Jimmy, he's hurt himself. Here...' She thrust the bundle into Morna's arms and ran from the tent.

A corner of the shawl had come loose and Morna lifted a hand to replace it, then stopped as she found herself looking at the dead child, its tiny face as white as a perfect rose petal. A tuft of dark hair stood out like a cockscomb along the top of the little head, and the eyelids, with their tiny stubby lashes, were closed as though in sleep. Moving carefully, unable to grasp that this child was incapable of being roused, she touched the little cheek with the back of a finger. It was as cold and hard as a china doll's.

She wasn't even aware that she was crying until a tear fell and splashed on to the baby's face. Carefully, Morna wiped it away with a corner of the shawl, then she jumped as Jess Kennaway said from the bed, 'Give him tae me.'

The woman was struggling upright, her arms reaching out for her child.

'Mrs Kennaway, he's...'

'I know that. Give him to me,' Jess ordered, and Morna placed the little bundle carefully into the arms waiting to receive it.

'Poor wee bairn,' Jess whispered, 'the road was too long and too hard for ye, wasn't it?' She eased the shawl back and bent to kiss the small face. 'It's a boy.'

'I know, and he's beautiful.'

'Just like all my other bairns. He has a look of my mother about him, God rest her. And something of his father too. My man's the handsomest in the whole street.' Jess smiled proudly, and in her smile Morna suddenly caught a glimpse of the beautiful girl lingering behind the older, careworn face – a girl still deeply in love. Then, with sudden concern, Jess asked, 'How have the other bairns managed without me?'

'I've been looking after them all day and they're fine, all of them. You've got a lovely family.'

'Did they get somethin' tae eat?'

'Oh, they've been well fed.'

'D'ye think ye could keep them busy for a wee bit longer? I just need tae spend some time with this one, then I'll get up and see tae the others.'

'But you need to stay in bed; you've just had a baby. Someone else will look after the other children until you feel strong enough to get up.'

'I'm strong enough now,' Jess said impatiently. 'This isnae the first, ye know. Women like me don't have the time tae loll about in bed as if child-bearin' was an illness instead of somethin' that happens naturally. This one,' she turned her attention back to the bundle in her arms, 'was tae have been wee Thomas, after Tom.' She smoothed the black curl down, then gave a little laugh as it immediately sprang up again. 'And he would have been a right wee character if he'd had the strength tae draw breath; wouldn't ye, my wee mannie? Ye know, Morna, no matter how many bairns a woman births, every one of them brings its own love, even the ones that don't stay for long. Would ye mind, hen, givin' us a wee while on our own, me and my Thomas?'

'Of course not. I'll go and see to the others.'

'Thanks. Could ye keep an eye on them tomorrow, too?' Jess asked as Morna turned towards the entrance. 'I'll need tae take wee Thomas home and see that he gets a proper burial. I'll be back before night-time.'

While Morna watched Jess Kennaway hold her stillborn child and Belle, in the back office of the shop in Dockhead Street, frowned over the ledgers, trying to make sense of them and Ena, Belle's maidservant, sat in her sister's kitchen on her afternoon off, explaining that she was thinking of looking for another position, Samuel Gilmartin let himself into the house he shared with Belle.

He stood in the hall for a moment, looking around with a satisfied smile, then called 'Ena?' As he had hoped, there was no reply, other than yapping from the kitchen. As Samuel opened the door Juliet backed away from him, growling.

'That's enough! Out ye go,' he ordered, opening the back door, and then, as the dog retreated to a corner, glaring at him, 'Out, I said – now!'

Slowly, the growl rumbling in her throat, Juliet inched her way to the door, giving him a wide berth, but not wide enough. She had almost reached the door when Samuel, impatient to close it, helped her on her way with the toe of his shoe. Juliet gave a shrill yelp of pain, and then, as he bent down to push her through the door, she turned on him, sinking her sharp little teeth into her tormentor's hand.

It was Samuel's turn to yelp. He rushed to hold his bleeding hand beneath the cold-water tap while Juliet watched, half-triumphant at giving him a taste of his own medicine, but half-appalled at what she had done.

'Right, milady,' Samuel Gilmartin said as he turned the tap off and wrapped his hand in the towel again, 'you've done for yourself now, haven't you? Done for yourself good and proper!'

'How can she do that?' Morna asked Tom the following evening as they cycled back along the coast road to Saltcoats. 'How can she just get up and get on with her duties right after giving birth, then bury her baby and come straight back as if nothing had happened?'

They had arrived in the morning to find Jess Kennaway dressed in her hat and coat, her gloved hands clutching the shopping bag that contained the body of her stillborn child. Tom, who was going to Glasgow with her, had offered to find a carter to take them to West Kilbride railway station, but Jess had insisted on walking. 'It'll be good for me, after spending the best part of yesterday in

my bed,' she had said, then instructed her subdued brood to behave themselves and not be a
nuisance.

'Stop here a minute and enjoy the evening,'
Tom suggested, and they cycled to the side of the
road nearest the sea. Tom laid his bicycle down
on the grass and when Morna had done the
same, he reached out a hand to her and led her
through the clumps of stiff grass towards the
sandy beach. Jumping down on to the firm sand,
he turned and put a hand on either side of her
waist before lifting her down to stand before him.

'All right?' he asked, and when she nodded he
released her. 'Look at that,' he said with satisfaction, indicating the vista before them with a
sweep of one arm. It had been a day of high cloud
and little sunshine, and now the slumbering sea
reflected the soft pearl grey of the sky. Arran
looked more like a fairy kingdom than a real
island as it floated on the cushion of thick mist
lying all along its shoreline.

Tom drew in a deep breath and stretched his
arms out, lifting them over his head before he
finally let them fall to his sides. 'I've been dream-
ing all day of standing on this beach, breathing in
the salt air. I wish I was an artist, then I could
paint that view in its every mood and hang it on
the walls of my flat in Glasgow. But even if I were
the best artist in the world, the paintings would
never be able to compare with being here in the
flesh.' Then, his eyes still on the sea and the island
floating offshore, 'You were asking how Jess Kennaway could do what she did today, and the
answer is, because it had to be done. She wanted

402

to let her husband see his new son, and then the two of them wanted to make sure that their child had the decent burial he deserved. That was the only thing they could do for him, and it was all done properly.'

'Did you conduct the service?'

'The Kennaways are Roman Catholics while I am a minister of the Church of Scotland,' Tom reminded her. 'Their own priest officiated but I was there as a friend of the family.' He paused, then said, 'I saw Christina Baird while I was in Glasgow.'

'She's out of prison?'

'Aye, she's served her time, but it's near killed her. Ruth wanted her to come back to Saltcoats for a long holiday, but she's going to her cousin in Dumfries. He's a doctor and he'll be able to look after her properly. I doubt if she'd be able to stand another prison sentence.'

'It's not fair!' Morna said passionately. 'Women shouldn't be treated like that just because they want the right to vote. How can Parliament allow such terrible things to happen?'

'Men had to suffer and die in their fight for the vote,' Tom reminded her. 'It's a sad way for a country that prides itself on being modern to treat its own citizens, but sometimes protesting is the only way to make the stuffy old men in Parliament change their medieval way of thinking.'

'Don't you worry about Ruth getting thrown into prison and suffering the way Christina suffered?'

'Every minute of every day, but I can't do anything about it.'

'You could ask her to be careful, for your sake.'

'No, I couldn't, because God gave us the freedom to choose the paths we want to follow in life.'

'We don't all have the freedom to choose. I had to leave the home I was born and raised in because my father left home and my brother married our servant girl. They were able to do what they wanted because they're men. Neither of them had any thought for the way their selfishness might hurt me.'

'Did your brother order you to leave home?'

'No, but–'

'So it was your choice. And it was your choice to accept Ruth's invitation to go and live with her and to teach the children in her little dame school. It was your choice,' Tom swept on as she opened her mouth to protest, 'to help with the summer camp. And I for one am very glad that you did.'

'I would hardly call those decisions freedom of choice.'

'Freedom comes in many disguises,' he said, amusement in his voice and eyes as he turned to look down at her. 'Sometimes it can be limited, but every single day of our lives we are all given a certain amount of freedom, even though we might not be aware of it. Look for it, Morna, and treasure it. As for now, let's go home. Ruth will have supper on the table and I am more than ready for it.'

They turned their backs on the sea, and on Arran, and headed towards the roadside and their bicycles. As they reached the grassy banking, Tom again took Morna by the waist and swung her up into the air, setting her down gently among the tufts of grass.

'Your turn now,' he said, and held out his hands. She took them in hers and he jumped nimbly up beside her, retaining her hands in his for a few seconds longer than necessary.

His firm, warm clasp and the intensity in his eyes as he looked down at her as though trying to fix a picture of her in his mind, suddenly caused an unfamiliar but pleasant fluttering throughout Morna.

32

August ended and the camp at Portencross resembled an ants' nest as the holidaymakers packed their belongings, took down their tents, unbolted the panels of their wooden huts and loaded everything on to the succession of lorries waiting to carry them off.

The final week was one of hard work and farewells. To Morna's surprise and pleasure, Jess Kennaway gave her a warm hug. 'Bless ye, pet, and thank ye for all ye did,' the woman said, while her children, faces rosy from sun and sea air, looked on, beaming.

'See ye next year,' they all yelled from the cab as their lorry jolted out of the field.

It seemed to Morna that an air of desolation began to blanket the field like a mist as the holidaymakers left, family by family. When Tom returned to his duties in Glasgow she was astonished to discover how much she missed him. She missed their cycle runs to and from Portencross, his stories about his work, their arguments and their laughter. She missed listening to his discussions with Ruth and she missed his cheerful whistling as he went about the house. Without him, it seemed a silent, echoing place, even when Ruth's friends gathered in the kitchen.

Noise returned to the place in September when classes resumed. The house was filled once more with the clatter of small booted feet and the chatter of childish voices, but busy though she was, Morna could not shake off a sense of loss, and a certain restlessness.

Guiltily aware that she had been neglecting her brother and sister, she first visited Argyle Road, where she found Sarah more confident and content than she had been since her marriage, thanks to Leez Drummond's calming presence. Wee Fraser, now seven months old, had begun to turn into a person in his own right. Watching him as he sat on his mother's lap, talking away to himself in some mysterious baby language and vigorously banging a rattle on the arm of Sarah's chair, Morna noticed that the poor little scrap still looked very like his father, but she had the tact to keep that thought to herself.

When she called on Belle the sisters spent a busy afternoon going through the possessions that had been stored for her. Most of the clothes were put aside to be sent to charity institutions, for Morna was now more in need of practical clothing than the pretty blouses, skirts and gowns she had once loved. 'It's like another world,' she marvelled. 'My life has changed so much since the days when I wore this sort of thing.' She spread a white lace evening gown over the bed in the back bedroom. 'I'll surely never wear that again.'

'Oh, you must keep it, Morna. You looked so pretty the last time you wore it, do you remember?' Belle fussed over the gown, smoothing out the tiered skirt and settling the cape-effect neckline and the tiered lace sleeves into place.

'The tennis club party last summer.'

'That's right. Mother had it specially made for you from a picture in a magazine and Papa thought that the sleeves were far too short, even though you were wearing long gloves. I wonder where he is now?'

'Papa? Riding an elephant in India, or finding gold in California, or perhaps working in someone else's ironmonger's shop in England. Wherever he is, I hope he's happy,' Morna said, and then as Belle raised her eyebrows, 'Hating someone is much more tiring than just letting go.' She studied the dress, her head to one side. 'You really think I should keep this one?'

'Yes, because it's still fashionable and you never know when you're going to need it.' Belle gathered the gown up and put it back in the wardrobe.

'My tennis clothes can definitely go to charity for I won't need them again.'

'That reminds me – did you know that Clarissa Pinkerton and Arthur MacAdam are engaged to be married?'

'I saw the announcement in the *Herald*.' Only a year ago, Morna realised, she would have been distraught at the news; now she wondered why she had ever wanted to marry Arthur. 'Were you invited to the engagement party?'

'I think my invitation must have got lost in the post.'

'Mine too. Isn't that a pity?' Morna said with a grin.

'It's good to see you smiling again. You're in danger of developing frown lines and they don't suit you. What's the matter?' Belle asked, concerned.

'Nothing – I don't know. I feel as if I'm standing at a crossroads and someone's removed the signs, so I don't know which road to take.'

'I can answer that – we'll take the road down to the kitchen. Ena's out for the afternoon so we'll have to see to our own tea.'

'Where's that annoying yappy little dog? I haven't heard her since I arrived,' Morna said as she set a tray with cups and saucers and plates. 'In fact, the house has been blessedly silent all afternoon, but I didn't notice it until now.'

'She – she's gone.'

'Gone where?' Morna asked, and then, realising that there had been a strange note in Belle's voice, she turned to see that her sister's eyes had suddenly filled with tears.

'Gone,' Belle said. 'She – she d-died.' Her voice broke and the tears spilled over.

'Oh, Belle, why didn't you tell me? Sit down here. Can I fetch you anything? Smelling salts, or a glass of water?'

'No, I'm just making a silly fuss.' Belle fumbled in her pocket for a handkerchief and wiped her eyes, then gave her sister a watery smile. 'Imagine missing a little dog – but I'd grown fond of her, Morna, and I think she was fond of me, if it's possible for dogs to care for people.' She began to get up. 'I'm being a dreadful hostess, you must be longing for your tea.'

'You just sit down again. I can see to the tray and make the tea. I know how to do these things now,' Morna said with a rueful smile. As she rinsed the teapot with hot water before measuring a spoonful of leaves from the tea caddy she said, 'I suppose she was quite old?'

'Elderly, perhaps, but still active. I always assumed that she would be with us for a while yet,' Belle's voice was still shaky. 'Samuel thinks she may have found something poisonous in the garden, and eaten it. He came home one afternoon two weeks ago and found her having a fit on the lawn. He was bitten on the hand when he tried to carry her into the house. She died shortly after he arrived and he buried her at once, to spare Ena and myself from seeing the poor wee thing.'

'Since you miss her so much, perhaps you should get another dog.'

'I couldn't. As you said, she was a yappy little thing, and so used to the company of womenfolk that she could never take to Samuel. When he was in the house she had to be kept in the kitchen or outside, and I know that she hated being denied the freedom of the house after having been used to it all her life. It's just that – Aunt Beatrice loved her so dearly that I feel as though I let them both down.' Belle got up to help carry the tea things through to the parlour. 'I can't think where she got hold of the poison.'

'Some ragamuffin might have thrown poisoned meat over the back wall – don't you remember that happening to Mrs Hepburn's prize Labrador years ago?' Then, as they went into the parlour, Morna stopped short so that Belle, carrying the teapot, almost bumped into her. 'You've moved all the furniture.'

'That was Samuel's idea. He thinks it looks better like this. Don't you think it does?'

Morna glanced around the altered room, frowning slightly. 'I'm not sure – it's not Aunt Beatrice's parlour any more.'

'I expect that that was what he intended. As he says, we must look forward to the future, not back at the past.'

'Are you happy in your marriage, Belle?'

'Of course I am. What a thing to ask!'

'Hearing about Arthur and Clarissa made me realise that you and Walter have both made marriages you would not have dreamed of when Mother and Papa were still here. Walter's very content – there's no doubt of that – and Sarah is beginning to look and sound like the mistress of our old home. And then there's you and Samuel – marrying out of one's usual social circle is probably quite a good thing. For myself, I'm convinced that I am very fortunate not to be marrying Arthur MacAdam. Clarissa is more than welcome to him – and he to her!'

'There's a letter for you – from Tom,' Ruth said casually when Morna returned to the house. 'I recognise his handwriting.'

'Why would Tom want to write to me?'

410

'Read it and find out,' Ruth suggested.

'Later.' Morna stuffed the envelope into her skirt pocket, waiting until she was alone before opening it. His letter was like Tom himself – cheerful, funny and enthusiastic about everything that was happening in his life. As Morna's eyes skimmed over the pages, it was as though he was in the room, talking to her. 'Write to me,' the letter ended. 'Tell me all about life in Saltcoats.'

Apart from school, Morna had never in her life written anything other than invitations and polite thank you notes. She bought a notepad, pen and bottle of ink the very next day, but in the evening, when she sat down in the privacy of her room to write to him, she hadn't the faintest idea how to go about it. She read his letter again, smiling over the things he said, then drew a deep breath before dipping her pen into the ink bottle. 'Dear Tom,' she wrote, and then suddenly her pen started racing over the page as she began to tell him about visiting Sarah and Belle, and about poor little Juliet, and the engagement between Clarissa Pinkerton and Arthur MacAdam.

Belle was used to seeing the assistants spring to attention every time she walked into the shop. Like her father, she was of the firm opinion that employees should be seen to be earning every penny of their wages and that being obeyed was more important than being liked. If the truth were told, she enjoyed the way the half-dozen people who worked for Forsyth's looked at her with respect.

But respect and guilt were very different things, and when she entered the shop on a particularly pleasant October morning, opening the door briskly and setting the bell overhead jangling, she was suddenly struck by the scene facing her. The cash desk was directly opposite the door, and since there were no assistants or customers to block the view she found herself looking straight through the window at Miss Campbell, the assistant cashier. The young woman was seated at the desk and Samuel was leaning over her so closely as they studied some paperwork that his auburn hair almost mingled with her fair curls.

As the bell jangled both heads, auburn and pale gold, lifted swiftly, and the guilt in the two faces brought Belle to a halt on the matting placed just inside the door. Samuel immediately straightened up and without a word to the girl he turned and left the small booth. For her part, Miss Campbell ducked her head down in a futile attempt to hide the deep flush sweeping over her pretty face.

Belle moved into the shop, nodding to assistants and pausing for a quick word with one of the regular customers. When she reached the office she found Samuel seated at the desk, working industriously. He jumped to his feet. 'Isabelle, my dear, I thought that we had agreed that you should have some time to yourself today.'

'I was doing some shopping nearby so I thought I would look in.' She drew her gloves off, glancing at the papers spread out before him. 'You're seeing to the invoices?'

'I know that you like to pay the accounts on time.'

'Yes, I do, but I was going to work on them tomorrow.'

'I thought I would make a start. You work too hard, and it's high time you let me take on some of the responsibility.'

'You already do an excellent job in the shop itself. And we have Miss Campbell to deal with the customers' payments.' Belle seated herself at the desk. 'What do you think of her, Samuel?'

'Miss Campbell? She seems a capable young woman.'

'You have no concerns about her work?'

'None whatsoever,' he said easily, and began to ask her advice about one of the invoices.

Belle had a lot to think about on her way home. For over a month now, she'd been aware of small but regular discrepancies in the shop's cash books. That, coupled with the scene that had greeted her on her arrival at the shop, was beginning to awaken the jealousy she had fought so hard to dispel. She tried to tell herself that Samuel had only been helping the girl with some problem, but a small, suspicious voice kept intruding, wanting to know why Samuel had hurried from the cash booth the moment his wife came into the shop, and why Miss Campbell had blushed so fiercely.

On the following morning she asked him to visit one of the Glasgow warehouses to decide whether a new brand of pots and pans they had in stock might suit the people of Saltcoats, and was in the shop just after it opened. It was busy, giving her good reason to ask her assistant cashier to go and serve customers while she herself took over the cash desk. In between dealing with customers she studied the cash book, glancing up now and again to see Miss Campbell watching her anxiously.

As soon as there was a lull in the rush of customers she called the girl into the main office at the back.

'I think you know why I want to talk to you,' Belle said when the door was closed.

'I have no idea.' The girl's head was high, though her hands were clenched into fists by her side, and there were two spots of bright colour on her cheekbones.

'Then I must tell you. I have noticed for some time now that the money being taken in does not agree with the stock going out. Figures have been altered in the cash book.'

'Are you accusing me of stealing?'

'Yes, I am.'

'How dare you!'

'I dare, my dear, because I have proof. You have been robbing me and my brother and I can't let it go on.'

Tears flooded into the girl's eyes. 'My mother's not been well – I needed money to buy things for her.'

'Then you should have come to me. We would have arranged something between us.'

'I won't ever do it again, I promise!'

A picture of the moment she had caught the girl with Samuel in the cash booth flashed into Belle's mind. 'No, you won't,' she agreed levelly, 'because you are leaving our employment here and now – and don't expect a reference.'

The girl drew herself up, dashing the tears from her eyes. 'I shall speak to Mr Gilmartin. He won't let you do this to me!'

'And what makes you think that?'

'Because ... because...'

'Kindly leave the premises at once,' Belle interrupted as she swept towards the door and held it open, suddenly afraid of what she might be about to hear. Then as Miss Campbell, now weeping profusely, scurried past her she added, 'And leave by the back entrance, please. I don't want customers to see you in that state.'

When Samuel returned in the early afternoon, she beckoned him to where she sat at the cash desk and told him what had happened.

'You dismissed her? But she was a good worker!'

'She was robbing us, Samuel. I'm surprised that you didn't realise it, since you seemed to give her special attention.'

His head came up quickly at that. For a moment his eyes met Belle's and then as she held her gaze unblinkingly, his own slid away, much as it had done the day she saw him with Miss Campbell. 'No more than any other employee,' he muttered. 'I was only trying to help the girl. She was willing to learn and I think that she was an asset to the shop.'

'She was, until she took over as assistant cashier. But it seems that working with money was too much of a temptation.'

'Perhaps we should give her another chance,' Samuel suggested. 'I'm sure she's learned her lesson by now, and she has a sick father to support.'

'Is that what she told you?'

'Yes, and I have no reason to disbelieve her.'

'Nor had I,' Belle said, 'when she told me not

three hours ago that she was only stealing from us in order to help her sick mother.' Then, as her husband stared at her in dismay, teeth nibbling at his lower lip, 'We must get back to work; we can talk about your visit to Glasgow tonight, at home.'

But that night Samuel went out after dinner, and when Belle asked where he was going he said curtly that he needed a walk to clear his head.

Left on her own, she tried to write some letters, but her mind was not on the task, and eventually she fetched her coat, told Ena that she too was going out for a walk, and went off to visit Morna and Ruth.

Life in the Gilmartin household was never the same after that day. Samuel lost some of his easy charm and began to spend time out of the house in the evenings. He refused to accompany Belle when she visited her brother and sister-in-law, telling her sulkily that he was tired of listening to Walter's self-important ramblings.

'When are you going to buy him out of the business?' he asked several times, but she found it hard to consider such a drastic step.

'The business has always been Forsyth and Son, even when my father was in charge of it.'

'Never mind what happened in the past – you know as well as I do that Walter's nothing more than a millstone around your neck. This is your chance to free yourself from him once and for all.'

'But it would take almost all that I – we – have in the bank.' Belle knew that Samuel hated to be reminded that the money, and the house that they lived in, belonged to his wife.

'We can make it up again once we own the business outright. I have plans for the place,' he said eagerly, 'plans that could make us both wealthy.'

These discussions invariably turned into arguments, ending with Samuel going for one of his long walks and Belle, who no longer took any pleasure from the house that had been a happy place when her aunt lived in it, usually putting her jacket on and going off to Ardrossan Road. She had discovered that sitting in Ruth Durie's kitchen listening to Ruth and whoever might have dropped in arguing about politics, education, or whatever else might come into their heads, soothed and refreshed her.

33

'I was wondering if you could recommend a trustworthy housekeeper.'

'Me?' Sarah gaped at her sister-in-law. Although Belle had become civil towards her once the shock of Walter's unsuitable marriage eased, Sarah was very much in awe of this capable woman who had the intelligence and ability to run a large shop as well as a home.

Belle, misunderstanding the younger woman's confusion, went quite red. 'I do apologise, Sarah – I didn't ask you to help me because you had been in service yourself, it's just that I'm so busy with the shop, and since you have managed to acquire such a good maidservant and nursemaid

I thought that you might be willing to help me.'

It was Sarah's turn to blush. 'I didn't think...' she began to stammer, and then, pulling herself together, 'Why don't we have another cup of tea and start this conversation again?'

Their eyes met in mutual embarrassment, which swiftly turned to mutual amusement. 'What a sensible idea!' said Belle.

'It is so nice to see you here, Belle,' Sarah ventured as she busied herself with the teapot. 'You don't call very often.'

'The shop keeps me busy Unfortunately, I had to dismiss our cashier, and that means that I have to be there most of the time at present. Once we get a new and trustworthy cashier I'll have more leisure time.' Belle sighed as she accepted her refilled cup. 'Ena could not have chosen a worse time to leave, just when I'm so busy. I'm going to miss her.'

'We can speak to Leez, the nursemaid, when we've finished our tea. She knows a lot of people, and if Leez speaks for them, you can be sure that they'll be reliable. If you wish,' Sarah offered tentatively, 'I could sit with you during the interview.'

'That would be kind,' Belle said gratefully. 'You probably have a better idea of my requirements. I've always left the running of the house to Ena, and the thought of starting all over again with someone new is not at all pleasant.'

'She was Mrs McCallum's housekeeper, wasn't she? I'm surprised to hear that she's leaving.'

'She feels that it's time to move elsewhere and there's nothing I can do about it.' Belle sipped at her tea, hoping that the sudden warmth sweeping over her face was caused by the hot drink rather than by embarrassment. She couldn't possibly tell Sarah, or anyone else, about the day Ena had handed in her notice, turning down Belle's panic-stricken offer of more money and more time off.

'I'm sorry, Mrs Gilmartin, but I won't reconsider. It has nothing to do with you, ma'am – I would be happy to stay on in your employment – but if I'm to be honest, I just can't get along with Mr Gilmartin. Nothing I do seems to be right with him, and so I think it would be best all round if I was to find work elsewhere.'

'Good riddance,' was Samuel's rejoinder when Belle told him that they were going to lose their treasured servant. 'She's a bad-tempered old bitch who thinks she rules the house.'

'Samuel!'

'I'm only telling the truth. She resents me being here and to tell the truth, I've had enough of her impertinence. It's just as well that she's decided to move on before she's dismissed.'

'I would never have dismissed Ena.'

'Tell the truth, my love.' Samuel came up behind her, put his arms around her, and nuzzled her neck. 'You insisted on keeping that noisy little dog because it had been your aunt's pet, you weren't happy when I rearranged your aunt's furniture...'

'I–'

'And you would never dismiss Ena, just because she had worked for your aunt,' he finished. 'When it comes to domestic considerations you're not as hard as you think.' Then, releasing her and turning away, 'It would have been better for poor Agnes Campbell if you had shown as much compassion for her as you're showing for our servant.'

'Miss Campbell stole from us!'

'And how do you know that that old harridan in the kitchen hasn't done the same thing? She could help herself to anything she wanted from the pantry and you'd be none the wiser.'

'She wouldn't do that,' Belle said hotly, and he shrugged.

'So no doubt you'll give her a good reference – which is more than you did for Agnes Campbell. D'you never wonder what became of her?'

'She's working in our coal merchant's office. I saw her there when I went to pay the last account.' Belle bit her lip at the memory of the insolent stare the girl had given her. 'So she managed to find work after all, even without a reference.'

'Oh, she had a reference, all right,' Samuel said casually. 'From me.'

'You?'

They had just finished dinner and Samuel, helping himself to a glass of Beatrice McCallum's port, smiled at his wife from across the room. 'Yes, she asked me for one.'

'And you did as she asked without speaking to me first?'

'The poor lass wouldn't have found a decent job without one. She'd already been turned away from the shop with no mercy at all, and I thought she'd had enough punishment. Why don't you try some of this excellent port, my dear? It might soothe your hurt pride.'

'You know that I hate port, and this has nothing to do with hurt pride. You recommended that young woman to other employers when you know very well that she took money from us.'

'A sixpence here and a shilling there – you and Walter won't miss that, and Agnes needed the money more than you did.'

'You're on first name terms with her, are you?' The white-hot jealousy that Belle had learned to dread and despise began to glow deep in her heart.

'I know her first name, yes,' Samuel said easily, sinking into a comfortable armchair. He raised the glass to his lips, his eyes challenging her over the rim.

Pain stung Belle's palms and she realised that she had clenched her fists so tightly that her fingernails were threatening to pierce the skin. She stretched her hands out and fought to keep her voice level as she said, 'And what if she steals from her present employers? What will they think of you – of both of us – then?'

'She promised me that she'd behave. Even if she doesn't, we can always swear that she was honest while she was in our employment.'

'You can lie if you wish, but I certainly won't.'

'Ah, but you will, if it's to protect my good name. Isn't that what you promised when we were married? To honour and obey me?'

Now, sipping tea in Sarah's front room, Belle flinched over the memory of that conversation.

'Is the tea too hot?' Sarah asked at once.

'Not at all – just a slight twinge in a back tooth,' Belle improvised.

'If you need attention, Mr Walker of Dockhead Street was very good when Walter went to him with dreadful toothache.'

'Thank you, I'll bear him in mind,' Belle said.

When Sarah and Belle went into young Fraser's nursery, Leez Drummond was kneeling on the floor, helping Fraser to make a tower from his coloured building blocks. He watched, bright-eyed, and every time the tower began to take shape he knocked it down with a sweep of his arm, laughing uproariously.

Leez scrambled to her feet while Sarah stooped to lift her son into her arms. 'Say hello to your Aunt Belle,' she said, then wiped his mouth with her handkerchief as he blew some bubbles. 'Leez, Mrs Gil–' her voice faltered and she choked slightly, then shook her head as Leez tried to take the baby from her. 'I'm all right, it was just a sudden tickle in my throat,' she explained when she had recovered. 'My sister-in-law is in need of a good housekeeper and I wondered if you knew of anyone suitable.'

'Livin' in, ma'am?' Leez asked, and then as Belle nodded the woman pursed her lips. 'I can't think of anyone at this moment, but I'll make enquiries. If a daily woman would do in the meantime, I know of someone – a good plain cook with clean habits and a pleasant nature. I could ask her to call on you.'

When Sarah closed the front door behind her visitor she stood for a moment, her hands pressed tightly against her mouth. She had enjoyed Belle's visit right up until that moment in the nursery when the words 'Mrs Gilmartin' had suddenly turned into a hot, hard lump in her throat and the old, familiar sense of loss had pierced her heart. She liked Belle, but how could she ever bring herself to make a friend of the woman who had won Samuel as her husband?

She whispered his name into her palms and the pain shot through her again. It took several minutes before she could compose herself and go upstairs, yearning to hold her little son and cover his face with urgent kisses.

The unresolved problem of what to do about Walter nagged at Belle over the next week. The matter, she knew, was not done with, and sure enough, the evening came when Samuel again raised the issue.

'There are premises for sale in Ardrossan – I want you to come and have a look at them. It's time we branched out and we can't do that while Walter has any say in things.'

'But if we bought another shop he could run it.'

Samuel looked at her with barely concealed impatience. 'Do you really think that he would agree to that? With the two of us keeping the Dockhead Street business going, he's able to laze about at home, enjoying the financial benefits. He's not fit to run a shop on his own. Be honest with yourself for once, Isabelle,' he surged on as she began to protest, 'you're much better at business than Walter is, and so am I, for all that I've come from nothing. I've got fire in here...' he thumped a fist against his own breast, '...and I've got the hunger a man needs to make something of himself. If Walter hadn't been born into comfort and security he'd be living down in the slums by the river right now, and probably working as a labourer in Ardrossan dockyard.' He gave a bark of laughter

423

at the picture he had just conjured up. 'And by God, he'd be having a hard time of it. Ah, to hell with it, I'm going out.'

'Out where?' She followed him into the hall, where he was pulling on his coat.

'Just out for a change of air.' He picked up his hat and his stick. 'And while I'm gone, will you for goodness' sake make up your mind about how you're going to tell that brother of yours that he's out of the business?' He opened the front door, then turned back for a moment. 'Go to bed when you're tired, I have my key.'

'Samuel, wait...' But he had gone out into the darkening night, letting the door slam noisily behind him.

Tears stung Belle's eyes as she returned to the parlour. Her marriage was scarcely five months old and already things were changing. She longed for the early days, when Samuel had been gentle and loving and considerate. They were both tired, she thought as she listened to the soft, regular ticking of the clock, both in need of a holiday. She thought of Ireland, that land of blue skies and soft green hills where Samuel's family lived. None of them had been able to come to the wedding because, he had explained, his mother had her hands full caring for her own elderly mother and an aged aunt, and his brothers and sisters were working hard to feed their growing families. He had promised that one day he would take her to Ireland.

'You'll love it,' he had said, 'and you'll love my family. We'll have a grand time there.'

It was time she met his kin, but on the other

hand, who would look after the shop? Certainly not Walter. Perhaps Samuel was right, she thought bleakly Perhaps it was time to buy Walter out.

Leez Drummond had not as yet come up with a recommendation for the post of housekeeper, and although the woman who had taken Ena's place on a temporary basis was adequate, she returned home to her own family every evening. Belle was alone in the house, which seemed very empty. She would have given anything at that moment to hear the sound of claws scuttering along the hall floor and Juliet snuffling at the bottom of the door before noisily demanding entry. But there was no Juliet, no Ena, and no Samuel. She was alone.

She thought of visiting Morna and Ruth, but then she thought that Samuel might well repent swiftly of his angry outburst and decide to return home to make up the quarrel with her. And it was time that the ledgers she kept at home were brought up to date. She had brought the cash books from the shop for that purpose, and had been about to start work when Samuel raised the subject of Walter. The books were piled on the table, waiting for her.

Belle sat down and started work.

It was late when Samuel finally returned home to find his wife sitting at the table, the ledgers in front of her. She knew by his flushed face and the way he swayed as he came to a standstill in the doorway, that he had spent the evening in one of the town's public houses.

'I thought you'd be in your bed by now, but here you are, still workin' away at this time of the night. My, my, Isabelle, but you're a conscientious woman right enough.'

'I've just finished.' She rubbed her sore eyes, smiling at him. 'I was thinking, Samuel, that we could both do with a holiday. Why don't we go over to Ireland to see your family?'

'Mebbe next year.' He went to the cupboard, straddling his feet wide in order to keep his balance as he bent down to get a tumbler and a bottle.

'Could we not go now?'

'Next year, I said.' He wrenched the cork from the bottle and poured himself a generous tot of whisky.

'Would you not rather have a cup of tea before you go to bed?'

'No, I would not,' he retorted, mimicking her precise voice. He took a gulp of whisky and reeled over to sit opposite her. 'So how is "Forsyth and Son",' he uttered the words with stinging contempt, 'doin', then?'

'Samuel, have you been working on these books?'

'Mebbe I have and mebbe I haven't.' He wagged a finger at her. 'That's for me to know and you to find out.'

'I think you have. I think,' Belle said steadily, 'that you've been altering some of the figures.'

'Oh God, here we go again! If it's not poor wee Agnes Campbell it's yer own husband. Ye always have tae suspect someone, don't ye, Isabelle?' he slurred. 'Mebbe it's all down tae you. Mebbe ye've just made mistakes. D'ye ever think of that? Or are ye too high and mighty tae make mis-

426

takes? Is that somethin' ye leave tae yer inferiors?'

'Have you been taking money from the till?' she asked, ignoring the drunken insults. He stared at her, working at focusing his gaze on her face. For a moment she thought that he was going to deny it – hoped that he would deny it, for she had already decided that she should have held her tongue. She would accept his word and that would be an end to it. Then Samuel laughed, loudly and open mouthed, leaning across the table towards her so that she was surrounded by the strong smell of whisky.

'Yes, my dear wife, I have been takin' money from the till. And what of it? Am I no' the manager? Am I no' a junior partner, thanks to your great generosity towards me when we married?' He grimaced with disgust. 'Dolin' out a manager's wage tae yer own husband while old man Pinkerton guards the money lyin' in the bank in your name. *Your* name, Isabelle, not mine. Is there any wonder if sometimes I take the bit extra that I deserve?' He flourished his glass in a toast and generous drops of whisky spattered the ledgers and Belle's hands. 'To you, Isabelle. You and yer oversh-overwhelming generosity!' He drained the glass in a few greedy gulps and then set it down, wiping the back of his hand across his mouth.

The room was warm, but all at once Belle felt chilled. 'And what about Miss Campbell? Did you stand by while I accused her of something she didn't do?'

'Poor wee Agnes. You can rest assured, my dear wife, that she wasnae entirely free of guilt. I let her have her share so's she'd keep quiet about the cash book being altered. By Christ, that upright woman that was your auntie fairly knew a good whisky from a bad one.' He refilled his glass with the last of the bottle of whisky he had brought to the table with him, and drank.

'Why didn't you tell me that you wanted more money? I would have given it to you.'

'Aye – given it. Doled it out, like the Lady Bountiful you are. Your house,' Samuel sneered, indicating the room with a wide sweep of one arm. The empty whisky bottle was knocked over and left to roll to and fro on the table, 'And *your* money – and *your* husband. Everythin' yours and nothin' mine! You Forsyths are always better than anyone else, aren't you?' he sneered at her. 'You get this place, Walter gets Sarah, and the rest of us can go to hell for all you care!'

Belle's head was beginning to ache. 'What has Sarah to do with it?' she asked, confused.

'She has everythin' tae do with it! Why d'you think I want Walter out of the business? It's what I've been waitin' for ever since he took Sarah from me.' He stopped to take another gulp or two of whisky.

'What do you mean?'

Samuel's chin was wet with whisky 'I'm talkin' about when she worked in the Forsyth kitchen and I delivered the vegetables – d'ye not remember?' he asked irritably. 'She tried tae get me tae believe that that bairn was mine, but I wasnae goin' tae marry her – oh no. I wasnae goin' tae live in a ditch just because she'd a wean in her belly. But she didnae tell the whole truth, did she? Women never do!' His gestures became wilder as he plunged into his story. Belle listened, appalled and sickened.

'Lied, she did! Instead of gettin' rid of it like I wanted so's we could go on as we were, she had tae marry that useless brother o' yours. An' when he saw me darin' tae speak tae his new wee wife he put me out of the house and lost me my job. But that...' he sprawled across the table, his chin almost resting on its surface, grinning at her, '...that was his mistake, 'cos I made up my mind on that very day tae do him down one way or the other. And now ye know why I want him out of the shop and why I'll not have any more of your arguin'. You just take heed of what I'm tellin' ye! We'll throw him out tomorrow, the two of us together so's I can see the look on his face.'

Belle couldn't stand another moment of it. 'I think we should go to bed now,' she said as calmly as she could.

'Go to bed with *you*? Sure, where's the pleasure in that? If you were Sarah, now, it would be a different matter. She's soft an' warm and eager tae please, while you – I'd as soon go tae bed with the garden gate, so I would. Now don't start that,' he added as her eyes began to fill with tears. 'I'll not have that. My oul' bastard of a da knocked my ma clean across the room when she turned on the waterworks, and he'd the right way o' it.'

Belle blinked the tears back. 'How can you speak to me like this, Samuel?'

'You know what they say.' He took another mouthful of whisky. 'It's easier tae tell the truth when ye're in drink. An' I've wanted tae tell ye the truth time an' time again.'

'So you only asked me to marry you so that you could find a way to punish Walter?'

'No, no, no, Isabelle, I'll not have that. Now it's your turn tae tell the truth. I never asked you tae marry me – it was you that asked me tae marry you. In fact, you begged me. Ye were desperate for a man, weren't ye? Desperate.'

Sour bile rose into Belle's throat, and for a moment she thought that she was going to spew out her disgust and shame there and then, like a drunken man emptying his stomach into the gutter after an evening's consumption of cheap, raw whisky. She swallowed hard, and once the sensation had eased she said quietly, 'How dare you speak to me like that?'

He laughed in her face. 'I dare because I'm yer husband and I can speak tae you any way I like. And because we both know that you're not goin' tae go running tae tell Walter or anyone else about this. D'ye really want folk tae know what a fool ye've made of yerself?'

'Buying Walter out won't punish him, it'll only punish us because we'll have to make up the money we pay him.'

Samuel shrugged. 'We'll make it up soon enough. But ye're right. The best way tae really hurt that brother of yours is tae take Sarah from him.'

'You wouldn't do that,' she said quickly, and then, as he closed one brown eye in an elaborate wink, 'You couldn't!'

'Could I no'? She's weakenin' already,' Samuel boasted. He picked up his glass and saw that it was empty. 'More whisky,' he mumbled, and levered himself up from the table. It took a few moments, and when he tried to walk to the cabinet his legs went sideways instead of forwards. Lurching like an ungainly crab, he reached the fireplace, and Belle jumped up, convinced that he was going to fall into the fire and burn himself. But he caught hold of the mantelshelf just in time, managing to swing himself round and into an armchair. 'Whisky,' he said petulantly.

'There's a fresh bottle in the kitchen press. I'll get it – and a blanket.' Clearly, he was in no fit state to climb the stairs to his bed. Belle picked his empty glass up from the hearthrug, where it had fallen when he almost fell into the fireplace, and went upstairs to fetch a blanket before going to the kitchen for a fresh bottle of whisky.

When she returned, Samuel, slumped like a sack of potatoes, legs sprawled across the rug, ordered, 'Fill the glass.' Once she had done so, he almost snatched the drink from her. 'Put the bottle on the wee table by my hand,' he slurred, 'an' make the fire up.'

By the time she had added fresh coals to the fire, which had begun to burn low, the glass was half-empty. When she stooped to put the blanket over him he batted her hands aside irritably. 'Stop fussin', woman, and let me be!'

'Good night, Samuel – sleep well,' she said, and went out, closing the door softly.

In the bedroom, she took a small, brown glass medicine bottle from the dressing table and put it back into the shabby tin box. Locking the box, she returned it to the wardrobe, pushing it right to the back, out of sight.

After that she went to bed and fell asleep almost at once.

34

'A party,' Ruth Durie said, clapping her hands. 'We shall have a party for all our pupils on Christmas Eve. It might be the only celebration some of those poor little souls will have. We'll have lots of food and lemonade, and play games, and we'll buy a present for each child and put a tree up in the classroom, with sweets and gingerbread men on it.'

Belle and Morna looked at each other across the kitchen table. 'But Christmas Eve is only five days away,' Belle pointed out, while Morna chimed in with, 'How can we possibly do all that in such a short time?'

'I'll see to the tree tomorrow, as soon as school's over. And we'll call in reinforcements – Anna can make gingerbread men, and I know that she'll be willing to help with the rest of the food. You'll help too, Belle, won't you?'

'I can't cook or bake, but I'm sure Ena would be willing.' On hearing that Belle had suddenly been widowed, Ena had given up all thought of a change of employer and returned to her former mistress's side.

'Do you think you could possibly choose suitable gifts for the wee ones as well? I'll give

432

you a list of names and ages. We shall dip into the bank to buy them,' Ruth added to Morna. The bank was an old tea caddy where they kept money to buy food and pay their other expenses.

'There's very little in it at the moment,' Morna pointed out, and Ruth shrugged.

'Then you and I must save money by living on porridge and soup and bread for a few days. It will be just like being in prison, only much more fun.'

'I will pay for the children's presents,' Belle said, and Ruth beamed at her.

'You are a darling. Isn't it helpful, Morna, to know someone who has money? You'll come to the party as well, won't you, Belle? So that makes three of us helping with the children,' Ruth swept on when Belle nodded, 'and then there's Anna – and Tom, of course.'

Something in Morna's breast gave a sudden skip, like a child jumping for joy. 'Your brother will be here?' He had said nothing of it to her in his regular weekly letters.

'He always comes for Ne'erday, and sometimes he manages to be home for Christmas too. I shall write to him and insist that he attends our party.'

Ruth's enthusiasm for everything she tackled, no matter how uninteresting or unpleasant, warmed Belle. It was Ruth who had given her the strength to cope following Samuel's death – from a sudden and unexpected heart attack, the doctor said, while his manner, as his sharp eyes noted the empty whisky bottle still lying on the table, the half-full bottle on the floor by the fireside chair and the glass that had fallen from

Samuel's hand to spill what remained of its contents over the rug, said clearly, without words, that excessive drinking must have played a part in the sudden death. It was later to come out that Samuel had been drinking heavily in one of the public houses down by the river on the previous evening. Belle had told everyone that she knew nothing of her husband's condition when he arrived home that night, because she had gone to bed early with a bad headache.

While those who had criticised and ostracised her after what they saw as her unsuitable marriage wondered whether they should call to express their condolences, Ruth Durie had not hesitated. Over the six weeks since the funeral she and Belle had become firm friends, and it was Ruth who had encouraged Belle to ignore the unwritten rules and return to the shop.

'You can't just sit behind drawn curtains for months with nothing to do,' she had said crisply. 'The boredom will drive you out of your wits and widowhood will do its best to make you old before your time. The family business needs you, and you must have something to do. Pay no heed to any old sweetie wives who might cluck and mutter about a sensible period of mourning – you can still mourn in your own way.'

Once the party had been decided on, Ruth was determined to find the ornaments for the tree she was going to buy The three of them hurried upstairs, where they carried a small table from one of the bedrooms to the landing.

'Tom can reach the trapdoor from the table,' Ruth said thoughtfully, 'but I can't.'

'Then let your brother search the attic when he gets here,' Belle's voice was firm. 'Or I can send one of the shop assistants along tomorrow morning if you want. Mr Lombard is very tall.'

But Ruth, too impatient to wait, went back downstairs and reappeared carrying an upright wooden chair from the kitchen.

'I'm not climbing up there!' Morna said nervously as the chair was settled on top of the table. 'It doesn't look safe.'

'It's perfectly safe, but you two must stay down here to hold the chair legs steady and pass the lamp up to me. If I happen to fall and break a limb, one of you can run for help while the other stays to comfort me,' Ruth said blithely, hitching up her skirts. She clambered on to the table and then got a firm grip on the back of the chair. 'Hold on, now,' she instructed, and in a moment she was balancing on the seat.

'I feel like a circus acrobat,' she crowed, and then, 'Oh dear, I can see a dreadful pile of dust above each of the bedroom doors! Remind me to do something about that before Ne'erday, Morna.' She reached up and managed to dislodge the trap-door leading to the attic. 'Give me the lamp, please.'

Belle clung to the chair legs as Ruth stooped down to take the lamp from Morna. She set it on the floor of the attic and then with a flurry of skirts, petticoats, black-stockinged legs and a yell of 'Alley-oop!' she swung herself up into the attic and disappeared.

For several long and anxious minutes the sisters listened to bumping noises overhead. Finally

435

Ruth reappeared, leaning over precariously in order to lower a box to the chair.

'Could someone take that out of the way?' she asked before disappearing again.

'You can do it,' Belle told her sister. Morna, her heart in her mouth, clambered on to the table and had just handed the box over to Belle when Ruth began to lower herself, feet first, from the trapdoor.

Once she was back on the landing and the dust and cobwebs had been brushed from her clothing, the three of them took the box down to the kitchen where they unpacked it, lifting piles of magazines, tracts and leaflets from the table in order to lay out a treasure trove of brightly painted wooden baubles, tiny dolls, nursery rhyme characters and an entire orchestra of miniature musical instruments. Ruth greeted each discovery with cries of delight, and it was quite late when Belle finally and reluctantly announced that she really must go home because Ena would be waiting up to make sure she got back safely.

'What about your sister-in-law?' Ruth asked as Belle was putting her coat on. 'Would she like to help us with the party? She could bring her little boy – and her nursemaid as well. The more the merrier.'

'Sarah? I don't know if she'd be able,' Morna was doubtful. 'She's not been well for weeks.'

'I'll call tomorrow to ask her,' Belle said. 'It's high time I visited her.'

What she meant was that it was high time she summoned up the strength to face Sarah, who

436

had succumbed to whatever ailed her the day after Samuel Gilmartin's death. She had fainted, and then gone into a storm of weeping once she was brought round. After that, she had taken to her bed. Walter was deeply worried about her, but Belle had a very good idea as to what lay behind her sister-in-law's collapse. In the bleak days following Samuel's death she had been tormented by the memory of what he had told her during their final confrontation: then gradually she reached the realisation that Sarah, like herself, had been Samuel's victim. They were two helpless flies caught in his web, but now they were free, and the past must be laid to rest. Armed with a new sense of purpose, she walked round to Argyle Road directly after breakfast the next day.

Mrs Forsyth was out of her sickbed, the little maid told her in a hushed voice, but she was still weak, and resting at that moment on the sofa in the parlour.

'Bring tea,' Belle said, sweeping past the open-mouthed girl and into the parlour, where she opened the drawn curtains to let some light in.

'Who – Belle?' Sarah's voice was feeble, her face ashen and her eyes darkly shadowed.

'I've come to invite you to a party at Ruth Durie's, on Christmas Eve.' Belle drew her gloves off and unbuttoned her coat. 'It's a children's party for her pupils. She needs all the help she can get, so I'll be there, and Morna of course, and you must bring little Fraser. It will do him good to be with other children. His nursemaid would be useful too.'

'I couldn't... I'm not well enough...'

Belle drew a light chair close to the sofa and sat down. 'Sarah, I know that you're mourning for Samuel, and I know all about your – friendship – with him. Not that he was my husband then,' she added swiftly as Sarah's eyes widened and she cringed back against the cushions. 'It was while you were employed by my parents, and was over before you married Walter.' There was no sense in telling this terrified young woman the true extent of her knowledge.

'He told you?' Sarah whispered. 'Are you going to tell Walter?'

'It's none of his business, or mine. I just wanted you to know that I understand how you feel. His sudden death came as a dreadful shock to both of us,' Belle said, her voice steady, 'but I know that he would want us to think now of getting on with our own lives.'

Nellie tapped on the door and brought in the tea tray. When they were alone again Belle poured out two cups of tea and then went to investigate the corner cupboard. 'Good – there's still some of Papa's brandy here.' She poured a little of the bottle's contents into each cup. 'Drink that up, Sarah, it will do you the world of good.'

The young woman took the cup in both hands and sipped cautiously. She grimaced, but sipped again. By the time the cup was half-empty, a little colour had returned to her face.

'You don't hate me, then?'

'Why should I? You knew Samuel at one stage of his life and I knew him at another.' The final stage, as it happened, but Belle had decided that she would not allow herself to dwell on that, ever.

'You must get better, Sarah, for Fraser's sake, and for Walter's. And you must bring wee Fraser to Ruth Durie's house on Christmas Eve. It will do you both good. Ruth has helped me so much through the past weeks.

'There's one thing I'd like to ask you – did Samuel ever tell you anything about his family in Ireland?'

'No, never. I don't think he had any family.'

'I see.' Before the funeral, Belle had searched in vain through Samuel's few possessions for letters that might have told her how to contact the mother and brothers and sisters he had promised that she would meet one day There had been nothing at all – no family, no background. Samuel had rushed into her life like one of the stiff winds that so often blew from Ireland towards the Ayrshire coast, whipping the Firth into a frenzy of white foam, and now he was gone, leaving nothing behind. It was as though he had never been a part of her world, and perhaps, Belle decided, as she drained her cup and put it back on its saucer, that was for the best.

'You'll come to the party?' she pressed, and when Sarah nodded, said, 'Good. Now I must go to the shop. Goodness knows what Wal – I mean, I've left poor Walter to deal with everything.'

She buttoned her coat and picked up her gloves. She was drawing on the second glove when Sarah, her voice stronger already, said, 'Belle? I – I think I'm expecting another child.'

Belle's hands suddenly stopped bustling about each other. She froze for a moment, and then forced herself to turn and smile at her sister-in-

439

law. 'But that's grand news. Does Walter know?'

'It's too soon to be certain. I thought that I would wait.'

'Very wise. He will be pleased, if your suspicions are correct.'

As Belle hurried to Dockhead Street she realised that Sarah's unexpected news meant that the wondering and the jealousy were not quite ready to be laid to rest. She had assumed, from Samuel's drunken ramblings on the night he died, that 'She's weakenin' already', meant that he had not actually seduced his brother-in-law's wife, although his intentions as to the future had been made very plain. But now she wondered...

For a moment the click of her boots on the pavement faltered, then they gathered momentum again. All she could hope, for the time being, was that if Sarah was right and another child was on the way, it would emerge from the womb looking even more like Walter than Fraser had.

As the children trooped into the house on the afternoon of the party their eyes rounded and their jaws dropped at the sight of the magnificent Christmas tree in all its glory, with brightly wrapped sweets, gingerbread men, coloured balls and miniatures hanging from its branches. Parcels were piled beneath green branches that smelled of pine forests, and the room had been festooned with chains of coloured paper and wreaths of holly.

It was, as Ruth had predicted, the best party anyone had ever known. There were games in the back garden, an elaborate treasure hunt indoors, more food and drink than even the hungriest and thirstiest child could demolish, and then came the highlight – opening the presents.

Little Fraser Forsyth, who had until then been convinced that he was the only small person in a world of gentle, softly spoken adults, was quite terrified when he found himself confronted by a pack of noisy, excited children. Leez Drummond had to take him into the small parlour, where he sat on her lap and thumped vigorously at the keys of the piano, a pleasure that was not allowed in his own home. Once he had calmed down he was introduced in gentle stages to the party and began to enjoy himself. His mother, among a group of children playing the games she herself had once played and loved, was in her element, helping the smallest children to play Blind Man's Buff and Hunt the Thimble. For the first time in many weeks she was happy.

Morna, too, was enjoying herself, but all the time, even when she was playing the piano for the sing-song before the party ended, her ears strained for the sound of the doorknocker, and Tom's voice. She had memorised the times of trains from Glasgow, and kept glancing at the clock, but the afternoon came to an end without any sign of Tom.

At least, she told herself as she helped to button excited, wriggling children into coats and stuff small hands into knitted mittens, there was Ne'erday. Ruth had said that he always came to Saltcoats for Ne'erday.

When Anna had taken the children home and Sarah, pink-cheeked, had departed with Leez and Fraser, who clutched a new velveteen ball that tinkled like a bell when rolled along the floor, Morna, Belle and Ruth started washing dishes and gathering up wrapping paper. Then Morna, longing for some fresh air, walked to Caledonia Road with her sister.

'Ruth,' Belle said thoughtfully as they crossed Ardrossan Road, 'is a most interesting person. I admire her passion for justice and the rights of women.'

'Does that mean that you're thinking of joining the suffragette movement?' Morna teased, and was taken aback when her sister said, 'I might.'

'Are you serious? You were horrified when you discovered that I was sharing a house with a suffragette!'

'That was before I got to know her and her friends,' Belle said calmly. 'Who knows what I might decide to do? We're approaching a new year – the perfect time to make changes in one's life. Come in and warm yourself by the fire before you walk back.'

It was dark, and it had started to rain. 'I'd better get home before this gets worse,' Morna said.

Glancing wistfully towards the town as she recrossed Ardrossan Road, her heartbeat speeded up as she saw a man hurrying along the pavement with long, familiar strides. She veered towards him, and as she approached he stopped beneath a street lamp to await her.

'I missed you,' she accused as they met.

'I tried to get away in time for the party but I couldn't.'

'I'm not talking about the party,' Morna said

impatiently, amazed by her own boldness. 'I mean – I've missed you.'

'And I missed you too. It's been a very long autumn.'

'Letters aren't enough.'

'I know. We must talk about this while I'm here,' he said. 'We must find a solution.' The rain had begun to fall in earnest and he pulled off one glove and ran the ball of his thumb along the top of her cheekbone. She shivered beneath his touch.

'You're getting wet,' Tom said. 'I would shelter you beneath my umbrella, but I must have left it on the train.'

'It doesn't matter.'

'It does to me. I don't want anything to happen to you. I couldn't bear it if something happened to you. Come on,' he picked up the bag he had laid down on the pavement when they met, and put one arm around her shoulders, drawing her close, 'let's get indoors.'

He adapted his long strides to her pace and Morna leaned her body against his as they hurried along the pavement together, beneath rain that sparkled like threads of spun gold as it slanted past the gas lamps.

Bibliography

The *Ardrossan & Saltcoats Herald*, issues from 1909–1910

Burgh of Saltcoats – a Brief History, compiled and published by the Local History Department, Cunninghame District Libraries, Ayrshire, 1985

Burgh of Saltcoats – Quarter Centenary, 1528–1928, published by Arthur Guthrie & Sons Ltd., Ardrossan, Ayrshire, 1928

McSherry, R. & M., *Old Saltcoats*, published by Richard Stenlake, Ochiltree, Ayrshire, 1995

The *Paisley Daily Express*, 30 April 1910 – a report on Mrs Emmeline Pankhurst's visit to Paisley Town Hall

This Large Print Book for the partially sighted, who cannot read normal print, is published under the auspices of

THE ULVERSCROFT FOUNDATION